All the Dark Air

Livi Michael has written two previous novels: *Under a Thin Moon*, which won the Arthur Welton Award in 1992, and *Their Angel Reach*, which won the 1995 Geoffrey Faber Memorial Prize and the Society of Authors Award, and was shortlisted for the John Steinbeck and John Llewellyn Rhys Awards. She lives in Lancashire with the poet Ian Pople and

BY LIVI MICHAEL

Under a Thin Moon
Their Angel Reach
All the Dark Air

Livi Michael
ALL THE DARK AIR

VINTAGE

Published by Vintage 1997

2 4 6 8 10 9 7 5 3 1

Copyright © 1996 Livi Michael

The right of Livi Michael to be identified as the
author of this work has been asserted by her in accordance
with the Copyright, Designs and Patents Act, 1988

This book is sold subject to the condition that it shall not by way of
trade or otherwise, be lent, resold, hired out, or otherwise circulated
without the publisher's prior consent in any form of binding or cover
other than that in which it is published and without a similar condition including this condition being imposed on the subsequent
purchaser

First published in Great Britain by
Martin Secker & Warburg 1996

The author gratefully acknowledges a generous grant
from the Royal Society of Authors

'Memory' text by Trevor Nunn after T.S. Eliot, reproduced by kind
permission of Faber Music Ltd on behalf of Trevor Nunn/Set
Copyright Ltd. The author and publisher have taken all possible
care to trace the copyright holders of material used in this book.
Any omissions will be corrected in subsequent editions provided
notification is made in writing to the publisher.

Vintage
Random House, 20 Vauxhall Bridge Road, London SW1V 2SA

Random House Australia (Pty) Limited
20 Alfred Street, Milsons Point, Sydney
New South Wales 2061, Australia

Random House New Zealand Limited
18 Poland Road, Glenfield,
Auckland 10, New Zealand

Random House South Africa (Pty) Limited
Endulini, 5A Jubilee Road, Parktown 2193, South Africa

Random House UK Limited Reg. No. 954009

A CIP catalogue record for this book
is available from the British Library

ISBN 0 74 939593 1

Papers used by Random House UK Ltd are natural, recy-
clable products made from wood grown in sustainable
forests. The manufacturing processes conform to the
environmental regulations of the country of origin

Printed and bound in Great Britain by
Cox & Wyman, Reading, Berkshire

In memoriam
Liz McCord, 1951–1996

The wall dissolves, you said,
dissolves into light. A passing through.

Walls, Hilda Cotterill

With grateful thanks
to Tony, Joanna and Steve

Julie swept dog dirt out of the back yard.

Bloody, bloody dogs, she said.

It was a communal cobbled yard, with little yards leading off. All the little yards had tall gates, and the yard to Mick's uncle's house had a tall brown gate, only it was hanging off its hinges, and all the dogs that sniffed around the big yard seemed to pick Mick's uncle's yard to do their stuff. The injustice of it made Julie sweep harder. It was no use complaining. The neighbours didn't care about the dogs, they hardly ever fed them, hardly ever let them in. If one of the dogs did something serious, like biting a baby, they'd probably say it wasn't theirs. Now that Julie was having a baby this bothered her a lot, this and the fact that whenever she left the house they came sniffing round her for food, but worst of all was the dog dirt. Babies should never play near dog dirt, she'd seen a programme once, it could make them go blind. Even now, in her condition, she shouldn't be sweeping it up, she'd forgotten that. There'd been a leaflet about it at the clinic, you could kill your unborn child that way. Julie dropped the broom and hurried inside as if she could protect herself there from what she'd already done. She held her back and stared at the crumbling plaster on the kitchen walls. Then, without thinking to wash her hands, she cut herself a thick wedge of the bread that wasn't hers and sliced chunks of butter onto it.

Mick had said he'd fix the gate.

Julie chewed the bread and stared out of the window. Though it was November the weather was mild, and all the builder's rubble was in the yard. Images of the baby as a toddler, crawling about in all the rubble with the dogs, flitted through Julie's mind. She finished the piece of bread and considered cutting another, but she was putting too much weight on, they said at the clinic, thirty-five pounds in four months was far too much.

We don't eat for two now, you know, the older nurse had said. But she was hungry all the time. When they'd asked if she was having any special cravings she'd just said, Food, and the younger nurse had laughed and waited for her to say what she really meant, but that was it. She craved food, all kinds of food, all the time, and there were all kinds of food she wasn't supposed to eat, like Brie cheese, which she loved, and a whole list of things she couldn't do.

Concentrate on what you can do, Medbh had said at the meeting.

Julie looked round the kitchen. It was full of bricks and old plaster and cement, they were trying to extend it. She couldn't do anything about most of the mess but she could wash up, rescue the dishes from the slimy water in which everyone except Julie left them. Then, while she was washing up, she could concentrate, as Medbh had said, on water, where it came from (rain clouds, mountain streams), where it was going (forests, the ocean), the miracles of cleansing and irrigation. And every day Julie could make use of this ordinary miracle, just by turning on a tap.

Julie turned the tap and remembered the last meeting of the Mind-Power group. Medbh had also said that if you wanted something to go away you could visualise it dissolving inside a pyramid of light. Julie had tried that often enough with the dog dirt, and now there seemed to be more of it than ever. Of course, it might be that she wasn't visualising it clearly enough, or not positioning it the right way inside the pyramid, or that it was all balls, Mick had said. He'd asked if she couldn't put the government in a pyramid so they could all sit round and watch them disappear, but Mick was like that. He didn't take anything seriously except, now that he was going to Socialist Worker Party meetings, everything they said. But he made her feel guilty about going to her meetings. He said it was decadent for one thing, and the worst kind of crap for another.

Julie sighed, though there was no one around to hear her. She'd caught herself doing that more often recently, as if life was really heavy and pressing down. She should live more in the present moment, she knew, she should set about the pots floating in their greasy foam, or scour uselessly again at the top of the cooker, without thinking about how much she didn't want to do it, that was the worst thing you could do. You had to find something positive to think about, like the grass in the yard, cracking the concrete all by itself, or an interesting pattern in the clouds. There was more to it than that though, according to Medbh. To really live in the present moment you had to concentrate on everything at once, not just the pretty things; the blackened blotches of grease on the cooker, the feeling in your arm when you scrubbed at them, the spider web in the corner of the window, the window itself. That was what you were supposed to do all day long, from the moment you got up, Julie couldn't see how. When she woke up it was to the sound of Mick coughing, and Uncle Si shuffling his way through the rubble downstairs, and to the thunderous feeling in her stomach, the anxiety that never settled onto any one particular thing but hovered over everything, the baby, Mick's health, money, work, the house and what was going to happen to them all in the end.

Julie cut herself the other piece of bread. She took it into the front room, stepping carefully over the joists since there wasn't a floor. Medbh had said that when you really lived in the present moment there was no fear, because you weren't thinking about the past or the future. The world transformed itself, she said. Julie wanted to believe that, and she did the practice whenever she remembered to, because she very much wanted to transform her world.

*

Let's see your money then, Benny Bennett said, and he opened her purse.

They had already taken her new maths set with its plastic protractor and set squares, now they stood round her eating her sandwiches, Benny Bennett emptying her bag.

Rick Higgins pulled her skirt up, she pushed it down, he pulled it up again.

One pound fifty, Benny Bennett said. Ta very much.

Julie could only wait for things to get worse. Any minute now they'd take her to the edge of the concrete hill in the playground and push her off. They'd done that to Naomi Brooke and she'd broken her leg. Julie could only wait for this to happen.

What're you at, said Mick. He pushed through the circle, between Rick and Chris Higgins. For the first time Julie dared to look up.

Mind your own, Fegan, Benny Bennett said.

Mind yours, Big Ears.

Who are you fucking calling Big Ears, said Benny Bennett, pushing Mick.

Fucking you, Mick said, pushing back.

There was a fight.

Julie backed silently away, but she didn't leave, she had to see what would happen. There were too many of them for Mick, though Mick was big, the biggest in their class, and known to be well hard.

Then an old man from one of the flats opposite came out waving his stick.

Clear off, he shouted. I'll have dogs on you.

There was a frenzied barking as he unlocked the door and a big black dog and a smaller brown one rushed out.

Jesus, Benny Bennett said, and all the boys rolled off Mick at once. Mick sat up slowly. Julie's stomach lurched as the big black dog reached him, but it only sniffed his face.

Hiya, Mick said to the dog.

Clear off, the old man yelled again. I'll have police –

Yeah, yeah, all right, Mick said, and got to his feet. He walked off coolly, Mick was always cool. He didn't see Julie. She followed him a little way, then ran back to pick up her things.

That was the beginning. In school that day Mick needed a rubber. Before he had time to ask the boy next to him Julie passed him hers. Mick looked surprised. Ta, he said. At break she offered him the only sandwich she had left, Mick was always hungry. Then the next day at break he left his pencils on the desk and Julie sharpened them all for him. She followed him to where he played football and watched, she took to bringing him an extra sandwich in her box.

As long as no one else was around Mick put up with this, and even sometimes asked her if she'd brought him anything to eat. But once when she was following him after school she saw the lads he was with start to nudge him and laugh. She'd thought she was hanging far enough behind not to be noticed, but then he turned round with a red, annoyed face.

Shove off will you? he said. Julie went forwards one or two steps, then stopped.

I mean it, he said. Sod off.

When they turned round again Julie hung back a bit, then went on following. They turned a corner. Julie hurried now, not wanting to lose them. As she turned the corner she ran straight into Mick.

What did I say? he said, and pushed her fairly hard. His mates stood a few yards away, grinning. When Julie didn't say anything he kicked her, not very hard. Julie hadn't cried in front of Benny Bennett's gang but she felt like crying now.

If you follow me again, said Mick, I'll kick your teeth in.

So Julie didn't follow him after that, but she did take notice, all the time, of where he was and what he was doing. In class she noticed the mole on the back of his neck, and the marks above the collar where he hadn't washed. Even when they went to the big school and everyone was streamed, so that Julie was usually in C or B groups and Mick in D or E (except for technical drawing, where he was in B and Julie C), she managed to keep track of him, finding out when he was doing well (usually at football), when he was in detention (most weeks), when he started smoking, who he hung round with. She caught glimpses of him in assembly or in the dinner room until he stopped going, and for one entire term his class played football outside the room where Julie had geography. Although she was careful about watching him, so no one would notice, she nearly failed geography, and once when three girls turned up to cheer him on, got so distracted she was given a detention, the only one she ever had. She hoped Mick might be there, but for once he wasn't.

Mick was suspended twice, once for fighting, once for sniffing glue. He didn't seem overly bothered about girls, but he went out with two: Amanda Cotterill for just over three months and Suzanne Edge for four. Julie went on as before, secretly nursing her warm, forbidden pain. She herself was never in danger of being suspended. The teachers who remembered who she was at the one parents' evening her mother went to said she was very quiet and always handed her work in on time. One said that he sometimes found it hard to get through to her.

You're not the only one, Julie's mother said.

Then, after the glue-sniffing, Suzanne's father

wouldn't let her go out with Mick any more, and he didn't bother with anyone else, though Julie lightened her hair for the school leaving disco and went on a diet. Mick turned up late with his mates, some of them weren't even from the school, and got drunk on cans of beer they'd brought in, and was thrown out before the end. Julie went home shortly after, very soberly, that was the last chance she'd have of seeing him regularly.

She did get to hear about him though; he was in the paper several times. Once because he'd got drunk with his friends and they'd smashed the lights on all the lorries parked near a local warehouse. Then he'd been done for joy-riding.

He wants to watch out, that lad, Julie's stepfather, Brian, said. No one'll give him a job, the way he's going.

Brian himself hadn't worked for several years. Julie's mother just said Mick wanted a good hiding. Once though, they read about him doing something good. He'd alerted a train when there was a blockage on the line.

Wonders'll never cease, said Julie's mum.

Julie kept her face lowered over her cereal. She herself hadn't been doing too well since school had finished, she'd had four jobs in eight months. It wasn't all her fault; the Wall's meat pie factory had closed down, then she'd had a temporary job at Boots, but they hadn't wanted her when the Christmas rush was over. She'd been sacked from Betta Drapes after seven weeks because she couldn't cut material, then she'd worked at the corner shop while Mrs Walter's daughter, Denise, had her baby, but Denise had wanted to go back soon after. Now her mother had put in a word for her at the biscuit factory where she herself worked, Julie was going to start on Monday. She wasn't excited. She never made friends at work. She hadn't at school either, but at least at school she could keep her head down and stay out of trouble, at work she was always getting things wrong.

The biscuit factory, though, was nearly as big as

school, so here again no one noticed her. She worked next to Alison on packaging and Alison was friendly enough. Julie thought she was pretty. She was a bit taller than Julie, and much slimmer, with long, pale hair and a pale face, lightly freckled. She laughed a lot, and talked all the time, but still managed to pack two boxes of biscuits for every one Julie did. She was very popular. Julie started to grow her hair, and when Alison bought an Alice band Julie bought one too.

Sometimes they got talking.

I see your friend and mine's left town, Alison said.

Eh? said Julie.

It turned out that Alison's brother knew Mick, they used to play football together. Alison knew that Julie knew Mick, from when she'd asked Julie if she had a boyfriend, and Julie had managed to give the impression that while she and Mick weren't exactly serious they had a kind of on-off relationship, off at the moment.

You'd have thought he'd let you know, said Alison.

Alison's brother, Steve, had talked to Mick two days ago and Mick had said he was leaving the next day, moving right out of the area, to a place where he'd heard they were training brickies. He was going with a group of mates and he'd said Steve should go too, but Steve hadn't liked the sound of it. He wasn't one for travelling, Steve, he always said something'd turn up sooner or later if he stayed put long enough.

So Mick had left.

Alison didn't know where he'd gone or for how long. She looked at Julie curiously and said she hadn't meant to upset her, anyway there were plenty more where he came from, and went on to talk about the works' disco, that Friday night. Julie wasn't listening.

Mick had always been around. Though they hadn't spoken for years there was always the chance it would happen, she'd run into him or at least hear something. It wouldn't happen now.

So might you come Friday? Alison said.

He might stay where he was for ever, find work, buy a house. She might never see him again.

Only it's a good do usually, Alison said.

Julie stared at her.

I haven't got anyone to go with, she said.

O, well, I'm going with Sean Bean, said Alison. You'll have to go with me, of course. And sit in the corner with the other wallflowers.

I'll think about it, Julie said.

The rest of the day passed slowly, Julie could feel her movements getting slower. She looked at the boxes as if they made no sense to her, then slowly picked them up, folded them and put them on the belt for packing. She put one box onto the belt for the crusher by mistake and was told off by Valerie the overseer. In the canteen she got coffee and chips and sat alone, staring at her reflection in the coffee.

The next day was no better. She'd got into the habit of expecting to see Mick, she couldn't help it. When she tried to pull herself up for doing it she kept making mistakes with the boxes. It seemed a long time till break. But as she queued for her coffee the thought came to her that he would come back, he had to. All his family were here and, anyway, those kind of jobs never lasted long. She picked up her coffee and hurried to a seat, more and more sure that she would see him again. It might be some time, but in that time she could grow her hair and lose weight and buy new clothes and be totally different when she next saw him, and he would be amazed, and she'd just smile, a dazzling smile, and walk on . . .

Julie hurried back to Alison.

Yes, I will, she said, as if they were still in the same conversation. The dance, she added, as Alison gave her a surprised look. I'll be there, Friday night.

Julie sat at a table next to Alison and Sara, another

packer. She'd bought make-up specially and was wearing her best dress, which was flowery and drop-waisted and looked old-fashioned next to Alison's Lurex leggings and off-the-shoulder T-shirt and Sara's dress, which was like an underskirt. Several lads from custard creams gathered round. Julie didn't talk much, but she listened and laughed in the right places. She thought one of the lads liked her, but she wasn't sure until he asked her to dance. Alison gave her a prodding look. Reminding herself that she had to practise for when Mick came back, she got up with him and thought she managed quite well considering she'd hardly done it before. It wasn't too bad really. If you didn't jiggle about too much attracting attention like Sara, no one looked.

The lad, who was called Stuart, stayed with her for three more dances then asked if he could take her home. When she said she was going home with Alison he asked if she wanted to see a film next week. Julie imagined telling the girls all about it. All right then, she said. She didn't get excited about it until later. She'd heard all about men on dates, how you had to fight to keep them off you; they had desert disease, the girls said, wandering palms. She sat through a film with Stuart waiting for this to happen, and when it didn't she decided it was because he wasn't Mick, they just didn't have the right chemistry. After the film they sat in McDonald's and talked about Stuart's collection of foreign coins, then he saw her to the bus. As she got on the bus he asked if she'd like to see another film next week and she said yes, but as the bus pulled away she changed her mind. So all the next day at work she avoided him. It drew her into a conspiracy with the other girls. She made out that he was keener than he was, and hinted darkly that he'd tried to go too far; they had to warn her whenever he came near. Although he didn't try to phone her at home, she told the girls he did, and that she always had to get her mother to say she wasn't in. She kept this up for a couple of weeks before everyone lost interest.

Meanwhile time happened. Julie never thought of it happening to her, but months passed, there was still no sign of Mick, and she was nearly eighteen. She'd spent her life waiting to be grown up, now it had almost happened. She launched into a new diet and lightened her hair again. Her eighteenth birthday came and went, nothing happened. She was still left with the mysterious sense of waiting.

More weeks passed. Julie lost five pounds then, over Christmas, gained six. She worked out she was the right weight for someone five foot eight and took to wearing heels. When Alison came to work wearing her hair a new way, taken back with combs, Julie decided she'd nip out in her lunch hour and buy a pair for herself. It was a dull day, and the wind was warm for January, and wet. Julie hurried along, holding the hood of her cagoule over her hair. When she turned into the precinct she saw Mick.

He wasn't alone. There were two of them, holding guitars and singing. Between them there was a small brown dog, and in front of them, on the pavement, a margarine tub for coins.

Julie had imagined many ways of seeing Mick again, this wasn't one of them. She stood and stared. They were singing a sad, tuneless version of 'Blowin' in the Wind'. Julie couldn't make herself walk past them, anyway, she'd forgotten about the combs. After a few more moments she turned and hurried away.

The next day she went back, going into Woolworths the back way so she could get a better look.

It was definitely Mick, taller and a bit thinner than before, his black hair a lot longer and scraped back into an elastic band. His face was scarred. Julie had been expecting to see him for so long she could hardly take him in. She didn't even know if she was pleased.

She didn't know how to speak to him. She couldn't

interrupt his singing ('The Streets of London' now), and she couldn't just drop money into the tub. She stayed where she was, in the music and video section, and considered buying a Mariah Carey tape as well as the combs.

Bloody awful row, the girl behind the till said.

I know, said the other one, and they only know two songs. I wish they'd clear off.

Julie stared at them.

I don't think they're that bad, she said.

She went back every day in her lunch hour, cutting it fine because really she only got forty-five minutes. They didn't only know two songs, they knew 'If I was a Carpenter' as well. Mick sang the lead, with the other guy joining in the choruses. Sometimes when they forgot the words, they hummed.

Julie watched them from different sections of Woolworths. She bought the combs, a new lipstick and a mirror for her handbag. Once she walked past them a little way off, but if Mick saw her he didn't stop singing. Though she didn't speak, she felt better just for seeing him, and for the possibility of seeing him somewhere else, just walking into him, he would stop and say Hi, Julie, and they would get talking.

Then, after only a week, they weren't there any more. Julie hung round Woolworths all lunchtime without a sign. As she was going back to work it occurred to her that they might be going at a different time, and for a moment she felt defeated. But the next morning she called in sick and hung round the precinct all day without seeing them. The day collapsed in on itself as Julie wandered round hopelessly. But by the time she got home she had other things to think about.

Brian met her at the door.

Your mam's been taken bad, he said.

Julie stared at him.

She was all right this morning, she said.

Brian sagged against the door, his usual bluff, edgy way all gone.

It happened at work, he said. I've been at the infirmary all afternoon. I've just come back to take you.

Julie's mother had had trouble with her stomach for years, irritable bowel, but this was something else, some kind of rupture, the doctor said. She wasn't conscious and she looked very bad and grey. Brian looked fairly bad and grey himself. He sat with his legs wide apart, as they always were, and stared at the floor. Julie didn't cry. She'd felt like crying on the way over, just because the day was turning out so badly, but now she couldn't seem to. Her mind ran round and round the things that might happen, like a hamster in a wheel, what had to be done if the worst happened, where she would stay.

She couldn't live with Brian.

She had to stay with him while her mother was in hospital.

She couldn't do it.

Julie shut this thought away and worried at other ones instead, when should she phone work, how did you sort out sick pay? And where was Mick? All the time she sat in the hospital room with its tubes and bags and monitors she felt as if somehow Mick was there as well. Whenever she left the room to get a drink from the machine outside she kept expecting to see him at the end of one of the long corridors.

In the end Julie went home with Brian. She kept well away from him, and the only time they spoke was when she offered to make him a cup of tea, and he said, Yes, thanks, and she made it and passed it to him and he stared down at it. Neither of them looked at one another. Julie edged round him and said, Goodnight. As she left the room he was still staring down at the tea. In her own room Julie started to undress then stopped, listened a bit, then pulled the dressing-table chair in front of the door, wedging it under the handle like they did in films.

Julie's mother died. Not immediately, it took several weeks. Weeks when Julie wasn't able to go to Woolworths to see if Mick was back yet. Weeks when, at times, even the thought that he might be failed to comfort her. She took time off work and didn't go back at the end of it, though she knew they were laying people off. But she had enough to do, travelling to and from the hospital, carrying flowers, fruit and bits of good news to her largely unconscious mother. When her mother was conscious she asked one of two things,

Where's Brian? and,

What about work, do they know at work?

Yes, of course they know, Mam, Julie said, every time. They've sent you these lovely flowers.

Sometimes her mother would just stare at her hopelessly, until Julie felt really uncomfortable.

At home she swept the kitchen floor, poured bleach down the toilet and kept the washing machine going. Later what she remembered most about this time was the dirt, crumbs and muddy rings of tea on all the surfaces in the kitchen and front room, hair in the sink, the smell of beer and smoke. Once she swept the stairs with the small brush only to see Brian walking up them and leaving a trail of cigarette ash and soil. So mainly she ignored the cleaning. She had enough to do, she told herself, with the cooking and washing. She stayed in her room and, if she saw Brian, they spoke briefly about who was visiting the hospital when. She never mentioned his dirt and clutter, he never mentioned the ironing. Every night she pulled furniture across her door then undressed quickly and lay awake until she was sure he'd gone to bed.

Then one night she woke up and he was standing over her. She sat up quickly, clutching the bedclothes.

What do you think you're at, eh? he said.

Julie could only stare.

Do you think I can't hear you every night, he said, moving furniture around?

He's drunk, she thought, and the little pulses in her forehead began hammering.

I mean, what do you think I am, eh? he said. Some kind of fucking pervert?

Then he was on the bed.

Julie shut her eyes and held the bedclothes as hard as she could.

Please, please, please, she thought.

Brian tugged at the bedclothes. Julie held on, but he tugged harder and they came away.

Julie felt the same way as she had that day on the council playground, waiting for things to get worse.

Nothing happened.

Cautiously she opened her eyes.

Brian was looking at her in a funny way.

You poor bitch, he said.

Then he got up and left the room, not looking at her again.

Julie stayed where she was quite a long time, staring at the floor. When she was sure she couldn't hear him any more she got up, and pulled the furniture back across the door.

One day Aunty Clare knocked at the door. She'd sent flowers to the hospital, and had visited once when Julie wasn't there, but mainly she was too busy. She had an important job, personal assistant to someone big at ICI, and always looked very smart. Julie was shocked to see her at the door.

Can I come in? she said.

Wishing the place was tidy, Julie led her in. The front room was full of the washing Julie hadn't ironed and the stale smell she couldn't get rid of. Aunty Clare stood in the middle of it all in her designer knitwear, not wrinkling her nose. Then Brian wandered in in his vest, and Julie felt an acute stab of shame, as if it was her fault he hadn't shaved, or probably washed, for days. She wished he would wear slippers on his feet, which were big and clumsy-looking.

When he saw Clare he started in exaggerated surprise. Well, hello there, he said. What can we do for you?

I've come about Christine, Clare said. To offer my help. If there are any arrangements, I mean. I'd like to help.

Brian glared at her suspiciously.

What arrangements, he said.

Aunty Clare perched on the edge of the settee, next to the washing. Julie admired her outfit very much.

Well, anything, she said. We have to face facts, Brian, and she looked at him very directly.

Brian blustered, What facts.

But Aunty Clare went on,

We don't know what's likely to happen in the next few days. I've spoken to the doctors and they all say the same. If the worst happens we must be prepared. I don't suppose Christine had any policies?

Looking a bit dazed now Brian shook his head. Aunty Clare had expected as much.

And you've not worked for some time –

Now hang on a bit, Brian said.

– So all I'm saying, Clare continued, is that we, Terry and myself, are prepared to take on the expense, and the arrangements, and so forth.

Brian's face congested. Julie looked at him in alarm, but Aunty Clare didn't seem moved.

O are you, he said. Well, aren't we the lucky ones, eh? You wouldn't help her when she needed you, but now, when it's all but too late, you think you'll step in and ease your conscience. My arse you will –

I can see you're not in the mood to discuss things, Aunty Clare said. Julie was amazed at her staying so cool. Perhaps when you're feeling up to it we can talk again.

She stood up.

When hell freezes over, Brian said. Aunty Clare picked up her bag and gloves.

I'll see you again, Julie, she said. Julie went with her to show her out.

Show your face round here again, Brian thundered after them, and I'll do it some damage. He pushed past Julie at the door. Do you hear? he yelled down the street. He shouted some other things too, about wills and folk thieving off their own flesh and blood, until Julie retreated in shame. She watched Aunty Clare from the lounge window. Aunty Clare didn't look back. Her high heels clicked smartly along the pavement to where her small white car was parked. It was a Fiat. It pleased Julie that Aunty Clare drove a Fiat, because she looked a bit Italian, small and dark, nothing like Julie or Julie's mother. She got into the car and drove off without seeming hurried. Julie didn't know when she'd admired anyone more in her life.

The next day, as if she'd been waiting for a signal from Clare, Julie's mother died.

Aunty Clare was at the hospital without being told, she said she'd rung the ward. Brian sat by the bed refusing to speak to anyone, but Aunty Clare took Julie to one side and asked if she'd thought about the funeral.

Not really, Julie said.

You'll need to think about whom to invite. She'll be cremated, of course, and there's a nice little hotel just down the road from the cemetery, with a very nice room. And they'll let us hire the caterers – something a bit different, you know – only I'll need to know numbers.

Over the next few days Julie thought a lot about Aunty Clare. She looked about half the age of Julie's mum, though in fact she was only about six years younger, which made her forty-one. She lived in a bungalow in the nicest part of the town, it had huge lawns to the front and side. She'd been married to Terry since before Julie was born, but they'd never had children; they had plenty of money instead, Julie's mother had always said. Julie couldn't see anything wrong with that. And the way she organised the funeral, everything went like a dream. Brian didn't object. He'd seemed a bit dazed by the price of everything and had backed out, letting Clare get on with it.

Julie thought carefully about who to invite, she couldn't think of many people. In the end she invited most of the people from her mother's section of the biscuit factory, Ada, who her mother used to go cleaning with, and, after much thought, Alison. But she was amazed at the numbers that turned up, people she didn't recognise at all, apart from a very old woman called Aunty Elsie, who had a shrunken, shrivelled face and a mouth very full of teeth.

They don't fit me, you know, she said to everyone. They're new this week.

Brian didn't say anything about all the strange people. He sat and stood stiffly throughout the service in his best suit and didn't cry. Julie stood beside him in the pew wearing navy blue trousers because she didn't have any black ones, and a black three-quarter-length jacket of her mother's. She didn't cry either, but she kept her face lowered so people wouldn't know. It was funny, she thought, that the people closest to her mother, including Aunty Clare, who looked very smart in a loose black suit and a wide-brimmed hat with a veil, weren't crying, when most of the people from the biscuit factory, and some of the people Julie didn't know (Aunty Clare said they were all relations) and Ada, wept all the time. The only time Julie felt like crying was when the vicar talked about life passing like a flame. It was true, she thought, like those wildlife programmes she watched on telly, all those creatures living and dying all the time, eaten alive, starving to death or falling in flight. Some of them, like butterflies, only lived a few hours anyway, and when they'd gone, what did it matter? That was like Julie's mother. She'd worked in a factory most of her life and had taken on cleaning jobs in the evenings when Brian had been laid off. She'd married one man, had his child, then left him for another. When she wasn't at work she was cleaning and cooking at home, but what did any of that matter? In a few years' time who would remember that Christine Morris had died?

The vicar said a few more words, about Julie's mother being a valuable member of the community and a good and devoted mother, it was clear he didn't know her at all. After that it was time for the reception.

Brian wasn't there, he just didn't go. People kept asking Julie where he was and she had to say he wasn't feeling too well. She could tell they found it a bit shocking but Julie was glad. It made it easier to ask Aunty Clare the question she'd been saving up. Anyway, once the buffet arrived everyone forgot about Brian. There were pastry boats with prawns, and salmon mousse, and things no one recognised, a big green savoury jelly that Aunty Elsie spat out straight away because it wasn't sweet. All the napkins were edged in black and there was an orchid by each plate, and different waiters for the food and drink. Aunty Clare had set up a little table with photos of Julie's mother when she was young, up to getting married, and a jewellery box she'd had as a child, even a hair-band, and in the background Nat King Cole sang 'When I Fall in Love', which had been her favourite song. Julie was glad she hadn't had to organise all that, she'd never have thought of everything. As it was she didn't have much to do at all, but she couldn't get to Aunty Clare for all the people stopping her to say what a grand woman her mother was, and how sorry they were, Julie had no idea she'd been so popular. She stopped Aunty Elsie poking her finger in the mousse and asking everyone where the band was, then she got stuck with a bunch of relatives who all said how much she'd grown. Finally she found herself in a corner with Alison, who was drinking too much.

I'm celebrating, she said in a loud whisper, I'm pregnant.

You never, Julie said.

Eight weeks, said Alison.

Alison had been seeing someone called Alan, who wasn't from the biscuit factory, for about four months. No one knew him, but they were going to live together, he had a flat of his own.

I was a bit worried about telling him at first, Alison said, but he was dead chuffed.

Well, Julie said, and Alison laughed.

I know, it's a shocker, isn't it? I nearly died when I did the test, but I feel great now. I don't suppose I should be celebrating at your mother's funeral though, she said, and giggled.

Julie said it was all right.

You shouldn't be drinking though, she said. They had quite a long conversation then, about whether Alison wanted a boy or a girl and what names she liked, and the cost of all the baby things. Then, before Julie knew it, it was time to clear away. People were leaving, saying what an unusual do it had been, and how nice it was to go to something a bit different from time to time. Julie followed Aunty Clare and the caterers around, wondering if she'd ever get her on her own. She waited as Clare spoke to one person then another. Finally, in desperation, she said,

Aunty Clare.

Aunty Clare turned, smiling in a frowning kind of way. Julie felt her face going pink.

I was wondering, she said, and stopped. The pink in her face deepened.

Yes, said Aunty Clare, not impatiently. Julie felt like she was praying.

I thought I – if you didn't mind – if I could stay with you just for a few days – until I get myself sorted.

Aunty Clare looked as if this was a not entirely unexpected blow, from which she rallied swiftly.

Yes, of course, she said, and went back to packing the photographs into a box. That was all she said, but Julie could tell she was thinking. Eventually she said,

It isn't right you staying in that house, and paused. Julie clung to the silence.

If you go home and pack, Clare said, I could pick you up later this evening.

For the first time that day Julie really felt like crying.

O thank you, she said. She couldn't manage to say anything else. Aunty Clare patted her arm.

That's all right, Julie, she said. I'm sure we'll get you fixed up soon.

Julie helped her carry stuff to the car then got in and Aunty Clare drove her to the top of Sefton Street and said she'd be back for her later. Julie thanked her again.

You don't have to keep thanking me, Aunty Clare said. But I don't suppose, she added carefully, I don't suppose you'd call me Clare, would you? Aunty Clare makes me feel so old. She laughed a bit as she said it, but Julie was horrified to think she'd been calling her the wrong thing all this time.

O yes, she said, anxious to make up for it now. I will A – Clare, thank you very much. She got out of the car, still thanking her aunt, and hurried to the house saying Clare, Clare, all the time, it stopped her thinking about Brian. She let herself in, praying that she wouldn't see him, and hurried upstairs.

The house was very quiet. Brian must have gone to the pub, Julie thought, and a great weight rolled off her, she could go without him even knowing now. She hummed as she pulled out her big going-away bag and began folding clothes into it.

Outside her window the trees were a blaze of light.

There weren't any gardens in Sefton Street, just the terraced houses and a row of laburnum trees down either pavement, which every year in spring were suddenly and violently transformed. It made Sefton Street one of the nicest streets in town, her mother always said. That was her mother, who wouldn't see the blossom any more, and as she thought this Julie felt the same tugging pain she'd felt in church, when the vicar talked about life being like a flame, but she wouldn't think about that now.

It was the small things you were likely to forget, like the dotted toilet bag, filled with cotton wool balls and a small jar of Nivea (her mother's) or her hairbrush. She picked up Emily, the rag doll she'd had since before they'd lived with Brian. She didn't need her any more and her bag was full, but Brian would throw her things out, she knew, there'd be no going back. Julie held Emily and gazed at the Lord's Prayer, stitched onto a sampler on her wall. She hated the thought of Emily just being thrown out, and she could always go to the kitchen for an extra carrier. She would go down, Julie thought, and she turned round, and jumped violently. Brian was there, leaning on the frame of the door.

You're leaving then, he said.

Julie held Emily tightly.

She didn't think I was fit to live with, eh? he said.

Julie couldn't think of a single thing to say. Brian looked away from her, down at the floor.

Well, I daresay you'll be better off, he said.

Now he wasn't looking at her Julie was able to speak.

It's not for long, she said. I'll visit.

Without looking up Brian nodded.

Sure. You'll have a better life there, he said. You don't want to spend the rest of your days with an old drunk like me.

Julie was paralysed by his smile. She could only think about how to get past.

Well, don't let me stop you, Brian said. Get on with it.

It was Julie's turn to look down now, clutching Emily and the handle of her bag. There was a silence in which she could feel Brian looking at her, it was like a kind of heat on her skin.

Then he said, Look. Why don't you stay? and without looking up Julie shook her head.

She thought he was going to say something else, cry, or beg her to stay and be really embarrassing, but then she heard him push himself away from the door frame with a grunt and go, she heard the door to his room close.

Julie stayed where she was, unable to believe that was it, sure he'd come back again. When he didn't she gripped Emily and almost shook her in a spasm of excitement. She'd done it, she'd told him, now she was free to leave. She gazed out of the window, but there was still no sign of Aunty Clare. As quietly as she could Julie crept downstairs. If Brian came down, she thought, she'd wait outside. Gripped by an excitement that was partly fear of seeing Brian again, she stood by the window and watched and watched.

A watched kettle never boils, her mother said.

Two little girls skipped along the pavement. The milk van turned into the street, he always called round about now, collecting money. Julie didn't have any money on her and she didn't want to be bothered changing the order, but anyway he was starting at the other end. Julie was just thinking about checking all the things she'd packed when she saw the Fiat. She ran to the door, calling out, Bye, up the stairs, and out onto the street, as if Aunty Clare might forget where she lived.

Are you all packed? said Aunty Clare without smiling, but then she rarely smiled. Yes, thanks, A –, Clare, Julie said.

Then they were off, to Julie's new life. At the corner Julie looked back at the house where she'd lived so long and was relieved when she couldn't see a face at the window. That was all she felt now, leaving the man she'd lived with since she was four years old, the house where her mother brought her up. Maybe she couldn't feel things like ordinary people, Julie thought, adjusting the seat belt. Except for Mick. And she closed her eyes and imagined herself owning a little white Fiat just the same, and driving Mick around in it with their three daughters, or no, two daughters and a son, for Mick, in the back. That was the first thing she'd do when she was settled, she thought. Go and see if Mick was back at Woolworths yet.

I forgot to ask, Clare said, are you working, Julie?

Julie thought about the biscuit factory, but that was part of her old life now.

No, she said. But I am looking.

Aunty Clare sighed quietly.

Well, we'll have to see what we can do, she said. She said a few more things, about it being unlikely that Julie would get anything from the house, her mother hadn't left a will.

Christine always was feckless, she said. She didn't even have her name on the house – everything's in Brian's name, so there's not much to be done about that. But if there's anything of your mother's you particularly want I will go back with you.

Julie didn't mind. She was still hugging herself at the thought of leaving, she certainly didn't want to go back.

We'll have to see, Clare said again, then she was turning into the street where Julie was to live, already Julie could see the bungalow with its long lawn, she recognised it though she hadn't been since she was small.

Later that evening they all sat in Aunty Clare's lounge. There was no telly, Julie realised with some dismay, she had hoped they'd have Sky. Uncle Terry read a newspaper and listened to a play on the radio, Aunty Clare knitted. She was the last person Julie expected to see knitting, but it was designer knitwear. She'd knitted the tight skirt and loose top she was wearing now, in bright zigzag colours, it looked like something from Benetton. Aunty Clare said it would cost up to four hundred pounds to have it made up in the shop.

Julie sat in the silence, leafing through *Better Homes and Gardens*. She would have liked to ask for something to eat, but they'd already eaten, food left over from the funeral, smoked chicken and creamed lentils and salad, with the raspberry sorbet for afters. She never had nice food like that at home. She cooked potato hash for Brian because he liked it and it was easy, and if she put a crust on top it was potato pie and if she used corned beef it was corned beef hash. Sometimes they got a chip supper. That was what she most fancied now, fish and chips, but she didn't know where the chippie was and she didn't like to ask. She hadn't even asked for extra chicken when it was offered, though there were only three slices on her plate.

Julie stared at the magazine and tried not to think about food. She'd have a figure like Aunty Clare's if she stayed. She thought instead about the funeral, and about Alison who was pregnant by somebody no one knew. Before she left Alison had slipped Julie her address and told her to call round, any time, and Julie thought she might. She thought about a good many things, and still it was only half past eight. The radio play ended, Aunty Clare's needles clicked. Brian and Julie never talked much, but the silence wasn't the same as this. Julie waited for an opening in the silence into which she could say, I'm off to bed now, or, I think I'll go to bed, but it didn't happen. She waited a bit longer, then Aunty Clare spoke, surprising her.

Tea? she said, and disappeared into the kitchen. Julie didn't know whether to follow or not, whether or not to offer to help. She looked at Uncle Terry, but he was still hidden behind his newspaper. She looked at the kitchen door, which Aunty Clare had shut behind her, she looked at the crystal ornaments in the cabinet.

I can't live here, she thought.

She heard the thought clearly in her mind before she could stop it. Then Aunty Clare came back with tea in a pot on a tray with cups, a tiny jug of milk and a bowl of sugar. Julie drank hers without sugar, though she always had two at home, and offered to wash up, but Aunty Clare said she should go to bed, she'd had a tiring day, so she went. Everything in the room was ready, one edge of the duvet turned back. Julie unpacked very little then climbed in beneath the duvet, which was a Wedgwood blue colour, patterned with pale yellow, like the curtains and the pillowcases and the lampshades.

Julie lay on one side then the other. She heard Uncle Terry's voice, then Aunty Clare saying, – not for long. Light came through the curtains from the quiet road. Julie lay, listening to the quietness and to the stupid, deaf beating of her heart.

*

When winter is at its most severe, the Arctic fox will leave her young to starve so that she herself may survive for the next breeding season.

Julie always used to like wildlife programmes, now they made her cry.

What's up with you? Mick said, coming in. Julie turned her face away. She didn't want him to see her crying again.

It's just a programme, she said.

Jesus, what's that? said Mick.

A young auk spiralled downwards from a high ledge, tumbling exhausted through the Arctic winds. Instantly one of the fox cubs pounced and began ripping it apart. It could only flutter feebly, and stare into the camera with mournful eyes.

Julie felt a sob break out of her.

Jesus, Mick said again. How can they just stand there, filming that?

Julie knew that the cub was also doomed, in spite of its temporary feast. It, too, would give up the unequal battle to live. And it was no use crying about these things, no use at all.

If it's bothering you that much, Mick said, why watch it?

Julie struggled for explanations.

It's just – they're only born to die, she said, her voice breaking with the effort of not crying aloud.

Now there's a new thought, said Mick.

Julie pressed the tissue from her sleeve to her eyes. She couldn't get at the heart of her grief, all these beautiful wild things, struggling into their doomed existence.

But – they're born in a place they can't live, she said and, abandoning all pretence, sobbed into her tissue, even though she knew how much this annoyed Mick.

What are you like, he said. Seventy thousand miles away some fox is having a hard time and here you are freaking out. Why don't you crack up over something real? Look at me, I'm having a hard time. What about all the people on the streets –

Mick was warming up now, this was his favourite subject. Julie lowered the tissues from her eyes.

I did cry about you, she said, when you were on the streets.

Something strange was happening to Julie and Mick. She wasn't trying to goad him, yet she said things, all the time, that drove him crazy. And she couldn't seem to help saying them. He was looking at her now as though, if she wasn't pregnant, he might have hit her. Then he said something, very deliberately, that he knew she'd find terrible.

Jesus fucking Christ, he said, and went upstairs, slamming the door between.

Soon after moving in with Aunty Clare Julie went to see Alison.

If you wait a minute, Alison said, I'll come out with you.

She seemed very anxious for Julie not to go in.

Alan's a bit busy, she said, hurrying out again.

They walked along the banks of the canal. It was a grey day, but all along the banks the broom was out, dropping buttery reflections in the still, green water.

Alison talked all the time.

Of course we're not staying there long, in the flat I mean, we want to move when the baby comes, Alan wants to travel. He's been all over the place already, India and Morocco and that, but he'd really like to go to South America, only it's probably not the best place for a baby. Eh, we were in the pub and this bloke said he knew someone who'd been to Ecuador and got chatted up by this gorgeous girl and he took her for a meal and the next thing he knew he was waking up two days later with only one kidney.

O God, Julie said. Alison laughed.

Alan thought that were great. They were at it all night then, him and this bloke, thinking up Useful Phrases for Ecuador, like, Give us me kidney back, or, Excuse me I seem to have been operated on. They even made a song up, but you have to sing it in a Scots accent – I kidney love you, if I didney love you, all the time – Alison sang the tune. He's a daft bastard, she said fondly.

Julie thought about Mick.

Shall I tell you Alan's favourite joke, Alison said. There's a pig goes to the Jobcentre and he says to the bloke at the desk, Can you help me, I'm looking for a job, and the bloke says, This is great, a talking pig, and he phones Billy Smart's circus and says, Eh, I've got a talking pig here, and Billy Smart says, Great, bring him round, and the man says to the pig, You're in luck, I fixed you up with Billy Smart's circus, and the pig says, But I'm a plumber.

Alison fell about.

He got that one off the Brian Conley show, she said.

Julie noticed how most of the wild flowers you saw were gold. There were all the different greens of the leaves and the occasional splash of cow parsley, but the buttercups, dandelions and broom were all bright yellow.

Alison told her what a good cook Alan was, and how he wouldn't let her do any of it, not that she was complaining.

What does he do? Julie said, and Alison went a bit vague.

O different things, she said. He's never short of cash.

They stepped carefully over rusted cans.

Alison said her parents weren't speaking to her yet, but they'd get over it. Anyway it was their lookout, she didn't care. She didn't look as if she cared, she was full of energy, her pale face glowed. Julie thought pregnancy must be a wonderful thing if it made you feel like that, and although she'd almost decided that a childless marriage would be best for her and Mick, she began thinking again about having a baby.

I've had a scan, Alison said. I'll have another one later, and they might be able to tell then if it's a boy or a girl. I'm not bothered really, but Alan'd like a girl. Three people at the clinic told me not to help out with the lambing – I must look like the kind of girl who goes round with her hand shoved up a sheep's arse.

Have you thought of a name yet? Julie said, and Alison said that at the moment she liked Sammy, for either a boy or a girl. Julie didn't know if she liked that or not, but she didn't say anything. They walked on a bit further in silence, though even when Alison wasn't talking she radiated energy. Julie felt the difference in her, she almost envied her. She waited a bit then said,

I saw Mick a bit ago.

O yes, said Alison.

Outside Woolworth. He was playing a guitar and singing.

They laughed.

I saw him a few times, Julie said, and then he just disappeared.

Alison didn't say anything.

You haven't heard anything, have you? Julie said, and Alison shook her head.

I don't see Steve these days, she said, and that was that.

They talked a bit more, about the biscuit factory, Alison wasn't going back either, they were making too many redundancies. She'd have to see what happened after the baby was born. When they got to the main road Alison said Julie must call round again some time and have a cup of tea. She seemed to be saying goodbye. Julie said she'd like that, and turned to go in a different direction. She considered going into town to look for Mick, but when he wasn't there she just got depressed, so she decided instead to go back to the bungalow.

She was getting used to being there, to living in other people's rooms. Her life felt a little flat and dull, with Mick not being there, and with not being at work, but there were things to do and she did them faithfully. Aunty Clare was growing orchids in the conservatory. They had to be fed and watered in tiny, regular amounts and turned round frequently. Then there was the dusting in the front room, with all the crystal ornaments in the glass cabinet, and blossom to be swept from the garden paths. Each day also Julie had her own secret ritual. She crept into Aunty Clare's room as if someone might hear her, and opened the fitted wardrobes. Every day she examined the forty-three pairs of Italian shoes and eighteen handbags, lifting them out, smelling the leather, looking inside. Aunty Clare was in love with Italy, she went there every year for a holiday. She was pleased when Julie said she looked Italian.

It's where I feel I belong, she said.

Some of the dresses and suits were Italian as well, and everything was co-ordinated. All the dresses had a jacket that matched, and shoes, and there were fourteen suits. If Julie had been anything like the same size she'd have tried them on, but she had to make do with holding them up against her and trying to imagine how they'd look. Next she opened the drawers with their silk teddies and stockings, but she didn't go through them because everything was beautifully folded, Julie couldn't leave things folded as well as that. Sometimes she lowered her face to them and smelled, Aunty Clare always kept scented sachets in the drawers. In one Julie found the photos Aunty Clare had set out at the funeral of Julie's mother and Aunty Clare when they were young, in frilly dresses at the Whit Walks, and in swimming costumes on the beach at Anglesey. One, taken in the same park Julie used to go in, showed Julie's mother, plump and smiling, helping Clare to walk; Clare, tiny and dark, was frowning in concentration. They were never alike, you could never have told they were sisters. And Julie was like her mother. She would never be like Aunty Clare no matter what she did. But she could sit at her dressing table and spray on just a little of her perfume, Nina Ricci, and smear the tiniest amount of moisturiser onto the tip of her finger. It was a restructuring, anti-ageing formula with a UV sunscreen and a collagen base, AHAs and liposomes. Julie hadn't been able to find it at Boots. She smoothed it onto her face, patting under her eyes like it said in the magazines, then looked at herself in the mirror as if expecting to see a change already. But it was still the same plump face with the tangled mousy hair. Aunty Clare had sleek black hair that was never out of place. But she always carried a comb with her, she'd told Julie, and whenever she went to the bathroom or passed a mirror she quickly ran it through her hair. Then, too, she had one of those cuts Vidal Sassoon called a bias cut, that you could just shake into place. Julie sighed. She didn't think her own hair would do that no matter how you cut it. So sometimes wanting to be like Aunty Clare just made her tired. And hungry. There was never enough food in the house, no snack-type food anyway. There was bread in the freezer, French sticks and packets of croutons, but no thick-sliced white, no biscuits, crackers or cake. And Julie didn't feel free to eat the food there was, the pâtés, tinned anchovies and capers. Aunty Clare was a good cook and always made something different every night, but she only served tiny portions. Julie didn't know how she managed off what she ate, she only ever had half a grapefruit and a black coffee for breakfast, crackers and cottage cheese for lunch. Then she insisted on doing all the cooking herself at night, so they never got to eat before seven, even when Julie offered to help. She watched Delia Smith and made her own pesto sauce with fresh pasta and salad, or baked fish and roasted peppers stuffed with anchovies and tomatoes. The food smelled so good while it was cooking that Julie thought she might faint before eating it. Then, when it was finally ready, Aunty Clare served her a tiny portion, just a bit bigger than her own, but smaller than Uncle Terry's. When she offered her more Julie knew she was expected to refuse. Sometimes she put dry bread on the table as well, for Julie and Terry, but again Julie knew she should eat less than Uncle Terry, who always left some that was taken away at the end. Julie took to drawing out her own money from the building society to buy packets of biscuits and crisps which she ate very carefully so she wouldn't leave crumbs or traces of grease. She walked into town every day, glancing in at the Jobcentre, where experienced bar staff and machinists were required, before buying herself a huge packet of chips in the precinct. She ate them, looking in the windows of all the clothes shops that sold fashionable clothes in small sizes, and one day, when she had nearly finished the chips, she saw Mick.

She almost didn't see him, he was just sitting in the side entrance of Marks and Spencer's, wrapped in a blanket. For weeks Julie had expected to see him singing again with his friend. She stood still for a moment, astonished, he was so different from the Mick she knew in her mind. She hesitated a bit, then said, Mick, softly, but he didn't look up. Julie stood by, not knowing what to do. She noticed the margarine tub by Mick's side with some coppers in it and a five-pence piece. When she took a step forward the small brown dog she'd seen with him before peered at her inquisitively from between the folds of the blanket.

So, Julie said. Where's your friend then?

Mick moved his head dully, she wasn't sure if he recognised her or not.

Darren's ill, he said, and looked down again.

You don't look too well yourself, Julie said. She wondered how she dared talk to him like that, after not speaking to him for years, but it was like talking to someone who wasn't there. She reached for her purse, found some change from the chips and dropped it, feeling less self-conscious now. Mick didn't look at either her or the change. Julie felt annoyed. She'd given more, a ten pence and a twenty, than anyone else apparently had. She squatted so that her face was almost level with his.

Mick still didn't look as if he knew her, and if he didn't know her, why wasn't he surprised that some strange woman was crouching down and talking to him? At this level Julie could see how bad he looked; greyish, unwashed. There was a cold sore at the corner of his mouth and his eyes were watering, a trickle of water ran down the long scar on his face.

You look terrible, Julie said, she felt the way he looked as a kind of blow. Mick seemed to be laughing to himself.

Where are you staying? she said, but Mick only laughed.

Here and there, sister, he sang at her suddenly. Nowhere.

Julie was frightened by his eyes. She got up slowly, tried to think of something to say but couldn't, then bent down again and left the remaining chips at his side. Mick didn't look up or move as she hurried away. By the time, she left the precinct she felt terrible, tears spilling down, she'd never cried that way, not even at her mother's funeral. Now in the middle of the street with everyone staring at her she couldn't stop. She hurried into the nearest side street and followed a complicated route back to Aunty Clare's, avoiding all the main roads.

The next day she made up her mind to take him some soup in Aunty Clare's flask. She bought some specially, and toured the precinct and market ground, but there was no sign of Mick. The thought struck her that if he was dead she might never know, there'd be no reason at all to let her know, she just wouldn't see him any more, and as she passed the fruit stalls with their bright globes of peppers and fruit, she felt her eyes filling again. She went back the next day and the next, then she stopped looking.

More days passed, then one evening Aunty Clare said Julie could really do with some clothes, she should meet her one day at lunchtime in town. Julie was worried.

I don't have much money, she said, but Aunty Clare told her not to bother about that, she was sure they'd see something affordable. Julie still felt worried, that they wouldn't find anything her size, she hoped it wouldn't be too embarrassing. But she was excited as well, she had been feeling the poverty of her wardrobe compared to Aunty Clare's. It hadn't mattered when she was working, at the biscuit factory everyone wore overalls, but now she just slopped around in the same old things every day, a pair of dark blue baggy trousers and a lighter blue baggy top, or a purplish Indian dress like a tent. She could hardly sleep that night for thinking about all the things she might buy.

The next day Julie put on her best dress, the flowery, drop-waisted one, and her mother's black jacket, and drew nearly all her money out of her building society. She was seized again by the worry that she wouldn't find anything to fit, but long, loose dresses were in now, they buttoned down the front and you wore them over leggings if you wanted and short stretchy tops with sleeves. Julie found one that fitted, though it was a bit tight around the bust and fell nearly to the floor. Aunty Clare was a bit doubtful, but Julie loved it and it was her money. It was black, with a close squiggly pattern all over it in cream, and they found a cream-coloured top to go under it which was miles too tight but you couldn't tell under the dress, and black strappy sandals with a two-inch heel. Julie wanted to wear them all right away and Aunty Clare laughed at her though she rarely even smiled, and helped her cut the labels off. It was like Aunty Clare to have scissors when you needed them.

Julie walked into the street feeling tall and proud, carrying her jacket though it was cold, she didn't want to wear it over her new clothes.

Then, when they passed Wallis, Aunty Clare pointed to a coat in the window, a long, silky cream-coloured coat. It cost more than the rest of the outfit put together and Julie didn't have much money left.

I can't afford that, she said, but Aunty Clare took her arm. Just try it on anyway, she said.

Julie tried it on. Though the dress was long the coat was longer, stopping just short of the black strappy sandals. It had caped shoulders and a belt, though Julie tied this at the back.

It doesn't make me look pregnant, does it? she said, but Aunty Clare assured her it was very flattering.

Julie didn't know what to say next, she'd already told

Aunty Clare she didn't have the money, but there was Aunty Clare, helping her off with the coat, and giving it to the assistant saying, I think we'll take this one, and the assistant was carrying it to the counter, and Aunty Clare was taking out one of those plastic cards her purse was full of, then she turned to Julie and said, My treat, and Julie wanted to hug her, but you didn't hug Aunty Clare, she was always too serious.

O thank you, she said instead. Can I wear it now? and they went out onto the street, Julie conscious at every step of the coat floating round her in the breeze. And she thought about Mick seeing her, he'd never seen her dressed up before. She imagined him standing at a corner, then seeing her and turning to watch her go by, and just as she was thinking this she saw him. He was standing outside the Arndale Centre with a stack of magazines at his feet.

Buy *The Big Issue*, he said to everyone who passed. Three people passed him, then someone stopped to buy a copy. Julie stopped too, then hurried to catch up with Aunty Clare who was fiddling with the clasp of her handbag.

You know, I paid a fortune for this bag, she said as they passed Mick. I've a good mind to take it back to the shop.

Julie couldn't look at Mick. She heard him pause, in the middle of saying *Big* and *Issue*, then he went on. Julie felt supremely self-conscious. She couldn't say anything to either Mick or Aunty Clare. It was only when they were well away from him, entering Marks and Spencer's, that she started to think about seeing him, and him seeing her, and what he'd thought of her coat.

Aunty Clare always did her food shopping in her lunch hour at Marks and Spencer's. Marks' stuff might be expensive, she always said, but you knew it was good. She'd once bought an iceberg lettuce at Marks and it had lasted nearly two weeks without going brown. The day

Julie bought her new clothes she carried all the shopping back on the bus and Aunty Clare said it was a big help. So from then on every Tuesday Julie went into town to meet Aunty Clare and carry the bags back. They went to Marks and Spencer's and to a little delicatessen in the Arndale which sold fresh pasta and capers and more different kinds of sausage than Julie could have imagined. Every week Aunty Clare asked Julie if there was anything she'd like to try and Julie got bolder about making suggestions.

How about pickled walnuts, she said, or that bread with the olives?

Then she could hardly wait to get home to try it all, it was painful to wait till evening.

Each time they went she saw Mick but she didn't let on because she was always with Aunty Clare. Then one week she decided to go early. She would take him some soup, or maybe coffee, the weather was warmer now. She thought about soup, then coffee, for a long time, finally settling on soup. Then she thought about what to wear. She put all her best things on and took up her hair with the two combs from Woolworths, then put on just a little of Aunty Clare's make-up, the lipstick and mascara. Most of it would have come off by the time she met Aunty Clare, in fact most of it would probably come off by the time she met Mick, but it made her feel better setting off.

Julie felt like a criminal though she couldn't say why. She left by the back door clutching a carrier bag with the flask inside. When she got to town she thought she'd missed him again, like the last time she'd taken soup, then she saw him, a bit further down than usual, talking to one of the other sellers.

Julie hung back. She didn't want to go up to him while anyone else was around. She stared at the window of Dorothy Perkins. They'd started doing bigger sizes now, and there was a magenta suit on display. Julie had never had a suit. She was wondering if she had enough time to try it on, but when she looked back Mick had stopped talking and was heading her way. Julie felt overcome by a nervous helplessness, but if she didn't speak to him now she never would, anyway she had to get on and meet Aunty Clare. She wished she hadn't brought the soup, it seemed a stupid thing to do. Mick was standing in his usual spot now, sorting out his magazines on the pavement. Julie walked towards him. She stood a little bit further off than she needed to and waited until he looked up.

Hiya, he said, and Julie could feel herself going bright red, but at least he recognised her this time.

I thought – you might like some soup, she said, and held out the flask in its bag, feeling terrible.

O right, Mick said, looking surprised. He opened the bag. What kind is it? he said.

Tomato, Julie said, relieved that she'd got the worst bit over.

O yeah, I would. Ta. Yes, thanks very much, Mick said, and Julie blushed even harder than before. Whenever she saw Mick she was conscious of the difference between the Mick in her mind, big and stocky and red-cheeked, and the person she could see, still tall, but greyish and shapeless. And he was definitely scruffy, hair scraped back and matted, ripped jeans and at least three sweaters. But he didn't look as bad as last time, at least his eyes were focusing.

Julie felt very conscious of her new clothes. She hovered a bit.

Well, she said. I'd better go.

Right, said Mick. So, how'll I get you the flask back?

Julie hadn't thought of that. She blushed again, feeling more stupid than ever.

It's all right, she said, thinking that she'd have to buy Aunty Clare a new one.

I tell you what, Mick said, don't you come past here

sometimes with a woman? If you come back later on I'll give you the flask back.

Julie was horrified.

O no, it's all right, she said. I don't think we'll be coming this way. I tell you what though, she said, gathering courage. I'll be here again next week, I could pick up the flask then.

Mick was scanning the crowd for possible buyers. He picked up the magazines.

Yeah, sure, he said.

Well – I'll be going then, said Julie, suddenly happy.

Right, said Mick. Then he smiled at her. He had a beautiful smile.

How would you like me to knit you something? Aunty Clare said later that evening. Maybe a cardigan, you know, a long one.

O yes, Julie said, then, But isn't it expensive?

O I don't mind, said Aunty Clare. I hate not having anything to knit.

They would go tomorrow, she said, and choose a pattern and some wool.

Julie was thrilled. So much had happened to her in the one day, the new clothes, a date with Mick, and now this. Aunty Clare was a wonderful knitter and long cardigans were still the in thing, though they'd gone out of the shops with it being summer. Julie couldn't help wondering how long it'd take to knit, but she didn't like to ask.

Aunty Clare was often very kind to Julie. She'd given her the black handbag with the broken clasp, and wouldn't take any rent, which was just as well, because the DSS money wasn't through yet, Julie could hardly afford the bus rides into town. Aunty Clare said she was going to visit Brian to try to sort something out, it wasn't right that Julie should have nothing at all from her mother. She asked if Julie wanted to go too, but Julie didn't. She didn't miss being with her mother or having anything of her mother's, she felt she was settling in quite happily where she was.

Then as she lay in bed thinking how lucky she was to be there, she heard Uncle Terry's voice raised a bit louder than usual.

Well, how long's it going to go on then? and Aunty Clare said something Julie didn't catch.

You said a few days at first and it's been nearly two months.

Julie hadn't understood that they were talking about her, but now she knew they must be. She lay very still and anxious, hardly breathing so she could hear.

Keep your voice down, Aunty Clare said.

Why can't she live with her stepfather? said Uncle Terry. That's where she belongs.

I can't just throw her out, said Aunty Clare. She's my sister's child, for God's sake. She doesn't want to live with Brian and I can't say I blame her.

Well, she can't stay here for ever, Terry said. If she'd get herself a job she could find a place of her own.

Aunty Clare said nothing to this, and Julie could imagine the look on her face which meant she wasn't going to discuss it any more. Terry was quiet too, and after a while Julie stopped straining to hear.

She didn't know what to do.

She would go in to them, she thought, and make it plain that she'd heard every word they'd said. You don't have to worry, she'd say. I won't stay where I'm not wanted, but minutes passed and it was no longer the right time. Then she thought she would leave the next day, just leave and not tell anyone, she could imagine the shock and dismay. She must have heard you, Aunty Clare would say to Uncle Terry. You should never have said those things. But none of these thoughts were any use, they couldn't take her beyond the fact that she had nowhere to go.

Minutes passed in the darkness, Julie wasn't sleepy at all. She lay restlessly as one scene after another played itself out in her mind. Some of them were very dramatic, others quiet and dignified. In the end, though, she couldn't see herself doing any of them, she could only settle for saying nothing, and looking round on the quiet for somewhere to go.

So you haven't got anywhere to go, Mick said. Julie shook her head.

You're fixed up, she said with a brave smile, and I'm homeless.

For Mick had just told her his astonishing good news. He'd run into his Uncle Si, who he hadn't seen for years, while he was selling *The Big Issue*. Uncle Si had obviously been upset to see Mick on the streets, and had come back two or three times to talk to him. Mick had mentioned that he'd trained for a while as a brickie, and it was then that Uncle Si had come up with his great idea. The council had slapped an order on him for house repairs; they'd said his house was a danger to the public, it was near enough falling down, and if he didn't get the repairs done they'd move in themselves, do the work and charge him top whack. They could do that, it seemed, even though the house was his own, so Uncle Si was stuck, flat broke, and he'd said that Mick could move in for a while if he wanted, rent free, in return for doing as much of the work as he could. And Mick had struck a deal. He'd move in providing Darren could move in too. Darren could help with the heavy work even though he wasn't trained. Uncle Si hadn't messed around at all. It'd be nice, he'd said, to have someone around for a change.

So I won't see you again, Julie said.

O yes, said Mick. He could still go on selling the mag until he was fixed up with a real job and a place of his own, though he wouldn't do it every day.

The way he told her, looking so pleased, brought her own situation home to Julie.

What's up? said Mick.

Julie tried to smile. She could feel she was making an impression, which made her even more emotional, Mick had to press her to speak. Then, as she said the words she'd overheard that night they sounded even worse, she was hard put to it not to cry.

That was two weeks ago, she said. And I've looked everywhere for a job or a room but there's nothing.

This was their second conversation since the day she'd given him the soup. The last time she'd dressed in all her best things, then taken them off and put on the old purple dress and her cagoule. This time she took him orange juice in a bottle and a packet of the chocolate biscuits she got cheap from a market stall.

Ta very much, he said. You don't have to feed me, you know.

O it's all right, Julie said. It's nothing.

Well, thanks, said Mick. He opened the packet with some difficulty. Want one?

Julie took the biscuit, then they were both grinning at one another until Julie suddenly felt shy. She said,

Where's your dog?

Dog's dead, Mick said, through a mouthful of biscuit.

It didn't seem like the best start for a conversation, but Mick began telling her how it had happened. The dog had caught a chill from being out so much and had just got worse. Then it had got the shits and no one would let them in the shelter with him. They couldn't afford a vet, but someone had told them the RSPCA'd put him down free, and Mick had said that'd be the kindest thing. Darren had been really cut up about it though. He used to sit up all night nursing the dog (whose name was Dennis) in a blanket, then go around stinking of shit all day. He went on a bender when Mick finally took Dennis away.

Julie remembered that Darren was the name of the lad Mick used to sing with.

Is Darren selling these as well? she said, meaning the magazines.

Darren wasn't selling, Mick said, he wasn't well enough yet. But he was going to rehab.

Julie wasn't sure what that meant and she didn't like to ask. She asked Mick where he was staying instead and he said, Just around. Mainly around Oxford Road station. He used to kip in Heaton Park which was nicer, but too far away to trek in every day. He'd had bed and breakfast for a while in Rusholme, but had fallen out with the landlord, who'd kept moving more people into Mick's room. And the landlord hadn't liked Darren, he'd thrown him out.

There was a pause while Mick sold a magazine. Julie couldn't think of anything else to say, she wondered if she should buy one and thought she would, then that she wouldn't. Finally she said,

I'll have to go, I'm meeting my aunt.

Yeah, sure, Mick said. Ta for the stuff.

That was the only other time they'd spoken, and now here she was telling him everything, about her mother dying and about not wanting to live with Brian. As she spoke she really felt like one of the homeless.

At least you've got the choice, Mick said.

What choice? said Julie.

Where to live, said Mick. Julie felt a bit offended.

You said you couldn't stand your dad, she said. It's the same thing.

It's not, Mick said. He threw me out four times. You can't just keep going back.

Julie didn't want to lose her new homelessness.

Yes, but Brian, she said. He – well – I couldn't live with him. He's not well – in his head ...

How do you mean? said Mick.

Julie didn't know how to say it.

He'd get drunk – you know, she said. Then he'd – do things – come into my room and stuff.

Mick stared at her.

The dirty bastard, he said. Julie felt a pang of joy.

That makes me really fucking mad, said Mick.

O no, Julie said, to mollify him, but she wanted to hear more.

No, Mick said. I mean it. If I ever saw him I'd kick his fucking teeth in. Julie felt a pang of alarm this time.

O no, she said. It wouldn't do any good, you know. He's just – sick. He's out of his head most of the time.

Mick hardly looked any calmer. Then he said,

You can come and stay with us.

Julie blushed hotly.

O no, she said.

Yes, said Mick. Why not? You don't want to sleep on the streets, do you?

Julie didn't want to sleep on the streets.

Well, she said timidly, remembering all the fancy food Aunty Clare made, I can cook. And clean.

It's a bit of a mess, Mick said. But it'd be better than sleeping rough. Until you get fixed up.

What about your uncle? Julie said. Mick hesitated a bit.

He'll be okay, he said.

Hadn't you better ask him first?

No. Look – you come with us Thursday and I'll – I'll say you're my girlfriend.

Julie's heart lurched with joy.

He's a good bloke, Si, Mick said. It'll be right.

I'll tell my – Clare – tonight, Julie said. And she did.

You never mentioned a boyfriend, Clare said, wrinkling her entire forehead into a frown. What does he do?

He's in sales, Julie said.

What kind of sales? said Clare.

Don't interrogate the girl, said Uncle Terry. She's entitled to have a boyfriend.

Well, the thing is, Julie said, he's moving soon. And he wants me to go with him. She said it all at once in a bit of a rush.

This is a bit sudden, said Aunty Clare. I mean, we haven't met him or anything.

She's not a child, said Terry.

Why don't you bring him round to tea, said Aunty Clare.

Well, he's a bit busy, Julie said, wishing she could get out of the conversation. He's moving on Thursday, she said. And – I'm moving with him. She stared at them both.

Julie, Aunty Clare cried, but Julie wasn't going to give in. She knew they didn't really want her.

Don't hector the girl, Clare, Uncle Terry said. Aunty Clare turned on him.

This is your fault, she said.

It isn't anyone's fault, said Julie. I want to go.

Well, then, said Clare, offended.

And I'm not rushing, Julie said. I've known him for years. We were at school together.

Aunty Clare seemed a bit mollified by this, and by the news that they would be living with Mick's uncle. She asked a lot more questions, but Julie wouldn't be drawn. She answered only when she had to. She was relieved that the worst was over, but she hadn't forgiven them. And she could sense Clare's relief beneath the concern.

Well, if you're sure, she said, and you really will have to bring him round some time.

Julie didn't answer. She said,

Do you think you might have finished the cardigan by then? and Aunty Clare laughed and said she'd certainly try. She was in a good mood now and she took Julie into the lounge to measure the cardigan against her. It was beautiful, black and lacy and calf length, with cream flowers around the hem, Aunty Clare had done it to match Julie's new clothes. She held it up against Julie and talked about sewing it up the next day, and Julie couldn't help feeling pleased. Then Aunty Clare put an arm around her for the first time.

You know you'll always have a home here, she said.

Julie didn't say anything, but she let Clare lead her into the kitchen and make her a cup of frothy cocoa. She sat up in bed and hugged her knees and drank it, and then lay awake, nursing her joy.

*

They sat on the clapped-out settee, munching Quavers from giant packs and watching a film on Uncle Si's TV. The set was old and had such a big screen all the actors' faces were pulled to one side. Even so, the film made Julie want to cry. It was about a couple who couldn't have a baby so they paid a younger couple to have one for them, but when the younger woman had the baby she didn't want to give it up. Julie couldn't hate her for it, she could see how she felt, pressing her fingers up against the glass pane between her and the tiny crumpled bundle in its cot. Julie felt the pressure to cry building up, and it got worse when the young mother broke the news to the older woman, who'd been trying to have a baby for ten years.

I don't know what to do, the young woman said. I can't keep him, and I can't give him up.

Leave it in a bin liner, Mick said. Solve everyone's problem, and Darren laughed, but Uncle Si said that wasn't a nice thing to say. But the young woman ran away with the baby, because she'd signed contracts. There was a heartbreaking shot of the older woman in the room she'd prepared for the baby she'd never have, the little mobiles above the cot. It was a gorgeous room and Julie's eyes filled up, partly for the woman and partly because her own baby would never have a room like that.

Julie had dreamed about Uncle Si's house. She knew it was run down now, but she could imagine the way it would be soon: a quiet end-terraced with a patch of garden at the front and hanging baskets full of fuchsia. In fact it was at the end of a row, but it overlooked a railway line, and when you opened the front door there were no floorboards, just a drop through to the foundations, you had to step very carefully from one joist to another. And every room had skipfuls of rubbish and junk in it, wallpaper hung in reams off the walls.

Mick stood in the middle of the front room.

It's got great potential this place, he said.

Julie clung to the wall. She could feel her dream coming away from her like a plaster being ripped from a wound. Mick said he'd show her upstairs.

Walk to one side, he said. They're a bit tricky in the middle.

At least in the bedroom space had been cleared for a single mattress on the floor, and another one was propped up against the wall. In one corner there was a pot sink, but Mick said the taps didn't work. He looked at her apologetically.

Er – he thinks you're my girlfriend, he said. So he's given us this room together.

Julie didn't say anything.

He said he'll sleep downstairs, Mick said. I said we could do that, but he said he quite often sleeps down there anyway – he falls asleep watching telly. Darren's in the little room next door. He pulled the propped-up mattress onto the floor.

You choose, he said. When she didn't say anything he said, What's up?

Nothing, Julie said.

Mick sat down on the mattress and began telling her his plans. He wanted to build a kitchen extension, that way they could have a small dining room, and then he would put a bathroom in the bedroom, where the sink was now. He wanted to open up the cellar, there was plenty of room down there, and maybe do something with the attic space.

It could be made into something, this place, he said. It's not one of them poky little terraces, these are decent-sized rooms.

Julie was hardly listening. She was wondering where to put her clothes, how she could get undressed. A train roared past and everything in the room rattled. Julie looked out of the window into the dying light. She was finally on her own in a room with Mick. She had never felt more lonely in her life.

Mick got up again.

Ah, well, he said. I'd better let you sort yourself out. The others'll be here soon.

Julie didn't want to be left on her own in that room, but she couldn't think of a single reason why he should stay. When he went the bad feeling in her stomach welled into the rest of her like water. She unzipped her bag, pulled out a towel and sat with it on the edge of the mattress, staring at the wall.

She couldn't go back.

Julie, Mick called. Darren's here, and Uncle Si.

Julie edged her way back down the stairs.

She stood awkwardly as the introductions were made. Uncle Si was small and balding, nothing like Mick. Darren was dark and very thin and wouldn't look at anyone. Julie helped them clear a space in the front room and dig the settee out, then the telly. Then Mick went into the kitchen and came back with a six-pack of beer.

This is to celebrate, he said.

They all sat on the settee. Julie got herself a mug because there weren't any glasses, the others drank from the cans. They toasted being there, then, because there wasn't much to say, they watched *The Bill*. Julie couldn't shake the feeling of being outside herself somehow. As soon as *The Bill* was over she said she was going upstairs, that way she could get undressed before Mick came up. Uncle Si said, Wait a bit, and started dragging a suitcase out from behind the settee.

There's blankets here, he said.

Julie carried two blankets upstairs as Mick began his third can. She could hear them all laughing downstairs. Now that she was alone the fear came back, uncertainty made all her movements slow. She didn't know which mattress to pick, she put her bag down on one side of the mattress then the other, she didn't know what to unpack. She stood helplessly in the dark because there wasn't a bulb.

Later, lying on one of the blankets and underneath the other, she heard Mick's heavy tread on the stairs. He opened the door, tripped over something, swore, and began pulling off clothes. All Julie's body seemed to be listening. He crossed the room, then sank down heavily on Julie's mattress, she shifted to one side just in time.

He didn't seem to know she was there.

Julie lay very still, taking this in. He lay turned away from her, already she could hear his breathing changing with sleep.

He was taking up both blankets.

Mick, Julie whispered. There was no response.

Julie put out a hand and pressed his shoulder through the thin material of his T-shirt; nothing.

She should move to the other mattress, she knew, there was hardly any room. But now he was here, so close to her, she didn't want to go. She pressed herself to one side, giving him as much room as possible and taking in the smells of him, mainly bad: unwashed clothes, cigarette smoke, beer. After a while, greatly daring, she let her hand rest on his back.

She slept fitfully, and in the longer periods when she was awake felt all over again the shock of being there, of Mick's body so near her own.

Mick was restless too. He slept heavily at first then

moved round, flinging out arms and legs and coughing. Even when he wasn't coughing his breath rattled in his chest. Once he rolled over facing her and stared at her in dull surprise before going back to sleep. Julie still couldn't bring herself to move.

Towards morning he began having nightmares.

No, God, Jesus, no, he wept.

Mick, Julie whispered.

Please, Christ.

What is it? Julie said. She held onto his shoulder, frightened now.

I can't, he cried in a high, broken voice. Leave us alone.

Julie was almost crying with him. She moved closer and held him tightly. Mick moaned aloud and Julie rocked him. Gradually he stopped crying and rested his face on hers, all his hair fell across her nose and mouth. Then he slipped his arms round her and his breathing quietened down. So, clumsily, inadequately, they fell into it; Julie not moving, Mick finding his way around her body. At one point he stopped and said, O, shit. But he tried again, and Julie held onto him as if he was the last thing left in her world.

The young woman was back now, at the older woman's house, clutching her little boy. Her face was all crumpled from crying.

I can't do right by this baby, she said, and held him out to the older woman.

When he grows up – tell him I loved him, she said, then she ran away into the night.

Julie got up from the settee.

I'll just get a drink, she managed to say, and almost ran into the kitchen. She leant against the door and sobbed.

Everything about babies made her cry these days, it seemed, she was always coming across something new and awful. Only two days ago she'd gone into the library to look up some symptoms she was having in a medical dictionary – pregnancy isn't an illness, all the pregnancy books said, and on the covers young women in leotards, still lithe in their eighth month, sat in improbable yogic positions and beamed – and she'd turned straight to two photographs of a battered baby, three weeks old, before and after stitching.

Julie stood, unable to turn the page. She shut her eyes, afraid she was going to cry, or be sick right there in the library. But even with her eyes shut she could still see the baby, and for days after she had moments of queasiness as the images returned.

Bloody, bloody kettle, Julie said. She'd forgotten how hot the handle got, and that it had been boiled. She found a cloth and tried again, lighting the burner with a match. That was another thing she'd noticed these days, her language getting worse, though she was always picking Mick up on his. She'd have to be careful when the baby was born.

Julie sat on the stool and stared at the flames licking the kettle base. At the meeting they'd said that people chose their own parents before they were born, whatever they were like, for the lessons they had to learn. That was karma. But Mick had said it was balls, it was the way society was everywhere you looked, the strong oppressing the weak. And Julie thought about one explanation then the other until she was tired, but nothing seemed to explain it to her at all.

If you look after your own garden, Medbh said, – never mind poking your nose over someone else's hedge – look after your own, that's all you're asked to do. It's all you can do. You can only look after your own garden your own way. Because if you do go into someone else's, even with the best intentions, the work you do'll be yours. And that might not suit them. You might be planting hydrangeas where they'd always wanted a rose bush, or digging a pond when they really wanted a big lawn – you don't know. Just because they've not got round to planting a lawn – and maybe they're complaining about it, saying how they wished they had a lovely one like yours – people are good at that – there's no need for you to go jumping over that wall with your Flymo. Because if you do enough work for them, what's going to happen to your own bit of green? And however hard you work for them, sooner or later they'll turn round to you and say, This is my patch. Clear off. Go and look after your own. And they'll be right. Whereas, she said, looking round at everyone with bright, severe eyes, if you tend your own garden well, and get it the way you'd like it, people'll walk past and say, What a lovely garden, however did you get it growing so well? or, Can I have a cutting? And that way you can be a real help. But if your own garden's like a council dump, people are hardly likely to want you butting in on theirs, are they? They'll say, Get back, and sort your own yard out.

Medbh was big on gardens. She used them to demonstrate nearly every point she made. When Julie listened she always imagined she was back at Aunty Clare's with its long neat lawns. She couldn't think about Uncle Si's because there wasn't a garden. But looking round at the others in the audience who were all listening and nodding their heads, Julie thought she must be the only one there with that problem.

Medbh's speech was her answer to a question from a rough-looking young man about international socialism. Didn't Medbh think that the wealth of the world should be redistributed, so that poorer countries got a share? Medbh had been very severe. There was nothing people liked better, she said, than organising a big do in aid of some downtrodden country thousands of miles away – the further away the better in fact – and anywhere so long as it wasn't on their own doorstep. When it came to doing some shopping for the old lady next door, or minding a neighbour's baby, there was always some excuse. O, no, I can't do that, I'm organising a jumble sale for Rwanda.

Medbh was against interference of any kind in other countries. Look where it's got us, she said. We've caused most of the problems they need aid for. If everyone minded their own business, and took care of the problems under their noses, the world wouldn't be in this mess.

The rough-looking young man hadn't finished.

I don't mean charity, he started to say, but Medbh had already moved onto someone else who wanted to know what you did about your garden when you had a bad back.

Well, if you ask someone to help, she said, and they agree, and you're willing to pay or do something in return, that's all right. Anything else upsets the balance.

Julie could see everything Medbh said very clearly, she always made perfect sense. She wished Mick would come to the meetings, because when she got home and tried to explain it to him, it all came out wrong.

Who's talking about gardening? he'd say. I'm talking about who owns the means of production, not who's mowing the fucking lawn.

Julie could see what he meant, but she saw it Medbh's way too. That was why she felt Mick should come, just to one meeting.

What, visit the Monster Raving Mind-Power Party? he said. No chance. All power to the one mind they've got and that, but I think I'll keep my own.

He thought Julie should come to a few of the SWP meetings.

I will if you come to mine, she said.

I don't want to know, said Mick. But Julie was sure that if he just saw Medbh once he'd be impressed. She stood centre stage in the Nicholas Crowther Hall, tiny, dark and ordinary-looking, but wearing a flame-coloured kaftan. Light streamed around her from a lamp behind as she spoke, in spite of the name, with a Lancashire accent. She was never phased by any question, or by anyone getting angry as they sometimes did, and she had a short way with intellectuals.

But if identity is social and determined by language, one young woman said, what you're talking about is a kind of no-space for people who meditate – a marginalised existence.

What I'm talking about, Medbh said sternly, is not feeding your brain so much it starts to get loose and runny. The trouble with education is that it trains the brain to think too much of itself. You've all heard that story about parts of the body, each thinking that it was the most important, you know, the liver said to the heart and the brain, You'd be no use without me, I get rid of all the poisons, and the heart said, Well, without me you wouldn't have any blood flowing through you and you wouldn't be able to get rid of the poisons. And the brain said, Yes, but without me neither of you'd know what to do in the first place. And so it went on, you see, until the bottom spoke up and said, You'd all be stuck without me. And they all laughed, you see, so the bottom decided to seize up. And first the liver jammed with all the poisons, then the heart got sluggish and stopped, and last of all to go was the brain, still singing about how clever he was, but in the end he had to pack in too. So there you are – left with the most important body part of all.

Everyone laughed. Medbh had a way of making people laugh.

Let's close the meeting, shall we? she said, and everyone had to close their eyes and sit with their legs uncrossed, and their hands palm upwards on their knees while Medbh talked them through the meditation. They had to relax each part of the body, then focus on the breathing, in, hold the breath, out, then on the tip of the nose where the breath came in and left, then on seeing the breath as a kind of light, cleansing each of the body's chakras in turn, green for the heart, blue, throat, then finally they were told to send out the healing energy to anyone who might need it, and Julie always thought of Mick.

Now, in your own time, Medbh said, bring yourselves round, and slowly, blinking or stretching their feet, people came out of the meditation smiling at one another; everyone felt great after one of Medbh's meditations even though the wooden chairs were so uncomfortable. Sometimes Julie felt a tingling in her hands and feet, sometimes warmth spread all through her body. When this happened she always felt that things were changing inside her, that anything was possible.

You can't change the world without changing yourself first, Medbh always said. Julie always left the meeting on a high.

Now that the meeting was over, several people gathered round Medbh asking questions, telling her about their meditations, nearly all of them kissed and hugged her goodbye. Julie always hung back, she couldn't make herself go forwards. Anyway she had to get home, she was walking to save the fare.

The Nicholas Crowther Hall, or Old Nick's as Medbh always called it, was near the top of a long hill called The Rise. Uncle Si's house was at the bottom and down a turn-off to the left. It was a good walk, nearly two miles. At the top of the hill the houses were very big, detached and surrounded by long gardens which set them back from the road, but the further down you went the more ordinary the houses were, big old semis, then small new semis, then terraced at the bottom of the hill. That was so all the sludge from the big houses would run into the houses of the poor, Mick said.

Tonight Julie got as far as the big semis when she saw someone she'd seen before at the meetings, a young woman walking a little way ahead. Julie hurried to catch up.

Hello, she said, a bit self-consciously, when she did.

O hi, the young woman said. At least she seemed to recognise Julie, but she didn't say anything else. They walked on in silence, Julie watching her in a sidelong way. She was thin and scrawny, with black, scrappy hair that looked as though a perm was growing out. She walked in a bent, energetic way and Julie found it hard to keep up. Then she found something to say.

Have you been to many meetings?

About four.

That was more than Julie, who'd been to two. She'd seen an advert in the local paper six weeks ago. It said:

Do you feel weighed down by your problems?
Do you suffer from any of the following stress-related symptoms:

    Nausea   •   Sleeplessness
    Dizziness   •   Groundless fears
    Headaches   •   Panic attacks

Do you not know which way to turn?

If help from others isn't working, why not tune in to the power of your own mind and TAKE CONTROL of your life? Come to our FREE meetings and learn to visualise your problems away.

As she read it Julie felt that she was suffering from all the problems on the list, so she thought she'd better go. She wondered if the young woman had felt the same way.

My name's Julie, she said.

– Annie.

Annie didn't say anything else, so after a pause Julie said,

What made you go to the meetings?

Well, mainly, said Annie, I was too knackered for aerobics and I wanted to get out. I've got twins, you see.

O, said Julie.

And I thought, just for one night a month, my husband could put them to bed. He goes out Tuesdays and Fridays, so I thought, I'm having a bloody night out as well.

How old are they? Julie said.

Eight months, said Annie. And they don't sleep at all except when you first put them down around nine. So if I come to the meetings I get to leave around half six and I get back around half nine and they're asleep and it's great. I know it won't last, and I'll be up with one or another of them all night, but just then when I first get in it's magic.

It must be hard work, having twins, Julie said.

It's a fucking nightmare, said Annie.

Julie didn't know what to say to that, but Annie said, That's the problem I have with the meetings – I keep falling asleep – it's too warm in that room. But I'm buggered if I'm giving up my one night out.

What are they called? said Julie.

Thomas and Jamie. Not Tommy and James or Jimmy. I called them after their grandfathers, Annie said as if Julie was arguing, and that's what I want them called.

They're nice names, Julie said.

I was going to let their dad choose, but he'd have called them Boy and George if he'd had his way. Or Kyle and Kylie like all the other kids round our way. Look at that poor cow, Annie said as a pregnant woman waddled across the road to the Late Shop. I look at them and I think, you poor daft cows, you don't know what you're in for.

There was a silence, then Julie said,

I'm pregnant.

O shit, said Annie. Sorry – I mean, congratulations. She shook her head. Jesus. And when Julie didn't say anything she said, I know you're supposed to congratulate people, but all I can think is, there goes another poor cow. I mean, it's the hardest job you'll ever do, and no one'll help. And make the most of going out now, because it might never happen again. And just hope to God it's not twins.

It isn't, Julie said.

Well, you're lucky then, I suppose. When's it due?

Julie wasn't sure. Her dates were different from the hospital's, but she should know.

Not for a while yet, she said.

Well, make the most of it, Annie said again. It's all downhill from here. Soon you'll be pushing a pram round night and day trying to keep a screaming baby quiet so your husband can get his beauty sleep, and running out of places to go by about ten o'clock in the morning. I push my two out every day round all the shops and then we feed the ducks, along with all the other poor cows with kids. They've got the fattest ducks you've ever seen in that park, it's a wonder they don't sink. But we've done all that by ten so we go home then and they start screaming the minute I sit down so I put the telly on – every day at ten-fifteen we watch *Thunderbirds* in Urdu – it's the only thing that shuts them up – they won't watch anything else. It took me six weeks to work out why I wasn't following the plot. But it keeps them quiet so I can have a cup of tea. And then we're off again, round the streets. But you'll find out, Annie said. Soon enough.

Julie pushed this vision aside.

Are you going to the new meetings? she said.

Eric, who was Medbh's right-hand man, had said he was starting some spin-off meetings in his own house so that smaller groups could work together more frequently. Medbh could only make it to Old Nick's once a month, she ran meetings all over the Northwest, so Eric in Julie's area and a man called Leonard and a woman called

Sophie in different areas had volunteered the use of their own homes for weekly meetings.

I don't know, said Annie. It depends how much they are, and Julie agreed. The meetings were free, but Mind-Power were saving up to establish four centres in the Northwest and you had to donate.

Annie stopped at a turning to the right.

I go up here, she said, but she didn't say where she lived. She said, See you again, and Julie watched as she walked up the road and then turned off again to the left. Then Julie walked down the last part of the hill to the street which led to Uncle Si's.

Lamps were fewer here and the street got darker as she went on. Julie remembered to do her practice, watching her breathing, imagining the breath surrounding her like a golden cloud. That way you strengthened your aura, Medbh said, and people left you alone.

No one bothered Julie as she turned from the dark street into the darker yard, so she thought it must be working. She was sure that if you practised hard, all the time, you could make anything work, and she was practising hard, but there hadn't been much improvement on the house yet, and as well as the rubble Julie now had to mind the broken glass. Mick had put new windows in the back, but he'd cut the bottom one a fraction too small and when the first train went by it fell out. Uncle Si had said not to mind, accidents were bound to happen. There was a toilet inside now though, and Mick and Darren had fixed the chimney stack and the little wall at the front of the house which was in danger of falling onto the railway line, so the council were off Uncle Si's back for the time being and he was grateful. They'd put some floorboards down as well, so it wasn't so dangerous – Julie was wrong to say there hadn't been any improvement. And at least the broken glass was keeping the dogs out, she should be pleased about that. But as she stepped over the crunching rubble, and struggled with the key, which would hardly turn in the lock, she felt the old anxiety that by the time the baby was born nothing would be ready at all.

*

Mick used to get drugs for Darren, when Darren was too ill to get them for himself. At first he used to twine for the money, then he did postal orders, lifting the stamp off with waxed paper, then he got into credit cards. He found a shooting gallery in a back-street terrace and met a dealer there called Big Dave. Big Dave was about five foot six and skinny and he laughed with Mick about his name. He once saw Mick in the pub, and instead of avoiding him as Mick expected, came right over to have a drink.

Drugs is a dirty business, he said right away as he sat down. A dirty business, but I'm clean. And I give my lads the best deal they can get. Because I'm not a user, you see. I sell it straight, just as it comes to me, I don't need any extra profits. Believe me, if you're buying, you're better off with a dealer who's not using.

Big Dave seemed straight enough. It was unusual to find a dealer who used his own first name, as he said it was. All the others Mick had come across had names like Ziggy or Waltzer. It turned out that he was new in the area and he thought Mick would know people in need of a regular honest dealer like himself. Mick didn't, but he was sure he could get to know them. And the more clients Mick brought to Big Dave, the better deals Big Dave could do for Mick on brown.

Why me? Mick said.

Because I can tell you're not a man with a habit, said Big Dave. You can never trust a user. But you and me, we can trust one another, see.

This seemed fair enough to Mick – cheap smack and a regular deal. He found more shooting galleries and mentioned Big Dave's name.

He's not a man who'd rob you, he'd say. He works for himself, not his habit, and people came to Big Dave through Mick, users who'd had a bad hit, or who found Big Dave's prices lower. Big Dave was pleased. Sometimes he let Mick have a bag or two without paying, saying he could pay later, and once or twice Mick sold the bag instead of giving it to Darren.

One night Mick was walking home to the squat where he was staying with Darren when four or five men came out of the alley behind the pub, raised what looked like baseball bats and began laying into him quite silently. Mick felt his teeth go, then his cheekbone, then a staggering pain in his shin. He thought he was being mugged, but as he lay on the ground and the beating went on one of them said,

Tell Big Dave it won't just be his arse-wipe next time.

Mick wasn't in a fit state to tell anyone anything. He crawled most of the way back to the squat where Darren was gouched out and couldn't help, but one of the girls wiped the blood off his face and gave him a green egg to kill the pain. By the next day Darren needed another hit, so Mick took another green egg and limped out to find Big Dave.

Big Dave was sorrowful.

There are some people who can't take a bit of free enterprise, he said. Jealous, they are, at bottom.

What will you do? Mick said.

Do? said Big Dave. Why, nothing, of course. I'm not a man to respond to threats and violence. We'll carry on as before. Then he winked at Mick. Not that I'm not properly sorry for the grief you've come to. Here, he said, pressing Mick's hand open. Here's a little something to tide you over, and he pressed a bag into Mick's hand.

Mick wasn't impressed. A bag was nothing, ten quid, and Darren's habit cost ninety quid a day. Ten quid was nothing for having damn near every bone in your body broken, but he didn't say any of this. He paid for an order for Joe, an elderly addict in the squat who wasn't always fit to get his own stuff, and bought some more bags for Darren, furious inside as Big Dave let him pay. They said goodbye as though they were still friends. But as Mick limped away he said to himself, What kind of a fucking game am I playing, paying through the nose to make Darren sicker, and Big Dave richer, and getting beaten up into the bargain?

Darren, he said when he got in. Have you ever thought of rehab?

Darren said he'd done rehab once, to avoid prison.

Mick squatted down beside him.

Have you ever thought about giving up? he said.

Darren said he'd thought about it.

Would you give it a try? Mick said. We could get you on prescription.

Darren was afraid to try, but Mick wouldn't give up. The last time Darren had gone into rehab he hadn't been serious. He'd smuggled syringes in inside the hollow frame of his rucksack, pierced the capsules they were giving him and injected the fluid inside. It was the injection he needed as much as the smack, he said.

They can give you stuff to inject, said Mick. You'll be all right.

Darren still wasn't keen, but Mick kept on at him, and in a few days he had him going to the CDT to try for a referral.

It wasn't easy to get them these days, he was told. They'd all been cut back. They could prescribe him some methadone and put his name down, but he'd have to wait.

This wasn't good enough for Mick.

We're trapped, he said, staring at Darren. Fucking trapped, and all that day and the next he never said a word.

Then Darren did a chemist's. He went out early and came back late, which was unusual for him, Mick began to get scared. He'd smashed a chemist's window while people were around, the alarm was shrieking and the police onto him before he got to the end of the street.

What did you do that for? said Mick.

Rehab, said Darren. Probation officer'll get me in.

And that was what happened. Soon after, Darren was booked into a detox unit for a fortnight.

Mick went to see Big Dave.

My mate's got to go away, he said. I was wondering if I could have a few bags for him till tomorrow – I'll pay you tomorrow.

How much? said Big Dave, and Mick swallowed and asked for a week's supply. Big Dave shook his head.

Where's he going? he wanted to know. Mick made up a story. His mate's sister was ill, he said. She'd lost a baby, and he'd always been close to his sister. He wanted to visit her for a few days, but he didn't know anyone he could score off round there. And he wanted to go tonight because her husband would be away and her husband hated Mick's mate.

Big Dave didn't look convinced.

I tell you what we'll do, he said. You take a bag or two for him for the night, and then take the rest to him after tomorrow, when you've paid for it.

Mick made up another story.

I could do that, he said, only I'm on bail and I've got to sign.

Where's his sister live, said Big Dave.

Cornwall, said Mick, hoping that Dave wouldn't ask any more questions. Look, he said. I've always paid you before, haven't I? And it's not as though I'm asking you to wait all week. I'll have it all for you tomorrow.

And when Big Dave still looked doubtful Mick said, Look – I got the shit beaten out of me for you – I thought I could ask you a favour.

Big Dave held up his hands.

All right, all right, he said. I'm a family man myself.

And you and me, we trust one another, don't we? You're not likely to run off anywhere, are you?

Sometimes Mick thought Big Dave was reading his mind.

Where would I go? he said, trying to laugh, and Big Dave laughed with him.

Exactly, he said. So I tell you what I'll do. You do a little errand for me, I give you a week's supply in payment. How about that?

He wanted Mick to take some smack to Brighton, collect the money and bring it back. Mick couldn't believe his luck. Big Dave went into a cupboard in the other room and came back with an ordinary sports bag. He gave Mick names, contacts.

It's a special mission, he said. Because I've always known I can trust you. And somehow, though Big Dave was friendly enough, Mick's heart began pumping like an engine. He couldn't wait to get the bag back to the squat to look inside. Big Dave punched him playfully on the arm.

Take care of the money, he said. Don't spend it all at once.

Mick walked away as casually as he could. Back in the squat he opened the bag. There was more brown in it than he'd ever seen in his life.

Mick packed up the few things he had. He was going to Brighton right away, he couldn't sleep with that much smack on him. And all the way he couldn't stop thinking. He would make the deal, he thought, then head off up north, back to Manchester, no, not Manchester, Big Dave knew he came from there. Newcastle then, though there were people he wanted to see in Manchester, Newcastle. And he'd use a different name and put all the money down on a flat for him and Darren . . .

Mick did the deal. It was easy. He walked away with another bag full of cash, and caught the first train he could up North. When trains to Newcastle were delayed he went to Sheffield instead. He didn't mind where he went, only he felt he had to get there fast. He couldn't shake the feeling of being hunted down.

Over the next few days, though, the feeling faded. He got himself a flat with basic furniture, and signed on. He wrote to Darren and shopped for food for when Darren came up. Then one day, walking home from the supermarket, he saw a smallish figure coming towards him and his heart fell to the floor, though Big Dave greeted him affably enough.

Did you get lost, Mick? he said. Only, it's taking you a while to come home.

Yeah, Mick said. I had someone to see. I was on my way back though.

That's good to hear, Mick, said Big Dave. But now I'm here there's no need. Let's go back to the flat, shall we, and settle things there.

Mick and Big Dave walked together towards the flat, Mick wondering all the way what he would do when they got there. He should lay into Big Dave now, he thought, and run. Leave the flat, Big Dave obviously knew where it was, he had to cut his losses and run. His thoughts ran on, telling him what to do, but somehow he couldn't make the first move. He couldn't just attack Big Dave in the street. Then anyway as they drew near the flat he became aware that they weren't walking alone. From the side streets behind them came two then four of the biggest men Mick had ever seen. Big Dave turned to Mick with a smile that was as affable as it could be, given the state of his teeth.

You were wondering, a little while back, where I got my name from, he said, and chuckled. Back home in Birmingham I was named for the size of my friends.

This is it now, Mick thought. He was in for another beating. He thought it calmly enough, but inside he began to shake. He hoped he wouldn't shit himself or anything like that. He just wanted to get it over.

Now then, Big Dave said as they reached Mick's flat, we were hoping you'd invite us in for a cup of tea, weren't we, lads? The lads said nothing. Sweating, Mick opened the door.

Now look at this place, Dave said. All the comforts of home. Even a gas cooker laid on, and the big bald man next to Mick went over to the cooker and switched it on, Mick couldn't see what he was doing. The others leant against the units.

You know, Mick, Dave said, drawing up a stool. You're almost big enough to be one of my friends, and I'll bet you've still got some growing to do. That's why I sent you on that little errand, as a kind of test, of our friendship. But you know, Mick, friends don't cheat on one another, or break one another's trust, now do they? Friendship, he said, shaking his head. It's a valuable resource, Mick, don't you forget it. But if someone lets you down now, betrays your trust, then you can't be friends any more, can you? And I'm sorry to see that that's the way things are.

Dave –, Mick said, but Dave held up a hand.

Don't trouble yourself, Mick, he said. There'll be no hard feelings. But I don't want to leave you without a small token of our former esteem, and the big bald guy turned round from the cooker, he was drawing up liquid from a foil wrapper into a syringe.

I know you're not a regular user, Mick, Dave said, but I want you to have this one on me.

Mick's tongue seemed to dry up and shrivel.

Give us a chance, he tried to say, but he was grabbed from behind, someone was dragging his jacket off his back. Mick hardly struggled at all, all the fight seemed to have gone out of him. He found himself staring upwards, into Big Dave's face.

Jesus, Dave, he said.

Now don't you worry at all, Big Dave said as someone tore up Mick's sleeve. A big boy like you'll come to no harm from a few grammes of brown. Of course, he went on, if it wasn't entirely pure now, mixed up with something nasty like, say, battery acid – it could kill a bloke. And that happens, he said, shaking his head. That happens even to the best of dealers.

Mick couldn't say anything as the hypodermic sank into his arm. He felt the familiar flood of warmth and goodness. Dave's men let go of him and he sagged in the chair.

That's better, Big Dave said kindly. Now you'll have to excuse us and we'll be going. But I want you to know it's been a very great pleasure, knowing you.

No – Dave –, Mick said, or thought he said it, because suddenly he was freezing cold, and his jaws clamped together. He heard them all leaving, he heard the front door go, and he knew he didn't want to be alone.

Come back, he said, between clenched teeth. Come back, Dave, you cunt –

He thought he was shouting but he couldn't hear much sound, and when he tried to get up he fell forwards and then he didn't know what he was saying any more. But he knew how cold hell was, he always said. He'd never been so cold in all his life. Then he heard a groaning in his ears and he knew he was going to die. But a little while after the vomiting began, so he knew he couldn't be dead yet. It was as though he was trying to throw up everything inside him, but the poison was in his veins so no amount of vomiting would ever be enough. He retched so hard and for so long he knew blood was coming up with the vomit and he shit himself as well. He remembered praying to die.

When he came to there was sunlight on the floor and the whole room stank like a sewer. And he felt so bad and weak he couldn't move. His first thought was that he couldn't be dead, he knew being dead couldn't be that bad. Then he fell back into unconsciousness and when he woke up again the sunlight had gone and his tongue seemed all stuck up in his mouth, there wasn't a drop of moisture in him. This time he managed to crawl to the tap and drink, the room rocking dangerously around him. That was all he did for the next few hours, it could have been days, drink and vomit. But he was still here, and this was the funny thing, and Mick leant closer as he always did at this point in the story. Even when I first woke up and I felt like shit, and I didn't know if I'd died or not – I knew I didn't want to die. He leant back.

This seemed to be very important to Mick, important and mysterious at the same time. He didn't know what had made him want to live. It was the most important point of the whole story to him, but it didn't affect Julie the same way. Whenever she heard the story she felt overcome by rage and helplessness.

Don't you hate him? she burst out once.

Why would I, Mick said.

He tried to kill you, said Julie. Mick shook his head.

No. If he'd been trying to kill me he'd have done it. He was trying to warn me. I tried to put one over on him so he had to do something.

Julie didn't understand it, the lack of hatred.

Look, he had a job to do, Mick said. I was getting in his way.

If he felt anything at all for Big Dave it was a kind of respect, just as, Julie could tell, he took a kind of pride in the story, surviving battery acid in his veins, it would have killed a weaker man.

Julie couldn't understand Mick at all, he didn't seem to hate anyone except for people he didn't know, the government, and people who voted for them, or people who refused to face facts, like the ones in the Mind-Power group, who helped the government indirectly by distracting themselves and others from the real issues.

Mick often told this story in Uncle Si's room whenever Uncle Si was out, as he often was for days at a time, and Mick could smoke dope there with Darren. Now Darren was on methadone he smoked dope all the time. But it was this episode, Mick always said, that convinced Darren to stay off smack for good.

He still shoots up though, doesn't he? Julie said. Mick looked uncomfortable.

Only once or twice a month, he said. That's nothing. It's not twenty times a day.

First the doctor had put Darren on methadone, but he'd tried to shoot it and all his arm came up in abscesses, so the doctor put him on the stuff you could shoot, and now he was off that and back on methadone, but he still smoked draw all the time and shot up occasionally, Julie couldn't see that he was cured, but Mick insisted he was better.

Julie had seen Darren gouched out. She'd called him down to tea one day, and when he didn't come she'd gone up the stairs to get him. The door to his room was open and Darren was slouched in a corner of it, head hanging over his chest and saliva running down his chin and chest. She turned away quickly and went back to the kitchen. When Mick came in she said,

Why does he do it?

Do what?

Shoot up.

Mick looked as if he didn't know how to answer, then he said,

He said it's the only thing that makes him feel warm.

Mick made out that he didn't mind Darren shooting up, but Julie wasn't so sure. She felt he was clinging to the hope that Darren would get better. She didn't say this to him because she felt it would be pushing her luck. They'd only just started talking again since the terrible day when Julie had told him she was pregnant, and he hadn't said anything at all. He'd just leant back in his chair, closed his eyes and said, Jesus, then left the room. After that he left every room as she came into it, and sometimes he left the house. It was better than that now, though he still never mentioned the baby. And Julie wanted to stay talking to Mick. So she went on with the shopping and the cooking and she didn't mention Darren's habit much, or the fact that there were more and more strange men around the house, Mick had asked them in, to help with the bigger jobs. They came from nowhere, these men, and they seemed to have nowhere to go. They slept on the kitchen floor, or the landing, Julie fell over one once when she got up to use the toilet. Uncle Si didn't seem to mind so long as the work got done, but Julie hated it, because they were supposed to be helping, but they were more likely to be sitting around in the kitchen, arguing, or helping themselves to food.

They're my mates, Mick said. They can eat if they like.

Julie didn't even feel as though she could go into her own room. And worst of all, they were all full of terrible stories, like Mick. There was Les, big and bony with lank hair, who'd been thrown out of a rented room by a landlord who'd had a better offer, and when he'd refused to go the landlord had had him beaten up, he'd been deaf in one ear ever since. Then there was Joe with one arm, who'd lost it tying cloth around it so the veins would come up, then shooting up and forgetting to untie it so all the circulation had stopped. And Tony, who was short and pock-marked, had had a girlfriend once, who was only fourteen but out on the streets like him. And they'd been shooting up one night and the next day he woke up and she was lying beside him, dead.

Julie didn't want to listen to any of these stories but she couldn't help it. They talked about them all the time as if they were stuck in a groove. Whenever Julie was in the house she couldn't help hearing the stories, and they filled her mind with terrible images like the smoke from their cigarettes filled her lungs. Sometimes she looked around and was surprised to find it was still daylight. And the worst of it was, it made her want to join in, to come up with terrible stories of her own, so she wouldn't be such an outsider, she found herself dreaming up terrible, unhealthy tales. So she went out a lot and tried not to complain, but it took a long time to shake the stories off her, it was like being infected by another world.

*

Besides dogs, the yard behind Uncle Si's was full of junk. There was old furniture from the two houses that stood boarded up, too dangerous to live in, the council said, though Mick had talked about it once. He had gone through the furniture when they first moved in, but anything good enough to use had already been taken. There was more furniture from time to time when people moved into the square or away. When a couple moved into the house opposite, for weeks the yard was littered with old chairs, a pot sink and a fridge that Mick and Darren took apart and put together again, but they couldn't make it work. Nobody ever came to clear this stuff and whenever Mick hired a skip it filled up right away with other people's rubbish and he went mad.

Then there was Des, who sometimes lived with Jude next door, and who messed with cars. He turned his radio up full and sat playing with engines and carburettors without ever seeming to fix them, so that car parts and halves of cars lay all over the yard as well. When people complained Des always said a firm was coming to pick up the scrap, only somehow they never arrived, though Des said he phoned them every day.

Kids played in the scrap, though Julie would have worried about rust. The woman opposite had two boys and a baby. The baby sat strapped in its pushchair while the older boys played and the woman watched them through the window with pale, hooded eyes. Jude next door had Tonia who was about six, she had pale brown skin and eyes, and mousy hair scraped back in an elastic band. She sat on the cobbles for hours digging the dirt out between them with a stick. Julie felt sorry for her and tried to talk sometimes without much success. But then Tonia had a bad habit of wandering into other people's houses without being asked, touching things. Once or twice Julie turned round in the kitchen, or even upstairs, and Tonia was there behind her, smiling with her pale brown teeth.

You shouldn't shock people like that, Julie told her, but Tonia only smiled, and ran her quick brown fingers across the sideboard in Uncle Si's room, which made Julie think she might be taking things. Certainly the milk kept disappearing; if Julie wasn't up early enough to take it off the milkman herself it always went, and Mick and Darren were always losing things. But she had to feel sorry for Tonia, she told herself, having Jude for a mother, because Jude was awful. She wandered round the back all day with a fag in her mouth, wearing only a dirty blue towelling robe.

I don't care, me, she said.

When the binmen came for the wheelie bins that had to be left at the entrance to the big yard every Thursday, Jude was always out at the back with her gown flapping open, showing her bare, slovenly body.

Come and get it, boys, she always shouted.

No one else but Jude was up so early, which also made Julie think about the milk, but she didn't say anything because Jude was hard, hard as nails, Julie's mother would have said. She harassed Uncle Si. Whenever she caught him letting himself in the back way she was there, holding her robe out wide.

Eh, Grandpa, get a load of this, she cried.

Uncle Si didn't like this at all, though he never said anything. He sidled past keeping his face turned away.

One day Mick was waiting for Jude.

He came up behind her as she came up behind Uncle Si. She'd hardly started shouting when he grabbed her by the neck and slammed her up against the wall.

Go and put some clothes on, he said, very quietly, and everything Jude was going to say died away as she saw the look on his face. She left, wrapping the robe around her.

Mind the gate, Mick called after her. I'm fixing it.

Julie admired Mick very much for that, he wasn't scared of Jude when everyone else was. Jude left Uncle Si alone from then on, and the milk stopped disappearing. Uncle Si was grateful. Perhaps that was why he put up with so much, Julie thought, Les and Tony and Joe always hanging round the kitchen and arguing, and not just them either, other homeless hangers-on, and sometimes some of the Pakistani workers who stayed in the remaining two houses in the square. These were owned by a big man with shifty eyes called Khalid. He had every room in them stuffed with beds, end to end, Mick called them hot beds because they never got a chance to cool down. The workers who did the day shift at Khalid's brother's factory slept in them at night and the night workers used them in the daytime. Mick said they even used one another's shoes, the night shift put them on as the day shift took them off. Julie thought that was disgusting.

And that's one of their own kind, she said, exploiting them. She wanted to make this point, because Mick was always on about the white middle-class people she was mixing with at the meetings, but Mick said it didn't matter what race you were, the only thing that mattered was capital.

No one spoke to the Asian workers except for Mick, even Jude said they were dirty and Tonia wasn't to go near them. But Mick went in the houses as he went everywhere else, telling them about socialism. Julie said Khalid should be reported, but Mick wouldn't hear of it.

They're just starting to listen, he said.

He took pamphlets and the *Socialist Worker* magazine, and stayed quite a long time sometimes, when the air was filled with the smells of their cooking. With the result that four or five of them hung round the kitchen along with everyone else, discussing the problems of the Third World, eating Julie's ratatouille and rice. Julie hated it. There was always someone in the way when she wanted to use the bathroom or kitchen. And it took her long enough to cook one of Aunty Clare's nice meals at Uncle Si's without having to push through a crowd of people as well. Some days it was impossible to do anything in the kitchen. She had to climb over bricks and planks of wood to get to the sink, then when she turned the taps on there was no water, and when she looked down water was gushing from a pipe beneath the sink, over her feet. So she had to use the sink upstairs. Then there were only three burners on Uncle Si's cooker and one of them wasn't working, so when another one started to gutter and flare Julie took to only cooking meals she could make in the oven. But the door was stiff and it got stiffer as the oven got hotter, and one day when she tugged it the whole thing came off in her hands. And no one even noticed until she shouted aloud. For two days they lived off takeaways, then Mick turned up with a camping stove.

Where'd you get that from? Julie wanted to know, but Mick would never say where he got anything from. So now she cooked and washed up upstairs, which was better because there weren't so many people, and because it was only a camping stove she gave up trying to cook anything exotic. She went back to potato hash and stew, and when Mick shouted up for more because someone else had turned up she just added water. She still had to carry the bowls downstairs though, and pass them round in the middle of whatever was going on.

– all doctors are bastards, Tony was saying. Mick had just told them that Darren's doctor was cutting back on his methadone. But Mick wasn't angry at the doctor. It was the system, he said. Tony disagreed.

Fuck that, he said. They just flog whatever's going cheap, so long as they've tested it on Third World first.

He said that for the benefit of Ali and Qasim who were at the table listening. Julie passed them the stew.

Mick didn't like doctors either, but he said, I'm talking about your average doctor – doing his best in a bad system.

They're drug dealers, nowt else, said Tony, and when Mick wasn't having it his red face got redder.

There's not one doctor in Manchester'd touch the homeless, he shouted. Tony always started shouting sooner or later, and soon everyone was shouting and banging on the table.

Excuse me, Julie said loudly, pushing past them with more bowls, collecting mugs.

Sometimes she thought she must be mad, feeding so many people, there wasn't enough money apart from anything else, though everyone's money was finally through. Julie had her social, Darren got some kind of invalidity now he was a registered drug addict, and Mick still got his NFA. It had all taken a long time, and for a while everyone was living off Mick. He hadn't complained. He'd gone out every day selling *The Big Issue*. Now they all had some money he was putting more effort into selling the *Socialist Worker*, so there was still hardly enough to go round. Julie didn't feel she could ask Mick to do any more. She cut back on the shopping, going out of her way to all the cheapest shops, but every week there was something new to buy because when she'd first moved in there wasn't a cloth or a brush or a duster in the house. She tried not to complain because it gave her something to do, and she couldn't imagine living there without feeling useful. But sometimes she felt she'd been landed with all the jobs no one else wanted, like keeping the new toilet clean with the brush she'd bought herself, or going round with a black bin bag for the dirty laundry. She was very glad there was a new toilet inside the house now that she had to get up two or three times a night, and it certainly needed cleaning with all the people using it, but none of the jobs got any easier, they all seemed to take up more and more time with all the dirt and clutter and people. Some days she couldn't see how she was ever going to get a chance to develop spiritually through the Mind-Power programme when it took her all day to get to the laundrette and back, and clear a path to the sink.

Mick and Darren didn't seem to be getting anywhere either. Often they couldn't do outside work because of the weather, then when they were putting floorboards down they found a dank pool of water in the cellar and they had to wait for days for that to dry out, and the first time they tried putting a damp-proof course in, they found the bricks were too porous and crumbly, and they had to wait for new ones. None of this seemed to bother them as much as it bothered Julie though. On the days when they couldn't get on, and Mick wasn't out selling, they would sit in Uncle Si's room, watching telly. Uncle Si was always out and Julie didn't blame him. Mick and Darren watched *Good Morning with Anne and Nick* in the week and the Disney Club at weekends, though Mick said morning television was funnier. There was a slot called Top Tips in which people who were famous or rich gave their most useful advice. Today Lady Belmont-Spencer was explaining how to clean your chandeliers with a water pistol so that the maids didn't have to climb high ladders.

Mick and Darren fell about.

My tip to you today, Mick said, is to have as many maids as possible lying under the chandeliers so that they soak up the dirty water.

Julie had never seen Darren laugh so much. She bumped her shopping trolley carefully over the joists.

Here we are messing around with the gutters, Mick

said, when the maids could have been doing it all the time. Hey Julie, he said, do you fancy being our maid?

Julie tugged the black bin bag out of the trolley.

I thought I already was, she said.

That's the best programme on telly, Mick said. They watched it every morning. Yesterday someone had told them what to do if they snagged their fingernails just before that vital dinner party. Mick and Darren thought it was great, and yesterday Julie had laughed with them, but today she wasn't amused. She wiped the streaming rain from her face and said,

Doesn't anyone know where Uncle Si is?

Uncle Si had disappeared the day before yesterday.

Out, Mick said.

Out, said Julie. In this.

They all looked at the window, where the snowy rain was making great wet splashes and trickling down. Mick gathered the mugs.

Well, I'm off too, he said. Work waits for no man.

He shouldn't be out in this, Julie said.

Mick and Darren looked at one another so quickly you could hardly tell.

I'll have to be going as well, Darren said. He was going to the drughouse, which was what Mick and Darren called the CDT unit, to get his methadone.

Aren't you worried? Julie said. Mick pulled on his jacket.

He knows what he's doing, he said. He'll not be on the streets.

Julie couldn't let it alone.

Shouldn't we tell someone? she said. She kept saying the wrong thing. Mick threw Darren a fag. She'd had this conversation with him before.

Look, he'd said, he's always been like this. He used to go walkabout when he was a little lad. My dad used to have to go and look for him. You're not going to change him now.

Now all he said was, I'll be back later, and Darren mumbled, Bye, in his downward way.

Julie stared after them. They didn't like her asking, that was the way they were. When you were homeless you got used to people disappearing for weeks at a time, you didn't ask questions even if you never saw them again. But Julie couldn't get used to it, it did her head in. She pulled clothes out of the black plastic bag and arranged them in piles on the back of the settee, trying to concentrate fully on what she was doing as Medbh had suggested.

Make each act a meditation in itself, Medbh had said, but Julie couldn't concentrate on anything. She sorted the clothes and stepped back over the joists and the tins of chemicals to the stairs. She climbed up the edge of the stairway to the bedroom and sat on her mattress in her coat and gloves.

Just five minutes a day, Medbh had said. There's no one who can't find five minutes if they try. But even in the bedroom it was hard to concentrate, Julie didn't know how the Asian workers got on trying to sleep. There was the noise of Des's radio and the car engine he was doing up in Jude's kitchen, starting and stopping and starting again. The kids were in because of the weather, but the dogs were out, barking and howling in turns. None of the noise was regular, if you had regular noise you could concentrate on it, Medbh had said, but this noise interrupted Julie's mantras and broke up her breathing exercises until in the end she gave up. All the others in the group would be doing the meditation practice, she knew, taking great strides towards enlightenment while she, Julie, got nowhere. And Medbh had said that if anyone was having problems with the practice they could talk about them at the meetings, but somehow Julie couldn't imagine talking about her problems there, it was the last place she would want to go and talk.

Julie had forgotten her sample.

She had been sent to the toilets with a plastic container. As she went in a woman leapt up, stubbing her cigarette out in the sink.

I thought you were the nurse, she said.

She settled back in the chair next to the sink and took the packet out again. She flicked it open and held one out.

Want one, she said.

Julie shook her head. Do they get at you about smoking? she said.

The woman inhaled deeply.

They would if I told them, she said.

But didn't they ask you? said Julie.

O yes, the woman said. I just lied.

Julie was very surprised. They had asked her a lot of questions and she always felt she had to tell them the truth.

Well, if I'd said yes, the woman said, they'd have given me all that crap about premature underweight babies. I mean, this is my third, and both my other two were over nine pound and had to be induced. But can you tell them that? She returned to her cigarette.

They get at me about my weight, Julie said, and the woman scanned her critically.

Putting too much on, she said. Well, I know. If they can make you feel bad they will. That's why I don't tell them anything. Keeps us both happy.

But they weigh me, Julie said. I can't not tell them.

You can tell them to get stuffed, the woman said. Stands to reason everyone's not going to put on the same. But I will say, she said, that's where a fag does help. Look at me now, and she stood and turned sideways. How far on do you think I am?

Julie shook her head. The woman didn't really look pregnant at all.

Six months, she said, and Julie gasped.

I know, the woman said, patting her stomach. My last baby was nine pound four and I only put on a stone. They'll weigh us now and I bet I've not put on more than ten pounds. And I go straight back after the birth, no problem. I mean that's what you want isn't it? Pregnancy's hard enough without carrying an extra load.

Julie felt more depressed than ever.

Mind you, the woman said, the hard bit's just after the birth when everyone's going on about the baby and you're there dying for a fag. But I've solved that one now. I'm having this one at home, and she smiled an artful smile. I'm only here now because my midwife's off sick.

Julie smiled wanly in return. It was hard to smile when she was about to be weighed in public.

Someone in the corridor announced a name.

That's me, the woman said, stubbing her cigarette out again. I'd best be off.

Julie was left alone in the toilets, clutching her container, for once not feeling even the smallest desire to wee. She considered going back to the drinks machine, then went into the cubicle instead and hovered over the seat.

Pregnancy, said the writing on the door, proof that God is a man.

Julie waited until her legs ached, holding the container in place until finally a thin dribble of urine trickled out, mainly over her hand, and she was able to go back to the queue.

Forty-three pounds, one nurse said to the other and both of them looked concerned. Blushing, Julie got down from the scales.

It's a bit much, love, the older nurse said, and the other one came over with a list of names.

Would you like to see the dietician? she said, and before Julie could say anything she had written her name down.

Nine stone five, the nurse said to someone as Julie left, That's very good, and looking back Julie saw the woman she'd been speaking to in the toilets.

She smokes, you know, Julie thought of saying, but didn't. She took the cards they had given her to another queue where she could sit down this time, outside a door marked DIETICIAN, and when it was her turn to go inside a smart woman with blonde streaked hair and coral fingernails asked her in a slow, clear voice if she knew what kinds of food went into salad.

Outside gales of rain battered her along the street. Julie walked past the main entrance to the hospital, averting her eyes from the block just behind, where her mother had died. It was hardly any better inside at Uncle Si's, she knew, with the rain running down the inside walls. Julie had had to move her mattress closer to Mick's because of a leak around the light bulb. She had pulled it right over, then thought better of it and moved it further away. Mick must have noticed but he hadn't said anything. She was almost within touching distance but not quite. On those nights when he slept in her room she could lie awake and watch the changing rhythm of his breathing, the mass of dark hair spilling over the mattress to the floor, whereas when he was awake she was very careful not to let him see her watching him, she had developed a downward, curbed glance, a way of sitting and moving half turned away, in case watching him her hunger for him would be seen, leaking out.

If she went home now, she thought, Mick wouldn't be in. And she was already soaked. She would go to Alison's, she thought.

An enormous man in a flowing nightie opened the door.

Are you friend or foe, he said.

Julie blinked at him.

Is Alison in, she said.

My own sweet love, the man who now struck Julie as being both old and fat called over his shoulder, are you in?

Who is it? came the faint reply.

Julie, Julie said.

A wandering damsel, named Julie, said the man.

O, the voice said, a little flatly. All right then, and the strange man stood to one side and bowed as Julie passed.

It was a small, square room in brownish colours, except for one wall which was pillar-box red. There was a big window in this wall through which Julie could see a balcony, and a strong smell of cooking from the kitchen. Alison sat propped up on a tweedy settee. Julie thought there was something wrong with her face, but as she got closer Alison turned it away.

Don't look at me, she said. I look awful.

You don't, said Julie.

I fucking do, said Alison, and burst into tears.

Behind them the man said,

Refreshments? Ambrosia? Mead?

Tea or coffee, Alison sobbed.

Tea, Julie said. She sat in front of Alison, on a pouffe which was lower than she expected it to be. Because the window was behind Alison Julie couldn't see her face very clearly, but she could see that her legs and hands were swollen.

Don't cry, Alison, she said. Alison sobbed even harder.

Look at me, she said.

It's not that bad, Julie said. I mean, look at me.

Alison looked, covering her face with one hand and managed a bit of a smile.

I'm only half-way through, Julie said. You must be nearly due.

Alison sniffed, still keeping her hand over her face.

It's due next week, she said. But the doctors say if the swelling doesn't go down they might induce me. I wish they would, she said with sudden energy. I'm sick of it. Stuck in here all day like the fucking elephant man – I hate it.

The man appeared again, carrying mugs on a tray.

He can't be Alan, Julie thought. He was much older than Alison, at least forty. And very ugly, she thought as he set the mugs down. Not a bit nice-looking like her Mick. He had a fat pink face with a big chin and slightly bulging eyes. At first Julie thought he didn't have any teeth, but when he talked she could see he did have some brownish, stumpy ones.

How can I ease thee, my morning star? he said to Alison, passing her a drink. A rub of thy tender feet?

Alison sighed, in the most dissatisfied way imaginable.

No, she said. She looked at Julie from behind the fingers of her hand. So how's things with you, she said.

Even through the fingers Julie could see that Alison's face was very swollen, her eyes were pulled back and her mouth had lost its shape.

Fine, she said, looking at the carpet. Then she looked up. I've just been to the hospital, she said.

Alison groaned in sympathy and the man said,

Into the jaws of perdition. He crossed to the only chair in the room, which was brown leather, and sat on it in a sprawled-out kind of way but as if he was observing them both closely. Julie began to feel that she disliked him very much.

I have to go every week now, Alison said. In this state. And Alan's never been. She shot him a look of hatred. He says hospitals are 'cultural deformities' and 'anathema to the soul', but I have to fucking go.

So he is Alan, Julie thought, and struggled with a wave of sickness.

It's always the same, Alison said bitterly. They get you in the shit and they leave you there. It's because they are shit.

My lady love, Alan said, suffers from an excess of charity.

What have I got to be charitable about? Alison demanded.

I make no apologies for the way I am, Alan said. As a very wise man once elucidated, I am what I am. Descartes. Or was it Popeye?

Fuck off, Alan, Alison said. Alan raised his shoulders and eye brows, and there was a silence into which Julie said that Mick never went with her either.

See, Alison said.

After that there wasn't a lot to say. Alan walked over to the window, Julie looked at his thick neck and shoulders, the flowing pink gown.

Why does he dress like that? she thought.

I was going into town, she said to Alison, to get some Christmas cards, but the weather's too bad. I thought you might like to come with me tomorrow, if you feel up to it.

Not in this state, Alison said. I'm going to hospital tomorrow to see if they'll induce me – I've had enough.

Alan turned back from the window.

Would either of you fair maidens, he said, care to partake of more substantial fare?

Why does he talk like that, Julie thought.

No thanks, she said.

Do not be precipitate, said Alan. There is, already prepared, the most tender, succulent lamb that ever frolicked in these fair hills, speared and spiced and roasted with the freshest vegetables the market is able to supply.

You might as well have something, Alison said. He can cook.

My lady speaks kindly, Alan cried. The angels have not forsaken me, and Alison managed an amused look at Julie as he disappeared.

I'm just so pissed off, she said, and Julie could see that. I just wish to God it was all over. They never tell you before you get into this how long nine months can take. Alan's all right really, she said, managing another of her queer, twisted smiles. He's been very patient.

So much praise in one day, Alan said from the kitchen. How can I stand it?

Well, make the most of it, said Alison.

Alan brought in the meat on dripping skewers. It smelled good. The lamb was covered in roasted nuts, and there were roasted chunks of tomatoes, mushrooms, courgettes. Julie wasn't sure how to eat the kebab. She held one skewer up and bit into the end of it tentatively. The meat was very good. Alan sat on the settee this time and turned his alarming eyes round to Julie.

Do you think, he said, that we can ever do other than that which is in us to do?

Julie swallowed the meat. She wasn't sure she understood the question.

Don't mind Alan, Alison said. He's always going on about something or other when people are trying to eat.

Alan swivelled his eyes round to her.

But I have been accused, he said, calumnised. Reviled.

I only said, Alison explained through a mouthful of kebab, that you haven't been to hospital with me. Which you haven't.

But the implication, Alan said, is betrayal.

Alison said nothing to this and Julie said nothing too, but Alan went on, saying that to him their journey was mysterious and profound, they had both embarked on a voyage into the heart of the feminine, and he could hardly hope to accompany them. He could only hope to serve, in the most limited way, whenever it might be appropriate.

All the time he was talking Julie felt a kind of sickness in her stomach, putting her off her food even though it was good. She ate anyway, chewing persistently on, and tried not to look at Alan. She stared downwards, at the frilly hem of his nightdress, but the sickness didn't go away. Alan didn't smell, he didn't seem dirty, she didn't know what it was.

So you see, he said. My role as I see it is to serve you as a knight would serve his lady.

O possums, Alison said, and Alan laid his great, unshapely head on her shoulder.

Julie quickly bit off the last chunk of meat, found a tissue to wipe her mouth with and stood up.

I'll have to be going, she said.

Alan, his head now on Alison's lap, raised it to lick her lips. At the door Julie looked back and they were still kissing, Alison's distorted face lowered to Alan's. She hurried out, her head filled with the strangeness of them both. She didn't know if she was disgusted or not, but as she got to the bottom of the stairs she knew that what she was feeling was a kind of pain, because she and Mick would never be like that. She could imagine what Mick would say if she called him possums.

Julie turned into the main road, lowering her face against the wind and rain, wondering what to make for tea. The trouble was she never knew these days whether or not anyone would be in for tea, because as suddenly as they had all arrived, everyone had disappeared again. There were no groups of people arguing in the kitchen, Mick and Darren were out overnight, or back late and they'd already eaten, because suddenly Joe had got a flat, they said. He needed help moving in. At least Uncle Si was back now though. She could add dumplings to the stew she'd already made. As she crossed at the lights she wondered what Aunty Clare would do in Julie's situation. She was sure that whatever she did it would be the right thing, she wouldn't just give up. Julie trudged along the street that led to Uncle Si's. All her clothes clung to her and there was hail in the rain. She remembered what Medbh had said about the present moment being wonderful, filled with wonder. Even the wetness was wonderful, according to Medbh. There was a mantra to say about water.

> Water flows from high in the mountains,
> Water runs deep in the earth.
> Miraculously water comes to us
> And sustains all life.

Julie turned the radio on.

A baby girl has been found abandoned outside a hospital, the voice said. Police are concerned for the mother ...

She turned it off again and sat at the table, thinking about the woollen feeling in her arms and legs, waiting for the slow light outside. She didn't know if this blurred feeling was a symptom of pregnancy or of some terrible disease. Already this morning she had stumbled down the stairs then spilt the milk. And it couldn't be eight o'clock yet.

Julie stretched her fingers, telling herself it must be the cold. Even though she wore gloves and a coat in bed, her fingers were numb with cold, but her legs felt numb too. And she had missed Mick again. He was never there when she went to bed, but lately he hadn't been there when she woke up either. She had trouble getting off to sleep, listening to the trains, following patches of light around the room, while the cold gnawed at her. Then sometimes she fell asleep briefly and woke to see Mick standing by the window, then she would wake up again and he was gone, she didn't know whether she had dreamed it. She knew he stayed up late with Darren in Darren's room, rolling joints, then sometimes she thought he went out, in spite of the weather. Sometimes she thought he just couldn't stand being in.

Julie yawned and stretched her legs. She couldn't feel her feet at all, it couldn't just be the cold. She should go to the doctor's later, or the library.

Don't rely on books, Eric had said at the first meeting she had been to at his house. That's the important thing. You have to learn to trust your own instincts, and he told them all about the Bushmen of the Kalahari, who followed their instincts, which they called tappings, for thousands of miles on hunting trails without ever losing their way.

Eric had travelled a lot. He'd been in Egypt and all over Africa with the army. Even now, though he wore open-toed sandals and a silk dressing gown over his shirt and trousers, he looked like an army major. But he told them all that he was a different man these days and had been since meeting Medbh.

I used to think life was a battleground, he said. I was so busy fighting I had no time for anything else. Now I've learned to give way a little, relax, smell the roses. Muriel, he barked suddenly, tea; and his wife ran in with a notepad to take their orders: tea, coffee, decaffeinated tea, decaffeinated coffee, herbal tea (rosehip, camomile, vanilla), barleycup.

Can I help, Muriel? Sylvia said. Sylvia was a large woman with shoulder-length white hair. She wore a silky top and a skirt tie-dyed in shades of black, magenta and electric blue.

O no, thank you, Muriel said, and Eric said,

She's done it often enough before. Besides, we have the meditation first.

They all had to make themselves comfortable, uncross their legs and turn their hands palm upwards. Annie hadn't come and Julie didn't know the other people there. Eric cleared his throat and began slowly,

Imagine darkness setting in all over the earth, he said. Fields and hills and mountains all covered slowly in darkness as the world turns in space. And as it turns slowly, over a dark hill, a single ray of light appears . . .

They had to imagine the sun rising over the hill, its rays energising the forests and fields, all the animals and finally the cells of their own bodies. When they had finished Julie felt none of the usual fuzziness or warmth. Eric was keen on what he called visualisations, but Julie wasn't sure that she liked them. She blinked across the room and on the other side of the candle a small, mousy woman smiled at her. Jean, Julie remembered. At the beginning of the meeting everyone had had to give their names and Julie remembered Jean's because she was the only woman there not wearing anything fancy. She wore a thick, ribbed jumper with leather patches on the elbows and corduroy trousers with flat walking shoes. Julie had felt worried about what to wear before she came, but at least Jean looked normal.

Jean turned to Eric.

That sounds as if it might be a good meditation for me to do, she said.

Certainly, he said, and for anyone with any kind of illness. He beamed at them all and snuffed out the candle.

More light, Muriel, please, he said, and Muriel switched on the overhead light, which was suddenly and unbearably yellow.

Time for refreshments I think, he shouted, and Muriel appeared wheeling a trolley with several cups, a jug of milk and a plateful of carob-coated biscuits on it. She hurried back into the kitchen for honey for those who preferred it. Julie was starving but she wouldn't touch the biscuits before anyone else.

Apart from Jean and Sylvia there was a much younger woman who had thick curly black hair and large brown eyes, you could see crescents of white beneath them. Julie thought she was very beautiful, and she had a beautiful name too, Josepha, Julie had never met anyone called Josepha before. She was very serious and thoughtful. Julie kept looking at her when she should have been meditating, but Josepha never looked up once.

Then there was Esther who was also dark and quiet, but smiling, and about forty, Julie thought, and a couple who sat together, holding hands and hardly spoke at all. They were young, both with longish mousy hair and longish pale faces, and Julie, who had worked hard at remembering everyone's name, couldn't remember their names at all. The last member of the group was Gerry. He had thick black hair and a red face and he spoke in a rough uneducated way.

Eric's front room was large, two rooms really, knocked into one, and all one wall was imitation stone cladding with a huge fireplace. People sat apart and weren't really talking, except for Jean and Sylvia, who seemed to have known one another before. It turned out they'd both had sons who'd died, Jean's died at seven from leukaemia, Sylvia's son Anthony had been born with cystic fibrosis, but had lived to be twenty-two. Sylvia had four other children, all girls, but Jean only had one other son, whose life was being ruined just as tragically, she said, by gambling. He had conned his own grandmother out of her house to pay for his debts. Jean had washed her hands of him now, he could go to prison and she wouldn't lift a finger, yet not a day went past, not one, without her worrying about him.

It's guilt, she said, that's all it is. No matter how I try to talk myself out of it. All the time David was dying in hospital Michael got no attention, he was passed round from one relative to another. And afterwards, well, things were bad afterwards. She clasped her hands round her knees and rocked. No one could give him the love and attention he needed – I certainly couldn't.

No one could blame you for that, said Sylvia.

No, no one could, said Jean. Except myself. Poor little Michael, he was only four at the time.

But he isn't four now, said Eric. He can't go on being poor little Michael all his life.

Julie felt let in to a private world, let in and shut out at the same time. She was embarrassed about listening, but they were the only people in the room talking, and they were talking loud enough for everyone to hear. She glanced quickly round at the others, they were all listening too. Esther listened nodding her head slowly all the time, whatever anyone said. She wore earrings of twisted metal and the different colours shone as her head moved. When anyone spoke she blinked a few times then went on nodding. It gave the impression that she was listening very intently. Sylvia was listening intently as well, leaning her large shaggy head forwards and resting her chin on the tips of her fingers, which were pressed together. Only Julie seemed to be thinking about the biscuits, but she tried not to be obvious about it, focusing instead on what people were wearing, the flaming crushed velvet of Josepha's dress, the satin leaves stitched round the hem of Esther's dark skirt. Julie was glad she'd worn her best dress and cardigan, but without wanting to she found she was watching the biscuits again. Then Gerry reached forwards and picked up a couple, so Julie did as well.

Jean said that of course she had more than Michael to worry about now that she had cancer herself. She was fighting it on all fronts, with conventional and complementary therapies.

Did you go to see that Qi Gong teacher? Esther said.

O yes, he was marvellous, said Jean, and she told them all how, without asking her anything, he had patted up and down her body and told her where the energy was blocked, and it was the exact location of her cancer. Then he gave her some exercises to do, she said, and she got up and showed them a series of bowing and stretching movements called Eight Brocades of Coloured Silk.

The thing that bothers me though, she said sitting

down again, is this idea of karma. You know if you ask any of these Buddhist chaps, or Medbh, why David should have to suffer so much and die at seven, or why Michael should have to go through so much in his own way, or why I should have to go on feeling so bad about both of them if it comes to that, they'd all say karma. You know they would, Eric, she said, lifting a hand to stop him speaking. And what no one ever tells you is, what is this bloody karma anyway? Just some kind of ongoing cosmic punishment? And can you ever change it, that's what I want to know. Because here I am now, with cancer, and I've completely altered my diet – I eat nothing I particularly like – and I practise my yoga and Qi Gong and I do the meditation every day, and I see a homeopathist as well as my consultant – if they came up with any new way of treating cancer I'd try it – I lived off potatoes and potato water for three months, didn't I? she said to Sylvia, who nodded. So what I'd like to know is – am I wasting my time? I mean, if karmically I've had it anyway I think I'd like to know, thank you very much, and I could lie around all day eating chips and drinking lager.

Everyone laughed.

Yes, but I think the idea of karma is precisely that you go through it all without knowing, Sylvia said. Or it wouldn't be effective.

But what for? said Jean. I mean, if I was fated to be the kind of mother I have been, and my boys were karmically programmed to be the way they were, why should I feel so guilty? I was the best mother I could be. I loved them both. I actually used to like all the bathing and changing them and taking them to the park. In some ways it would have been easier to go to work, we could certainly have done with the money. But I was determined to be there for them. Then what happens – one dies of leukaemia, the other one's slowly killing himself in less obvious ways, and logically I know it's no one's fault, but the question you always ask yourself is, what have I done wrong? That's my problem with the idea of cosmic punishment – if you don't know what you're being punished for, how can there be any point?

I don't think karma is about punishment, Sylvia began.

No, said Eric. Consequences. It's not the same thing.

I think it's more like housework, Esther said. You always notice the bits you haven't done.

Yes, said Sylvia. And if you don't do the ironing one day it'll definitely be waiting for you the next. But it isn't to do with punishment at all, is it? she said, appealing to Eric. It's about learning to love.

Jean laughed a bit.

If you've seen anyone suffering to the point of death, she said, and you should know, watching Anthony – you should surely know that suffering doesn't teach them anything ennobling. It makes the world close up around them, it doesn't teach them to love at all.

Perhaps it calls out love in other people, Esther said, nodding.

Julie had never heard such things discussed so openly before. She listened to everything everyone said with great interest. Jean had a small vivid face and Julie liked watching it. Yet all the time Mick's voice kept breaking in.

What a pile of crap, she heard him say. Karma. Just another way of getting more people to eat more shit.

I think what you've got to get over, Eric was saying, is the idea that karma has anything to do with morality – it's not the same thing at all. Morality is by and large a Christian affair.

Well, what is it about? Jean said.

I suppose in the end we would have to say we don't fully know, said Eric. Maybe we're not able to know. Maybe we have to accept the mystery.

More turd pie, Mick said.

Jean thought a bit.

And yet I'd still like to know, she said. Because it is the most promising solution after all. I mean look at the alternatives. If you're not a Christian the alternative is really the idea of meaningless suffering. And I just don't think I can live with that, she said.

She can't live with it, so it can't be true, Mick said.

Shall we close with another meditation, said Eric, and Julie tried with the others to relax and to clear her mind of Mick's voice. But Mick's voice wouldn't be cleared. It rattled on, about capitalism being the real source of suffering, even illness, and how these middle-class people were just pissing in the wind.

Julie got up from the kitchen table and brought the packet of cornflakes over from the cupboard. She opened it neatly so that she could fasten the flap down again like Aunty Clare always did, rather than just ripping the top off like Mick.

If you are pregnant you are recommended to increase the amount of folic acid in order to reduce the risk of spina bifida and other neural tube defects, it said on the box.

Julie ate three bowls of the cornflakes. Then she started preparing a breakfast for Uncle Si, tea and toast. She had started doing this whenever she knew he was in. If someone was looking after him, she thought, he wouldn't wander off so much. So whenever she made a cup of tea for herself she made one for him as well, knocking on his door before taking it to him. He would always open the door just a little each time and take it from her saying, Well, now, that's very kind.

Julie set the table, putting out cereal, butter and jam, then while the toast was grilling she tapped on Uncle Si's door.

Breakfast, she called, then knocked again in case he didn't hear. She went back into the kitchen to get a tray for the toast and tea, if he didn't come out she would take it to him. Before buttering the toast she wiped the plate carefully, Uncle Si had been known to put pots away without washing them. She poured hot water into the little teapot she'd picked up specially for him at Age Concern, then carried the tray into the corridor.

Uncle Si, she called, through his door.

Julie knew he was in, at least he had been last night. Surely he hadn't gone out in the middle of the night. She knocked on the door again, then pushed it open. Uncle Si was standing in the corner, wearing only a vest, and staring at her as if he'd never seen her before.

Julie didn't drop the tray. She went out carefully and closed the door behind her, then she put the tray down on the kitchen table. She stood still a moment, pressing the tips of her fingers to her forehead, trying to remember what she was doing.

Cards, she thought. She had to go to get the Christmas cards.

She stayed where she was, not moving.

She'd once asked Mick what was wrong with Uncle Si.

What do you mean? he'd said.

Well – what's wrong with him?

Mick stopped trying to prise a tack out of the sole of his boot and looked up.

He's all right, he's fine. He just – can't cope with stuff sometimes.

Has he always been like that? Julie said.

He's not mental you know, said Mick. He's had a bad time. He used to have a bad time at school. My dad had to look after him.

This was the first time Mick had said anything about his dad except that he hated him.

But isn't your dad younger than Uncle Si? Julie said.

Mick went back to tugging at the nail.

He is younger, yeah, but he was the one who'd fight. And Si didn't move up many classes at school. They used to call him Simple Simon, of course.

The nail came out with a final tug. Mick looked at it and said,

That was stuck right in my toe.

Well, shouldn't someone be looking after him now? Julie said.

Yeah, Mick said. Like who – the tooth fairy? He laced his boot up again. I suppose you could say we're looking after him.

Julie hadn't thought of it that way, but that was when she decided to start looking after Uncle Si.

It was nice of your dad though, wasn't it? she said. To look after him, I mean.

Mick looked up briefly.

My dad, he said, is a wanker and a bastard.

Then he started whistling and Julie knew that meant the end of the conversation. She wished he wouldn't use such terrible language about his father and for a moment considered telling him so, then thought better of it and went downstairs. But she remembered what he'd said and from that time on tried to make sure that Uncle Si got some food down him every day, and several mugs of tea. He didn't say much, Uncle Si, even when they were in the same room together eating. Most of the time he acted as if she wasn't there at all, and she never knew what to say either. So she got on with things in the kitchen and he ate, or hummed folk tunes to himself. But he was polite, and always thanked her for whatever she did. But now look, she thought. Look where it had got her. She was living with mad people, she thought, and felt a wave of despair. Then clearly she heard Medbh's voice.

It doesn't matter what the people around you are doing, she said. You have to get on with your own life. And that was what Julie was doing. She was going out to buy some cards.

Julie reckoned up how many cards she would have to buy

as she walked down the hill to the lights. She wanted to send one to each person at the Mind-Power meeting, there was just one meeting left before Christmas, and one to Alison, and Annie, and Darren and Uncle Si. And Mick. She didn't know as yet what to do about Brian, or Uncle Terry and Aunty Clare. None of them knew where she was living, though she had promised Aunty Clare to send her the address as soon as she was settled. She was afraid of any of them turning up to see her, and she didn't want to post their cards by hand in case she bumped into any of them. So there was plenty to think about, and as she walked towards the thick flow of people in the town centre she began to feel better. She always liked being out in town, even if she didn't see anyone she knew.

Today Julie saw two people she knew. As she reached the main road to the market she stopped and looked up the long street that led to Aunty Clare's, wondering what to do. She often thought about visiting them, and remembered what it was like living there. She liked to think of the two of them still doing the things they did when she was there, untouched by the world around them. You would never think that a few streets away there was the yard, and Uncle Si's. And as she was thinking this, and wondering if she could possibly visit them without giving away where she lived, she saw Annie coming down the long slope, pushing a double buggy.

Julie waved and called, Annie, and Annie looked, but her expression didn't change until she was nearer.

Hi, she said.

Julie was really pleased to see her.

Are these your twins? she said. Identical faces gazed at her from beneath corduroy hats.

This is Jamie, Annie said, pointing to the blue hat. And this one's Thomas. Thomas was in a brown hat.

Are you going to the shops? Julie said, but Annie said

she'd already been. And to the market. She was just on her way to feed the ducks.

I told you that's all you do once you're a mother, she said, with a sidelong glance at Julie. Look around the shops, feed the ducks.

It's all I do now, Julie said. Except that I don't feed the ducks, and they laughed. Julie followed Annie though it was out of her way, trying to keep up. She said,

I've got an aunt lives up there, on Fairview. I used to live with her.

Annie accepted this without comment, then she said, I don't live that far up. I live on Harker Street.

Julie remembered this, though Annie didn't give her the number and she didn't feel she could ask. She said,

I went to the meeting at Eric's house. I thought you might be there, and Annie said she was going to try to get to some of them, but it wasn't easy with the twins.

I didn't know anyone there, Julie said. There was a woman called Jean, who's got cancer, and another one called Sylvia.

O I know them, Annie said. They're nice. I've been to Sylvia's house, she has dos there sometimes.

Julie wondered if she would be invited to a do. Annie knew Esther as well, but she wasn't sure about Josepha.

Do you do the meditations? Julie said.

Fat chance, said Annie, tugging the buggy up a kerb. I used to, at first. I used to visualise these two staying asleep, but it never worked.

Julie told her about the dog dirt. But I think you've got to keep trying, she said, and stopped. She could feel an ache in her lower stomach.

I think I'd better get back now, she said. I've got some shopping to do.

Right, Annie said. She didn't know if she could get to the meetings at Eric's, but she would definitely come to the next one at Old Nick's.

Julie walked back slowly, suffering queasy fears about

the weight in her stomach, that the muscles might give way and it would all fall through bloodily onto the pavement. Usually when she felt like this she liked to sit down, but there wasn't even a low wall nearby for her to sit on. Perhaps she should have gone to the park after all, where there were benches.

Julie made herself think about something else, like Medbh said, concentrate on the things around her. She looked around and noticed how many churches there were at this end of town, Baptist, Mormon, Methodist.

Carpenter seeks Joiners, said the poster on the side of the Jehovah's Witness hall, and the notice on the door of the Salvation Army read,

> Believing Christ died – that's history
> Believing He died for you – that's salvation.

When Mick's dad was a lad he'd seen some Methodists coming out of their church and a big group of Unitarians set on them, and they all tried to stone one another and the police had to break it up. That's how Christian they were, Mick said.

Julie couldn't see that it was any different from SWP members fighting the WRP at Blackpool, but Mick said it wasn't the same. Religious groups were all suffering from the same delusions, whereas the SWP and the WRP had a real argument, about how the proletariat were to be organised during the revolution. Anything that divided the workers at that stage, he said, would be disastrous. So that made the WRP Enemies of the People.

Julie had given up in the end, as she usually did when arguing with Mick. She could never seem to get across exactly what she meant whereas he was very clear. She didn't want to start the argument off all over again in her head so she thought instead about how Mick would love the baby when it was born. If it was a boy he would teach it to play football. She was sure Mick wanted a boy really, and she did too. And she thought how nice it would be to be like Annie, not wandering around on her own any more but with a pram to push, people would stop and talk to her about the baby.

All these thoughts took Julie's mind off the ache in her stomach and off Uncle Si, what Medbh said definitely worked. And soon she was walking along what used to be the main shopping street of the town before all the old shops, Barlow's hardware and Arthur Lees herbalist's had been closed down and new ones like Dorothy Perkins opened instead in the precinct. Now at this end of town there was only a store selling computer games and an arcade full of fruit machines, until you passed Vernon's car spares and there was a new shop, Krishna, that everyone had been talking about at the Mind-Power meeting. Julie looked in. There were dowsing crystals, tarot cards and scented candles in the window, and inside there were crystal balls and copies of *Psychic News*, and a stand full of greetings cards. Julie went in to look at them. They had pictures of the Qabalah or zodiac signs or photographs of stone circles on them, but they were expensive, too expensive to buy for everyone in the group, and she couldn't imagine giving one to Mick or Uncle Si. So she looked instead at the aromatherapy oils and the books: *Mysterious Britain*, *The Way of Heaven*, *Palmistry and You*, *The Booke of Spelles*. The shop assistant was reading behind the counter, she didn't seem interested in Julie at all. Julie took *The Booke of Spelles* down from the shelf and read the back cover.

> Kazovar, a practising magician, has for many years used his magical powers to help those who consult him achieve better health, longevity, riches or romance. Now at last he has decided to make his wisdom and power available to a wider public . . .
>
> Whether you want to attract the attention of that special person, lose weight or improve your bank balance, *The Booke of Spelles* is for you.

Feeling as though she was doing something wrong, Julie flicked through the contents page.

Spelle to increase potency, she read.

Spelle to cure sickness in the young.

Then towards the bottom she read,

Spelle to increase desirability, and,

Spelle to arouse devotion in the one you love.

When she turned to the page everything was set out like a recipe.

> One sachet angel hair
> One sachet St John's wort
> One old penny, faded.
> Lavender oil, six drops.

But what was angel hair, and where would she get it? And how much would it all cost?

We sell a lot of those, the assistant said behind Julie. They're on special offer at the moment.

Julie glanced at the price.

I was just looking, she said, quickly putting it back. She went back to the cards and found a packet with a picture of a rainbow and *Peace on Earth* on the front. She bought these for the group and left the shop, looking briefly at a pair of aura goggles on the way out. Medbh could read auras, Eric had said. She could tell you everything about yourself at twenty paces. Julie had never seen anyone's aura, but she remembered looking at Alan and feeling sick, she wondered if that counted. It would have to, since she couldn't afford the goggles. She couldn't even afford to eat while she was out, though the smell from the tandoori takeaway made her feel very hungry. She'd saved up some money for Christmas, but she had to spend it very carefully. She wanted to buy Mick some gloves for the cold weather, and a new mug for Uncle Si to thank him for letting her stay there. She couldn't think what to get for Darren. And really, above anything, she needed to start buying things for the baby.

That was, after all the cards. There weren't any cards up in the house yet, it was really depressing. Mick had had one, from the SWP. It had a bunch of reindeer glaring at Father Christmas on the front with Have a Revolutionary Yule at the bottom, but he hadn't put it up, it was just lying around the bedroom floor. Uncle Si had had one from a friend at the Mechanics', but that was it. Darren hadn't had any of course, Julie sometimes wondered if anyone had ever known Darren apart from Mick. And Aunty Clare and Brian didn't know Julie's address, so Julie wouldn't get any unless she sent some out. Alison and Annie might send her one back, and she might even get some from the meeting. She was going to put all the cards they got up on the mantelpiece in Uncle Si's room and string up some tinsel underneath. That was as far as she dared go without Mick going mad, but she was worried about food. She didn't know who would be in when, and Mick wouldn't discuss it, but she wanted to cook something special. It was their first Christmas together and there was the baby, it was the baby's first Christmas too.

The town centre was strung with lights, there was a big tree in the marketplace and an inflatable Santa on the town hall roof. All the shops were offering last-minute Christmas bargains and interest-free credit, and people Julie had never seen before hung around the shop doorways begging. The old man with his penny whistle was there as usual, but there was a younger man with dreadlocks and a dog, and a young woman with scabs all over her face, and a couple with children, two little girls with dirty hair. The couple just stood by the crowds looking dazed, not really begging at all. Julie got past them, then she was stopped by a young lad who couldn't have been more than fifteen. She gave him some change then pushed past the next two on her way into Boots, aggrieved that they were asking her. She was poor too, she wanted to say, then she felt guilty remembering Mick.

There was only a week till Christmas so there wasn't much choice on the card counter. The ones that were left were being sold for Oxfam and Dr Barnardo's. Mick hated charities. Then Julie found one that was just right for Mick, with a picture of Good King Wenceslaus on the front watching the beggar carrying sticks. Good King Wenceslaus sees for himself the results of VAT on fuel, it said. Julie took this card and a small packet of ordinary-looking ones for everyone else to the till, and as she stood in the queue she was nudged from behind by a pram.

Alison, she said, feeling a rush of guilt. You've had the baby then.

Looks like it, Alison said. I said they'd induce me.

Julie peered round the pram hood. She could just see an elderly, bluish face in a pink bonnet.

A little girl, she said. Did you call her Sammy?

Sadie, Alison said, and Julie thought that was much nicer. Several older women shoved and pushed past them. Look, Alison said. Do you want to sit down there – she nodded towards the deep window seat on which several people were sitting, waiting for prescriptions. Julie payed for the cards and followed Alison.

I'm not supposed to be out really, she said, manoeuvring the pram along the narrow aisle, only I couldn't stand being in any more.

They squashed themselves in on the end of the ledge.

Well, you look better anyway, Julie said.

I know, said Alison, or I wouldn't be out. I didn't leave that flat for a month – I thought I'd die there.

Sadie was one week old. They'd induced Alison and it had taken ages, a day and a half, though the midwife said she'd only been properly in labour for eighteen hours.

Bloody well long enough, Alison said, and Julie agreed.

Then Sadie had been underweight, and not breathing properly, and they'd taken her off for tests. But it had been all right, they'd let them both out yesterday, though she didn't weigh five pounds yet.

She's down to four pounds three now, Alison said. But they always lose weight the first week.

Then she said,

When we got back from hospital Mick was there.

Mick? Julie said.

I forgot to say we'd seen Mick, Alison said. A few weeks ago in the pub. The last time I went out in fact. Him and Alan got on like a house on fire –

They did? said Julie.

– And Alan said he could borrow some music some time. So when we got back from the hospital there he was. Talk about timing.

But we don't have a record player, Julie said. He never told me, she thought.

Alison shrugged, then shifted about on the seat.

I just feel like I've been kicked all over, she said. And the stitches are the worst.

The queue for prescriptions was getting longer and a large lady next to Julie gave them both a prodding look.

Shall we go for a cup of tea? Alison said. Might as well while she's asleep, and she eased herself off the ledge.

Julie was still thinking about Mick not telling her he'd met Alan, and Alan and Alison not saying anything either, when she went round.

I've got to get back, she said.

A cup of tea won't take long, said Alison. I'll buy you one. And they went across the precinct to McDonald's.

She only sleeps when I'm pushing her, Alison said. All the books say to try to get some sleep when they do, to make up for being awake all night. They don't say what to do if they'll only sleep when you're pushing them across a main road. She went to order the tea.

Julie looked at the photos of BigMacs and chicken burgers on the walls, but told herself she hadn't the money.

Alison came back and sat down. Almost at once there was a sharp little cry from the pram and then another. Alison groaned.

See what I mean? she said. Julie peered into the pram. Sadie's lips were curled back over tiny gums, her eyes were shut tight.

She knows when I sit down, Alison said. Little cow.

Don't say that, said Julie. She's beautiful.

Alison laughed shortly.

So where's your white stick, she said.

Can I hold her? said Julie.

Be my guest, said Alison.

Sadie was very light and scrawny. She wore a green BabyGro that was too big for her, and a knitted pink cardigan and bonnet. She squirmed all the time Julie held her.

If I'm not pushing her out, Alison said, I have to walk with her, up and down, up and down, wearing a bloody track in the carpet. The only way I can get to the loo is if Alan takes over, then he has to walk up and down.

Julie cradled Sadie awkwardly, her wobbling head bumped into Julie's shoulder.

How's Alan taking it? she said.

Like every other man – lying down and snoring, said Alison. I've never known anyone sleep through so much noise.

Sadie cried again, in a sharp, peevish way.

Maybe she's hot, Julie said, and she pulled the bonnet from the bobbing head, but Sadie only cried harder.

O she's got black hair, said Julie. Alison said nothing. Lots of pretty hair, she added, in case she'd said the wrong thing, but Alison only said,

They quite often lose their first hair and it grows back a different colour. She's got dark skin as well, she said, before Julie could say anything. But that's because she's a bit jaundiced. In a week's time she could look like a different baby, the midwife said. I wish she was a different baby. One that slept.

Am I holding her right? said Julie. Sadie kicked and squalled and Alison helped Julie shift her into a different position.

I didn't know how to hold her either when they gave her to me, Alison said. You think it'll be natural, but it isn't.

Sadie's cries took on a harsh sawing note, people in McDonald's were looking round.

You'd better give her to me, Alison said, unbuttoning her coat. She took Sadie and pushed her inside. Sadie struggled and cried, then Alison winced as she latched on.

This isn't – ow – like you think it'll be either, she said, and Julie had already guessed that it might not be.

The day after I got her home I had to sit and feed her all the time, she was on-off-on-off all day. You think she's had enough so you put her down and she starts crying again for more. The midwife says she's got a lot to gain. But after two days of that I said to Alan, sod this, go and get some SMA. I don't mind doing it some of the time but I can't sit around all day being chewed.

Julie looked at Alison's face and thought about how many kinds of pale there were. There was Alison's ordinary skin colour, then the glowing pale she'd been when she was pregnant, now this old dead white. Alison looked downwards, concentrating fiercely on Sadie.

Ow, shit, she said as Sadie came off the breast. She held her against her shoulder and patted her back. Sadie puked copiously over Alison's coat.

Then when you get her fed she throws it all back, Alison said, and for a moment Julie thought she might cry.

Shall I help you push her back? she said. You shouldn't be out so soon.

Together they tucked Sadie into the pram and Julie

held the door while Alison pushed her through. Outside Julie pushed the pram through the crowds and Alison held onto her arm, walking slowly like an old woman. But Julie was delighted by the feel of the pram, which was a new one, navy with white flowers. It pushed smoothly and when she looked inside she could see Sadie's little face, furiously sucking her dummy. They walked slowly past people laden with shopping and trees, clutching children.

All ready for a family Christmas, said Julie, feeling suddenly happy.

Not us, said Alison. My family still aren't speaking to us. They've not even been to see Sadie. So it'll just be us this Christmas. Alan'll probably do something like a potful of Bolognese and we'll see who turns up.

After that they said very little as Julie pushed the pram up the long slope and Alison held onto her, breathing hard. Sadie stopped glaring at Julie, her head dropped to one side and she shut her eyes.

I think she's settling down, Julie said.

I told you, said Alison. So long as you don't ever sit down yourself she's fine. Alan'll have to push her out when I get in – it's my turn to sleep. I don't know what I'd do if he wasn't there. I think I'd kill myself.

O no, Julie said.

I bloody would, said Alison. You don't know what it's like, day and night. But you will, she said.

A feeling of nervous doom settled round the edges of Julie's happiness. She was quite glad when they turned the corner into Alison's street and the hill levelled.

I have to be getting back now, she said, and Alison took the pram from her.

I'll call round soon, said Julie, feeling as though she should say something else, offer to help, but Alison had already turned away. Julie walked on, looking at the hills with their ribbons of snow. It was only at the end of the street that she remembered she'd forgotten the tinsel.

And she still didn't know what to make for a Christmas meal.

Music, more powerful than the trains, vibrated through the floorboards from Darren's room, John Martyn, Yes.
This is the real stuff, Mick said.
I thought you liked Ralph McTell, said Julie.
That was just what we could play, said Mick.
Now the Steve Miller Band came thumping through the floorboards.

> Some people call me the space cowboy
> Some call me the gangster of love

That was all the stuff Alan liked, from the sixties and seventies. Mick had picked up an old record player from a scrap heap and had spent hours with Darren trying to get it to play.

Julie hadn't said anything about Mick seeing Alan. Instead she'd decided on a new regime of cookery now that Mick had picked up a proper stove. Because it was Christmas she was doing a cooked breakfast every day, but she didn't take Uncle Si's into his room any more. She set out the table for everyone and called them down and tried to ignore it if they didn't come.

Today it was scrambled eggs. Julie put the pan on a low light then wiped the table again, she could never get it looking really clean. She poured hot water into the teapot and set out the plates. She felt pleased with herself for being so organised. Yesterday she'd bought all the presents and posted all the cards, except for the ones she was taking to the meeting. She'd posted Alison's and Annie's by hand. Alison hadn't been in so she'd pushed the card and a little mobile for Sadie's pram through the door, then she'd wandered up and down Harker Street until she'd found the house she thought must be Annie's, with all the toys on the floor when she looked through the window and the double buggy in the hall. Annie wasn't in either so she left the card, then, after some thought, put stamps on the ones to Brian and Aunty Clare. She'd written, With love, Julie, on all of them. Now she buttered the toast and put it on a big plate, then went into the corridor again.

Breakfast, she yelled up the stairs, then, Uncle Si, she called through his door.

No answer except for a shuffling noise inside. Julie went back into the kitchen and considered squeezing the oranges she'd bought.

Outside there were footsteps in the yard and the postman left letters on the windowsill, no one could get to the letterbox at the front. Julie always expected bad news, from Brian, or the DSS. But it was only an envelope with advertising on the front. *You have definitely won a cash prize*, it said on the front. Julie tutted, and turned on the radio.

The search continues for little Rebecca Hughes, who disappeared three days ago . . .

Inside her Julie felt the faint wobbling motion of the baby. At first she hadn't been sure it was kicking, but now she knew it was. And she hadn't talked about it to Mick yet, she kept meaning to mention the baby to him but it was too hard.

Is there tea? Uncle Si said and Julie jumped. He was standing behind her in his vest and trousers, Julie thought he didn't look pleased. The music was so loud the pans on the stove were rattling.

O yes, she said, there's scrambled eggs, but Uncle Si said he only wanted tea. He poured it and took it back into his room.

Upstairs the record changed and there were several loud thuds. Then from the yard someone yelled, Shut that fucking racket up, and several dogs started barking. But if anything the music got louder, and there was a small thud, then a terrific one, and a yell.

Julie thought she had better go upstairs. She cared about what Uncle Si thought if no one else did.

The stairs rattled as she went up them and Julie could feel a similar vibration in her chest bone as she got closer to the noise.

Going on up to the spirit in the sky –

The door to Darren's room was open and Julie paused in surprise. Darren was dancing. Around the house he rarely even moved, but now he leapt onto the old chair in his room, thrust his hips forward and pretended to play the guitar.

That's where I'm gonna go when I die –

Then, with one foot pressed to the back of the chair, he brought it crashing down and jumped back onto the bed.

When I die and they lay me to rest I'm gonna go to the place that's the best –

Mick tried to follow him, tripped over and fell, laughing helplessly, but Darren was unstoppable. He leapt on and off the bed, then did some weird steps of his own, and arched his back until his head nearly touched the floor. Mick got up again to join him.

Never been a sinner, they yelled. I never sinned –

Well you're having a good time, Julie said, laughing a bit. No one heard.

Breakfast's ready, she shouted.

Mick frogleapt over Darren and they both crashed to the floor. They lay on the floor, tangled up and laughing, and Julie backed out of the room. Her heart was beating a little uncomfortably. She went back down the stairs to the kitchen and served herself some of the scrambled egg before it was all ruined.

Soon the house went quiet and Mick came down, followed by Darren.

Breakfast! he said as if he hadn't heard her before. He went over to the pan. Scrambled eggs.

Darren sat down at the table, turned away from Julie. Julie chewed and swallowed.

They're cold now, she said, sounding stiff without meaning to, so she added,
Uncle Si hasn't had his either.
Mick got the plates.
You eating? he said to Darren, and Darren said he'd have a piece of toast and Mick passed him one.
Anyone would think they were joined at the hip, Julie thought.
You know who came round yesterday? Mick said through a mouthful of egg. They waited. Jehovah's Witnesses, he said and Darren laughed.
There was this old bloke, Mick said. Wanted to know if I ever read my Bible. He gave me a leaflet, look, and he fished it out.
RESIST WICKED SPIRITS, it said.
He said did I know that wicked spirits ruled the world? I said I knew that and he looked dead chuffed, well made up, poor old sod. I bet he'd taken some stick before he got round here.
Julie read the leaflet.
True, many scoff at the idea that wicked spirits rule the world, it said.

> That is because wicked spirits are so clever that they can assume many disguises. The Bible says, 'Satan himself keeps transforming into an angel of light' 2 Corinthians 11:14.

So he asked me, Mick was saying, if I'd read the Bible with him. And I said I would of course, only something funny kept happening to me whenever I picked it up, or even when there was one in the same room, I could feel a burning pain in my right arm and the room going dark –

> Be particularly wary of those who try to turn your mind towards the spiritism of the so-called New Age, astrology, palmistry, conversing with the dead,

said the leaflet.

Worrying stuff, eh, Mick said, watching Julie.
What is? she said.

All that about the Mind-Power group, and Lucifer – sorry, Medbh.

It's not about them, Julie said.

Of course it is, said Mick. I told the old bloke all about it, because he wanted to know why I was having the trouble with Bibles. He said was there anyone around me who might be invoking evil spirits. So I told him all about you.

Don't be silly, Julie said, getting up.

Straight up, said Mick. He was dead interested. He was talking exorcism. He asked if I've ever seen you reading a Bible and I had to say no. So that proved it.

I bet I know more about the Bible than you, said Julie, who had been to Sunday School. I can quote it.

So can I, Mick said. 'The', he said to Darren, that's a quote from the Bible. 'And', there's another one.

Julie turned away shaking her head, and ran water and washing-up liquid into the sink.

Anyway, I promised we'd take you to the next meeting, said Mick. Julie didn't say anything. Mick pushed his plate away.

Well, I'm off, he said to Darren. Have you finished?

Darren said he had.

Where are you going? Julie said without turning round, and Mick said, Out. When they left he said, See you later, but she didn't reply. They were always out these days and nothing was getting done around the house. The only good thing was that all the others had stopped hanging round as well.

Julie dumped the pots into the sink, then thought uneasily about Medbh and the group. She sat at the table again and re-read the leaflet slowly. It seemed very clear. She stared at it for a while then got up, and walked up the stairs to Darren's room.

The chair was upended and all the blankets were on the floor, and the bed itself was askew. On the window-sill there was a bottle. Julie stepped carefully over the bedclothes and picked it up. The label was printed in small letters, METHADONE. Julie got the top off with some difficulty and smelled. It reminded her of something she couldn't place, then she remembered the nail polish remover at Aunty Clare's. She tilted the bottle and touched a drop of it onto her finger. Green liquid. She licked it off but it didn't taste of anything. Then she felt afraid for the baby and put the bottle back. She looked around. Underneath the shifted bed she could see polythene packets near the wall. She knelt on the bed. They were full of white stuff, CITRIC ACID, the labels said. And there were several bits of silver paper, then, as she reached right under the bed she drew out a bag of hypodermics.

Julie sat on the bed. She stared at the needles. They looked terrible to her though she'd seen them often enough at the hospital. She took one out and felt the tip. Darren did this, she thought. He took the needle and pushed it all the way into the vein. Julie could see the veins in her own wrist and the long point of the needle. She didn't think anything, as if for the moment she wasn't able to think. Inside her she felt the slow, crawling movements of the baby.

And this is lapis lazuli, Sylvia said. You can actually use this one to help children sleep.

Julie craned forwards. It was a bright blue colour, with speckles.

I keep it in a little pouch that I wear around my neck, and I think it really does help me to relax. Or what you can do, she said, is to leave it in rainwater for a few hours and then wash in it. It's supposed to be good for neuralgia and eye trouble that way. And it's one of the cures for depression.

Everyone was interested now.

Yes, it has the influence of the sun and Jupiter, Sylvia

said. So it's a protective stone, it wards off danger and strengthens your energies.

She put it with the others, rose quartz, jasper, onyx.

Esther had told the group about how she liked to prepare her own fragrant oils from an almond oil base, and how different oils were best used at different times of the day. She had brought some in so that everyone could smell them. Jean had shown them some more Qi Gong, soon it would be Julie's turn.

Julie had forgotten that they were all supposed to be giving a talk this week, on any aspect of New Age philosophy that interested them. She hadn't a single idea of what she could say. She sat very quietly and hoped all the others would talk for a long time, that was what she used to do at school. Sylvia seemed to like talking, Julie thought she might go on for a while.

Well, that's it really, Sylvia said. There are lots of others. I only brought a selection or we'd have been here all night. But I do believe in the benefits I get from them. I wouldn't go anywhere without my rings, and she spread her fingers to show them the moonstone, jade and aquamarine rings she wore on one hand, and the topaz and amethyst on the other.

Does it matter which hands you wear them on? Josepha wanted to know.

I don't think so, Sylvia said. But you can also get chains of different stones made into necklaces if you prefer. I haven't got one. I always wear this, she brought out a white stone on a silver chain and told them it was a rock crystal.

I think you have to be careful which energies you combine, she said.

There was a brief discussion between Sylvia and Jean as to whether you could grind the stones to a powder and mix tiny amounts in a drink, or whether that would be a waste of time. Julie looked round. There was only Julie,

Josepha and Gerry left, but she still had hopes of being overlooked.

Let's keep the ball rolling, Eric said. Anyone else?

Josepha said that she would talk for a bit about Bach flower remedies, she'd used them on herself and on her little boy, Stanley.

Julie was surprised to hear Josepha had a son, she didn't seem the motherly type at all. She watched Josepha's long slim fingers as she moved them delicately around, explaining, and noticed that there wasn't a ring. But then as she watched the coffee-coloured oval of Josepha's face she remembered a picture on an Oxfam Christmas card, of a brown Madonna and child. She did look like that, Julie thought, mysterious and angelic, then she remembered the leaflet. Satan himself keeps transforming into an angel of light, it had said.

I used mimulus and chicory on Stanley, said Josepha, because he was getting clingy. And rescue remedy on both of us for stress.

I used Star of Bethlehem once after an accident, said Jean. And I definitely felt better. They have such lovely names, don't you think?

Everyone agreed.

Josepha said she used to buy them all separately, but now she had a kit.

And when I put Stanley to bed, she said, I always give him a few drops of vervain or rescue remedy. He expects it now. If I forget he says, Bye-bye dops.

Everyone laughed and said, Ah.

Well, that's it really, Josepha said, and smiled. She hardly ever smiled. Julie thought she looked better when she was serious, her teeth were a bit crooked. She wondered how old Josepha was, and decided she couldn't be much older than Julie herself.

How old is your little boy? Jean said.

Seventeen months, said Josepha. His birthday's in July.

Well, is that it then? Eric said, and Julie dug her

fingernails into the palms of her hands. What about you, Gerry?

I'm afraid you'll have to give me a miss, Gerry said. I'd forgotten all about this.

Julie felt intensely relieved.

I forgot too, she said.

O well then, said Eric. Perhaps you'd like to prepare something for next time. Julie looked worried all over again.

Now Eric, Jean said, not everyone likes the sound of their own voice you know. She smiled at Julie.

O no, I wasn't suggesting, Eric began, but Jean laughed at him and poked him in the ribs.

Yes, I don't think this should necessarily be a compulsory exercise, Eric, Sylvia said, and everyone agreed.

O well, Eric said, puzzled. Right you are. Muriel – lights, and the lights immediately went dim.

Now, said Eric I thought we'd end the meeting with a spot of chanting. So if we all arrange ourselves into a circle.

Everyone stood up, holding hands. Julie found that she was holding Gerry's and Josepha's hands but she wouldn't look at them and they didn't look at her. Even without looking she was aware of Gerry's roughness in contrast to Josepha, the skin of his hands was rough and he hadn't shaved. In spite of all the grease, his hair wouldn't lie down properly at the back. Josepha's hand was smooth and cool, she wore silk patchwork trousers and a flowing top, Julie could smell her perfume.

Eric began on a single note.

Oooohhhmmmmm.

Everyone else joined in at different times. The chant rose and swelled, faded a bit then came back stronger than before. Julie joined in quietly then got louder with everyone else, the noise spiralled upwards and outwards. Julie's ears were humming and her chest bone vibrated, she couldn't help wondering about the neighbours. She could feel the note coming from a deeper and deeper place inside her, then, just as it became nearly unbearable, it began to fade on its own.

Eric sang.

Om, shiva-a ya-a va-shi.

And everyone sang with him, then it all died away. People looked round at one another and laughed.

Well, Eric said happily. That raised the energy levels a bit, eh?

Julie was glowing. And as the meeting ended and people got their coats they were all talking and laughing, even Gerry was joking with Esther as they left. And Julie, finding herself next to Jean in the porch, managed to say what she'd been meaning to say all evening.

I brought you a card.

O lovely, said Jean. I almost forgot my cards too, and everyone stood round while Jean and Julie handed the cards round.

No one had brought cards for them.

Mine are all in the post, Sylvia said, and the others murmured something similar. Julie would have felt embarrassed, handing cards out on her own, but with Jean there it was different.

You've not bought me a card, have you? Jean said to them all. I can tell, and I should hope it is in the post, it better had be, and everyone laughed. And afterwards Sylvia offered Julie a lift.

Sylvia and Jean talked in the car, about Jean's new diet, no fluids at all except from fruit, and Sylvia said she didn't know, but Jean said it definitely worked. Julie didn't say anything. She was wondering where to get out. She didn't want anyone in the group to see where she lived, so when Sylvia drew up at the lights at the bottom of the hill Julie said she would get out there.

O no, Sylvia said immediately. Let me drop you at the door.

I don't think you can get the car round, said Julie.

Well, I don't like the thought of you walking, Sylvia said, and Jean said,

How far do you have to walk?

It's just behind the road, Julie said. I walk all the time.

Let me take you, said Sylvia, and Julie began to feel desperate. Then the lights changed.

The lights are changing, she said, opening the door.

Take care, Sylvia called, I shall worry, you know, and as Julie crossed the road her last impression was of Sylvia and Jean waving anxiously as they drove away.

Julie brought the milk in from the back.

There was a wafer of moon in a pale clean sky and a leaflet stuck between the two bottles. Julie picked up the leaflet and, as she stood up, was frightened by two faces staring at her over the gate.

We're swinging on your gate, one of the faces said.

It was the two kids from across the yard. The one who had spoken to her had a shaved head and a harsh, quacking voice. When he had finished speaking his mouth snapped shut like a trap. The other one was a bit smaller, but apart from this they might have been twins.

So you are, Julie said carefully. You'd better watch out though, it's not very safe.

The boys stared at her unwaveringly and Julie felt a bit unnerved. The whole family were a bit horrible to look at, Mick called them the Plug-Uglies. Even the baby looked the same, only very sad, permanently strapped into its trolley, watching the comings and goings in the yard with remote, unhopeful eyes.

Julie had better things to do than stand in the back staring at two ugly boys.

You might have a nasty accident, she warned, and went back into the kitchen with the milk and the leaflet.

Immediately the two boys set up a chant.

We're swinging on your gate, we're swinging on your gate, they quacked.

A vision of the gate crashing suddenly off its hinges and burying the two boys in rubble flitted across Julie's mind, but she didn't let herself dwell on it. She sat at the table and opened the leaflet.

> The Natural Law Party Wishes You
> PEACE ON EARTH THIS CHRISTMAS

it said.

There was a picture of two smiling men hovering in midair.

Yogic flying correlates with maximum orderliness of brain functioning, said the caption. It produces bubbling bliss for the individual.

Julie chewed her toast and read on.

The rest of the leaflet explained how, if everyone who read it took time out on Christmas Day to meditate on world peace, crime and violence everywhere would be reduced, and there was a graph illustrating this. Then there was a summary of Natural Law policy, the aim of which was to produce perfect world health in three to five years. This was to be achieved by:-

- The cultivation of orderliness in world consciousness.
- An increase in collective creative motivation to free the economy of unemployment and debt.
- The elimination of collective stress which causes world enmity.

A group of seven thousand yogic flyers on each continent was to maintain a high degree of satisfaction and integration everywhere, preventing refugee and immigration problems.

EXPERIENCE A LIFE FREE FROM MISTAKES AND SUFFERING, the next heading said. This sounded good to Julie, but it was hard to concentrate with the gate creaking and banging and the two kids chanting on.

Mick appeared from upstairs.

What the fuck's going on? he said. He flung the back door open.

Oi, he roared. Fuck off you little twats.

The two boys disappeared.

Fucking little bleeders, Mick said, closing the door. What's for breakfast?

Julie wasn't cooking breakfast any more, no one ever showed up to eat it. Mick opened the fridge door.

There's nothing in, he said.

There's bread, said Julie. And eggs.

Mick meant there were no sausages or bacon, he loved fry-ups. He got the frying pan out now and cut a large chunk off the cheap margarine Julie bought in to stop Mick buying lard.

I suppose bread and eggs'll have to do then, he said, and he cracked two eggs into the sizzling oil.

Where were you last night, Julie said, trying to sound interested in a friendly way, while her stomach turned at the smell of the oil.

Out, said Mick, cracking a third egg.

What time did you get in?

I don't know. We had a few at the pub, then we all went round to Joe's place. Les has moved in with him you know. We're helping them do it up.

But what about all the work here? Julie said.

Joe'll help us later, said Mick. He can get us some stuff.

Julie watched as he turned an egg over and threw in two hefty slices of bread.

I don't know how you can, she said, sickened. Julie couldn't eat fried food now.

Can what? said Mick, turning the other eggs.

Eat fry-ups when you've been drinking all night. She could never stop herself sounding prim with Mick.

Luverly jubberly, said Mick. He noticed the leaflet. What's that? he said. He read the first bit and started to laugh.

A group of yogic flyers in each country will reduce

crime and eliminate the need for nuclear weapons, he read. Yeah, right, forget the ICBMs and cruise missiles, there's some prat in a yashmak trained on Iran. Eh, Darren, he said as Darren appeared. Get a load of this. They read the pamphlet together, Mick falling about and Darren smiling.

Is this your lot, Mick said, waving the pamplet at Julie.

No, it isn't, Julie said.

It's your leaflet though, innit?

No, said Julie. She was about to explain that she'd found it outside with the milk when Mick fell around laughing again at the photograph.

Yogic flyers bring you Peace on Earth, he read. And I thought that was the Angel of the Lord. Eh, maybe that's who Mary and the shepherds really saw that time – but it doesn't say anything here about getting virgins pregnant and scaring sheep.

Both Mick and Darren were laughing now, so Julie laughed with them. She carried a cup of tea through to Uncle Si, knocking on his door and lowering her eyes when he opened it, just in case.

Well, now, that's kind, said Uncle Si. He was in his vest and trousers. Julie carried her own mug upstairs. If she hung round Mick and Darren long enough she would only feel left out. Or start asking questions no one would answer, like when would the house be ready for the baby, and where were all the new tools coming from. Every time Mick stayed out late he seemed to come back with more – a circular saw this time and a rivet. The last time she'd asked he'd said he'd got them from Les, but Les wasn't working, and all the tools seemed brand new.

Julie knew if she kept thinking about what Mick was doing it would drive her daft. She had to take her mind off him somehow. The more independent you are with a life of your own, she'd read in a magazine recently, the more *he'll* be interested. And Medbh was always saying you had to get on with your own life. So Julie put her coat on over her cardigan because the bedroom was freezing, there was ice on the inside walls now, draped her blanket round her and sat cross-legged on her mattress.

She tried counting the number of breaths she took, but she couldn't make it as far as ten, her mind wandered off somewhere between five and six. But Medbh had said that the point of the exercise was not to get to ten, but to notice when the mind was wandering and try to bring it back. Julie tried this two or three times, then she tried relaxing her body from the feet up, because she'd forgotten to do that first. Then she visualised light, a golden light all around the house for healing, and a pink one for love, because the next day was Christmas Eve and she wanted Christmas to be nice. If it was really nice, she thought, she might get to speak to Mick about the baby.

Julie sat for a few minutes as the cold bit through the gloves she was wearing to her fingers, waiting for something to happen. All kinds of things could happen, she knew from listening to people when they talked to Medbh, anything from astral projection to visits from spirits. But the only thing that ever happened to Julie was that the darkness behind her eyes swam a little and changed colour. She liked it when that happened, it meant that the meditation was working. And though she didn't feel the tingling or warmth she sometimes felt in group meditations, she was sure that something was happening. And that it was bound to help somehow, though she didn't know how.

It was Christmas Eve. All the NSPCC adverts were on the telly.

Somewhere a child is being battered, the voice said. Left alone for days in a dark room. Black and white pictures of huge-eyed children filled the screen.

Julie went back and forwards from Uncle Si's room to

the kitchen. In Uncle Si's room she was cleaning, making neat piles out of the junk, scrubbing brick dust and cement from the frayed carpet. In the kitchen she was making spaghetti Bolognese on the new cooker Mick had said he'd found on a scrap heap. She didn't know if anyone would come in to eat it but she kept visualising everyone coming together, putting out the energy.

Toddler's life of suffering and brutality, the headlines read on the screen.

Every time Julie passed the window she could see Tonia, out by herself in the square, wearing only a jumper, leggings and pumps in the sharp rain. Sometimes she dragged the toe of her pumps between the cobbles where the dirt was, sometimes she sat on her back-yard step, staring at nothing.

There had been trouble at Jude's recently, screaming rows with Des who had driven off in one of his clapped-out bangers. Then the police had been round, and last night Jude had screamed and howled at Tonia, Julie could hear everything through the walls.

Please let it stop, please, she had prayed. Then towards midnight there had been a deathly quiet which was almost worse. Mick and Darren were playing music in Darren's room and didn't seem worried, Uncle Si was out, Julie had lain awake wondering. Nothing had been seen of Des for over a week and Jude was acting funny. No one saw her in the day any more, but there were shouts and laughter late at night when no one else was there, and sometimes Julie was sure she locked Tonia out. So now every time she passed the window she looked anxiously at Tonia and considered asking her in. She didn't want her in. Tonia wouldn't talk but she would follow Julie around, touching everything, Julie would feel her like a prickle beneath the skin. And if Jude was out who knew what time she would come home.

Just fifteen pounds will pay for that crucial visit, the voice on the television said. Julie turned it off. They probably could get fifteen pounds together between them, but Julie knew what Mick would say. She stuffed more rubbish into a black bin bag and caught sight of Tonia again, hopping from one foot to the other with her arms flung wide and her face turned up towards the rain.

Why wasn't Jude letting her in?

Julie tugged the black bin bag into the kitchen, muttering under her breath. She didn't know, after all, that Jude wasn't letting Tonia in. Maybe Tonia wanted to play out on her own, in the rain, without a coat. Medbh had said to look after your own garden, and Julie's garden had enough problems in it already without Tonia. Or Jude. Jude was unpredictable. If she found Tonia with Julie she might go mad. Or worse, start coming over herself.

Julie turned her back on the window and went back into Uncle Si's room. She pulled out the bedding chest from behind the sofa, she was sure she'd seen curtains in it somewhere. Then she thought, maybe she should tell Jude, go over there and just say something, she didn't know what. She pulled the curtains out. They weren't too bad, green and leafy. They didn't go with anything but the material was good. She carried them over to the window and made herself look out. Tonia had gone. Julie looked carefully round the yard but there was no sign of her. She felt vastly relieved, almost happy as she struggled to hang the curtains on the old rail. Then part of it came away from the wall and Julie almost fell. She stared at it in despair for a moment, then went over to the box where Mick kept the screwdrivers.

Later that day everything was ready. She had cleaned and tidied the front room and put all the cards on the mantelpiece, including the unopened ones she had written to Mick, Darren and Uncle Si. She had found some tinsel in the end, in another box in Uncle Si's room, and had looped it beneath the cards. That was as Christmasy as she dared go, although she had been tempted by a little tree. But then she needed some new clothes in the January sales, the purple dress was the only thing that still fitted. And she had to buy everything for the baby. So she'd settled for making the mantelpiece pretty with a candle in a beer bottle at either end. And the curtains were finally hung. They stopped short of the windowsill but they were better than nothing. She'd shifted all the furniture and cleaned behind it and scrubbed all the surfaces in the kitchen until her aching back and lower belly told her to stop. And she had made a huge panful of Bolognese with garlic and peppers. Now she poured water from the kettle into the upstairs sink because the taps in the kitchen still didn't work, and washed her hair, fixing it back with the combs from Woolworths. Then she put on the big black cardigan Aunty Clare had knitted over the purple dress and thought about make-up. Mick hated make-up but sometimes it made Julie feel better. In the end she put on just a touch of lipstick. Then she went downstairs to wait.

Julie waited in the empty room. The rain had stopped but frost was setting in, thickening on the windowpane so you couldn't see out, which was an improvement, she didn't have to worry about any of the children. Inside the fire was lit and everything was bright and cheerful. It wasn't Aunty Clare's, but Julie tried not to think about that, or about all the extra little things Aunty Clare would do to make Christmas special. She raked over the coals to keep the fire going, then sat down again. She fluffed up her hair, there was still some perm left, and tried not to think about how fat she was getting.

She wondered what she would do if no one came back.

Eat the Bolognese, she supposed. Watch some telly. Go to bed. She closed her eyes.

Let them come, she prayed. Then she sat back on the settee and fell asleep.

She woke up to a shuffling sound and someone tugging at the hanging gate.

Is that you, Uncle Si? she cried getting up clumsily, then, remembering the Bolognese, she hurried into the kitchen.

Uncle Si was there, red-faced with cold, but smiling.

Hello, Julie, he said, then he stood as if not knowing what to do.

Just sit down, Uncle Si, said Julie. I'll get you a drink. Suddenly she felt nervous and clumsy. She stirred the Bolognese vigorously and turned the light down as far as it would go, it seemed to be all right. Then she opened the sherry and carried it through. Uncle Si was staring out of the window at the ebbing light.

The lamp's pretty, he said.

The council had put a lamppost up in the big yard. Before it had been totally dark, now a hazy light shone through the frosted glass. Mick had said it was about time, and now all they needed was the yard paving over, which was true, since many of the cobbles were broken and before the lamp came it had been an adventurous business, stepping out after dark.

Do you like the curtains? Julie said.

O they're wonderful, yes indeed, said Uncle Si.

Julie didn't think wonderful was quite the right word, they were shabby and uneven, but she was pleased that he was pleased.

Take your coat off, Uncle Si, she said, and she helped him then sat him down with the sherry.

Now then, that's lovely, he said, and she thought, as she had thought before, what a nice man he was and how strange it was that he'd lived all his life alone.

Are you much older than Mick's father, she said, sitting down with him.

O yes, he said, and Julie waited. About six years, he added at last.

That's just like my mum and Aunty Clare, Julie said pleased. Only my mum was the older one.

Uncle Si said nothing to this, but Julie had more

questions. That was her project, she'd decided, to get to know the people she lived with better.

How did you come to live here? was her next question, but before she could ask it there was more noise in the back yard.

It's Mick and Darren, Julie said, and she ran to let them in. It was working, she thought. It was all working.

Mick looked pissed off. He stamped his feet on the mat.

What's all this? he said.

Nothing, said Julie, hurrying past him to the garlic bread. I just thought we'd all eat together for a change.

The kitchen table was too small for them all to eat at, and anyway, the only warm room was Uncle Si's. Julie put the oven on for the garlic bread and set the water heating for the spaghetti, then she carried the cutlery through.

Mick was talking.

He was sick of selling *The Big Issue*, he said. There were so many people out selling and begging, you were lucky to get rid of two copies a morning. Then there were always the twats who tried to pick an argument with you. One had said that he bet Mick's bank account was healthier than his own, and Mick had shouted after him down the street, when you didn't have a job or a fixed address, he'd shouted, it was a bit difficult to get a bank account, you twat, and the bloke had come back to sort Mick out. Then the shopkeeper had come out. They didn't like you arguing in front of their shops, Mick had been banned from three spots in town already. So he'd been cleared off from there, and all the other spots were taken, town was heaving with the homeless, all the families were out with kids and babies, you didn't stand a chance. Mick was sick of it all.

Julie hurried back to turn the spaghetti down. She got out a six-pack of beer from the cupboard and took it through.

O right, Mick said. Thanks.

Can I get you anything, Darren? Julie said, but Darren didn't drink when he was on methadone. Julie went back to the kitchen to stir the Bolognese.

There's this kid called Roxy, Mick was saying when she got back. And these dickheads came up to him to buy a mag – so he thought, and they dropped the money on the pavement – I mean, it's an old one, but he didn't see it coming. So he bends over for the money and one of them knees him in the face. I mean, that's the kind of shit you get. And you have to take it. Or they can stop you selling.

Julie began to dish the food out. Mick was talking in a brittle, worn-out way she'd seen before and didn't like. She poured the spaghetti into the colander she'd bought specially and unwrapped the garlic bread. It all smelled good. She carried the steaming platefuls through.

For a while all the talk stopped. Julie knew it was good from the concentrated silence. Even Darren was eating with something like enthusiasm. Julie resisted the urge to cut Uncle Si's spaghetti up for him and got on with her own. It was good. After a bit Mick looked up.

Nice one, Ju, he said, and the others mumbled agreement. Then he leant forwards and switched on the telly.

This wasn't part of Julie's plan, but she didn't say anything. She passed the garlic bread round again and they all watched the Christmas edition of *Blind Date*. Mick cheered up a lot.

Look at that plonker, he said, and,

Is she a dog or what? And he asked for more Bolognese.

Then for afters Julie had bought a couple of tinned treacle puddings, and she managed not to burn the custard. Darren couldn't manage pudding, but the others ate up and Julie began to feel very happy. Outside it was cold and dark but inside was so warm and bright that people began to talk.

This is a bit better than last year, eh, Mick said to

Darren, who smiled his lowered smile. This was just what Julie wanted.

What were you doing last year? she said, and Darren laughed unexpectedly, but still without looking at anyone.

Last Christmas was when we met up, Mick said. Wasn't it, Darren? But Darren said nothing, he just went on smiling with Mick looking at him in a funny way.

What's so funny? Julie said.

O we were just sleeping down the same alley, Mick said through a mouthful of pudding. And it was fucking freezing.

That was all he would say, but Julie was sure there was more, something that bound Mick and Darren together the way they were. She would find out one day, she thought.

There was a silence.

So what were you doing, Uncle Si? Julie said, but Uncle Si said he couldn't remember. But this is nice, he said.

It is, isn't it? said Mick. We ought to drink to that, and Julie went back into the kitchen for more beer.

I met a right bastard the other day, Mick was saying when she came back. I keep meeting them – it's because it's Christmas. Season of goodwill. Anyway, I didn't have any change so he said, I suppose you think I'm going to forget the change.

You what, I said, and he starts then. That's what you were thinking, isn't it? he said. That I'd just give you the pound and forget it, I bet you make a pretty penny that way.

O yeah, I said. I'm saving up for a Porsche and a holiday home.

What did he say to that? Darren said.

Nothing, said Mick. But he took his pound back, the dickhead.

Julie had hoped to talk about other things, but since he seemed to want to talk about it she said,

Do people ever keep the change?

Sometimes, said Mick. You don't always have change for a pound.

No, I mean on purpose, Julie said.

I don't know, said Mick. They might do. They're not going to get rich off it, are they, a few pence here and there?

Julie was about to say it would add up, but she didn't want a row on Christmas Eve.

I mean, what are they going to do with their left-over twenty-five p's, eh? Mick said leaning over. They won't notice what they do. Unless they think some poor bastard on the street's picking it up. Then suddenly it's a major crisis. And what does it matter, eh?

Julie wouldn't argue, but Mick could see what she was thinking.

Look, he said. There's no sense to it. That guy – he had a coat on him must have been worth four hundred quid. It'd've been made somewhere for nothing and marked up 500 per cent. But that's all right. So long as some poor sod on the street's not getting twenty-five pence more than he should.

Julie could see she wasn't going to win this one.

Another drink? she said and went into the kitchen. When she brought it back Mick said,

I saw Darren in *The Big Issue* once.

When? said Julie, and Darren lowered his face even further.

A while back. They have this page on missing people with a photo and a just-let-us-know-you're-okay kind of thing. I was reading it one day and there was Darren, large as life and twice as ugly. His mam and dad and sister wanted to know if he was still alive.

And didn't you tell them, Julie said.

No, said Mick.

Julie was very shocked.

Why not, she said.

Not my business.

Did you tell Darren, she said, looking directly over to where Darren sat, hunched up with his arms around his knees.

He'd already seen it, said Mick.

Darren, Julie said, didn't you think of just letting them know you were all right.

Everyone was silent waiting for Darren to reply. There was a long pause. I thought about it, yeah, he said eventually. I wanted to. But I couldn't stand it.

Stand what, said Julie, and when he didn't answer she looked to Mick, but Darren said,

Hearing from them again.

Julie waited, but he didn't say anything else. Mick watched telly and Uncle Si seemed sunk in his own thoughts.

Eventually she said,

What do you mean, Darren, and Darren shifted about on the floor.

I didn't want to hear about them being upset and that.

Look, Mick said. They don't just want to know you're all right, do they? They want to know where you are and when can they see you and when are you coming home. And two weeks later they'd want to know it all over again. It's best to just cut them off, he said and he drained the last drop of beer.

Uncle Si said nothing.

What do you think? Julie asked, but he only looked troubled and said no doubt each case was different.

But were your family that bad, Julie said to Darren. Darren laughed a bit and shook his head.

You don't have to talk about it, Mick said to him. What is this, twenty questions, he said to Julie.

I just want to get to know Darren a bit better, Julie

said. We live in the same house but I don't know anything about him.

Mick shrugged.

They weren't bad, Darren said unexpectedly. There was nothing wrong with them. It was me. I was doing their heads in – shooting up and that.

He leant back against the wall and shut his eyes. Julie noticed how pale his face was.

My dad couldn't hack it – it was tearing him up.

Darren's dad's a doctor, Mick said. His mother's a teacher.

O, Julie said, and she stared at Darren. It wasn't what she'd imagined about him.

No one spoke and there was a depressed feeling in the room. Julie didn't want the evening to end like this. Then Mick farted in a loud, impressive way and Darren laughed. Uncle Si laughed a bit too, shaking his head, but Julie didn't.

Sorry, Mick said to her, not looking very sorry. Gut rot.

I thought you were going to the doctor's, she said. He'd been complaining about his stomach all week.

Not me, Mick said. I hate doctors. They make you ill.

He seemed to have changed his mind since the argument with Tony. Julie didn't point out that she was the one cleaning the toilet.

The last time I went to the doctor's, said Uncle Si, I told him I was having a bit of trouble, and he told me to bring up a chair. And I said, Doctor, if I was bringing up chairs I'd really be in trouble.

Everyone laughed, surprised that Uncle Si was telling a joke. Then he told another one.

There was this doctor, he said, wide-eyed, who said to his patient, I'm very sorry to tell you this but you've only got three minutes to live. And the poor man was very upset, he said, Jesus, Joseph and Mary, is there nothing you can do? and the doctor said, Well, I could get you a lightly boiled egg.

Everyone laughed again, it was hysterical.

Eh, Mick said. What's the difference between a Tory MP and a prostitute? You have to pay a prostitute extra for the kinky stuff.

After that they all told jokes, even Darren. Julie told the joke Alison had told her about the pig and it went down well. Darren told spider jokes. Where do you find a spider with no legs? Where you left him, and, What's this? holding his hand palm upwards, the fingers twitching – A spider with epilepsy. But Mick and Uncle Si told the most, Julie would never have believed it of Uncle Si. She watched his face as he told them, the curiously blank, light eyes. Sometimes he looked like Mick, though she'd never seen it before. When Uncle Si was only four, Mick had said, his mother had left him in their back yard in Salford, and when she came back he was gone. Two days later the police brought him back from Huddersfield. He'd been all that way on public transport, with everyone thinking he was with someone else. That was the first time he disappeared, but from then on he never stopped. He drove his mam and dad daft. Mick had once asked him about it, if he had anywhere to go to, but he'd just said if he had he wouldn't want to go there. So that was it, Mick supposed. Something just got into him and he went.

Watching him now, Julie felt the mystery of him keenly, he would always be a mystery to her. The people she lived with were all mysteries to her, all unknowable, even Mick, though she'd set out to know them better. You couldn't really get to know anyone, she thought.

The police came to pick this bloke up, Mick said. And they said, Where were you between three and four? and he said, Nursery.

Everyone laughed. Julie wasn't going to let herself get depressed. The evening wasn't over yet. She thought about the presents she'd bought them, but it didn't feel like the right time to give them out.

Then Uncle Si asked if they played cards.

We come from a card-playing family, Mick said.

They played poker, gin rummy, red dog. Julie lost all the time, and after a while she started yawning and couldn't stop.

It's Christmas Day, she said, and it was, nearly one o'clock. No wonder I'm tired, she said, I'm off to bed.

Darren smiled. Mick said, *Yes*, to Uncle Si as he cleared his cards, then, You go up, to Julie. We'll be up soon. It was the first time he had ever made any acknowledgement of her going up to bed alone.

Julie didn't move. For the first time she felt how embarrassing it would be to hand out presents when she knew no one had bought her one. But she didn't want to go through it all tomorrow either. She pulled the carrier bag out from underneath her chair and stood up.

I just bought a couple of little things, she said, and she put the carrier bag down in front of the table between Mick and Uncle Si and, without looking at anyone, left the room.

That wasn't so bad, she thought, as she climbed the stairs.

Later, still cold beneath her blankets and coat, she heard Mick and Darren coming up. She expected Mick to go into Darren's room but he didn't, she listened to him sitting down on his mattress, pulling on an extra sweater.

Julie was very awake. There were so many things she wanted to talk to Mick about: the baby, and the two of them, and Darren. She didn't know what to say but she had to get him talking before he went to sleep. She sat up and said,

Mick.

Mmmm.

Mick –

Uhhh – thanks for the gloves.

That's okay – I thought they'd be useful outside.

Yeah, Mick said, sleepily. Inside too.

Yes, Julie said and laughed a bit. Mick rolled over again.

Mick, she said.

What? said Mick.

What happened to Uncle Si?

Mick shifted about.

I don't know. His dad happened to him, like mine happened to me. Only his seems to have been an even worse wanker.

Julie waited. Mick propped himself up.

His dad believed in fighting. He thought boys should fight. So him and his mates used to get their kids together – the boys, that is – and take bets while they thrashed the shit out of each other. My dad told me that. I'd never have believed it but my mam knew him then and she said it was true. Only Uncle Si – he'd never fight. He wouldn't fight and his dad wouldn't let him out of it, so every night he got twatted. Until my dad got bigger, then he twatted everyone. So Grandad won all the bets. Which kept him happy. Trouble was, when my dad got older, he couldn't stop beating people up.

Mick stopped talking and lay down again. Julie felt sick. She felt sick, but she still didn't want him to stop talking to her, so after a moment she said,

Mick –

Mmmm.

What happened when you and Darren met?

In the darkness she could hear Mick turning over.

Some other time, he said.

Julie was quiet. She lay down quietly, but running through her mind like a train were terrible images, of Uncle Si as a small boy, and of the NSPCC adverts. She lay in the darkness running her hand over the slope of her belly, thinking terrible thoughts without wanting to. She thought about how if Uncle Si died, and this house was his, he might leave it to Julie and Mick, then, ashamed of this thought, she thought about Darren instead, and his parents. If she could get back copies of *The Big Issue* and find the one with Darren's picture in it, she could write to his parents. She thought about this for a long time, his parents coming to the house, the tearful reunion, them taking Darren away. It would all be Julie's doing, she would have brought them back together, but even as she thought this she could tell somehow that this wouldn't be the way Mick saw it. From Mick's point of view she would have done a bad thing, the very worst thing she could do.

And then I saw this beautiful lady, Josepha said. In a long robe of midnight blue. And she was holding something up like a big pearl. And I'd asked at the start of the meditation about this problem that's been on my mind, and she said – I heard her speak to me – she said, *Let it happen*. Then she showed me a door, and when I opened it there was just the wide sea.

Mmmm, said several people, impressed.

So you got your answer then, said Sylvia.

Yes, Josepha said. Julie thought she had a very earnest, spiritual face. And things always happened in Josepha's meditations, it made Julie feel quite bad about her own. All she ever saw was darkness, a swirling kind of darkness if she looked hard enough behind closed lids, patterns formed and disappeared again, but they never formed themselves into anything she could understand.

What about you, Jean? Eric said.

Jean was sitting on the floor and frowning, her hands clasped around her knees. Well, she said and sighed. I realised something I've never realised before. You know when you told us to go back in time – to any time at all in our lives. I went back to the hospital when David died. I was sitting beside his bed. I think he'd just died, I could feel the pain – not directly, but I could feel how much pain I was going through. And I knew suddenly how much I'd loved him – more than anyone else. She put her head back and closed her eyes. I knew that if I'd had twenty children I'd still have loved David the best.

That's a good thing to know, Eric said. You can't feel bad for not having loved him enough, right to the end.

Jean opened her eyes and looked at Eric.

It's not very good for Michael though, is it? she said. Eric didn't seem to know what to say to that.

But I realised something else, Jean said. I realised that I hadn't *chosen* to love him more than anyone, any more than I could choose to stop loving him once I knew he was dying, though that would have been infinitely less painful. Jean's voice shook a little, and Sylvia reached forwards from the settee and squeezed her shoulder. Jean didn't shake her off, though Julie could tell she didn't really like it.

I didn't choose to love David any more than I chose to be five foot one instead of five foot ten. You don't choose who you love, do you? she said, looking round at them all, but especially at Gerry, who had told them that his wife had died six months ago.

That's what I'd like to understand, Jean said to Eric. You don't have the choice about any number of things, but you do have guilt. Now why should you feel so guilty about something you didn't choose?

Well, if you listen to Medbh, Eric said, we all do choose at some level.

But why? Jean said sharply, and Sylvia said,

Because we all need to *learn* to love.

But I already did love David, Jean said, then she shut her mouth tightly as if she wasn't going to take up any more time. She clasped her hands round her knees and rocked a bit.

Eric said,

What about you, Julie, do you have anything you'd like to share?

This was the moment Julie had been dreading and waiting for. She thought of all the things she'd been thinking about recently, the suffering of babies, and how, if you were damaged when you were little, like Uncle Si, and you never really recovered, was that karma? Because if you never got over it, how could it work?

Everyone looked at Julie and Julie's brain jammed with all the thoughts. Eric looked as if he might speak again, then Julie blurted out,

Pink.

I saw a lot of pink, she added. She didn't know where that came from and everyone else looked surprised too.

Josepha said,

You mean like a pink light? and Julie nodded.

It made me feel warm, she said. And sleepy.

The others laughed. Sylvia said,

Well, pink is the colour of loving, you know. You must need to attract more love into your life.

Julie looked at her surprised. She did want to attract more love from Mick.

Maybe it's love for the baby, Jean said. Or *from* the baby, and Josepha said slowly,

I bet there's a lot of pink in your aura. You look like a pink person to me.

That's just the heat from the fire, Jean said, and everyone laughed, including Julie, for the first time she didn't mind being the centre of attention.

There's a lot of pink around Medbh, Sylvia said. Especially when she's healing. It's a creative colour as well.

Julie was pleased. She'd noticed at school that sometimes, if you lied well enough, people began to support your lie, and it became a kind of truth.

How about you, Gerry? Eric said, but Gerry didn't want to say anything. Julie felt sorry for him, that was how she used to be. Esther wasn't there, and neither were the young couple who'd been to the first meeting, they'd never come back. Sylvia had already spoken, about sensing her mother close by, so Eric said it was time for refreshments. Muriel hurried in with the tray.

There wasn't enough dandelion coffee, she said, a little breathlessly, to Sylvia. So I did you a barleycup. I hope you don't mind, and Sylvia said it was quite all right.

Everyone was unusually quiet as they drank their herbal teas. Julie thought about what she'd said, and how everyone had been interested, even Josepha. When Eric said it was time for the next meditation she found she couldn't concentrate at all. She kept bringing her mind back to the meditation, as Eric told them to, then she found herself thinking about the silverfish in the bedroom sink that morning, they'd all come crawling up through the plughole, dozens of them, and Julie had turned both taps on at once before remembering that neither of them worked. Then she'd grabbed the kettle of hot water she'd brought upstairs to wash her hair with and poured it all over them and they'd all curled up and writhed and Julie had felt quite sick. Now the memory of it returned, the hot water flushing the little bodies away, and Julie felt a wave of guilt because Medbh had told them that all life was sacred. She brought her mind back to the meditation. This time she saw Brian's face quite clearly. And she remembered going all the way to Sefton Street the day before Christmas Eve and how everything was quiet, a dull day, no traffic, and she'd thought about Brian being in the house alone. But she hadn't been able to post the card herself through the door.

When she thought about this Julie felt so bad she couldn't meditate any more, but when she opened her eyes a bit and peeped round no one else had finished, so she had to close them again.

She remembered Eric saying that there were parts of the mind where time didn't exist, that kept playing old scenes and bringing back old feelings of pain and guilt. He hadn't said what you could do about it though.

Now when you're ready, Eric said, bring yourselves

back to the room. Julie opened her eyes right away and sat up, waiting to be asked about her meditation. The mug was passed round for contributions to tea and coffee, but then it looked like everyone was leaving.

Julie didn't want to let the chance to speak go again. She thought over what she had to say once, twice, then she said, Eric, loudly, into the middle of a silence.

Everyone looked and Julie went very pink.

Yes, Eric said encouragingly.

Julie looked at Jean.

What happens when – she said, then started again. You know, what you said – about old memories, and you can't get rid of them –

She couldn't explain it, but Eric said,

You mean when the mind keeps repeating them – as if time doesn't exist?

Yes, Julie said. What can you do about it. And inside her she felt a sense of relief so intense at having spoken at last she could hardly listen to the answer.

One very good remedy for that, Eric was saying, is to stay with the memory, no matter how painful, and really see yourself in that situation, and send out some love to yourself.

How do you mean? said Jean.

Well, you see yourself in the situation at the time, Eric said, and then see yourself surrounded by a loving light, yellow or pink, or you can imagine the you that you are now putting your arms around the you that you were then.

Julie wasn't sure she understood. She was trying to find the right question to ask when Gerry said,

And that changes everything, does it?

Julie was surprised by the tone in his voice.

What do you mean? said Eric carefully.

What happens after you've changed it all?

I'm not sure I follow you.

Look, Gerry said. My wife's dead, right? It's not going to bring her back, is it, eh?

O well, no, of course not, Eric said. If you want to bring back the dead I think you're talking about our advanced course, and he beamed broadly around the room.

Gerry didn't smile.

But what I mean is, he said, Shirley's dead and I can't do anything about that. So maybe I shouldn't be feeling that happy about it – you know what I mean?

Well, Eric said. We all have to let go of pain some time.

Why? said Gerry.

Well, you don't have to let go before you're ready, but surely at some point you'd want to.

Eric's right, Sylvia started to say, but Gerry shook his head.

Why should you expect to go through life without pain? he said, and several voices spoke at once telling him that no one expected that, of course they didn't, but Gerry's voice overrode them all.

Well, that's what you're all talking about though – at every meeting I've been to so far anyway – how you can get rid of stress and depression and painful memories – I mean maybe life's just like that – you know what I mean?

Julie began to think she'd never get her question asked.

I mean look at me, Gerry started to say, but Eric said, I don't think anyone here would agree with you, that all we want is to get rid of pain – anaesthetise life, so to speak, he looked round the room and Sylvia and Josepha shook their heads and Julie did too. I think what we're talking about here is a question of *perspective*. The perspective that you have on suffering is what counts. Whether or not you make it into a way of life, he said, and there was a moment's pause. Julie nearly asked her question, but he spoke again.

If you have a lot of painful memories, he said, and

you're carrying a lot of baggage, then something you might want to consider is rebirthing.

Everyone wanted to know what that was.

Only Medbh could do it, Eric said, out of all the people he'd ever met. She had seen him and known right away that it was what he needed. It was a form of hypnotic regression that made you relive everything you were carrying around, so that when you came through it you never had to carry it again, you were like a new person. It's painful though, he said. It's the most painful process imaginable. I wouldn't recommend it unless you feel seriously bogged down. Utterly handicapped as it were. Most of the time I cried like a baby, he said.

There were ripples of interest around the room.

I wonder how much she charges for that, Sylvia said, and Jean said maybe it was the baggage that made you ill.

See what I mean? Gerry said suddenly and quite loudly. You're all talking about the same thing again.

I think what we're talking about, Eric said, and this time there was a sharp note in his voice, is the process of change, and letting go, and not turning your suffering into a way of life. There's an old Chinese story that illustrates this point rather well, about an old sage whose wife dies and he starts singing and clanging pots and pans about and generally making a racket. And one of his students is very shocked by this, you see, and asks the sage whether he doesn't think he should be in mourning.

The Tao comes and the Tao goes, the sage replies. It liberates the spirit into all life. Is that not a source of rejoicing?

That's one of Medbh's stories, Jean said, and Eric said, Absolutely. You can always depend on Medbh for a good story, and everyone laughed.

And on that note, Eric said before Gerry could say anything else, I think it's time to close the meeting.

Julie didn't get to ask her question after all. She couldn't help thinking about all the questions she never asked, and she felt annoyed with Gerry. He had stopped her this time, she thought.

Can we all see if we can bring someone to the next meeting? Eric said as she got her coat on. The numbers are getting a bit low. And it's in two weeks' time, remember. Every two weeks from now on – I'm starting my course.

Eric was starting a course in hypnotherapy, Jean stayed behind to talk to him about it.

Well, that suits me better, Sylvia said to Josepha. It's getting so that there's something on every night, and Josepha agreed. But Julie felt that she needed more meetings if anything, more chances to ask all her questions. And it was somewhere to go, away from Uncle Si's.

As she stepped out of the porch Gerry was right behind her.

Can I drop you off anywhere? he said, but Julie didn't want a lift from Gerry.

No, thank you, she said, a little coldly.

Julie hurried out of the house. The electric man had come to read the meter, and she knew for a fact it was fixed. Mick had rigged it up with a bent hairpin, it hardly went round at all. Julie thought it looked dead obvious but Mick had said they were all estimated these days, and the only time you had to worry was if it actually started going backwards. But now the man was here at the back door, and Julie was having to fight her way out of the front. The weeds were high and the path between the houses and the railway embankment no longer existed.

She should keep calm, she told herself as she clambered through weeds and bracken. But it wasn't only the electric, it was the gas as well, and they didn't have a licence for the telly. Then there were all the new tools and building materials lying around. Only last week

Mick had been moaning about the price of silicone, then two days ago a load of it had turned up all at once. Now Julie felt that somehow all these things would be found out at once. When she got to the end of the row she could feel pains in her chest and she stopped. This was stupid, she told herself. She had to calm down. Then she felt ashamed, she should have stayed in the house with Mick. But she couldn't go back now.

Julie pressed her hands to her face and tried to think what to do. She didn't want to go back. And she couldn't go to the shops, spending money, there might be a fine.

After a moment she opened her eyes. She would go to see Alison, she thought. Alison would understand.

Up the hill she went slowly, slowly, it was getting harder to walk these days with the breathlessness. She hoped Alison would be in, or no one, she didn't want to sit in with Alan, but she needed to sit down.

No one answered when she knocked on the door, but she could hear Sadie crying so she knocked again. After another long pause she saw Alison through the glass panel. Alison came towards her very slowly. She stumbled twice, then swore when she couldn't get the door open. Then, when she opened the door, she didn't look at Julie, her long hair hid her face. She turned away, leaving the door open and stumbled back along the corridor, Julie didn't know what to think. She followed Alison into the front room. Alan was there, on the settee, his head lolling backwards. Julie could hear Sadie but she couldn't see her.

Where's Sadie? she said, then she saw the carrycot pushed partly behind the settee.

Sadie had no clothes on. She had kicked off the sheet covering her and the sheet beneath her was very wet. There was a draught from the big window.

O she's cold, Julie said, and crouched down to pick her up. No one said anything.

Sadie's body was mottled and there was a bad rash

between her legs that looked as though it might have been bleeding. Her toes curled like tiny bluish caterpillars. Julie clasped her tightly and stood up.

Where are her clothes? she said.

No one answered. Alan went on gazing at the ceiling, Alison seemed to be mumbling something. Julie held Sadie very tightly and took her out of the room. In the bedroom she found a BabyGro and cardigan. She put Sadie down on the bed. Sadie kicked and squalled.

Alright, baby, all right, Julie muttered. Under the bed she found a pack of nappies.

Julie had never put a nappy on before. She laboured carefully, getting it the wrong way on at first, then Sadie kicked it off again. Getting the kicking legs into the BabyGro was very hard, Julie had to sit down on the bed.

It can't be this hard, she told herself as she got all the studs wrong. By the time Sadie was finally dressed she felt quite tired and she couldn't think because of the relentless crying, she could hardly see. She carried Sadie back into the front room.

No one had moved. Julie dragged the carrycot from behind the settee to the middle of the room where it was warmer. All the time she felt a tight feeling in her chest and throat, but she wouldn't cry. On the floor she saw the little mobile she'd bought for Sadie at Christmas and she picked it up and jingled the bells for her as she lowered Sadie into the cot. But when she tried to tuck her in, Sadie drew her legs up and screamed.

Julie picked her up. She went over to where Alison sat, slumped in the chair. A long strand of spit hung from Alison's mouth to her hand.

Alison, Julie said, I think she's hungry.

Alison said nothing.

Many things ran through Julie's mind. She should take Sadie away, she shouldn't leave her there. Then she thought about trying to make up some powdered milk. She felt a spasm of anger and shook Alison's shoulder.

Alison, she said, Sadie needs feeding. She knelt down and held Sadie out.

After several moments Alison took hold of Sadie. Slowly, slowly she unbuttoned her shirt. She held Sadie to her, rocking and crooning and Sadie latched on. Julie stood up. She didn't want to leave Sadie, but she didn't know what to do, nothing she could think of to do made any sense. So she left them all and went out of the door and down the stairs.

Outside, between the clouds, there were milky, chill patches of sun. Julie laboured along the street. She couldn't take Sadie, she told herself. There was no way she could keep her at Uncle Si's. They just weren't ready for a baby, she thought. Then, as she turned the corner onto the main road she thought about Darren, and it seemed to her that it was Darren's fault they weren't ready. She remembered the times she had seen Darren strung out just like Alison and Alan, Mick not getting any work done because he was with Darren in Darren's room. She didn't want her baby growing up with that. Darren, she thought. She didn't want her baby growing up with Darren.

Phone Watkins' Windows now, the voice on the radio said, and female voices crooned,
0–2–7 2–7–7 7–2–7–2.

Now, said the DJ. We've got a lovely lady on the phone, Joan. We've got Joan on the phone and it's her birthday today, and she's just sixty-five years young.

Julie picked up the post from outside the door. A reminder about the council tax and a card with little silver squares, you had to scratch them off to see if you'd won anything. Julie put the reminder on the table and dropped the card in the bin.

So you mean to tell me, the DJ said, that at sixty-five years of age you're thinking of running off for a naughty weekend with the man from the Prudential?

Helpless giggling down the phone line.

Julie propped the reminder up so that Mick was more likely to see it. She was sure it was the second one, and the first one had mentioned court.

Well, I'm shocked, the DJ said. And you a grandmother.

Mick never worried about bills. Sometimes she thought he didn't quite know what to do with them. You didn't get them, she supposed, if you didn't have a home. Then, when the reminders came in, he started getting angry. People own you, when you own a house, he'd said once.

I mean, I thought grandmothers were people who rocked you to sleep and sang nursery rhymes to you . . .

He hadn't even worried when the electricity man came the other day. He'd been very smug about that.

We couldn't see your arse for dust, he'd said.

Julie had looked at him sitting with Darren on Darren's bedroom floor.

What happened? she said.

Nothing happened, said Mick. Darren was down in the cellar and he took the pin off like a good man when he heard us coming down. So. The bill'll be about fourteen quid.

Julie could tell how clever he thought he was.

So there was no need to leg it down the road like Linford Christie, he said.

Julie looked at them. Darren's eyes were shut, one finger tapped out the music. Mick was skinning up, but the way he was sitting was the same as Darren, one leg bent at the knee, one stretched out on the floor. She turned to leave the room and looked back at them over her shoulder.

You were just lucky, she said.

Joan was still giggling on the phone.

He's a nice man, she said.

A nice man? A nice man? I should hope he is a nice man. A very nice man. A very, very, very nice man.

Don't do it, Joan, several voices shouted.

Julie ran her finger along the dial until she found some music she liked. She poured cereal into a bowl and sat down.

> Do you have to let it linger-er
> do you have to
> do you have to let it linger?

She wasn't making breakfast for everyone that morning. And she didn't want to wait around to discuss the reminder with Mick either. She would only start noticing the way he was with Darren, talking to or for him all the time, echoing the way he sat or stood, as though Darren, not Mick, was the stronger one. She didn't know why she hadn't noticed this before, but now she had she couldn't stop. So she was going out this morning, before they were up. She was going to visit Annie.

Annie, looking seriously harassed, let Julie in. Both twins were crying, one sitting on the carpet with no nappy on, the other face down with only a nappy on. There were toys and spilt cereal all over the carpet.

They won't let me get them dressed, Annie said. She walked past both crying babies into the kitchen and stood with her back to Julie. Then suddenly she lowered her face into her hands.

I'm all right, she said. I'll be all right. It's just that I've been trying to get them dressed for the past hour and a half. And Jamie takes his clothes off while I'm putting them on, then he takes them off Thomas. And I'm supposed to be going to the dentist's, she said. She looked up, rubbing her forehead. I don't suppose you'd mind them for half an hour while I go, would you?

Julie hesitated.

It's only a check-up, Annie said.

Of course I will, said Julie. She needed the practice, she

told herself. Annie grabbed her bag off the washer and was half-way out of the back door.

Thanks a lot, she said. I'll go this way, then they won't know I've gone. Make yourself a cup of tea, she called over her shoulder.

Julie went into the lounge.

Now you two, she said above the noise, which of these clothes are which?

She found a pair of brown dungarees and a pair of green ones, an assortment of socks that didn't match, identical jumpers and bootees. The twins stopped wailing as she sorted the clothes out and looked at her in surprise. Julie felt very mumsy and organised.

Now which one of you shall I get dressed first? she said, then, I don't know which one of you is Jamie and which one Thomas, do I? But you need a nappy on, she said to the one sitting up, and she found a bag of Pampers near the telly. She switched the telly on, hoping to distract them with children's programmes while she got them dressed, but it was only Richard and Judy. She left it on anyway and picked up the twin without the nappy.

This was the second time she'd tried to get a nappy on and she got it the right way up this time, but then ripped the sticky bit off one side and had to start again with a new one. Both twins were as good as gold while she dressed them, staring at her the whole time rather than at Richard and Judy. Julie began to feel that she must be good at looking after babies. When she finished dressing one twin, the other one started trying to take his bootees off, but Julie said, No, sternly, and he stopped right away.

When Annie came back, Julie thought, she would be surprised at how well Julie had coped. They're not this good for anyone else, she would say.

She scrubbed the cereal up from the carpet while one twin began to crawl around the other. Then she sat them both in front of Richard and Judy while she made herself a cup of tea, and they stayed where she put them, still as stones.

Annie's kitchen was very well organised. Everything was in pink or blue. Tea, coffee and sugar were in pink and blue containers near the kettle. Julie couldn't help peeking into the cupboards to see what kinds of food she bought in, but there were mainly jars of baby food and tubs of pot noodles.

A squawk made her run back into the lounge. One twin was pulling the plug lead at the back of the telly, the other had got the top off the talc. Julie ran towards the kitchen for a cloth, stopped herself, then ran back to pull the first twin away from the telly. He screamed but she tucked him under one arm and went back into the kitchen.

She couldn't see the cloth she'd used for the cereal.

Bloody, bloody cloth, she muttered, putting the baby down and banging cupboard doors to no effect.

When she gave up and went back into the lounge the other twin wasn't there. Julie stared for a moment, then she heard bumps and a scream. She flew into the hall and there was the baby, crying at the bottom of the stairs.

O baby, Julie cried, picking him up, but he only cried harder. Julie carried him into the lounge in time to see the other twin climbing up a shelf towards the fish tank.

No, Julie screamed, forgetting herself and making both twins cry. She grabbed the second twin and sat down, holding them both tightly. The noise of their crying clawed at the inside of her skull. She stared at the clock wondering how long Annie would be, she seemed to be taking a very long time. Suddenly she thought she would take them both out. She would go to meet Annie.

For days the weather had been too bad to go out, but now it was only raining, a steady, vertical downpour. And the trolley already had its raincover on. After a brief intense struggle she got the twins into their outdoor suits, strapped them into the trolley and tugged it through the door, thinking hungrily about the bakery at the end of the road.

It was uphill all the way to the shop and the trolley was heavier than Julie had thought. Soon she was completely out of breath. She'd had attacks of breathlessness before, rested a bit and been all right. But now here she was, hanging over the trolley in the rain.

I see you got them dressed, said Annie, behind her. I'm sorry I was so long. Have they been playing you up? Are you all right?

Julie straightened slowly.

I'm fine, she said. It's fine. I was just going to the shop for something to eat.

Annie took the trolley.

Let's have a cup of tea, she said. I could do us some toast if you like.

Julie followed Annie, conscious that Annie was going slowly for Julie's sake.

You should have made yourself something, she said over her shoulder. Julie remembered the talc.

Er – the lounge is in a bit of a mess, she said, catching up. I wiped up the cereal, but one of them got the talc.

O don't worry, Annie said. It's always the same. Shit, she said tugging the trolley up the doorstep. This thing's getting heavier.

Julie helped her lift the trolley up, then unstrap the twins and carry them through.

It's all hard labour, Annie said as Julie sat down heavily with a twin. Twenty years. The baby wriggled off Julie's knee and Julie didn't try to stop him. She felt very tired.

Sugar? Annie called from the kitchen. Julie was about to say she'd had a cup of tea, then she couldn't remember whether she had or not.

Two, she said and leant back. Then she remembered what she'd meant to say.

There's another meeting at Eric's next Thursday, she

said. We're all supposed to bring someone. I was wondering if you'd like to come?

Annie brought the tea through. I'll have to see, she said. These two are giving me a bit of a time at night. And Chris is working away.

What does he do? Julie said, when Annie came back with the toast.

Leave the fish *alone*, Jamie, she said, then pulled him away and sat down next to Julie.

Toast, she said. Julie took a piece.

Transports skips, she said through a mouthful. All over. Sometimes abroad.

Julie thought she would remember that for Mick. But she didn't know who else she could ask to the meeting. Alison, she thought, but she wasn't keen to ask. She didn't think Alison would want to know.

Annie leapt up to stop Thomas pushing a car into the video.

I had hoped they'd be a bit late walking and crawling and that, she said. But now look at them. She put Thomas down. Are you okay? she said again to Julie. Only you look a bit pale.

Julie chewed her toast slowly because of heartburn, then she told Annie about the breathlessness.

Well, it'll only get worse, Annie said, tipping out some toys from a box. I tell you what might help it though, she said, swimming. She looked up. I keep meaning to go myself now they're running a crèche at the pool. I mean the pool's a bit of a pit, but I'd go to hell, me, if they were running a crèche, and she grinned at Julie in quite a good-humoured way.

O I don't know, Julie began. I've not got a costume.

Annie looked at her consideringly.

My mother's got a costume, she said. From when she put on a lot of weight. She doesn't use it any more. I bet she'd let you have it.

Julie felt very embarrassed.

O no, she said.

Why not? said Annie. Then we could go together. It's better than going on your own, she said, looking at Julie.

Julie knew she should try to lose weight. And maybe she should ask Alison, she thought. She might want to go swimming if she didn't want to go to the meetings.

All right then, she said doubtfully, but you've got to come to the meeting.

Annie brought two dishes of baby rice in from the kitchen.

I'll go to the next one Medbh does, she said, picking one twin up and settling him on her knee. They won't go in their high chairs, she said. Do you fancy feeding Thomas some rice? The books all say they should be feeding themselves now, she went on as Julie picked up a dish. But they don't tell you you practically have to redecorate afterwards.

Julie scooped up baby rice onto the spoon. She knelt in front of Thomas on the carpet and he watched her all the time. As she lifted the spoon he opened his mouth like a bird.

I used to have terrible migraines, Sylvia said. Especially when Anthony was dying. When they hit me I'd be completely unable to do anything except lie in bed with the curtains drawn. It made things much harder for the girls, especially Suzanne, she took a lot of the burden. I still feel guilty about that even though I don't suppose I could help having the migraines. Isn't that strange?

Not at all, Jean said. That's just what I was saying. We always do feel most guilty about the things we can't help – like me loving David more than Michael.

Well, one day, Sylvia went on, I had this terrible migraine. Really bad. I thought my head was going to burst. And I just lay down on the carpet. I couldn't move or think. And then suddenly – I don't knew how to describe it – I felt this kind of *space* inside the pain – and

I was able to move into it somehow, and it all became manageable. And since then I've had the migraines but they're nowhere near as bad.

Well, that's what it's all about, Eric said. Who are you? You're not your emotions – they come and go, so do your thoughts. You're not your job – that's just something you do. And you aren't your pain either.

That was the meditation they'd just done, Who are you? but Julie couldn't say she was any wiser. She'd felt for a moment something pressing behind her eyes as if the darkness was about to give way to something bigger. But then, either because she wanted it too much or because she was afraid, the feeling disappeared and she was left with the ordinary darkness.

Sylvia was doing the closing meditation. This was to be a new thing, Eric had said. He would always do the first one, but anyone who wanted could do the second. Julie hoped she wouldn't have to. She always seemed to have to worry about the meetings. She'd worried about not bringing anyone to this one, but in fact no one else had. So there were no new people, and Esther and Gerry weren't there either.

A lot of people are down with this bug, Eric had said.

Sylvia said she would do the meditation on the colour blue.

Blue is a peaceful colour, she said. It's the colour of forgetting, of letting go.

As she talked Julie leant back and almost fell asleep. She imagined the blue light filling her body, then spreading outwards into the room, then to all the people who might need it, especially Mick, and Uncle Si and Darren, who all had the terrible bug. Even Julie had a sore throat though she was trying to keep out of their way, and Mick had taken to sleeping in Darren's room so that he wouldn't give it to her. She had thought about not coming with the weather being bad, but it was miserable staying in. So now she concentrated on the healing, Mick going back to work, and on Darren suddenly finding another place to stay. She had thought a lot about this, but had given up the idea of trying to contact his parents. Because she didn't want to upset Mick, and she didn't wish Darren any harm. She just wanted what would be best for all of them. So after she imagined him leaving she sent out extra blue light to him and to Mick, so that Mick would accept him going.

The meditation seemed to go on for a long time, and Julie had trouble seeing the blue light. It would fill the room one minute, then change colour and then disappear. She concentrated as hard as she could, then realised she was all tense from the strain. She took a deep breath and sank back in her chair.

Suddenly, in the centre of her mind she saw a butterfly, a large blue butterfly very close, close enough to touch if you could touch anything that far inside you. She watched its velvety wings slowly opening and closing as if the butterfly breathed with them. She saw its feelers quivering and the round, lidless eyes, all blue. She sat astonished, and only as Sylvia was closing the meditation did she remember about Mick and Darren and Uncle Si, and tried quickly to see them in the blue light surrounding the butterfly.

When everyone came to, Julie couldn't wait to tell them all what she'd seen, but Sylvia didn't ask. She talked a bit about blue being the colour of the throat chakra, and how that could be useful at the moment with this bug. And no one else seemed inclined to talk much, perhaps because the weather was so bad and everyone was thinking about getting home. Eric thanked Sylvia and said it was always good to get back to some colour work, and people started getting up.

Hail clawed at the windows as they all got their coats on. Julie tried not to mind too much about not telling the group about her meditation. She couldn't wait to see how everyone was at home when she got in.

Julie got to the door with Josepha. Esther usually gave Josepha a lift, but she wasn't there. Julie had never spoken to Josepha before, but now she thought she would.

How are you getting back, Jo? she said cheerfully. It's a bad night out there.

I'm getting the bus, Josepha said a little coldly.

O not tonight, Sylvia called to them. You can both have a lift from me – I'm not having you wandering around in this weather.

Josepha was already out in the garden, her head lowered against the wind.

Jo, Julie called, Sylvia says she'll give us a lift.

Josepha turned back.

It's Josepha, she said as she reached Julie. I always use my full name. Otherwise people might think I'm called Josephine. Or Joanne, and she walked past Julie into the lounge.

Julie followed Josepha and Sylvia out to Sylvia's car. The hail whirled round them and Sylvia had some trouble getting the engine started, then the heater.

We should all sing, said Jean. That'd warm us up.

Sylvia ignored Jean.

I'd better drop you off first, Julie, she said, easing the car slowly down the hill.

Julie sat next to Josepha in the back. Their hands had touched briefly, fastening the seat belts, but Julie didn't look up.

You know I don't remember a year when there hasn't been snow on my birthday, Sylvia said. The end of January. Next Sunday, in fact. Which reminds me. I'm having open house that day and you're all invited, noon onwards. Don't bring anything except yourselves, please, it's all provided, and she gave them all her address.

Is it all right if I bring my little boy? Josepha said, and Sylvia said of course it was, and Jean said,

What's his name?

Stanley, Josepha said. Not Stan. I always use his full name.

Julie began to think she didn't like Josepha at all.

Now there's a name you don't hear any more, Jean said. How old is he?

Eighteen months, said Josepha. But he's big for his age and he's been walking since before he was one.

Josepha likes Jean, Julie thought. She said nothing all the journey, thinking about going to Sylvia's house. She didn't know how she'd feel, going there on her own, and she didn't know what to buy. Sylvia had said not to take anything, but she couldn't go without some kind of present. She wondered if other people would start inviting her round to their homes and whether she would be expected to invite them back to Uncle Si's.

You're very quiet, Julie, Jean said. Are you all right?

Yes, thanks, Julie said. I've got a bit of a cold.

As she said this she suddenly noticed that her sore throat had entirely gone. Her heart beat a little faster but she didn't say anything. Blue was the colour of the throat chakra, Sylvia had said.

Jean was saying that she hadn't noticed much improvement from the Qi Gong yet, but she was sure it must be working. Mainly because it was costing her a fortune.

Nice when you've got it to throw around, Mick said.

They're not all rich at the meetings, Julie told him. They're not all middle class.

O yeah, Mick said. Who does the talking?

The question surprised Julie.

What do you mean? she said.

At the meetings, said Mick, who talks the most?

Julie had to think about that one, and when she did she realised she couldn't remember a single time when Jean and Sylvia and Eric hadn't done most of the talking. Esther didn't talk though, and she was middle class.

Mick was waiting for an answer.

Anyone can talk if they want to, Julie said.

Yeah, yeah, said Mick.

They can, said Julie.

But I bet they don't, said Mick. I bet there's just one or two of them talking about *their* problems and *their* feelings. Like no one else fucking has any.

It's not like that, Julie said. She always found what Jean and Sylvia had to say very interesting, but Mick wasn't having it, and he had taken to calling their meetings the Jean and Sylvia show.

I don't suppose anyone in the SWP is middle class, Julie had said, but Mick said that was different. They were aware of the class struggle. You couldn't help the class you were born into but you could help being ignorant.

Is it left here? Sylvia said at the lights.

This'll be fine, said Julie, unclipping her seat belt.

O no, said Sylvia. You're not wandering about in this weather. Tell me where it is and I'll drop you at the door.

Julie remembered this argument from last time.

You can't really get to the front door, she began.

Unexpectedly Josepha helped her out.

It's the same where I live, she said. Esther has to drop me off at the end of the track.

Well, Sylvia said as if she was still going to argue, but the lights changed to amber and Julie opened the door.

I'll be fine, she said, clambering out. Thanks very much.

Sylvia tapped on the window.

See you at my place, a week on Sunday, she said, and drove off.

Julie curved her shoulders as she walked into the hail and made her way towards the yard. She would have something to tell Mick tonight, she thought. Then she slipped on the icy rubble and banged her shin on the cement mixer Mick had borrowed a week ago but hadn't used yet because of the weather.

Bloody, bloody thing, she muttered, letting herself in. She switched on the light.

There were pots everywhere and broken glass. A length of guttering had come off and smashed into the window at the top, obviously no one had felt up to fixing it. There were pools of wet around the rubble on the floor. Julie stared at the mess.

If you want anything doing, do it yourself, her mother said.

Julie felt a flare of anger, cold and dark. She stepped over the wet rubble to the bread tin, tore off a chunk of bread, dug it into some butter and chewed it slowly, not looking round. Then she realised she was standing on the tea towel which had been left on the floor in the muddy water. There wasn't another one, Julie hadn't done the laundry that week yet.

Julie turned her back on the kitchen.

It'll all be the same in a hundred years' time, her mother said. Certainly it would all be there for Julie tomorrow. And she remembered Medbh saying stay centred, keep calm. She took deeper breaths. Then as she was going upstairs she remembered the blue light around the butterfly. She tapped on Darren's door.

Yeah, Mick said.

Julie opened the door.

Darren lay on the bed with headphones on, Mick sat in the chair reading. Mick's eyes were swollen and watery with cold.

I just thought I'd see how you are, she said, nicely. How are you feeling?

Like shit, Mick said. I feel like shit.

Julie sat in the water at the shallow end of the pool, next to Annie and Alison.

Christ, kid soup, Alison said.

It seemed as though every school in the area had

brought a class in for swimming, you couldn't move for kids thrashing about and leaping in.

Julie had almost changed her mind about asking Alison, but they had to walk right past her flat and at the last moment she felt guilty. Alison needed to go out more, she thought. She needed a friend. So she asked Annie if she minded and Annie said not at all, and she'd waited at the bottom with the twins. Julie climbed the stairs slowly, hoping Alison would be in a better state this time. Even as she climbed she could hear Sadie wailing, so she knew they were in. Then when she knocked no one answered, and she knocked again and her heart thumped at the thought that maybe they weren't in after all, only Sadie was in.

Alison opened the door.

O hello, she said slowly. Come in.

Julie explained that she'd come to ask Alison out.

The baths –, Alison said. Well – I don't know if my cosi still fits.

She looked tempted.

There's a crèche, Julie said.

I bet they won't take Sadie though, said Alison. She's too young.

A loud cry from Sadie seemed to make up her mind.

Hang on, she said. I'll see if I can find my cosi.

Alan's not up yet, she said, reappearing with a towel. But he can get up. Alan, she shouted through the bedroom door. You'll have to get up now – I'm going out.

Silence. Alison opened the door.

I said get up, she yelled. I'm off out, and out she came, stuffing the towel into a carrier bag.

That'll teach him, the lazy bastard, she said on the way down. I'm dead glad you came, I've been stuck in for weeks. We had Sadie in hospital over New Year with gastroenteritis so that was a great start – she stopped as she saw Annie, and Julie introduced them both.

Christ, twins, Alison said. I don't know how you cope.

I said to Alan, the only thing that could be worse than this is twins. That's the thought that keeps me going.

I think about triplets, Annie said.

Alison and Annie talked all the time about how dreadful it was, having babies. Alison said she knew someone who printed T-shirts and she was going to get some printed with anti-motherhood slogans on them.

Like kids are for goats, Annie said, and Alison said, You too can be a hassled, haggard woman.

They talked and laughed all the way to the baths. Julie began to feel a bit left out, and as if they were aiming some of it at her, to make her feel bad for being pregnant.

Now they were in the baths Julie felt very self-conscious. She had hoped the swimming costume would be a nice neutral colour, but it was a shade of pink the label called sizzling. She squatted in the water so that only her head and shoulders could be seen. Annie wore a black sports swimsuit. She had an entirely flat stomach and long legs for someone so small.

How did you get your stomach so flat after twins? Alison said, and Annie said it was easy, they never let her eat. Alison wore a crinkly turquoise costume. Her stomach was a bit rounded from Sadie, but not much. Only Julie looked enormous. She got into the water quickly, only glancing round once she was in, but no one else looked as big, except for one big, awful-looking man with scabs.

Just think, Alison said, ducking to avoid a small boy who had jumped in right over her head. Ours'll be like this one day, and Annie said at least they'd be at school then, that was the day she was waiting for, but it was another 1,786 days off.

O don't, Alison said.

Next to Julie the big man with the skin complaint blew his nose straight into the water.

Dirty git, Alison said clearly, and Julie moved away.

Come on you two, she said. We did come to swim.

It was impossible to swim in lengths, they just had to swim in any clear space they could find. This suited Julie, who couldn't swim much anyway. She kept moving and tried not to think about the scummy water, though once when she opened her mouth a plaster drifted in and she stopped in horror. From then on she kept her mouth shut all the time. Whenever she looked round she could see Alison's fair head and Annie's dark one bobbing about together. It seemed they liked one another better than either of them liked Julie, but Julie told herself that that wasn't positive thinking, she should just get on with the swimming. She dreaded the moment of getting out of the pool, when the soggy swimsuit would cling to her bulging body, but that wasn't positive thinking either. It was amazing how many negative thoughts went through your head once you started being aware of them, like Medbh said. That was what made people ill, she'd said.

On either side of Julie, clearing the water in miraculously straight lines, two elderly men thrashed up and down. They never raised their heads so everyone, even the kids, moved for them. Julie carried on bobbing about, dodging children, wondering when Annie and Alison would have had enough. She got out when they did, hobbling self-consciously to the changing rooms. Annie and Alison went to the showers but Julie found herself a cubicle right away, and even inside it dressed cautiously, because none of the doors were locked and the changing rooms were full of kids, running and pushing the doors and screaming. She sat on the narrow bench to put her socks on and looked at the graffiti, Pete is gorgeous, Michaela has VD, and suddenly she wondered what was wrong with her, she never seemed to make friends like everyone else. She had often felt lonely before, from being a little girl, but now it was as if all the separate feelings of loneliness had come together in a big wave and washed over her. She sat in the cubicle with her head slightly bowed, waiting for understanding of her friendlessness to come.

Later they all sat in McDonald's. One twin was fast asleep and Annie fed the other one chips.

Alan'll be well cheesed by now, Alison said. I might not go back until tea.

Julie looked down at her plate. Though she hadn't managed to swim much she was starving now, but she had only bought herself a small packet of chips. She'd been putting money aside since before Christmas meaning to pay off, all by herself, one of the many bills that were due, without saying anything. Then, when they were all talking about bills and the usual arguments were boiling up, she could just say, You don't have to worry about that one, I've already paid it, and Mick would be surprised and pleased. It was a hard choice to make, because she really needed some clothes, especially now that she was going to Sylvia's, and what she wanted most of all at the moment was a BigMac. She tried not to stare at Alison's and Annie's plates. Alison had a BigMac and a large portion of chips, Annie had chips and a smaller cheeseburger, only she didn't seem to be eating them and Julie couldn't help wondering whether she wanted them or not. She didn't like to ask in case she was saving them for when the other twin woke up. She sighed in a depressed kind of way and wondered how many calories she had used.

What do you think Mick'll be like, Alison said, when the baby comes?

They had just been talking about how what men said before the baby came and what they did after were two different things. Even so, Julie wasn't prepared. She thought a bit, then just shrugged.

I wonder what he thinks he'll be like, Annie said. Chris thought it'd be great, having twins, but he's changed his tune now.

Julie said nothing.

Well, what's he said? said Alison.

Julie wasn't going to say anything, she didn't want to talk about Mick, then suddenly she said,

He never says anything. He never talks about it.

Annie and Alison looked at Julie and Julie looked back at them.

What do you mean? said Alison, and,

Why not? said Annie.

He won't talk about it, said Julie. He doesn't want to know.

As she said it she felt almost tearful. There was a silence, then both Alison and Annie spoke at once.

That's terrible.

That's no good, is it – you mean he's leaving it all to you?

Julie knew she had their complete attention now, at the same time she felt she wasn't being loyal to Mick.

I don't think he can face it, she said.

But you'll have to, Annie said, and Alison said,

Bloody typical.

Then they both started talking about what she should do. She should make him sit down and listen to her, in front of the others if she had to, then Annie said maybe she should talk to the others as well, get them on her side and they'd talk to Mick. Julie couldn't see that working. Then Alison said that the next time Mick called round to see her and Alan she'd start talking about the baby just to see what he said, but Annie came up with the best idea.

I've got some baby things I've been meaning to pass on, she said. I'll bring them to the house. And if Mick's there I'll pass them on to him, but if he isn't he'll have to take notice when you start building up a pile of things for the baby.

Yeah, Alison said. Leave them where he'll fall over them.

Julie was grateful to Annie, she knew she had to start getting things ready for the baby and stop waiting for

Mick. But everything cost so much she hardly dared start. It was a great relief that she was going to be given some of Annie's things. But she was still worried about anyone seeing the house.

We're in a bit of a state, she said, but Annie told her not to worry, she should have seen Annie's house when they first moved in, no ceilings, only a couple of floors, so Julie felt a bit better. And she felt a lot better thinking that something would finally be done about Mick.

I bet you haven't bought anything for yourself either, Alison said, taking in Julie's clothes. You can't wear that dress for ever, you know.

Julie blushed.

I know, she said, but Mick needs a lot of money just now for the house.

Sod that, Alison said, and Annie said,

Never mind about him.

There's a sale on at Mothercare, Alison said. I bet you'd get fixed up there. Or in the market, and she and Annie agreed that they should all go, right away.

Julie felt embarrassed, and a bit worried, and when she got to Mothercare she felt worse, because everything on the rails was a small size.

This is nice, Alison said, holding out a baggy top that buttoned down the front and a long pinafore dress both in the same dull pink.

Mulberry, Alison said. That's the in colour now.

The label said one size only, and reduced to £19.99.

Well, go on, Alison said. You'll never know if you don't try them on.

Julie didn't want to tell Alison her size. She took the outfit into the cubicle and pulled it on somehow. But once it was on it didn't look too bad. There was only a bit of pulling under the arms. Julie was so pleased she decided she would buy it, but when she went out Alison was waving a pair of leggings at her, mulberry again, with yellow and violet flowers.

O no, Julie said.

You'll need a change, Alison said. And they're only £6.99.

Julie went back into the cubicle.

The leggings had very soft elastic round the waist, so they fitted too. And they would go with her old blue top which she could still get into. So it was four outfits for the price of two. Even so, she felt a bit queasy inside, though it might only be heartburn from the chips. Slowly she pulled her old dress back on.

I'll take them, she said to Alison. Annie was busy pulling the twins away from the toys.

I'm going to have to take these two outside, she said.

Julie and Alison went to the till.

That colour really suits you, Alison said, but Julie still felt bad, handing the money over. Alison bought Sadie a frilly BabyGro, and Julie thought about all the things she needed for the baby. Then they joined Annie outside.

Julie clutched the bag tightly as she walked.

You'll feel better now, Alison said. You've got to keep yourself looking good when you're pregnant.

Those coats are nice, Annie said, and Alison followed her into the store. Julie waited outside. The old man with his penny whistle was back outside Boots and the young man with the dreadlocks was sitting outside Woolworths, just for a moment Julie thought it was Mick.

Annie and Alison came out talking about holidays. Annie was going to Eastbourne for a week in May with the twins. Chris would be working away, but she had an aunt down there she could stay with. Alison said that Alan had plans to travel. He wanted to go to Mexico, though it would be hard enough getting to Oldham with Sadie.

It wasn't exactly snowing, but particles of snow flew around in all directions like fluff. The light was cold and yellow. Julie walked a little way behind Alison and Annie. The things she'd bought would go with her other things, she told herself. They would go with her black cardigan as well as her old blue top. And she still had half of the money for the bill.

Better than a poke in the eye with a sharp stick, her mother said.

Julie was thinking so hard she didn't notice they were nearly at Alison's. Alison invited them in for a drink but Annie said she had to get back to start tea and Julie said she had to get back as well. Then Alison and Annie talked about meeting up again and Alison mentioned karaoke. Eventually they all agreed to meet again, and Annie turned off to go up the hill, waving, and Julie walked home slowly, through the old yellow light and the light, whirling particles of snow.

There were more posters on the sides of the churches.

Brush up on your Bible, one said. Avoid truth decay.

There are many roads to sin, the poster on the side of the Congregationalist Church read, and beneath it someone had written, Try Wellington Road, no. 34.

There was a pain in Julie's side and all her old fears of losing the baby returned.

I can get home, she told herself. It's only a hundred more steps, and she counted them, thirty-six, thirty-seven.

No one was in when she got to Uncle Si's and she let herself in thankfully and sat down. The house looked just the same, there hadn't been any disasters while she was out, no walls had fallen in, the ceilings were still there, the new wood for the kitchen units Mick had decided to build was propped up against the old cupboard. Julie didn't know why she should feel so bad when nothing had changed.

It'll all be the same, her mother's voice said. In a hundred years' time when we're dead.

Julie pressed Sylvia's doorbell and it played a tune. The knocker was shaped like a hand and on every finger there was a ring. Ivy overhung the wooden door and light flakes of snow fell on it and on Julie. Julie clutched her jar of garlic and tarragon in oil. She nearly hadn't bought it but she'd still felt she couldn't go without buying something. Now she felt it was the wrong thing to buy and not enough.

It took Sylvia a long time to answer the door.

O good, I was hoping you'd make it, she said, then, How lovely, taking the jar. We could try some of that in the salad.

Vastly relieved, Julie followed her inside.

Sylvia's house was very grand. There were oak panels and polished floors and tapestries. Sylvia herself looked very grand in a black silky outfit, decorated with tiny mirrors. Julie was glad she had her nice things to wear, though she had changed quickly and put her coat on before leaving the house, so Mick wouldn't see them.

The room Sylvia led her into had the biggest oak table Julie had ever seen, heaped with food. There were photographs all over the walls. Sylvia took Julie's coat away, and Julie tried to make out the faces of people she knew. Jean sat talking earnestly to Esther, then Julie saw Josepha walking round and round, holding onto her little boy's hand. She smiled as she passed Julie and Julie was so surprised she forgot to be shy.

Hello, she said the next time they passed. Is this Stanley?

He's going through this phase at the moment, Josepha said over her shoulder. I have to walk round with him all the time.

Julie caught up with them.

I could walk round with him for a bit if you like, she said.

Well, thanks, said Josepha, but I think it has to be me, and she smiled again in a resigned kind of way. Julie suddenly felt shy after all.

I have to see Jean, she said and hurried away. But Jean and Esther were still talking, so Julie went to look at the food.

A small card at one end of the table said,

All food is suitable for vegetarians. A green leaf next to the plate means it is also suitable for vegans.

It didn't look vegetarian.

There were sausages on sticks and sausage rolls, bacon kebabs, meat pie and gravy and big steaming bowls of chilli and rice. Julie helped herself to the bacon kebabs and rice and wandered round the room looking at the photographs.

They were mainly of Sylvia surrounded by children, her own, then a big group of African children, and one of the children at Dr Barnardo's. There were some photos of people in a group called CAFOD, and more of children in hospital. One, blown up large and framed, was of Sylvia leaning over a young man's hospital bed. The young man was very thin, with high cheekbones and light brown curly hair. Light from a window behind made a kind of halo around both their heads.

That was Anthony the week before he died, Sylvia said behind Julie and Julie mumbled something about being sorry.

It's an old wound now, Sylvia said. Though it aches sometimes, as they do, and she showed Julie round the other photographs.

There were the graduation photographs of each of her four daughters, Suzanne, Jayne, Victoria, Emily, and pictures of them all as children with Anthony always in the middle.

He was such a beautiful child, Sylvia said. We all loved him.

Julie didn't know what to say.

At the end of a bookshelf were the wedding photos of the two older girls and a large black and white one of Sylvia's wedding. Sylvia was slim and very good looking, with a white train arranged around her on the floor, and the man beside her, plump and dark in uniform, looked very proud.

I married at twenty-two, Sylvia said. I always said I would and I always said I'd have five children, though I lost a couple as well, miscarriages, you know, not very far on.

Arthur was twenty-seven and very handsome, or so I thought at the time, though he was always prone to gaining weight. He got very heavy towards the end of his life. In the end his heart gave way. He died just before his fifty-second birthday.

Sylvia took Julie round all the photographs, speaking a bit like a tour guide in a museum. Julie had noticed before that she tended to speak like that, as if the person in front of her wasn't really there.

There are fourteen years between Suzanne and Emily, she said. I was thirty-eight when I had Emily and I thought, Well, that's me finished, thank goodness. Now I can get on with my life. Funny, isn't it – how I couldn't think that until I'd had five rather than two, say. Medbh would say that I'd made the choice before birth and I was simply sensing my own destiny, but I don't know. I suppose, in that case, I should be grateful it was five rather than fifteen, and she smiled and squeezed Julie's arm.

Anthony again, she said, and she paused for a moment before going on to the next photograph.

Here's one of Arthur and Anthony, he was so pleased to have a son. We called him Anthony Arthur, you know, though they were never very much alike. I always thought Anthony was more like my brother. But Arthur loved him very much, I was always glad he didn't have to see him die, and again she paused. Each time she paused Julie felt as though she should say something but she couldn't think what, and it didn't seem to matter, Sylvia went on anyway. She took Julie through a selection of sepia photographs on the wall, which were all of people Julie didn't know, and she found it hard to concentrate.

But I'm boring you, Sylvia said.

O no, said Julie.

And you haven't had a drink yet, have you? Let me get you a drink.

Julie followed her to the table, where Sylvia poured

grape juice and Perrier water into a tumbler for her, then she was called away. Julie helped herself to more kebabs.

Lovely food, Josepha said, appearing suddenly. Stanley lolled sleepily against her shoulder.

O yes, Julie said through a mouthful of rice. Josepha manoeuvred a chair into position and sat down.

He's heavy, she said, shifting Stanley from her shoulder to her knee.

He's beautiful, Julie said. He had a mass of soft, light-brown curls but his skin was a darker coffee colour than his mother's. He was dressed in a baggy suit with a waistcoat embroidered with little stars. Josepha wore an assortment of clothes that didn't match, a big, tie-dyed shirt with splashes of green and pink, tweed trousers and a stripy waistcoat. She always wore a lot of jewellery, two or three necklaces, an armful of bracelets and big earrings you could just see through the curly dark hair. She didn't seem to want to leave Julie, she sat and talked about doing the meditation and how much it had changed her life. Julie pulled up a chair and sat down, and she hardly had to say anything, she just listened and watched Josepha's hand stroking Stanley's hair, and thought how nice it must be having a beautiful, unusual kind of a mother like Josepha, she felt hungry for a mother like that. Then, when Josepha paused, Julie said,

What made you think of calling him Stanley?

It's in the family, Josepha said, and she started telling Julie all about her family. Her great-great-great-grandmother on her father's side had been one of the last slaves in England, brought over from the Caribbean. Her name was Josepha Augustina May, and she'd been freed in England when public pressure brought an end to slavery, and she'd married a retired servant, and together they'd set up a corner grocer's in Collyhurst and ran it the rest of their lives. Then, when Josepha was very old, nearly fifty, she'd had their only child, a son called Stanley. There was a rumour in the family that she'd had other children when she was a slave, but Stanley was the only one she'd been able to keep. No one knew what had happened to the other children. Josepha paused and looked down at her sleeping baby, and Julie thought again that she looked just like the Madonna.

If he'd been a girl, Josepha said, I'd have called him Augustina May.

Julie was very impressed. She thought it must be wonderful to have an interesting family history like that. Some people just seemed singled out to be interesting. She wondered what Mick would think about Josepha's story, then she thought she wouldn't want Mick knowing Josepha, she didn't even like him knowing Alison.

Is this a private meeting, Jean said, or can anyone join in? and she smiled down at Stanley who was frowning hard.

Such concentration, she said, touching his cheek.

Josepha was telling me why she called him Stanley, Julie said.

O yes, said Jean, sitting down. It's an amazing story, isn't it? Have you chosen a name yet?

Julie felt as though she should have, but she didn't want to choose a name without Mick. Besides, there weren't any interesting names in her family.

I'm not sure yet, she began, and Jean said,

I had the most terrible problem with names. I wanted names from the family, but whatever I chose someone was offended. I'm sure that's why I only had two in the end. Medbh of course says, in her typical way, that the child chooses its own name. But I'm sure I'd have picked something a bit more interesting than Jean, and she grinned at them both. Julie couldn't help smiling back. Out of all the people there Jean was the only one who hadn't dressed up at all, she wore corduroy trousers and a jumper as she always did. Julie liked Jean, but she didn't like the name at all.

So Medbh says the baby chooses the name, Josepha said.

Yes, said Jean. You have to look in their eyes when

they're born and they tell you. You could probably start asking the baby now, she said to Julie. Julie wondered what Mick would think of that.

Would you like a boy or a girl? Josepha said, and Julie said she didn't mind.

I always knew Stanley was going to be a boy, Josepha said, and Jean said she'd known with David but not with Michael.

What do you think it is? she said, but Julie only smiled in an embarrassed way and said she didn't know.

I bet Medbh'd tell you, Jean said, and went on to tell them about the time when a young woman had come to the meeting, and no one else had even known she was pregnant, but Medbh said to her, That's two babies you've got there, a boy and a girl, and she was right, though not even the doctors had picked it up at the time.

But isn't there anyone in your family you'd like to call the baby after, Josepha said. What about the father's family?

Julie thought about Mick's family.

I don't think so, she said, and Jean said,

If I'd had girls my mother-in-law would have wanted them called after her – Agatha Wallis Pemberton, if you please. And what an evil old sow she was. Do you know what she told me to do with the afterbirth? Eat it, my girl, eat it, it'll make your milk strong.

O no, said Josepha, and Julie felt quite ill.

So on the whole, Jean said, I was glad I'd had boys. Though I have heard it's the done thing in some parts of the world. We're dreadfully squeamish, aren't we?

Well, I'm a vegan, Josepha began, but she was interrupted by an announcement at the top of the table.

I'd like to propose a toast, an elderly man said. To Sylvia. And he went on to make quite a long speech, about Sylvia's work for charity, especially with the terminally ill, and her hospitality to her friends, and everyone clapped and drank and sang 'Happy Birthday to You', and some people hugged Sylvia, it was clear they all liked her very much.

Outside the light had nearly gone and wet snow splashed against the windows, but inside was warm and bright and full of friends. Julie felt a powerful ache for a home just like Sylvia's, maybe smaller, but with the same oak panels and the garden, and three little boys with old-fashioned names, Arthur and Stanley, and maybe George.

Jean leant towards her.

I'm thinking of inviting a few friends over to my place, she said. In two weeks' time.

Julie felt uncomfortable. They would all start inviting her back, she thought, but she couldn't invite them.

I don't know if I can make it, she said.

O, well, call round anyway, any time you like, Jean said. I don't think we live too far away from one another, and she told Julie her address. Julie was very surprised.

Aren't those –, she said

– The council flats, said Jean. I live on the ninth floor. It's a long story. Involving my renegade son, and she winked at Julie and disappeared.

I'd better be going too, Josepha said as Stanley stirred. I'm going to my parents' later on.

Julie wanted to ask where Josepha lived but she didn't. She felt ashamed of the kind of thoughts she'd been having, because sometimes she thought like Mick, What did any of these rich people know?, but here was Josepha, descended from slaves and Jean lived in a council flat on the roughest estate in town. Mick had no right to say the kind of things he did, Julie thought. Just because someone had a posh voice.

The party guests started to leave. Annie hadn't come, or Gerry. Julie didn't want to leave without trying some of the sweet stuff. There was a big pudding called pond pudding, set on the table over little burners to keep it warm, and a hazelnut meringue and a chocolate mousse. Only the fruit salad had a green leaf next to it, Julie felt quite sorry for Josepha. She put a helping of all three puddings onto her plate, in spite of the heartburn, when no one was looking.

As the room cleared Julie felt a bit self-conscious being the only one left eating and she ate as fast as she could.

Don't feel you have to rush off, Sylvia said as she walked past. Jean and I thought we'd have a session with the cards.

Julie wasn't sure what Sylvia meant, but she certainly didn't want to rush off. What did she have to go home for? She swallowed the last of the hazelnut meringue and felt the burning pain beneath her ribs, her face becoming congested. She tried to breathe deeply and hoped she wouldn't be sick.

Sylvia showed the last of her guests to the door. Jean was already setting out cards on a small carved table. Julie burped two or three times as discreetly as she could and then went over to join her. They weren't like any cards she had ever seen before, there was an ox and a bear and several birds.

Are they tarot cards? Julie said.

No, said Jean. Native American Medicine Cards. And these are runes, she said, rattling a small velvet bag.

Julie pulled up a chair.

The runes are my favourites, Jean said. But Sylvia's daughter's bought these for her birthday. They're very expensive, I believe.

Sylvia came back from the door.

What shall we do first? she said.

Well, it's your birthday, said Jean, but I hope you've got a book for these cards, because they don't mean a thing to me.

We're supposed to be developing our intuition, Sylvia said, but she got the book anyway, then shuffled the cards.

Jean read from the book, taking a long time to find the right page.

Swan, entry into the future accidental and confused, she read. Spider weaving, horse.

They couldn't make sense of them all put together.

It looks like you're going to foreign lands to knit jumpers and lead a coup, Jean said. Sylvia laughed.

Perhaps you'd better read the runes, she said.

Jean laid out the runes in what she said was a runic cross.

O dear, Sylvia said. Aren't they all reversed?

That's not necessarily bad, you know, said Jean, and she began to read.

In the immediate past, she said, you've gone through experiences that have quickened your development and now you have to pause to take things in. So although this period may feel like a standstill, it's really time for you to take stock.

Sylvia nodded.

In the immediate future, said Jean, there's a kind of movement but it won't truly lead anywhere, it might even seem to create more blocks because it's not time for it to move. If you can, avoid doing anything, because at the base of the situation, she tapped the stone at the bottom of the cross, there are people who aren't open to the truth. Really this rune means that you have to face up to the fact of loss and let something go. The challenge – she pointed to the next stone on – is to try not to overreach yourself, exceed your own strength, but to operate quietly within restraints and wait for the wisdom of instinct. And the outcome is –, she paused, – very favourable. Union. Uniting or partnership on a true and equal basis. Now does any of that make sense?

Sylvia said it did indeed.

She had just fallen out with her son-in-law, which meant that Victoria wasn't speaking to her, and she hadn't known if or when to make the first move. So it was all very accurate.

Well, it seems so to me, said Jean, because you're always taking on too much, and this is a warning against that. You're to stand back, and keep your size nines tucked in, and Sylvia laughed and said she'd certainly try.

Now it's your turn, Jean said to Julie.

Feeling a bit nervous and self-conscious Julie picked the stones out of the bag and Jean spread them out for her. One of the runes looked like the letter H, one like M upside down and one like an arrow.

O now that's the fertility rune, Jean said, pointing to one that looked like two x's, one on top of the other. And this one's harvest, fulfilment, so all that looks fine. But there's a big disruption on the way, she tapped the letter H. There's a situation here where you feel you're not getting anywhere and it will take a big disruption to clear the air. Then a kind of journey.

What kind of journey? Julie said. She didn't want to go anywhere.

It can be inside yourself or a physical journey, said Jean. But this rune here, she said, touching the arrow. This is the real journey. To the foundation of your soul.

Julie hadn't a clue what that meant.

Does it say whether I'm having a boy or a girl? she said. Jean laughed.

It's not quite like that, she said. But you're carrying high, so that should mean a boy. Or is it a girl?

Sylvia said she could never remember.

Your turn now, she said to Jean, but Jean shook her head.

Why not? said Sylvia. Jean dropped the stones back into the bag.

I don't want to know, she said.

Julie sat in the kitchen, reading the book Sylvia had lent her, *Astro-Geography*.

Have you ever wondered if a move could change your destiny? it said on the cover.

Are you afraid of making the wrong move?

Julie had been sitting with the book for over an hour. Since she didn't have an exact time of birth for either herself or Mick she was doing the calculations the best way she could. It seemed she should move further east, but

Mick should be somewhere in the Pacific Ocean. She did all the sums twice over but couldn't get him near land.

What's cooking? Mick said, coming in.

Julie was trying to cook the kebabs she'd had at Sylvia's. Sylvia had given her a packet of veggie bacon to try and instructions. They were quick, cheap and filling, she said. Mick picked up the packet.

Oligosporus bacilli incubated with Rhizosporus culture, he read. Yum, yum.

It's just like bacon, Julie said.

It doesn't look like bacon, said Mick. It looks like sticks of Plasticine.

Well, it tastes the same, said Julie, annoyed. She'd been hoping to surprise him with the food, then, when he said how good it was, tell him it was all vegetarian.

I think I'll go to the chippy, Mick said.

Julie felt a spark of rage which surprised her.

You could give it a try, she said.

There was a knock on the door. Annie stood outside in the driving rain with the twins. There was the usual clutter behind the door, but Mick helped Julie and Annie to lift the twins through.

I've brought you that stuff we were talking about, Annie said, dropping a small rucksack onto the kitchen table. There were more bags around the handles of the trolley.

O thank you, said Julie, not looking at Mick. She helped Annie to unstrap the twins.

Mick, she said, still not looking at him, would you put the kettle on?

She'd never spoken to him like that before, as though they were really together. She feared he might say something, but he put the kettle on without a word.

Annie began unloading the rucksack. There were several BabyGros, patterned with rabbits, elephants or bears, and some knitted cardigans to wear over the top. There were vests and bibs, two rattles and two mobiles for the pram and cot.

At least you get one spare with everything, Annie said, starting on the other bags.

There were four little outdoor suits, several socks and bootees, and some cot and pram bedding.

There's more stuff at home, but I couldn't carry everything, Annie said. But I was thinking, we don't use the pram any more, so if we load it up later with the other stuff you could push it back if you like.

Julie was overwhelmed.

This is great, isn't it, Mick? she said. She looked at him for the first time. Every muscle in his face seemed to have tensed at once.

Well, we can't use it any more, Annie said. And we can pass more stuff on as these two get older.

Julie managed to thank Annie again as Mick went out of the room. She stared after him.

See what I mean? she said to Annie. He doesn't want to know.

Well, he'll have to know sooner or later, Annie said. Wait till the baby stuff really starts piling up, and she went on to tell Julie that there was a new stall on the market selling second-hand baby stuff, then there was a crash from Uncle Si's room and screaming. Annie ran in and Julie followed. Thomas had tipped the small table over on himself and Uncle Si's new mug was smashed to pieces on the floor.

It's all right, Julie said as Annie picked Thomas up. It's my fault. I should have moved it.

Mick's voice came from up the stairs.

Up here, he shouted.

Julie hurried onto the landing. Mick stood near the top of the stairs, holding the other twin out. As Julie went up the stairs for the baby their eyes met briefly.

Perhaps they'd like to play with the plug sockets, he said. How about a hair dryer in the bath?

He wasn't smiling at all. Julie carried Jamie back down the stairs.

I'd better be going, Annie said, before they do any more damage, and she strapped Thomas back into his pushchair. Jamie kicked and squawked as she strapped him in, and then sat still looking very stern. Julie helped Annie to get back out of the kitchen with the trolley.

Don't forget, said Annie. There's a pram full of stuff waiting for you whenever you want to call by.

Julie thanked Annie again absently, her mind on Mick. It was a start, she told herself. She couldn't expect much, it was only a start. She began to sort through the baby clothes on the kitchen table. She needed a suitcase or something to keep them dry in the damp bedroom. She could ask Uncle Si, that way she could get talking to him. Then suddenly she thought she didn't want to talk to Uncle Si, she wanted to talk to Mick. She picked up an armful of the baby clothes and went upstairs.

Mick was in Darren's room. Julie knocked on the door and no one answered, but she knew they were there. After a moment she opened the door.

Mick and Darren lay on the floor. Darren, with just his trousers on, was staring up at the ceiling. Mick's arm lay across Darren's body. His face was on the floor and all his dark hair spread about. Julie could see a needle, and bits of silver paper.

Julie shut the door. She stood behind it for a moment, hardly breathing. She went into her room, then came out of it again, still clutching the baby clothes. Then she went back in, put the two piles down on her mattress and stood still, pressing her fingers to her face. After a while she went down the stairs, feeling the familiar breathlessness, clinging to the handrail with both hands like a child. She stood in the kitchen staring at the remaining baby things and at the pot of tea she hadn't used, and nothing at all made any sense.

She had to get out. It was raining outside but she had to go. And because she couldn't face going upstairs again for her coat she went out as she was, into the rain.

Out of the yard, onto the street that led into the yard she went, skidding on the slippery cobbles. Watching her step gave her something to think about as the rain came down hard, harder. She tried to remember about rain coming down from the mountains into the valleys, but all she could really think about as she turned into the main road was the way it soaked into her clothes and made her dress stick to her legs. Cars driving down the hill sent up great flares of water and light. Julie could hardly breathe in the sudden torrent, with the rain in her mouth and nose and eyes. She didn't know where she was going but still she pressed on, up the hill, unmindful of the shops she passed or the people in their cars and how she looked to them, aware only of the wild, hard beating of the rain.

Medbh was teaching everyone to circle dance.
Two three four *change*, she called.
Everyone held hands and tried to follow the steps. It was warm in the big room and all the chairs had been moved to one side. Julie had expected the worst when she'd gone in, and when Medbh said they were all going to dance she'd thought for a moment of leaving. Circle dancing sounded depressingly like Music and Movement at school, when you skipped around the smelly hall with thirty other flat-footed kids and there was always a hole you were desperate to hide in your vest. Julie had always tried to be off on those days. But before she could leave everyone was forming a big circle and Medbh herself caught Julie's hand. She was surprised enough by this to allow herself to be pulled along, but when the music started she wished she hadn't come at all. She felt more self-conscious than ever, right next to the teacher. It reminded her of the time when she'd been made to stand out at Brownies for getting the steps wrong. These steps kept changing, and sometimes Medbh went fast and then slow.
O I can't do this, someone called out.
Don't worry about it, Medbh said. Just keep going.

Julie kept going, her eyes fixed on Medbh's feet. From time to time she glanced up quickly. She could see Jean, and Annie was there, but not Sylvia, or Josepha.

It was hot in the room, Julie was sweating. Other people looked sweaty too, but Julie suspected she was sweating more. She wouldn't look at Medbh's face or at the face of the other person holding her hand, a grey, grizzled man.

All at once Julie realised there was a pattern to the steps, they weren't all changing at random. She even found that if she concentrated she could follow the pattern, and other people seemed to feel the same, because the circle, which had been moving in uneven waves, suddenly came together smoothly and everyone looked a lot happier.

Then Medbh increased the speed.

Two three four *change*, she shouted, and everyone hurried round almost running. Julie began to worry about her breathlessness, but a strange thing happened and as long as she concentrated on the steps she felt fine. She even felt a surge of energy as she went round the room, a kind of flow through her hands. When the music stopped the circle fell apart, everyone laughing and beaming at one another, some people still holding hands. Across the room Julie saw Josepha and she smiled at Julie.

Well, I think you've earned a rest, Medbh said, and they all went back to their chairs. Annie sat down next to Julie.

Thank God that's over, she said. I felt a right prat. But Julie felt much better than when she'd come in. Because all the way up she'd been thinking about Mick and Darren, Darren and Mick, as if she couldn't think about anything else any more. She hadn't said anything to Mick, they'd hardly spoken, but all the time her thoughts ran round and round her head, so that all day she hardly noticed where she was going, or anything around her, except briefly the moon, which looked like the bald head of a baby, wrapped around with greenish cloud.

Medbh was talking about energy.

That's what we've created here tonight, she said. That's

what the whole universe is made of, and we've just made some more. So it's there now, to be used, to heal, or lift depression or to change a state of mind. You see this table? she said, tapping on it. It looks solid. But it's all energy. Everything in this room is energy in different forms. You can't destroy energy, it just changes form. You burn this table and what do you have – another form of energy. The same with the body – it doesn't go, it simply changes form. Breathing and movement make energy and so does love. When you love someone you create an energy that draws you together for all eternity.

Mick, Julie thought, but Annie said,

Christ, does that mean I'm stuck with the twins for ever?

Learning to make energy is learning to let go, Medbh said. You can't hold onto it. When you hold onto something, whether it's anger, grief or hatred, you make big blocks, so there's a lot of energy in a little space for a while. But if the energy can't flow, it goes. It won't be trapped. That's why any negative emotion is very draining.

Everyone was listening. Julie felt she'd understood something very important. As always when Medbh was talking, everything seemed beautifully clear.

But how? said a woman's voice suddenly from the other side of the room. How do you let go of something that hurts?

Everyone turned to look. It was a fat woman, very well dressed with a perm, but Julie could tell she was very nervous.

If it's hurt you a lot, she managed to say when Medbh didn't answer, how do you let it go?

All eyes turned to Medbh.

It depends on what the hurt is, Medbh said kindly.

The woman considered this, then she said,

What if – I mean –, she stopped, then started again. Three years ago, she said, my daughter and grandson were murdered, and a shocked murmur ran through the room.

The woman took a hanky out of her handbag and pressed it to her eyes. I'm sorry, she said, but I can't get over it, and the woman sitting next to her put an arm round her as she began to cry quietly, heaving great, restrained sobs.

Every day it's like this, she said, looking up. Every day I wake up with a pain here, she clutched her chest, and I have to drag myself through the day, and it doesn't get any better. She cried again and on either side of the handkerchief her cheeks wobbled. That's what I can't get over, it doesn't go away. My husband's never been well since it happened. How can it go away? she said, looking up again at Medbh. Every time I remember that I had a daughter I also have to remember that she was murdered.

How did it happen, someone wanted to know, but someone else shushed her, and the woman who had her arm around the fat lady said that she didn't have to say anything if it made her feel worse. But the fat lady said she couldn't very well feel any worse than she already did, and she blew her nose a bit and went on.

Her name was Erin, she said, because there's Irish ancestry in the family. Sometimes I think – I know it's silly – but I think it was all my fault in the first place, giving her that name. She was always in love with Ireland, you see, and she smiled weakly at her own silliness.

She had a little boy – brought him up herself, and she'd never say who the father was – she always was a headstrong girl, Erin, but kind – she'd do anything for anyone. She called him Liam, the little one, and she wouldn't come to live with us – she got a flat nearby. But we were always to hand if she needed us, you know. Little Liam was always round at our place – he could play in the garden, you see. He was a lovely little boy –, the poor woman was overcome again and Julie felt near to tears herself. She looked quickly to see how Annie was, but Annie's face was turned away.

I looked after Liam while Erin was at work, the woman went on. She did art therapy, at a couple of old people's homes, and a restart centre for people who had been in

184

prison. And her dad took her shopping, and there wasn't a week went by without Liam staying over so his mother could have a night out. We helped as much as we could, just as if he was ours. We had our ups and downs with Erin like any parents, but they meant the world to us, both of them. And then one day out of the blue she tells us she's got this full-time job in Donegal. The fat woman raised her eyes to heaven. We were devastated, she said. We begged and pleaded with her not to go, but there was no stopping Erin once she'd made up her mind. I felt even then that we'd never see them again, but Erin said of course we would. There'll be holidays, she said, and long weekends. But we wouldn't go and see her off, I don't know why but we wouldn't. Sometimes I think that's what hurts the most now – we never went to see them off at the end, and she pressed the hanky to her eyes again while the woman next to her hugged her hard.

The next thing we heard was from the police, she said. We had a phone call – they'd not been gone a week and the police came round to say they'd found the bodies of a woman and a little boy over the cliff at Coleraine. I don't know what they were doing there. But we had to go and identify the bodies and it was the worst thing I've ever had to do. She sobbed into the hanky. There's nothing worse, she said, seeing the life you've brought into the world lying on a slab – you brought it in and you don't expect to have to see it go out.

She was crying freely now and a few people in the audience were crying with her. Julie felt tears rolling down her own cheeks and even Annie looked emotional. When the woman was calm again she said,

It seems Erin had hired a car – it was found abandoned a little way off. And they'd been stopped by two men with guns and made to walk to the edge of the cliff – no one knows why, no one can tell us. They stood there holding hands and the men, whoever they were, just shot them in the back of the head. Her voice shook and another horrified murmur ran through the crown. Again the woman pressed the hanky to her eyes.

When they found the bodies, she said, they were still holding hands, and she rocked herself for a moment with the hanky still pressed to her face.

And that's what I see all the time, she said. In my dreams or even when I'm awake – Erin and Liam on the edge of that cliff, holding hands. I can't see the men, though I've tried. But I'll just be doing something or watching telly and things'll be fine, and suddenly all I can see is Erin and Liam on the edge of that cliff, waiting. And nothing, nothing I do makes it go away, and there was the sound of fresh sobbing behind the handkerchief.

No one said anything. A few people looked at Medbh, but it was impossible to read the look on her face. Then the woman looked at Medbh again.

So what can I do? she said. How can I make it go away?

Everyone looked at Medbh now, but Medbh didn't take any notice. All the time she had been listening to the fat woman's story, now she shook her head briefly, as if twitching a fly away, and crossed the room. She knelt down in front of the woman, took hold of both her hands and kissed them, it seemed like the most natural thing in the world.

What's your name? she said.

Margery Bowden, said the woman in a hesitant way, as if wondering what Medbh would do next.

Well, Margery Bowden, Medbh said, and she stood up, still holding Margery's hands so that Margery stood up with her, blinking and surprised.

This woman, Medbh said, turning to the audience and holding up one of Margery's hands, has suffered a terrible thing. The worst thing a woman can suffer. Should she just be able to forget it?

Several people spoke at once and Margery spoke, but a woman at the front spoke loudest.

But she wants to know how to let it go, she said.

Medbh held her own hand up.

Pain and grieving are a natural part of life, she said. We're all on the wheel of karma and sometimes it feels like we're being broken on that wheel. If you lived in another culture, one of those with all the primitive, barbaric rituals, you'd be taught how to face that pain. But in this culture, she said, we have painkillers. She turned to Margery.

Did the doctor give you tablets when it happened?

Well, yes, said Margery. To help me sleep, and Medbh turned back.

That's this culture's response to pain, she said. You have a headache? Take an aspirin. Having a baby? Go for a shot of pethidine.

Too right, someone said, and people laughed.

O yes, said Medbh, I know what it's like. I've had children too. But I also know there's no quick way to get rid of pain. Sooner or later you have to face it. And if you don't get through it at the time it can take years. The important thing is to let the pain happen, let it hurt, and, she paused, lifting one hand again, know that you are not that pain. You are not your pain, any more than you are your thoughts, or your moods that come and go, or the job you do. Now, she said, turning back to Margery. How did you feel when you were doing the circle dance?

Fine, Margery said, I felt fine then.

And afterwards? said Medbh.

Afterwards was when I felt it – all the pain and grief coming back out of nowhere, and there was a murmur of interest round the class.

That's what it's about, Medbh said, rounding on them all. It's about learning to let it happen, releasing the pain, and all the time knowing that there's a little part of you not caught up in all the turmoil, a tiny, still part, calm, aware of your breathing. And the more you do the practice the stronger that part will be. And the more able you'll be to let the pain go.

But will it all go? Margery said, and Medbh hugged her.

What will happen is that you'll become ready to let it go. You won't need it any more. Now, she said to everyone. I want us all to join hands, and soon all the people in the room had made a circle round Margery, who smiled at them in a confused kind of way as they all began to dance. Sometimes they danced close up to her and sometimes further away, and from time to time someone broke free of the chain and hugged her before returning, more and more people as they kept going round. Julie thought about it but she couldn't make herself go up to a strange woman and kiss her. It happened a lot at the meetings, people hugging and kissing, especially at the end. It was nice in a way, Julie supposed, part of the general niceness that she couldn't join in, that Mick would despise. But Margery seemed to like it, she wiped her eyes and laughed as more and more people came to hug her.

You see how much love there still is out there, Medbh said as the dancing stopped. Don't close yourself off from it, the more you turn to it, the more you'll be ready to let go. And when that happens Erin will become a beautiful space in your life, not a painful memory, and she kissed Margery again and told her that any time she wanted she could come to see Medbh personally, about learning to let go.

When Margery sat down Medbh had a few more things to say, and she introduced a new teacher, a young, good-looking man, Julie had seen him dancing round before. Medbh said his name was Pierre and that he would be taking meetings with Eric from now on. Julie hardly listened. She was thinking about what had just happened with Margery, and how amazing it was that Medbh had been able to help her. She kept searching out Margery's face as Medbh spoke. She definitely looked better, listening intently, turning to smile once or twice at the woman next to her. Julie felt gripped by a peculiar excitement. She noticed how everyone looked better, their eyes were bigger and brighter, as they were sometimes after meditation, though when she'd said that to Mick he'd said they probably all had thyroid, like his mam. Julie knew he was wrong now, everything he said about the group was wrong.

When Medbh finished and people surged forwards to speak to her, Julie just grabbed her coat and hurried out, forgetting all about Annie. She'd lost sight of Annie anyway, in the last circle dance. She hurried out into the night air which was fresh and almost warm, spring-like. There were new baby buds on all the bushes and trees though it was only February, lamplight shone on them and on the drops of water clinging to them and they quivered as Julie passed.

If someone like Margery could be helped, Julie thought, anyone could be, and all the doubts that had been accumulating in her ever since she'd started meditating on Darren leaving and he hadn't gone yet, seemed to blow away in the fresh night air. Everything Medbh had ever said came back to her, about changing your way of thinking if you wanted to change your life. It seemed possible right then to change the way she saw everything, and even that horrible scene that had hurt her so much, Mick and Darren lying together on Darren's bedroom floor, seemed different now. They were just messing around. She'd always known Mick shot up from time to time. She didn't know now why she'd let seeing them get her down so much. As she walked through the moist, dusky light she looked around her all the time, at all the surrounding hills and the lights on them, it looked like they were studded with stars. She realised that there was nothing to be frightened of any more, if people like Margery could be helped then it didn't matter what happened, nothing was so bad that it couldn't be sorted. Julie didn't think she would ever be frightened again. She wasn't even frightened when a car pulled up at her side. She looked once, twice, it was Pierre, the young man Medbh had just introduced.

Hello, he said. I have seen you walking alone and I thought, maybe she would like a lift.

Julie never accepted lifts from strange men.

O yes, I would, thank you, she said, getting in.

In the car she didn't know what to say, but Pierre said, Did you enjoy the meeting?

O yes, I did, Julie said. It was wonderful.

Medbh is a wonderful woman, Pierre said. People live their lives in fear of what might happen and never realise that there is an alternative. Just tell me where to let you out.

At the bottom, please, Julie said. She searched for something else to say. Have you known Medbh long?

About three years, Pierre said. I was just drifting from one country to another, drifting through my life. Then I met Medbh and she gave me my direction, and he smiled at Julie in the driving mirror.

Julie blushed.

It's just here, she said, and Pierre pulled the car up.

Maybe I will see you at the next meeting, he said, looking at her with dark, intent eyes.

O yes, I mean, thank you, Julie said, and she hurried away.

He wouldn't fancy a pregnant woman, she told herself as she turned the corner. He was just being nice, that was all. Mick was never nice. And he had nothing good to say about the meetings, and yet look what they did for people, Julie thought. Look what they were doing for her, she felt stronger every time she went to one, and as she stepped over the cement mixer and sacks of sand she felt that she would never let anything get her down again.

Julie, Julie, wake up, Mick said, shaking her, and Julie pulled herself out of a deep, awful sleep. You'll wake the whole street up, he said.

Julie sat up slowly. Her face was wet.

I was dreaming, she mumbled.

I could tell, Mick said, going back to his own mattress. Julie held her head in her hands. She felt the pressure of the dream all around her.

What were you dreaming anyway? Mick said.

Brian, said Julie, I dreamed Brian was dead, and she stared in despair at the window.

I thought you hated Brian, Mick said, but Julie didn't answer. She couldn't tell him the awfulness of the dream, the woman coming to tell her no one had seen Brian for days, and all the neighbours thought Julie should go, she was the only family. And just as she meant to say she wouldn't go she was already there, inside the house, going through the dark rooms, smelling the peculiar smell.

Well, anyway, Mick said, lying down, if he's dead maybe you'll get the house. Eh, that's right, he said, sitting up again. You're his only family, aren't you? Maybe you should go and check. Julie shook her head. She didn't want to speak. Well, you didn't get anything when your mam died, did you? And someone's got to get the house.

Julie hadn't had anything when her mother died. None of that had been sorted out, though Aunty Clare had said she would. But Julie hadn't seen Aunty Clare for months.

We could all use the money, Mick said, and Julie shifted uncomfortably on the mattress. She didn't like Mick talking like this.

I'll go with you if you like, he said.

It's all right, Julie managed to say. She didn't want to go back, and she especially didn't want to go back with Mick.

But you will go though, Mick said.

It was only a dream, said Julie. She wished she hadn't said anything now. She turned herself slowly on the mattress and inside her the baby shifted too. She thought of having a proper home for her baby. But she couldn't imagine going back there. Surely they would let her know, she thought, if anything happened to Brian. But she couldn't think how, and anyway, who were *they*?

See, we could sell the house, Mick said. You wouldn't have to live in it.

Julie noticed he said we.

Money'd come in all right, Mick said, turning over. Julie didn't say anything. After a while she could hear him sleeping, but Julie herself stayed wide awake, in the grip of bad dreams and bad memories. She remembered Brian so well she could almost smell him, having to walk past him in the hall, and the lumbering rage that was always in him after he lost his job that might make him push her, or say something, or laugh suddenly, she never knew what he would do. And something had happened to her memories, turning them into a single big cloud, everything to do with Brian became somehow part of it. She couldn't remember in detail the things he'd done, or if the things she'd said to Mick were true. But he did used to do things, he squeezed her bust once, right in front of her mother. Eh, she's growing up, he'd said, and her mother had just ignored it, pretended not to see. And he used to walk into the bathroom when she was having a bath, because there wasn't a lock on the door. He was always unpredictable, she never knew what to expect. Julie and her mother used to live around that, trying to guess, never knowing if the things they said or did would make him feel better or much worse. And she hated it, and she hated him. In her memory he was always lurking round dark places, waiting for Julie. Then suddenly she wondered how Brian remembered it, and how Eric had said there was more than one past.

What do you think I am, a fucking pervert? Brian had said.

Yes, she'd wanted to say. Maybe she had said it.

He wouldn't remember things the way she did though, maybe he wouldn't remember them at all.

Julie lay in one position then another, but she couldn't stop herself thinking about Brian and the past that was maybe only her past.

You have to let the past go, said Medbh.

Towards morning she crept downstairs. Tired of the silence she turned the radio on.

The parents of Joshua Corbie, the two-year-old found battered to death, appeared in court today charged with his murder, the voice on the radio said.

Julie turned it off, and sat at the table, rubbing her forehead. There were so many bad things in the world, what could meditation do? She wondered hopelessly how she could fend off the big cloud. The day could only get better, she told herself, then she caught sight of a card on the table.

It was her appointment day.

Julie groaned aloud.

She had to go more often from now on.

Julie stared around the kitchen in despair, as if something would tell her it was all right, she didn't have to go, but nothing did and Medbh said,

If you have to do something, do it the best way you can.

She could go to the park first, Julie thought. She never went to the park, though it was only half a mile down the road. She should start now, set off early, get some exercise, it was better than sitting in, thinking negative thoughts.

It was a still, brown day. The ducks and the water and the reeds and the bare trees were all different shades of brown. It wasn't raining but the air was wet. All the ducks gathered round Julie, quacking furiously as she drew out the bread, some even snapped at her hands, and Julie felt quite nervous. But when the bread ran out they just waddled and swam away towards two people on the other side of the pond, leaving long trails in the smooth brown water.

Julie sat back. She tried to relax and become aware of everything around her as Medbh had said; the smooth round buds on spiky bushes, the reflections of trees in the brown water, almost more real than the trees themselves, and the sudden, trackless flights of the ducks. All of this is energy, she told herself. If she concentrated hard enough she might see all the particles of energy from which everything was composed. Then if she went further, to the point of stillness towards which all meditation was directed, she might not only see them but see them transformed, she might transform her world. Julie tried this for a long time, but maybe she couldn't concentrate fully enough, because she only began to feel bored and cold. Medbh said there were people who spent their whole lives sitting still, aiming at the point of stillness, but maybe it was warmer. Mick once said that that was the problem with meditation, people sitting round on their arses doing nothing, but somewhere inside her Julie still believed that if you did it properly it would work, things would change. The trouble was she never felt as though she was doing it properly.

Julie pressed her hands to her stomach and told her baby how beautiful it all was. We'll come here when you're in a pram, she said, but the baby was quiet. Then she realised that she couldn't remember when she had last felt it move. She had read somewhere that she had to start counting the movements soon, it had to do ten by a certain time of the day. But what did it mean if it didn't? Julie prodded her stomach a bit but there was no response. Then she felt afraid. That always happened whenever she sat down quietly for a bit, all her fears and anxieties surfaced, it wasn't relaxing at all. Julie got up stiffly. The hospital, she thought. They would tell her what to do. And pushing away her dread of going she began walking out of the park towards the antenatal clinic as fast as she could, hoping that the movement would wake the baby up.

Fifteen stone two, the nurse said in her loud voice, and the other nurse wrote it down. That's an overall weight gain of sixty-three pounds. What height are you – five foot two.

Three, Julie said, stepping back off the scales and not looking at anyone in the room

I think we'd better get the doctor to take a look at you,

said the nurse. We don't want to take any risks, do we? and Julie took the card she was given and left the room.

Nine stone eight, she heard the nurse say to the next woman. That's very good.

Julie sat in a cubicle. Another nurse had taken her blood pressure and said it was slightly high, so now she was waiting to see the doctor. She had taken her clothes off and was wearing a white cotton gown that hung open at the back no matter how she tried to pull it together. Although the cubicle was small there were two notices on the wall which she could see very close up. One was a list of statistics about Down's syndrome and how the chances of it increased with age, the other was a phone number you could ring in case you had a stillbirth. Julie sat with her eyes closed and focused on her breathing. Since her panic in the park she had felt the baby moving, she could feel it now faintly. And she put her hands on her stomach and told her baby to kick harder, and keep kicking. She tried to listen to her breathing, but all she could hear were the clinking hospital noises, voices and footsteps approaching, then passing by. She waited so long she thought about putting all her clothes on again and leaving, but then a nurse opened the door.

Can you come through now, please?

Clutching her gown at the back, Julie walked through the door to a room with a bed and sink.

Just lie down on your back, said the nurse, turning to wash her hands.

There was no way of climbing onto the bed without letting go of the gown, Julie tried twice. Then she gave up and clambered on any old how, nearly falling off again as the doctor came in behind her.

The doctor looked very young, about Mick's age. He consulted with the nurse for a long time but Julie only heard the words 'obese' and 'premature'. Then he turned to Julie.

Good morning, he said in an entirely different voice. Can I feel your tummy?

Julie tugged the sheet up over the lower part of her body, then she lifted the gown.

Fifteen stone and five foot two, said the nurse.

Three, Julie said. And a half.

The doctor prodded carefully all round Julie's stomach.

Now breathe in, he said, and gripped hard at the base of the womb.

Just trying to assess the position, he said as Julie writhed. How many weeks did you say? he said to the nurse.

About thirty, the nurse said.

Thirty-two, Julie corrected them in her mind.

A little early to induce, the doctor said.

Behind him the door opened and a much older doctor came in with a younger, Asian one.

This is Dr Protheroe, your consultant, the young doctor said to Julie. And Dr Rashid.

Dr Protheroe prodded Julie's belly.

How far on did you say? he asked the young doctor.

Thirty weeks, chorused the doctor and nurse.

And a weight gain of sixty-three pounds, the nurse added.

Too many chocolate puddings, eh? Dr Protheroe said to Julie in a slightly louder tone, as though she might be deaf. I think we'd better do an internal, he said. Just bend your legs, please, and let them fall apart.

When Julie was a little girl she sometimes used to pretend she was dead, to see what it felt like, or when anything awful was happening. She knew that if she shut her eyes and stayed very still the world would eventually go away. So now she drew her legs up and shut her eyes and took the tiniest breaths she could.

Dr Protheroe pushed two fingers inside her and worked them around.

Now then, he said to Dr Rashid. That's interesting. Would you like to try?

Dr Rashid pulled on plastic gloves. His fingers entered Julie and squirmed around a bit.

How about you? said Dr Protheroe to the young doctor, who pushed his fingers in as far as they would go.

I will be dead I am dead I will be dead I am dead, Julie chanted to herself, and she made no noise even when it hurt.

Tell me what you feel, Dr Protheroe said.

The cervix is rather soft, said Dr Rashid.

Precisely, said Dr Protheroe. And what does that tell us?

The young doctor withdrew his fingers.

I'd say she was a bit further on than thirty weeks, he said.

Thirty-two weeks, Julie screamed at them in her mind, then went back to chanting.

Excellent, said Dr Protheroe and the young doctor went pink. How much farther on? and Dr Rashid suggested she might be thirty-two or even thirty-three weeks pregnant.

Absolutely, said Dr Protheroe. So here we have a patient thirty-two, maybe thirty-three weeks pregnant and severely overweight. Which means that over the next four weeks we can monitor her weight carefully and if there are any further untoward increases we can induce.

The young doctors wrote this down, then all three of them left the room.

Julie couldn't sit up. She tried three times, then stared at the nurse.

Want a hand? the nurse said, eventually noticing her, and she helped to heave Julie into a sitting position.

Now if you get dressed, she said, speaking clearly, and take this card through to reception, they'll make you a card out for next week.

What did he mean, induce, Julie said, and the nurse seemed to her to look cagey.

Well, we'll monitor your weight every week from now on, she said. And your blood, in case of diabetes or pre-eclampsia – we don't want any of that, now do we?

Julie had only the faintest idea of what it was.

And if there are any problems, the nurse said, Doctor might want to start labour off, you know. Get it all over and done with.

So I have to come every week, Julie said. The nurse dried her hands.

Just while we sort out what's best for baby, she said.

Then she checked her watch, clucked softly, and left the room. Julie stared at her retreating back.

But I don't want to be induced, she thought. That would mean she'd have a premature baby, and she didn't know what to do with a premature baby. Besides, she wasn't ready.

Julie pulled her clothes on and went back to reception with the card, doing as she was told even though the thought of coming back again in a week's time was almost as bad as the thought of being induced. But she didn't know what to do, and as she walked away from reception towards the main doors she hated herself for not knowing what to do.

She should have done something, she told herself. Kicked up a fuss, refused to let them mess with her like that, it wasn't right, and as she reached the pelican crossing she hated herself so much for just doing nothing that she started to cry. Great shaking sobs welled up and she was mortified, it was broad daylight on a busy street. Everyone was looking, but there didn't seem to be anything she could do about that either.

When the sobbing died down Julie looked up and saw ahead of her through the clear cold the tower block where Jean had said she lived. Julie stopped for a moment, rubbing her eyes.

Come round any time, Jean had said at Sylvia's party, and, You will call round, won't you?

The lift smelled strongly of wee but the floor was dry. There was a rough notice stuck to the wall as there had been in the foyer. If you want to mess up your own life with drugs, it said, that's your business. But please don't leave your needles where our children can play with them.

Jean opened the door right away. She looked at Julie and took hold of both her hands.

You look as if you've been having a rough time, she said. Come in.

Julie could only cry again at Jean's kindness, but Jean wasn't phased.

You sit here, she said, patting Julie's shoulder. I'll make us a nice cup of camomile tea.

Julie sat where she was told, in a reclining chair, facing a big window. Beyond the window was a balcony, but the angle of the chair meant that you could only see the sky.

That's what I call my comfort seat, Jean said. It's very soothing, staring at the sky.

Julie stared at it. It was a blank grey. She watched it for a while but it didn't change, so she looked around the room instead.

On either side of the other, smaller window there were masks, a bird mask and a star mask. By the door there was a mask with the sun and moon combined into one face, and around the bookshelves jesters and a wolf. The only other furniture was a folded-up kind of sofa bed, Julie had seen one in one of Aunty Clare's magazines and knew it was called a futon.

I can't always meditate, Jean said, coming back in with a tray. But I can sit on that seat and stare at the sky. When I first moved here I didn't think there was going to be much to be grateful for, but the sky has been a great gift. Honey?

She went on talking as she poured the tea, about the masks which were all from Venice, a magical place, she said, her favourite city, and Julie took the tea and remembered Aunty Clare, who went to Italy every year but had never bought a mask.

Julie picked up the tea but it was very hot. Jean put hers down. Shall I show you the views? she said.

They went out onto the balcony. Julie gazed around at

sights which should have been familiar but everything seemed different this high up. There were the flat tops of maisonettes, then the Lex Motor company, the Akbar Cash and Carry, the big new Norweb building and the precinct beyond. She searched in vain for more familiar landmarks, Krishna's, Sefton Street, Uncle Si's. Gradually she oriented herself to the view. Everywhere she looked people were working on the town, tearing up roads, putting up scaffolding on buildings. Great cranes swung loads of concrete and bricks slowly around. There was clearance work going on by the canal, a multi-storey car park being built to one side of the precinct and the church was being cleaned. Julie had never seen before how much work went on every day, building and pulling down. It was a town with a long history, long before the Industrial Revolution, Julie remembered that from school, yet all the old past had been torn down and covered over, built over, torn down again and rebuilt, it was still going on. It was hypnotic, watching the big machines as they tore it down and built.

The other side is prettier, Jean said, and she led the way to her bedroom.

In the bedroom there was just a bed, wardrobe and locker in white, but from the window you could see more of the town, the railway which ran in front of Uncle Si's, the park and the hills beyond. Julie could just make out the boating lake.

I always wanted a room with a view, Jean said grinning. A lot of people were shocked when I gave up the house for a flat in a tower block – I was a bit shocked myself – and some of the neighbours are, well, not necessarily people you'd choose to live with, but these views are a great compensation. Especially at night. I find that just looking at the night sky puts most things into perspective.

There was noise from above, the sound of children shouting and footsteps thudding across the ceiling.

I always think it's a shame for the little ones, Jean said, turning away. Nowhere to play.

Julie noticed two photos on the locker, a big one of a family group and a smaller one of a single child.

That's David, Jean said, passing it to Julie. David's face was slight and pointy, he had fair, silky hair.

He looks like you, Julie said.

Do you think so? He looked like his father as well, and Jean picked up the big photo, of Jean and her husband and the two boys. They were all fair and slight with short silky hair. Jean's hair was a bit darker, but apart from that they all looked the same.

Norman died two years ago, Jean said. But we'd divorced a long time before that. Do you want to see the garden? she said, and she showed Julie a tray she hadn't noticed before standing in the corner of the room. It was full of soil, with small rocks set in it and tiny rock flowers growing round them. There was a miniature tree with oranges on it and Jean had added a small mirror for a pond.

It's beautiful, Julie said. She hated the way she sounded, dull and hollow, even when she meant what she was saying. It was because she wasn't used to saying nice things to people. Josepha would have said it better, she thought.

Medbh got us all going on gardens, Jean said. And since I couldn't have a real one I thought I'd start this little one. I find it a kind of meditation in itself, she said, and she led Julie back into the lounge. The noise upstairs increased into a regular thud, thud, thud as if someone was skipping and there weren't any carpets, but Jean didn't say anything. Julie sat back on her chair and sipped her tea and it didn't taste at all nice.

Now, Jean said. Why don't you tell me what's wrong.

When Jean said that, so many things flooded into Julie's mind that for a moment she couldn't speak. Then she began to tell her about the hospital. Some of it was hard to say, it was so awful. When she told Jean about the doctors examining her she nearly cried again.

I'm surprised they didn't bring in the porters and let them have a go, Jean said and she laughed. I always remember having this rod shoved up my back end, she said. It took three of them to get it past the blockage in my bowel. And just as they got it into position the cleaner wandered in looking for her machine.

O no, Julie said.

Yes, but the worst thing was, these young doctors have all been trained to keep you chatting, you know, to take your mind off the fact that you've got a three-foot pole up your rear, so there they were, the three of them, wielding this immense rod around and saying things like, Are you going anywhere nice this year?

Julie laughed aloud.

And another time, Jean said, this old lady in the bed next to mine – she died eventually of the cancer – but while she was in she was visited by the top specialist, and after the examination he stood at the foot of the bed with all the students, you know – I always think they look like a flock of penguins – and he said to them in this penetrating voice, We don't often get anything as wrinkly as that to look at.

O God, said Julie.

Well, the old lady, Charlotte her name was, she was terribly upset. And we were all mortified, for him, not for her. Even the students were mortified, you could see that. And I tried telling that to Charlotte but it was no use. She was just too upset and humiliated.

I know how she felt, said Julie.

Yes, well, it shows them up, not you, said Jean. And don't you forget it. But I have to say, she said, they were kindness itself when David died. They stopped the machine, you know, and we all stood round and watched him die – I felt as though I'd just been killed myself. And afterwards I walked away from everyone, from Norman and Michael, I couldn't bear to speak to them or touch them. I walked away, right out of the ward, through the doors, into the gardens. I hadn't a clue where I was going and I couldn't see a blind thing, but one of the doctors came running after me. And he said, Come back to your family, Mrs Pemberton, they need you now. And he held my hand very tightly and said, The only way you'll get through this is by keeping going. I always remember that because it's true. They give you sedatives of course, because all you want is to blot out the pain, but the only real way to deal with it is to keep on going – straight through it.

Julie wondered where Michael was now, Jean never mentioned it and she thought maybe she shouldn't ask, but then she said,

Does Michael live near here now? and then wished she hadn't because Jean looked very sad.

Michael? she said. I don't know where he is. I haven't seen him since Norman died. And then he was asking for money. I told him then, Michael, I have no more money. And if you can't come to see me for any other reason, then maybe you shouldn't come at all. Since when of course, she said, I haven't seen him.

Julie didn't know what to say, but Jean said,

But as far as your problem goes, if the hospital's getting you down that much, why go?

She laughed at Julie's face.

Well, they're not going to come after you with police helicopters and hunting dogs, are they? I know they always make it sound as if you have to go through one indignity after another, but in fact of course the choice is entirely yours.

Julie still looked as if she didn't quite believe it, but Jean said,

I didn't go for treatment for quite some time. I tried every alternative therapy there was. But in the end the idea that we're all somehow mysteriously in control and if we just lived perfect, stress-free lives there'd be no sickness, was getting me down more than the chemotherapy. When I wasn't getting better I just felt guilty and incompetent as well as ill. I mean, she said, pouring more tea, when I first found out I had cancer I blamed Michael for giving me so much stress. He was always in trouble in his teens, he left home twice and was brought back by the police, he tried drugs, the lot. It broke up the marriage, you know, his father couldn't stand the strain. And that's what they say about cancer, isn't it – that it's all unresolved emotional pain. So I hated him for a while. I think that's why I gave up my house in the end, as a kind of apology for having hated him. Because mothers aren't allowed to hate their children, you'll find that out. Anyway, it's not useful, is it? going around hating people. So eventually I stopped. And I came to this conclusion about suffering. You can't avoid it, it's not a simple matter of getting everything right all the time, it just is. It affects everyone all the time and no one quite sees the extent of it. But to think, O, God I'm suffering, I'd better not suffer or I'll be ill, is just nonsense. It's got to be accepted, like an animal accepts it. That's the powerful act, my Qi Gong teacher says. The act of powerful surrender.

Jean looked at Julie and Julie hoped she looked wise.

Well, anyway, Jean said. Here I am, talking about me all the time and you've got problems of your own. So tell me about them.

Julie couldn't think of anything to say, then she said, Sometimes I don't think meditation's for me.

O I know, Jean said. When I first started I couldn't take to it at all. There I was, surrounded by all these smiley, happy people, and I was weighed down by all the problems in the world, and I thought, what do any of this lot know about trouble, eh? Real capital T-type trouble. The biggest problem they've got is deciding whether or not to buy shares in a holiday home – I was very bitter when I first started. But I don't think that way now. You get to know people and you realise they've all had their crosses to bear. Look at Sylvia. And Eric – he was crippled with arthritis when he first met Medbh. The diet and visualisation and all the rest of it really worked for him. It's no wonder he's a bit of an evangelist.

Julie hadn't known that about Eric, but she nodded because she'd come to the same conclusion about the people in the group. But her problem seemed to go deeper than that. It was to do with the way they lived their lives and she lived hers. She couldn't tell them anything about herself.

Do you live with your boyfriend? Jean said unexpectedly.

Yes, Julie said. She hesitated a bit and then said, And his uncle, and his friend Darren.

Jean didn't seem phased.

Well, that'll be nice for you when the baby's born, she said, having two built-in babysitters.

Julie almost laughed at the thought of Darren and Uncle Si babysitting.

Well, I always maintain, Jean said, that childcare should be spread out. This one-to-one business is monstrous. It's inhuman and unhealthy.

Julie shook her head. She wasn't contradicting Jean, she just couldn't explain. Jean watched her closely for a while, then said,

Well, Julie, you know, sometimes I can tell things about people, and I've thought for some time that you know about capital T-type trouble, don't you. Am I right?

Julie didn't say anything. She thought of denying it, then she felt confused, then she leant back in the chair and rubbed her forehead. The sky had changed, she noticed. Around the edges there were splashes of intense yellow.

How did you meet Mick? Jean said.

Bit by bit Julie told Jean about Mick, about knowing him at school, then about leaving school and Mick being homeless, and Julie's mother dying, and moving in with Uncle Si and the state the house was in. All the time she talked she was conscious of leaving things out, about Brian and about Mick and Darren, but she didn't think Jean would notice.

So the house isn't ready for the baby, Jean said.

Nowhere near, said Julie, and she couldn't entirely keep the bitterness from her voice.

Isn't there somewhere you could stay until it was ready – what about your Aunty Clare?

Julie had glossed quickly over Aunty Clare, now she shook her head. She couldn't just go back there with a baby. Besides, though she really didn't know why, she couldn't imagine herself leaving Mick. She didn't think he was wonderful any more, but that was still the way she felt.

And Darren, Jean said. How does he feel about all this.

Julie shook her head again. She didn't know.

Well, how did Mick meet Darren? Jean said.

This Julie did know, because Mick had finally told her, one night when neither of them could sleep. He'd been looking for a place to kip on a night near Christmas, and he'd gone round the back of Victoria Station and seen three lads standing round something on the floor. A step or two closer and he'd seen it was a body, and the three lads were pissing on it. The alley was full of bottles. Mick picked one up and crept closer, then quick as lightning he smashed the bottle and grabbed the nearest lad by the throat.

Fuck off, he said to the other two. And fuck off now.

When he told Julie this she could see by the orange light from the window how much he had wanted to draw the bottle edge across the thin, thin flesh of that throat.

The three lads ran off, who wouldn't? Mick was six foot three and in a white rage. He dragged Darren out of the rain into a doorway. Darren was in a bad way, stoned out of his head and beaten. He started shaking and spit ran down the side of his mouth as though he was having a fit. Mick thought he might die. But he'd stayed with him all night, holding him when the spasms started and wrapping him in his own jacket, it was all he could do besides wait. And towards morning Darren came round.

That's it really, Julie said. They've been together ever since. I think Mick thinks Darren needs looking after.

So he looks after him, Jean said, and she took the cups and put them back on the tray, then she picked the tray up.

It's funny, isn't it, she said, what makes one person start to love another.

What? said Julie, but Jean didn't look at her.

Love, she said, getting up with the tray. You work for someone, you give them everything you have to give, like your children. You'd think they'd be a burden, they keep you up at night and drive you to the point of exhaustion, and the end of it is, you love them.

Jean said something else but Julie wasn't listening. The image of Mick lying across Darren returned suddenly and horribly to her mind. But she hadn't told Jean that, she hadn't told her anything.

Jean went out of the room with the tray, then came back and sat down and looked at Julie in an odd, compassionate way. Julie didn't move or speak. Finally she said,

I'd better be going.

Jean looked as if she was going to say something, then didn't. She stood up instead, and helped Julie up and held onto her hand.

Take care of yourself, she said.

Julie read the housing pages of the local newspaper.

Well-appointed end-terrace, she read. Convenient for all local amenities, and,

Ideal for the first-time buyer.

Julie knew all the phrases by heart.

Deceptively spacious mid-terraced accommodation, she read. Requires some renovation.

Really she was looking for places to rent. Since seeing Jean she'd only been able to think about getting away. But the rented places cost more than she would ever be able to earn, and anyway, she couldn't get a job. So she stopped looking at them, but she couldn't stop herself looking at the properties you could actually buy. Owning a house seemed to her to be the best thing in the world.

Tastefully decorated, garden, terraced, she read. Two/three bedrooms, pleasant outlook.

In her mind these houses were all the same. They were all like the ones in the row of cottages behind the park, the ones she used to walk past with her mother, whenever her mother took her to the park.

Eee, there's some lucky people, her mother used to say.

It was a private row of six cottages overlooking the boating lake. They all had small gardens at the front and a communal grassy bit behind. Though the gardens were small, they were packed with all kinds of flowers and shrubs, there was a hanging basket by every door. Some of the bushes, hydrangea, lavatera, looked too big behind the tiny walls. But when you walked past on a summer evening you could smell the flowers and all the colours glowed pure and pale.

They'll have bought them for nothing, years ago, her mother said, and there was an ache in her voice. Her mother had always wanted a little house like that, and it seemed to Julie that she had too.

Everyone dreams about having their own home, Mick said. But maybe you didn't just dream about any home, maybe there was always just one. Julie didn't want a house like Sylvia's any more. When she tried to imagine any of the properties in the paper she could only see the houses near the park. And the wanting them made her feel hungry, it made her want to eat.

Even the hard cases on the streets want a home, Mick said. It's not something you ever stop wanting.

And yet Mick wasn't getting on with Uncle Si's at all. He was always out at meetings or arguing in the kitchen. There was one cupboard built in the kitchen, that was all. That morning Julie had climbed over more rubble than ever before, all up the stairs, planks of wood, plaster, tools and sawdust. There was so much mess it made her feel lost.

A charming new development of town houses, the advert said. Each with private garden and conservatory.

Without a home you couldn't get the smallest thing together; everything was massively difficult, like living in a hole. It drove you into dreaming instead, about things that weren't real, as though without a home to live in you lived in a dream. That was the way Julie felt anyway, lost in a dreaming hole.

Uncle Si came in.

Julie jumped up, moving the paper. She didn't want him to see her looking at houses.

Would you like something to eat, Uncle Si? she said.

Well, now, that's kind, said Uncle Si in his hesitant way. He never failed to say she was kind whenever she did anything for him, only she wished he wouldn't scratch himself so much. He was scratching now as he sat at the table. It reminded her that her own leg was itching and there were small red bumps near the ankle.

She turned to the pans on the stove. She had made up a curry to use up the vegetables: potatoes, cauliflower, peas. It had taken her mind off the mess on the stairs and given her something to do. She was getting good at curries and at using things up. But all the time she was preparing it the terrible weight of not knowing what to do never left. Mick and Darren, that was all she could think. Darren and Mick.

The rice wasn't quite ready. Julie stirred it, not knowing what to say to Uncle Si, she had almost stopped trying to speak to him. Finally she said,

Do you ever wish you lived somewhere else?

She waited a long time for an answer, so long she thought his mind must have wandered; then he said that sometimes he thought it must be nice to live on a ship.

No, I mean a real home, Julie said.

No, said Uncle Si. I never think that, and he looked at

her with his light eyes that sometimes seemed so penetrating and sometimes just blank.

But you know, Julie said, somewhere to come home to. A real home. She thought of warmth and light and armchairs, she couldn't explain how she felt.

Uncle Si scratched his head and said that he never thought of houses like that. Where there were houses there was always dirt and clutter and things to do.

You have a home and then you have to work for it, he said. It takes up all the room in your head.

Julie thought about that as she served the rice. It was certainly true of Uncle Si's. There was always the mess, and bills to pay, new guttering to order. She had to tell the council about the drains. But that was just here, she thought.

There was a silence while they ate the curry. Julie chewed slowly. When she was hungry she felt sick, when she was full she got heartburn. At least it would probably stop her putting on so much weight. Uncle Si chewed slowly too. Julie thought about the home she wanted so much she could almost smell the polish on the furniture, and about Uncle Si not thinking about it like that.

What made you buy this house then? she said.

I didn't buy it, said Uncle Si. It was left me. In a will.

O, said Julie. She wanted to ask who had left it, but she thought it wouldn't be polite. Anyway she could tell that he had switched off now in that way he had, his eyes were empty. So they ate in silence again, but when they weren't speaking all Julie's misery returned, and she wondered if she'd ever have a home of her own, or ever stop dreaming about one. Then she thought that maybe if you ever stopped dreaming about home you really were lost.

When the burning pain beneath her ribs started she stopped. Uncle Si stopped too.

Have you had enough, Uncle Si? Julie said, and Uncle Si said it was very nice, lovely, only the rice got under his teeth. So Julie scraped the plates into the bin and rinsed them under the tap. She couldn't think of anything else to say to Uncle Si, she half expected him to go, but when she turned round he was still there. He said,

Would you like to see some photographs?

O yes, Julie said, surprised. She hadn't imagined him having anything like photographs, but she followed him into his room and from a drawer on the floor he took out a bundle held together by an elastic band.

That was my mam, he said, showing her an unsmiling woman in a big hat, before she married my da.

Julie felt she should say something nice, but people always looked so grim on sepia photographs. Uncle Si drew another one out.

My da, he said.

Julie craned her neck. This was the terrible father. He didn't look so terrible, young and clear-eyed, in uniform. If anything, he looked nicer than the mother.

He was in the army then? she said.

Yes, said Uncle Si. He stroked the picture with a movement of his thumb. His skin was nearly the same colour as the sepia.

Was he in the war? Julie said, prodding for more, but if there was any pain at the memory of his father, Uncle Si didn't show any sign.

He was away a lot of times, even before the war, he said. But when the war came it was very bad. He shook his head.

The next photo was black and white, a young boy in long shorts and a baby in a pram.

Is that you? Julie said, and she took it to get a better look. Is that Mick's father?

She could tell Uncle Si from the shy half-smile. On the back of the photo someone had written 1945.

That was when the war ended, she said. But Uncle Si only looked young on the photo. He couldn't be that old now, she thought.

Were you born before the war? she said, and Uncle Si

said he was born in 1938, but Dan wasn't born until nearly the end.

Not even sixty, Julie thought. She had thought he was nearer seventy, though that would have made Mick's father very old as well.

My da was away, you see, Uncle Si said.

Julie looked at the chubby baby who had grown into another terrible father. You couldn't tell that from the picture, you couldn't tell anything. Julie looked at the little boy who became Uncle Si and the baby who turned into Mick's dad, and wondered how much of what they became was already in them then. There were other pictures of Si and Dan as they got older, Uncle Si took them out of the bundle one at a time, one with their parents at the seaside, the happy family.

Weren't there any other children, Julie asked. Uncle Si shook his head.

There was one who died when he was just a baby, he said. A long time after.

Julie's hands went to her stomach.

That's terrible, she said.

Yes, said Uncle Si. He was baptised though, properly baptised, he said. His name was Jonathan.

The next picture was of Uncle Si in the army with a lot of other men, but Julie picked him out.

You were quite good-looking, she said, and Uncle Si shook his head laughing. Julie found it hard to believe that he'd ever been in the army. Or that he'd never married. She wanted to ask about that, but the next photo was of Dan's wedding. Julie looked closely. Mick was just like his dad.

Mick doesn't get on with his father, does he, she said, and Uncle Si looked very serious.

Too much blood, he said, and Julie wasn't sure what he meant by that. She wanted to make him say more, but he had already gone on to the next photo, a colour one of Uncle Si with his arm around a middle-aged woman who had dyed black hair.

Who's that? Julie said quickly before he could slip it away, but Uncle Si only muttered something about it being a woman he used to know, and he got up, turning away from Julie. He just stood there, shuffling through the photos until it dawned on Julie that he wanted her to go away.

I'll just go and wash up, Uncle Si, she said, and went past him into the kitchen.

Through the window she could see one of the boys from the house opposite, Jordan or Ryan, she never knew which, playing with a stick near Uncle Si's half-open gate. Julie felt cross. She couldn't shut the gate properly because it still wasn't mended and she didn't want another run-in with Dawn. The other day she'd done a load of hand washing because the sink was working now and she didn't fancy the long pull up the hill to the laundry. She'd hung it out, glancing up all the time at the soiled clouds, and each time she looked up she saw Dawn's baby, strapped into its trolley the way it always was, unmoving but not asleep, its eyes followed Julie dully around the yard.

Julie went in, made the beds in her room, swept the kitchen and had a cup of coffee.

The baby was still there.

As Julie carried rubbish out to the wheelie bin she was sure she felt a spot of rain.

It was a shame, she thought. He couldn't do anything strapped up like that, he couldn't crawl around or play. Julie would never treat her baby like that. And as she swept Uncle Si's yard she thought over, in the way she often did, how well she would treat her own baby, nursing him and bathing him (she was sure now it was a boy) and singing songs. She would make up all the nutritious food in the baby books: mashed banana, pureed carrot and apple, toast soldiers and soft-boiled egg. She could see him opening his little mouth for the spoon, just like Jamie. And she would take him out for walks, wrapped up warm. All these thoughts took her through mopping the kitchen floor, a job she hated, then she sat in Uncle Si's room reading the free paper, since he didn't seem to want to talk, while she waited for the floor to dry.

When she went back into the kitchen she could still see the baby.

Julie went to the back-yard gate.

Hello, she said.

The blue dummy moved a little more, but apart from that there was no response. Julie went over.

The baby was dressed warmly, in a blue outdoor suit, but his hands were pink, she noticed, and his eyes watering. She looked around but there was no sign of Dawn. Julie wondered if she ever took him inside, even to feed him or change his nappy. She crouched down.

What's your name? she said. The baby stared back. There was a green stream from one nostril. Julie found a tissue in the sleeve of her coat and wiped his nose carefully. Even this didn't make the baby move. He seemed to be staring very intently at a place just beyond Julie's face. Julie wondered if she might make him laugh. The twins laughed with their mouths wide open, Julie loved to see them. She began pulling faces and playing peek-a-boo, but the baby only stared and Julie began to feel daft. Anyway her legs hurt, so she stood up.

She wondered what to do.

She didn't want to offend Dawn, who looked hard and was friendly with Jude. You could hear their loud, hard laughter late at night sometimes out the back.

If she pulled the trolley into Uncle Si's, Dawn would definitely come looking.

She ought to knock on the door.

Dawn, she could say. I think your baby's getting cold.

She could smile as she said it.

Dawn, she could say. I think it's starting to rain.

It actually was starting to rain, she would have to bring the washing in. She pulled the trolley cover over the baby's head.

It would never be a home here, she thought suddenly. Not when she had to keep worrying about the neighbours.

Cautiously she stepped into Dawn's back yard and peered in at the window. It seemed very quiet.

Julie began to be afraid. What if no one was in? She tapped on the door, still not knowing what to say, then the window.

Just then footsteps crunched over gravel at the entrance to the big yard and Julie hurried out of Dawn's back. It was Dawn, with Jude.

I was just talking to your baby, Julie said.

Jude looked at her with big leering eyes. Dawn, thickset and pale, never looked at anyone. She pushed past Julie now.

His dad's in, she said, though Julie hadn't said a word. He's on nights. Come on, Kane, she said, taking the trolley. Time for din-dins.

Julie hurried back to Uncle Si's, her face hot. Medbh was right, she thought as she took the washing in. You shouldn't ever interfere. You never knew what Dawn or Jude would do. When someone had stuffed a lighted rag through the letterbox of one of the Asian houses some weeks ago Mick had said he was sure it was one of the lads who used to hang around Jude's after Des had gone. Jude knew all about it, he said. Julie was glad she lived with Mick. Nobody messed with Mick.

But now here was another one of Dawn's kids, whacking the gate with his stick. If it wasn't one kid it was another, Julie thought. She went into the yard.

You'd better stop that, she said. That gate's broken. Then she went back in.

Do you want a cup of tea, Uncle Si? she called, but there was no answer. His door was open and timidly Julie poked her head round. He wasn't there. Then she noticed that the front door was open and felt a spasm of annoyance that he'd felt he had to leave without her knowing. She went into his room.

The photos were back in the drawer, Julie picked them up and sat down. She went through them again slowly, as if looking for clues. She looked at the eyes. Sometimes the same pair of eyes looked as if they were smiling, sometimes not, the longer you looked the harder it was to tell. The baby's eyes looked full of knowledge. Julie went through all the photographs and it occurred to her that all these lives were involved in her baby's life; even, somehow, the woman with the dyed black hair. Her baby wasn't just one person at all, all the people in Mick's family and Julie's family, everything they had done and said and suffered, all of it was passed on somehow, to Julie's baby. With all that inside him he would hardly be able to choose how he would be, it was all already there.

Julie put the photos away. She stood up slowly and caught sight of her reflection in the window, the bent head straightening, already old. She stared and it was her mother staring back at her, she had never seen it so clearly before.

Julie went into the kitchen and sat down. At the meetings people often talked about seeing their dead relatives when they meditated, but that wasn't like this, it couldn't be like this, the feeling that she was only waiting to become her dead mother.

There was brick dust on the table. Mick and Darren had been demolishing the outside loo. Brick dust got everywhere; as soon as Julie swept up, a thin layer of it settled again. She worked hard to keep it away from the food, but it was a losing battle.

You've got to keep on top of the little jobs, her mother said, before they get on top of you.

That was her mother, who had done three cleaning jobs as well as her full-time work. And died.

Julie stared, hardly seeing the half-demolished toilet, until she noticed Dawn's little boy again, trying to climb up the bricks.

Stay away from there, she shouted, getting up. That's dangerous.

Dawn's boy climbed back down unsteadily. He stood in the yard staring at Julie.

What? she snapped. She felt suddenly that she couldn't stand to see him any more.

Go on, clear off, she shouted. Go and play in your own yard.

The little boy's face crumpled. Suddenly he was crying, right in front of Julie, his shoulders hunched and his mouth pulled into a big distorted hole. He sobbed as he turned away.

Julie felt stricken, only partly because of Dawn. She hurried after him, trying to remember his name, and caught up with him easily, because he could hardly move for crying.

I'm sorry, she said, and touched his shoulder, which was stiff and shaking. Julie didn't know why he was so upset. Probably he had grown up being told to go away, she thought. She bent down to look at his face, but he wouldn't look at her.

Eh, come on, she said. Suddenly she picked him up, he hardly weighed anything. She took him in and sat down heavily on the kitchen chair nearest the door, and pressed him to her; for once the ampleness of her body didn't seem a burden. Holding him so close, she could feel his sobs shaking her own body, he cried in the heartbroken way of the very young. Julie almost felt like crying herself. She rocked him and was suddenly aware of the slightly aggressive rhythm of her rocking, that it had come from a long way back. It was the way her mother used to rock her, she remembered, only as she got older her mother only used to tell her to go away. Julie clasped Dawn's boy very hard, and prayed that she would love her baby when it came. She didn't think any more that it was automatic, or even natural, if anything it seemed to be a hard thing to do, loving a child, especially if you had to work all the time, and live with a man who wasn't working. Maybe it was just hard anyway. Julie relaxed her grip on the little boy but went on rocking. If she was going to grow into her mother, she thought, she had better get on with it, even if it meant she spent the rest of her life cleaning up other people's dirt. Only she wanted to love her baby.

Dawn's little boy stopped sobbing, only the occasional sob caught his breath. He sucked his thumb as Julie rocked him, she looked down at the small, shaved head and felt pleased that she could comfort him so well.

Later, after she had sent him off with a biscuit, she started to work. There was nothing else to do, nothing that had happened that day had helped her to decide what to do next, so she began stuffing rubbish into a black plastic bag. Maybe she should go to Citizen's Advice, she thought, or even a solicitor, if they still did free sessions. As she carried the bag out the full misery of her situation returned.

Then, as she was carrying the second bag out, it came to her that what she had to do was nothing at all. She had been thinking about Mick and Darren and wondering what would happen to Mick if he stayed with Darren. It wasn't a situation she could imagine going on for ever. As she swept sawdust into the dustpan it occurred to her that while she didn't think any more that Mick would choose Julie if it came to a choice between Julie and Darren, there was more to the choice than that. If Mick stayed with Darren there was nothing for him but drugs and homelessness, whereas, if he stayed with Julie there was the chance of a home, and work and family, a normal life. Once the baby came, the council would give them a home, she thought, and she began to sweep with more energy. Once Mick saw the baby everything would be different, she knew, and she had to stay around long enough for that to happen, long enough to give Mick a chance to do the right thing. It would be the right thing for all of them, Julie, Mick and the baby, even Darren in the end, Julie thought, and the weight of her situation lifted. Because she didn't have to leave now, she didn't have to go through all the hard hassle of trying to move, she had to wait. All she had to do was wait.

Julie knocked on Annie's door, but when Annie opened it she didn't seem too happy.

O it's you, she said, and went back inside. Julie hesitated, then followed her in.

Have I called at a bad time? she said, but Annie only muttered something about there being no such thing as a good time.

I mean about the pram, Julie said timidly.

Annie sank down on the settee. There was the usual clutter of toys and clothes, but Julie could only see one twin, strapped into his high chair, his face covered in soup.

Thomas is asleep upstairs, Annie said. They've started sleeping in shifts now, so I don't get to sleep at all. She dipped a small piece of bread into the soup and gave it to Jamie, who opened his mouth.

He eats well, doesn't he? Julie said.

O he eats, said Annie. And the other one won't eat at all, Jamie eats all his as well. The health visitor said to try to feed Thomas when Jamie's not there but he won't eat, I've given up.

Jamie splashed his soup with his open hand and beamed at Julie.

Don't, Annie said, wiping it up, but Jamie went on beaming and splashing. Julie laughed.

You're a cheeky one, she said. Annie didn't smile. She just went on mopping up the soup. Julie sat down heavily.

What's the matter? she said.

Annie didn't say anything, then she said,

Chris is going away. Only for two weeks, she added when she saw Julie's face. He's got to take a load abroad. So I'll be on my own with these two.

Julie felt as though she should offer to help.

Is there anything I can do? she said.

Annie smiled wanly.

Thanks, she said. I'll manage. I had to last year when he went away, the lucky bastard.

When does he go? Julie said, and Annie said, Sunday. Then she was silent a while and Julie thought about Annie being stuck in with the twins, and about being stuck in herself with Mick and Darren and Uncle Si.

Maybe we should go out, she said. Before he goes, I mean.

Annie wiped Jamie's face and hands with a wet wipe and lifted him out. She didn't say anything.

Alison wanted to go out, Julie said, remembering at the same time that this might mean she would have to go round to Alison's to arrange things, and Alan would probably be there. Maybe you could come to the meeting while Chris is away, she said, but Annie shook her head.

Who'd babysit these two, she said.

Upstairs Thomas wailed and Annie went to get him. Jamie started to follow but Julie picked him up and held him for a moment, feeling how solid and soft he was, smelling the baby smell and the smell of soup. When Annie came down Julie said,

I could do with going out myself, and Annie sighed and said, I suppose so, and went into the kitchen to make more soup.

Do you want to go round to Alison's? Julie called through, but Annie said she couldn't, she was waiting in for the telly man.

Where did Alison want to go? she said, carrying Thomas' dinner through.

Karaoke, Julie said. They grinned at one another. Well, it might be a laugh, Julie said. She couldn't think of anywhere else they might go. I just want a night out, she said. It occurred to her as she said it that she wanted it quite badly, she was sick of staying in, and soon she would have to stay in all the time.

Well, I don't mind, Annie said. She lifted Thomas into

the high chair but he kicked and screamed. This always happens, she said. It's because Jamie's here.

Julie took Jamie into the back yard where there were some toys and tried to distract him there until he cried for his mum, then Annie came out and Julie went in to feed Thomas, who was so surprised that he forgot to cry and ate some of the soup. Between them they managed pretty well, until about half the soup was gone, then Thomas refused the rest. Annie came back in with Jamie.

Well, that's better than usual, she said.

They put the twins in the back yard again while Annie washed up and made a cup of tea, and they agreed that Julie should go round to Alison's and sort things out. Then they took it in turns to chase the twins and drink the tea, and Julie left. It was only when she was nearly at Alison's that she remembered she'd forgotten about the pram.

Strange music pulsed behind Alison's door as Julie knocked on it, feeling qualms already. Even before Alan answered she could see it was him through the glass on the door.

Is Alison in? she said.

Alan stared at her impassively until she didn't know what to think. Then he stepped back, holding the door open for her. After a moment Julie went in.

Alison, she called over the music. There was no reply, and no sound from Sadie either.

The light of my life, Alan said in a deep voice, has been eclipsed. He said it in such a way that Julie didn't know if Alison was out, asleep or murdered.

What do you mean? she said, rounding on him, and she thought she could see a glint of amusement in his eyes, but all he said was,

Tea? waving his arm towards the kitchen.

Julie followed him in, wondering whether or not to just leave.

Pots littered the work surfaces and an LP jacket lay half covered in beansprouts, the Velvet Underground. Behind this, next to the radio, there was a microwave. Julie hadn't known Alison had a microwave. Inside it a little dish turned round slowly, and on it there were crystals like large crystals of salt. There was a beeping noise and Alan switched it off, then gazed intently at Julie.

The spirit of the valley never dies, he said.

That is called the mysterious female.
The gateway of the mysterious female
Is called the root of heaven and earth.

Fortunately he didn't seem to expect an answer.

That is from the *Tao Te Ching*, he said. Are you at all interested in Eastern mysticism? I'm making spring rolls, he went on without waiting for Julie to say anything. I always find the cuisine of the East calls to mind its great philosophies. Can you understand that? he said, and he swivelled his great eyes round to her again.

Julie decided she was definitely going, but then the front door opened.

Ah, said Alan. The mysterious female, and he went into the hall.

She's gone off at last, said Alison's voice. She screamed all the way to the Jobcentre.

You have a visitor, my angel, said Alan, and Alison looked up at Julie.

O hi, she said, and seemed quite pleased to see her.

I'll have to be getting on, Julie said, but Alison said she could have a cup of tea, surely. Put the kettle on, she said to Alan.

It is already done, said Alan, and Alison and Julie went into the lounge.

Alison wanted to complain about Sadie.

She's always ill, she said. She threw up everything I gave her last week, and it was all brown, you know – that's not right from just milk, is it? I took her to hospital one night, I'd had enough, but they made us wait four hours in Casualty – four hours – and then they said it was a virus and there was nothing they could do. And this stupid cow asked me what I'd been feeding her. Milk, I said – what did she think I'd been feeding her – steak? So then she said, had I thought of changing the brand, so I said that since I was feeding her myself that might be a bit hard. So then she said I could bring her in next week if I liked and they'd check her over again. Don't bother, I said. Just don't bloody bother, and Alison sprawled on the settee in a depressed kind of way. I'm not going back there again, she said.

Julie sat on the edge of the big chair. If she sank back into chairs these days she had trouble getting up.

Maybe Alan could take her, she said.

Alan won't go near hospitals, said Alison. I told you.

Alan came in carrying a tray with tea and a big plateful of steaming spring rolls.

O Alan, you are a love, said Alison.

May I offer you a small delicacy? Alan said to Julie.

You'll have to try one, Alison said, her mouth already full. These are fantastic.

Julie realised she was very hungry.

Well, just one, please, she said, and Alan put two on her plate. Then there was an agonised wail from the pram. Alison sank back in a position of hopeless despair.

Not again, she said. Alan raised a calming hand.

I will go, beloved, he said and left. Alison looked quite emotional.

O you know, he takes really good care of us, she said. I don't know what I'd do without him.

Julie looked at Alison's face, a washed-out pale. She didn't wear her nice clothes any more, just jeans and a sweater.

Did you say you've been to the Jobcentre? she said, and Alison nodded.

I can't stand being in all the time, she said. And we could do with the money. Alan likes being in, and cooking. He doesn't even mind babysitting. So we might as well give it a try. But there was nothing in apart from carpet cleaning, and you had to have experience for that. I'm thinking of trying the biscuit factory again, she said. Just in case.

Julie finished her roll. It was good, spicy and moist. She couldn't resist starting the second one, and she bit into it and told Alison what she and Annie had said about going out. Alison pounced on the idea.

That place near the park, she said, they're doing karaoke evenings on Saturdays. I've fancied going for ages, only it's not Alan's scene.

Julie wasn't sure it was her scene either, but she didn't have any other suggestion so they agreed to meet up Saturday night at eight.

Alan came in with Sadie writhing in his arms. He stood in the doorway in his pink nightie, rocking her and looking ridiculous, Julie thought. He held her absently with one big hand and Sadie couldn't seem to get comfortable at all. Julie itched to take her off him. Her hair hadn't changed colour yet, she noticed. Sadie knew she was being watched. She drew her legs up and squalled.

Here we go, Alison said, and Julie was struck by the sunken look in her eyes. She stood up.

I'll have to go, she said. I'll see you Saturday, and Alison nodded without looking up.

Julie felt bad about leaving but she didn't know what she could do. She didn't want to do anything, she didn't want to get involved. It was Alison's fault, she thought, going down the stairs, for getting mixed up with someone like Alan, nothing had gone right for her since she met him. Outside the rain was starting again and Julie pulled up her collar. If you made mistakes you had to learn from them, she thought.

Julie leant against the bus stop. Only a little way up the hill she had been overcome by breathlessness, she felt as though she was going to fall down. She wished she knew Sylvia's phone number to ask for a lift.

Really she needed to sit down.

By Julie's reckoning she had less than seven weeks left, but even now she couldn't walk very far. She would be helpless and stuck inside by the end, she thought, and part of her wished very much that it was all over. She couldn't remember what not being pregnant felt like.

Julie gazed down the road into the space where the bus should come. She had been waiting a long time. She should have checked before she came out but she had been desperate to leave. All Mick's friends were back again, for a while they hadn't been there and Mick had been out, but now they were all back again, Tony and Joe and Les and two others Julie didn't know, all talking about the men who had been sleeping behind the railed windows in Chinatown, they packed them with cardboard and slept behind them regularly, only last night this gang had come along and torched the cardboard. They had talked about this for a long time, then finally the talk had shifted, to Mick's hands, which kept bleeding from the work, and Joe had told him to piss on them.

All at once Julie was sick of all the talk. She had put the kettle down in the middle of brewing up and left.

An old couple joined Julie at the stop.

Is the bus due? the old woman said.

I don't know, said Julie, and all three of them stared down the road.

Then four lads came up to the shelter. Julie and the old couple stood closer together. One of the lads thumped the glass of the shelter.

This is that reinforced stuff on the adverts, he said. You can't break it.

I bet you can.

You fucking can't.

You're not supposed to be able to, even with a hammer.

I could break it easy.

Go on then.

I bet you could break it with a really hard kick, and he kicked it, really hard.

Julie and the old couple moved a little way away from the shelter. The first lad jumped up and swung from the shelter roof. He drove his feet into the panel at the back. The glass shook but didn't shatter. Then they were all up, swinging and kicking, driving their boots into the glass, which started to splinter.

Julie didn't know what to do. The lads didn't care that people were standing right next to them, and cars were passing, it was as if they couldn't see anyone outside themselves. And no one tried to stop them.

These were the people Mick was trying to save, she thought.

When the glass finally shattered over the pavement and road the gang shouted, *Yes!* and went on their way down the hill.

Julie and the old couple moved further apart. Julie felt foolish and ashamed. The old woman looked at her and the old man shook his head, they were old, she was pregnant, but Julie still felt bad.

Finally the bus arrived. Julie sat down thankfully. She watched the windows of the houses she passed, a woman ironing, a toddler on a little bike, an old man watching TV. It was as if the scenes in lighted windows never really changed. Julie wasn't comforted by this, she still felt disturbed. She thought about the vandals at the bus stop and how Mick would say it was all the system. If he had been there he would probably have tried talking to them about Organised Subversion as opposed to Random Violence, that was one of the discussions she had listened to in the kitchen. He would probably have tried to recruit them, she knew people just like them were in the Party already. Then her mind jumped to the new materials in the kitchen, and suddenly it focused on to one terrible thought. She knew that Mick used stuff that was knocked off, though he never said. He had mates who stole, who broke into people's vans or even their homes. What if the house they burgled was Eric's, or Sylvia's? She had never thought this before, but now she could see how likely it was, the houses at the top of The Rise were always being burgled. She would be at the meeting one night and Sylvia or Esther would say they had been broken into, and Julie would say nothing but she would know. All the way up the hill Julie worried and worried about this and nearly missed her stop.

It's like being given a whole new lease of life, Eric said. You come out of it a different person.

Julie slunk quietly to the nearest empty chair. She seemed to have missed the opening meditation, but no one took any notice. She looked quickly round the room. Josepha and Esther sat together. Jean was there, she smiled quickly at Julie as she sat down, and Sylvia of course, and a woman Julie didn't know. Pierre wasn't there, it was only Eric. Julie tried to relax, but she could only wait for someone to start talking about burglaries.

But how does it work, this rebirthing? said Jean.

Well, basically, Eric said, it's regression. Medbh takes you all the way back through your life to birth, all your memories come back from your childhood, things you thought you'd forgotten, it all comes flooding back.

Well, that sounds terrible, Jean said. I can remember my childhood quite well enough thank you, and Julie felt the same way.

Ah, but can you? Eric said. We all think we remember, but what is memory, eh? Part fantasy, part fact distorted by guilt and fear – no two people remember the same event the same way, and yet we allow ourselves to be crippled by what we think we remember. But, he leant forwards, this is more than memory. The full experience comes back, and once it's back, and fully taken in – bingo – it's gone. He sat back. It's the most liberating experience, he said.

Julie thought about Brian.

And did you say Medbh's running a day on it? Sylvia said.

Twenty-ninth of April, said Eric. But I'd get my name down now if I were you, there'll be a queue.

How much will it be? said Josepha.

Two hundred for the day and bring a contribution to food, said Eric. Even Sylvia gasped.

I know, I know, Eric said, raising a hand. But what price liberation, eh? I tell you, you're a different person afterwards. Free from the weight of the past. And Medbh works tremendously hard, it's a terrific strain.

People nodded their heads, they could see that it would be.

But not everyone's going to be rebirthed, are they? Josepha said. She won't be able to do everyone.

No, but she'll be explaining it all in detail, Eric said. And giving demonstrations. Apparently it's one of the things she gets asked about most at the meetings, so she's decided to explain it all to everyone in the one session. And anyone who wants to can volunteer, but it's powerful stuff. Blood, sweat and all the rest of it. Not for the faint-hearted.

And that's just the lunch, Jean said.

Everyone laughed.

No, seriously, Eric said, if you want to go, if you're thinking about being a volunteer, I'd get onto Medbh right away. It's a marvellous opportunity. I'm a living testimony to that.

But if it costs that much for the day, Esther said, nodding her head, how much would it cost for the actual thing – you know, to make an appointment?

Eric was vague. I think it varies, he said. You'll have to ask her.

You mean she does discounts, said Jean.

Well, I think she takes some account of income and circumstances, yes, Eric said. But whatever the charge I think you'll find it well worthwhile. I mean, before I was done, so to speak, I wasn't really getting anywhere with the meditation, I was held back by all this stuff from the past. But afterwards, well, I came on leaps and bounds. Anyway, he said, I think it's time for the next meditation.

Everyone stopped talking and sat with their eyes closed while Eric talked about being a baby in the womb. Julie tried to listen, she tried to focus it all on her baby, but all she could think about was the rebirthing, and how she'd never be able to afford it. She'd wondered why she wasn't getting anywhere with the meditation. She couldn't go on that day anyway, she told herself, the baby was due around then. But she knew she'd never be able to afford any of the other days Medbh ran.

Afterwards Josepha sat talking to Eric and the new woman moved forwards to listen. She had silky, cream-coloured hair and a wide mouth but almost no lips. Josepha was asking Eric all about the regression, and the new woman took out her diary and started writing in it. Sylvia smiled at her.

Are you thinking of going? she said.

O well, I'd like to, said the new woman. But I'm not sure I can get my children minded that day. I do have a child minder but she's always busy. And I'm too frightened of her to ask.

Everyone laughed.

I'm frightened of my child minder, Esther said unexpectedly. Well, I am, she said, looking round at everyone.

If I'm five minutes late, the new woman said, she's there at the door, and both Anna and Kirsten have their coats and hats on, and she always mentions her contract.

Mine tells me when I can bring them, Esther said. She's not very accommodating at all.

Well, I had a nanny when the children were young, Sylvia said. A marvellous woman, I couldn't have coped without her. But Suzanne has a child minder who frightens her to death. She says child minders come just after serial killers on the scale of terror.

Everyone was off, talking about child minders and how

guilty they made you feel. Julie stopped listening, she wasn't ever likely to have one.

Then Jean said, I wonder what Medbh would say about it, and there was a critical tone in her voice Julie hadn't heard before.

The new woman was called Suzi. Julie watched her laughing and talking to Esther on the way out, as if she'd been going to the meetings for months, whereas she, Julie, had never yet talked to Esther. But as she went into the garden Sylvia touched her arm.

Lift? she said.

Julie felt embarrassed, being offered lifts all the time.

I've been thinking, Sylvia said, taking Julie's arm. There's no reason why I shouldn't give you a lift up here as well as back.

O no, Julie said.

It's hardly out of my way at all, said Sylvia, steering her along. And I don't like the thought of you being out in the dark. And it'll get harder, you know, she said, opening her car door. It can be hard just moving from one room to another at the end of pregnancy, never mind getting up that hill. I can meet you on the main road, she said, as Julie opened her mouth, and she looked at Julie very kindly until Julie felt quite uncomfortable, and all at once she was struck by the thought that Sylvia must have been talking to Jean. That was a horrible thought, and Julie felt quite sick as she got in the car. Everyone would be feeling sorry for her now, she thought, and all the way home she couldn't think about anything else. She could hardly look at them as she got out of the car and hurried away along the dark road to Uncle Si's.

Julie stood in front of the health-food counter at Boots, looking at bran grains and dried fruit. There was also a bottle called Lactulose. Works gently to improve normal bowel activity, the label read. There weren't many laxatives you could take in pregnancy, so after some hesitation Julie loaded her basket with one of everything and took it to the checkout, calculating the extra expense on the way.

The man in front of Julie turned round and smiled.

Hello, he said. Julie held the basket partly behind her.

Gerry, she said, I didn't realise it was you. She laughed a bit and Gerry smiled again. He had a nice smile, Julie thought. She hoped he wouldn't notice what she was buying. Then she noticed that he was buying Odor-Eaters and haemorrhoid cream. He took these out at the till, not seeming very self-conscious at all.

I haven't seen you at the meetings, Julie managed to say.

Gerry picked up the Odor-Eaters.

No, he said. I don't think it's my kind of thing. He stood to one side while Julie checked her items through. She shovelled them quickly into a carrier.

Don't you like the meditation? she said.

No – well – I mean – it's not that I don't *like* it. I just don't seem to be getting anywhere with it. You know what I mean?

Julie moved away from the till.

And they're a funny lot, aren't they.

Julie looked blank.

I mean Eric and that –, Gerry shook his head. They're all a bit loose in the screw department, don't you think? I think so anyway.

Julie didn't know what to say. She thought they were all very nice.

Anyway, they're not my types, Gerry said. I went for a while after Shirl died to see if it'd help me come off the tranquillisers. And it did help a bit. But nothing really helps, if you see what I mean. Time might help, and getting on with things, but that's about it.

That was what Jean said, Julie thought.

And as for all that about a man losing his wife and banging pots and singing, that's neither use nor ornament.

I thought to myself then, there's someone who hasn't a clue.

So you won't be coming back then, Julie said, and in spite of herself she sounded a bit offended.

I don't think so. No. But that's not to say that it wouldn't work for some people. Some people might get a lot out of it, I suppose, but it never seemed to do much for me.

I see, Julie said. She could tell that she sounded as if she didn't know what he was talking about, but really she knew just what he meant. Everything he said made her feel pangs of fear, that Mind-Power might never work for her either. She considered telling him about Margery, and what Medbh had said to her, but she didn't want to get into a big discussion.

Anyway, how are you? Gerry said, and Julie mumbled on.

Well, he said, that's nice, and they stared at one another for a bit until Julie said she'd have to be going. Gerry opened the door for her and said he'd see her round, and Julie was stuck for something to say until she remembered what Jean had said to her.

Take care, she said.

She made her way through the precinct, it was nearly empty today except for all the people asking for money, and for once Julie hardly saw them at all. She kept thinking about what Gerry said, and how, if Mind-Power didn't work for her either, she didn't know what would. Then she thought about Jean and the others and how much she liked them, and how she would never fit in. And she couldn't afford any of the special courses. But then everyone agreed you didn't need money to meditate, not just to do the basic practice. And that was the important thing, doing the practice every day. And Julie had to admit she hadn't done that. She couldn't give up until she'd really given it a try.

As Julie stepped over the buckets in the yard she heard music coming from the bedroom. That meant Mick and Darren were in. She pushed open the door and the music got louder. If she really decided to do it nothing could stop her, that's what Eric said, you went along the road so far, not doing much, then suddenly you knew that it was what you wanted and there was no more messing around. You did it seriously, twice a day no matter what, and the real changes started. You couldn't expect much until then.

Riders on the storm, throbbed the music. Julie knocked on Darren's door.

Could you turn that down a bit? she called. She went into her room and sat on her mattress, pulling her coat around her because she really felt the cold when she sat still. She tried to make her body less tense, starting with her feet as she'd been taught. This is what she should have been doing every day. She had meant to do it every day but other things always got in the way – she let them get in the way. Julie straightened her spine and started to think about her breathing, breathing out more deeply than she was breathing in.

Breathe in, one, two; out, three, four, five.

All the time she was willing something to happen, and she tried to let go of that, it wouldn't work if you wanted it to. She tried to clear her mind of everything but the breathing.

Behind her she could sense someone watching. She opened her eyes and Mick was there, leaning against the doorway. He shook his head as she looked at him.

Haven't you given that up yet? he said.

I'm not giving it up, said Julie.

Mick walked over to his mattress and sat on it.

What do you think you'll get out of it? he said. No, tell me, I'm serious.

Julie wasn't going to be thrown by Mick.

Well, she said, what do you think you'll get out of the Party?

Change, Mick said. Change for the better.

Right, Julie said.

Mick thought.

Yeah, but look, he said, leaning forwards. Just think for a minute. How is sitting on your arse with your eyes closed going to change anything?

Well, Julie said, how is what you do going to change anything?

Mick wouldn't be put off.

Well, I'm getting out, aren't I? Speaking to people, trying to make them see.

Yes? Julie said.

Mick got annoyed.

Well, if you sit on your arse from now until it drops off nothing's going to happen, is it? I mean, tell me – what's going to happen?

Julie had to think for a bit.

I might change, she said.

How?

Julie remembered the different things that had been said at the meetings.

Well, if I'm calmer, she said, I might see things more clearly. And if I see things more clearly I might do things differently. And then things around me might change.

Mick said nothing to this so she went on.

And it's about potential. Medbh says we're all only using a tenth of our potential, and she stopped, remembering that he hated her to say what Medbh said. Already he looked scornful, as if he would say something, but then he changed his mind.

We don't use our potential because of the society we live in, he said. And he explained to her then seriously, as he never had before, about capital, and how, if your labour was taken off you so that you worked for money you couldn't fulfil yourself, you were pitted against the next person and the value of what you did was nothing.

I mean, money doesn't mean anything on its own, does it? How can you say that a piece of work is worth a coin, or a sackful of coins? It's not the same thing. Money doesn't mean anything, it's just a way of making divisions in society, and keeping the powerful in power.

Julie thought she understood, but she said,

You're not going to change all that, are you?

Yeah, of course we are, Mick said. If you want to change the world you've got to start with people.

Haven't you got to start with yourself? Julie said.

You've got to see the way things are, yeah, and then you've got to make other people see.

And then what?

Then you guide them – towards revolution.

Julie felt quite calm. At one time she would never have argued with Mick like this. She said,

But if you have a revolution, and the people haven't really changed, you can't make a different world.

Mick shook his head.

No. That's what I'm trying to tell you. You change society and then people change, not the other way round. You sitting on that bed isn't going to change anything.

It'll change me, Julie said.

You don't believe that. And even if you do – what then? If you change and the rest of the world stays the same, that makes you a nutter.

Julie shook her head.

If I change and what I say and do changes, she said, that affects other people. And that means the world around me changes. And if enough people change then their worlds change as well, and it makes a difference.

Mick shook his head in disbelief.

You don't believe that, he said.

Julie stared at him.

I do, she said very firmly.

Mick closed his eyes and rubbed his forehead. He let out his breath in a long gust. Julie waited. She wasn't going to give in. But as she watched him preparing to reply she felt something else, the urge to go over to him and rest her head on his stained jacket and say Mick, Mick, and make him talk about something that wasn't politics. But the urge that she had had before, many times, to agree with him, to try to believe what he believed just so that he would look at her and like her, and they could talk, had entirely gone.

Mick opened his eyes and changed tack.

What do they do anyway, he said, your Mindblown friends?

Julie thought he meant at the meetings. She said,

What do you mean?

For a living, Mick said. Don't any of them work?

Julie thought. She didn't think any of them did work, at least, she couldn't think what they did.

So what do they do for money then? Mick said.

Well, Jean's ill, Julie said. I think she gets Invalidity, and she paused. Sylvia worked for charity, but she knew better than to mention that. She didn't know if she was paid for it, or what Eric and Josepha or Esther did for a living.

Mick was looking at her triumphantly.

So none of them work then.

None of your friends work, said Julie.

Correction, Mick said. All my friends work. They're just not given a living.

Julie wasn't getting into this.

It doesn't matter, she said.

That set Mick off. Of course it mattered. If you didn't work you weren't a part of society, you didn't belong in the real world, you were living in fairyland, and people in fairyland were hardly qualified to tell everyone else how to live . . .

Julie waited for him to finish, she wasn't shaken at all.

That's your opinion, she said. It isn't mine. And she turned her back on him and closed her eyes. She had never done such a thing before and she could feel him staring at her back, wondering whether to start again. Julie made herself concentrate on her breathing, and after a moment or two he left.

Julie felt triumphant. It showed what you could do if you

stayed with the meditation. She was glad she'd had the argument with Mick, glad she'd shown herself to be strong for once, and glad because, after arguing it all out, her doubts had gone away. She knew she wanted to keep going to the meetings even, somehow, after the baby was born. Because if she lost touch with the people there she would only have Uncle Si's, and Julie didn't want to belong to the world of Uncle Si and Mick and all Mick's friends. She wanted to belong to the world Sylvia and Josepha and even Jean lived in, whatever Gerry or Mick said about it, and if she couldn't belong she would stay in touch with it somehow. It was the only way she could feel any hope.

Memory, the man on the platform sang, all alone in the moonlight.

Sing something cheerful, Alison muttered. Everyone was a bit cast down, Annie because she was about to be left on her own with the twins, and Alison because she'd had a row with Alan, so far as you could ever row with Alan, she said. The house was always full of lowlife. And Sadie was ill again. Julie hadn't felt cheerful for a long time. She was drinking lager in spite of being pregnant. She didn't mind the singing since she wasn't in the mood to talk. Smoke stung her eyes. For a moment she imagined herself getting up through all the smoke and singing her favourite song, 'I Will Always Love You'. She would stand in front of everyone and the song would flow out of her in a low, pure voice. And everyone would listen as Julie gave it everything she'd got, just like Whitney Houston, and Mick would be sitting there in the audience, amazed.

Alison was still complaining about all the people in their flat.

Mick's always there as well, she said.

Julie snapped out of her dream.

Mick, she said.

Every other night, said Alison, and she went on to tell

them how she'd thrown everyone out last night she was so sick of them being there.

Julie didn't want to let on that she hadn't known Mick had been going to Alison's, but in the end she had to say something.

What's Mick doing there? she said. Alison shrugged.

You'd better ask him, she said. Julie sat back in her seat. She knew Mick went to see Alan sometimes, she'd asked him about it the other week.

What do you want to see him for? she'd said.

Mick was reading the *Socialist Worker*.

Who? he'd said.

Alan, said Julie.

Mick looked as if he might tell her to mind her own, then he said,

Recruiting, and disappeared behind the paper again.

This made no sense to Julie.

Recruiting, she said. To the Party? Mick lowered the paper again.

Why not? he said.

Alan? said Julie.

Well, why not Alan? said Mick, as if Julie was stupid, and she snapped,

Well, why would you want a great fat fairy like Alan in the Party? and Mick had laughed. Julie had never made him laugh before and the surprise of it made her forget to be cross and laugh with him. They had been getting on better recently, for some mysterious reason, ever since Julie had stood up to him about meditation, in fact. Julie had even started telling him about the little things that happened in her day and he sat and listened with a willed patience. But that was when he was in. He was out a lot. At Alison's.

He fancies Alison, she thought, in spite of everything Jean had said, and the pain she felt was very pure.

Annie waved her hand in front of Julie. Lost to the world, she said, but Julie didn't smile.

On the platform two women sang to 'Without You' by Mariah Carey.

This needs livening up, said Alison.

Annie yawned. I'm not up to this any more, she said.

It's this place, said Alison. It's a wonder we aren't all asleep.

Maybe I'll get an early night, Annie said.

O no, you can't go yet, said Alison. I want a go.

You don't.

I do, said Alison. Why do you think I wanted to come here? And when 'Without You' stopped she ran to the karaoke machine. Annie laughed as Alison started dancing to Take That. Julie remembered that Alison always used to like Take That at the biscuit factory. Before she met Alan.

Annie made a great show of being embarrassed as Alison started to sing, but Julie couldn't stop watching her. She was wearing the same clothes she wore at the biscuit factory do: shiny leggings and the off-the-shoulder T-shirt. Her hair hung nearly to her waist. Anyone would fancy her, Julie thought.

The track ended and Alison came back to her seat.

That feels better, she said, and she downed her rum and Coke in one go.

So can we all go home now, Annie said.

You're a right miserable lot, you, said Alison. Look, I tell you what. Why don't you both come back to my place.

Annie said she was definitely going to bed, and Alison told her she'd only be up all night anyway, but Annie wouldn't be budged. Julie said she'd have to get back too, and she stood up with Annie.

Party poopers or what, said Alison and she caught Julie's arm. Come back with me, she said. She was very determined. And Julie suddenly felt that she wanted to know why Mick was going round there so much. She might even meet Mick, she thought, and her heart gave a hollow thump. She allowed Alison to pull her along, away from Annie who waved as she turned the corner. Alison didn't seem to care about Annie now that someone was coming back. She was full of a hard, brittle energy, she didn't even try to talk until they were nearly at the flat. All the lights were on.

That's Alan, she said, with his mates, and there was a savage edge to her voice.

They trudged up the stairs in silence and Julie had to stop twice. Then they met people coming down, a walleyed man in a donkey jacket and a bald boy, younger than Julie, with a pin through his nose and a tattooed face. They stood aside to let Julie and Alison pass.

Alan's circus freaks, Alison said, quite loudly as they passed. At least they're going.

Alan himself stood framed in the doorway, in a long white shirt with a ruffle this time. Julie thought he looked more of a circus freak than either of the other two.

My pinnacle of light, he said to Alison as she reached the landing, but Julie thought there was an edge to his voice too, and he disappeared before they got to the door. Sadie wailed from the bedroom.

O God, is she still at it? Alison said.

All night long, my beloved, said Alan from the kitchen. All night long.

Alison went into the bedroom.

Christ, Alan! she shouted. She's soaking wet. Couldn't you even change her?

No, I could not, my dove, Alan said. He came out of the kitchen and fixed Julie with his prominent eyes.

Are you here for a specific reason? he said. Julie couldn't think what he meant.

Can't you see she's pregnant? Alison said, coming out of the bedroom with Sadie.

Indeed, said Alan, and went back into the kitchen. Julie wanted to ask what they were talking about, but Sadie cried and started to puke.

Look at her, Alison said. All the bed's wet. She held Sadie out to Julie and without wanting to Julie took hold of the light, squirming body. Sadie banged her head into Julie's shoulder and puked again.

Alison, Julie called. I think she's been sick.

She's always like that, Alison called back from the bedroom.

Julie took Sadie into the lounge, sat down and laid her on her knee. Sadie quietened down, chewing her hands and gazing round the room with bright, unfocused eyes as Julie dabbed at her coat with a tissue. Her scrimpy hair was as dark as ever, the blue eyes had deepened to a definite brown. Julie wondered if she had grown at all.

Alison came in with a changing mat and nappy, took Sadie and began peeling the damp layers off. Julie passed her things as she needed them.

That rash looks bad, she said.

Most of Sadie's body was covered in a rash, but between her legs it was actually bleeding.

There's cream in the bedroom, Alison said, and Julie went to look for it.

She had never known before how much babies suffered in such ordinary, everyday ways, rashes and colic, sticky eyes and wet, uncomfortable clothes. She had only known about the kinds of suffering that got on the news.

Next to the cot in Alison's bedroom there was a cupboard with a basket on top. Julie rummaged through the basket and found three tubes of cream, but she didn't know which was which.

There are three tubes here, she said returning, then she stopped as she saw Alan. He had draped himself round Alison as she wiped Sadie clean and was nuzzling her neck. Julie wouldn't look at them, but Alan spread his arms wide.

Sustenance, he said, but Julie had decided to go. She picked up her coat.

I saw your *amour* today, Alan said, with his ever-present companion.

Julie turned back. Alan licked the fingers Alison was winding in his hair.

He has increased his order, which is gratifying, but I did warn him of the quintessential – angel?

For Alison was burying her face in his hair and murmuring in a warning way.

Julie saw everything with a sudden, freakish clarity, she didn't know how she hadn't seen it before.

Alison knew, she thought, and she felt her face going blood-red.

Then suddenly Sadie lunged and fell, right off the changing mat onto the floor.

I'll get her, Alan cried, and he picked her up tenderly and jiggled her, but she only screamed.

O what's wrong with her? Alison cried, but Alan only jiggled Sadie harder, then began to shift her from one hand to the other. He was almost juggling her, and Sadie started to squeal instead of screaming.

There my baby maiden, Alan cried and Alison laughed. Julie prepared to go now that the crisis was over. She couldn't ever be friends with Alison again, she thought as she buttoned her coat and Alan swung Sadie in a long arc almost to the ceiling.

She would never come back, Julie thought, picking up her bag. She would leave the flat and that would be it. She never wanted to see Alison again.

Alan, Alison screamed.

Julie saw Sadie tumble from the high point of the arc, smack her head on a shelf corner and hit the floor. She made no sound at all.

Shit, Alan! Shit, Alan! Alison screamed, and they both crouched over Sadie. Julie stood absolutely still, then she knew what to do.

I'll call an ambulance, she said, and hurried out, down the steps to the phone, as fast as she could for the terrible racing of her heart.

When she got back, Alison was clutching Sadie and

crying. Sadie was very white and there was a trickle of blood from one ear.

Look at her, she's not moving, Alison sobbed. Julie moved over slowly and looked. She felt very calm.

The ambulance'll be here soon, she said. Alan moved swiftly.

In that case I had better – er – beg to be excused, he said, and he whipped the ashtray out of the way, and returned with a room spray and a pair of loose trousers over his nightdress. Julie watched him coldly. She considered telling the ambulance man what he'd done.

Alison rocked Sadie.

Sadie, Sadie, she moaned, then she looked up. We'd best pack some stuff for the hospital, she said. Alan looked grave.

I can hardly bear it, he said, but I cannot accompany you. I'm expecting guests, remember, later in the night.

Alison looked as if she couldn't believe what she was hearing. Her face whitened.

You fucking will, she said. You fucking, fucking will.

Alan started to explain that he would be happy to come later, when there was a loud knocking at the door.

That was quick, Julie thought, opening it.

Ambulance here, the man said, and he came in with a woman behind him. They looked at Sadie and asked what had happened.

Alan dropped her, Alison said, looking at him with hatred.

Alan raised his eyes to heaven and spread his arms helplessly but said nothing.

Are you both coming in the ambulance? the man said.

Yes, we are, said Alison, and Alan started to say he couldn't, he had to stay.

I'm afraid that won't be possible, the ambulance woman said. You might have to answer some questions, and she looked at Julie. Julie started to say she had to go and Alison looked up.

Julie didn't see anything, she said, unexpectedly. She was on the loo.

All right then, let's get going, said the ambulance man, after checking Sadie's limbs, and the woman held the door open. Alison went through holding Sadie, then Alan, wrapping himself in a coloured cape, and Julie following after. They all followed one another into the night, and as Julie turned to go home, the last she saw was Alison's white face disappearing into the ambulance.

Julie stayed in her room. If Mick came in she didn't say anything and neither did he. She sat on her mattress and sometimes she lay on it, and sometimes she stood by the window and saw how thickly the plants were growing by the railway. It was almost spring, and she could feel the baby kicking most of the morning, then there was a long quiet spell, then it started again in the early evening. Julie stood by the window and watched trains carrying people backwards and forwards, a long way away. At night they were empty, with long chains of lighted windows. When the baby was born, she thought, they would stand there together and watch the trains. Then she thought she was mad, she couldn't live here with the baby, and she walked up and down a bit, scrubbing the fingers of one hand up and down between the fingers of the other. Because she couldn't stay here, but there was nowhere for her to go.

Julie knocked on Brian's door.

Well, well, well, he said, and Julie heard the echo of her mother's voice.

Three holes in the ground with water in them, it said.

I can see you've been busy, Brian said, almost at the same time, and he looked her up and down.

Julie felt bad, bending and swaying slightly. There wasn't anything to lean on.

You'd best come in, Brian said, and she followed him along the smoky passage.

Brian sat down and sucked on his cigarette.

Well, he said again, what can I do for you?

Julie felt worse inside. The place stank with almost the smell of her dream and there wasn't a clear space to sit in. She perched on the edge of the settee as Aunty Clare had done all those months ago and wondered why she had ever come. Brian flicked his cigarette ash onto the carpet.

Lacks a woman's touch, he said, and he looked at her with a look that brought everything back, all the rage.

I've come because I never heard anything after the funeral –, she said, and Brian sat back with triumph in his eyes, but Julie went on, – if my mam left anything, I mean, and she hated herself for faltering over the words.

O yes, Brian said, I thought that might have something to do with it. And he just went on looking at her, he wasn't going to help her out at all. Julie looked down, but then the memory of all the other times he had been like that with her came back with a flash of hatred. She stared at him and Brian said,

Didn't your Aunty Clare tell you anything?

Yes, Julie said. She told me there wasn't a will.

And that this house is mine – not your mother's – it's my name on this house.

Yes.

So what else did she tell you? Brian said, leaning forwards, Julie could smell his breath. She told you your mother owned nowt and had nowt to give – I bet she didn't tell you why.

Julie waited.

She didn't tell you that your mother had nothing when she came to me – except you. Because when her mother died she cut Christine right out of her will. She never liked her coming here, you see, leaving your dad. Never mind that he was knocking her about and you too for that matter – never mind about him having his own bit of stuff on the side – Christine should never have left. Holiness of matrimony and all that. Stand by your man. Eight months after your mother came here to live with me her mother died, but she'd changed her will. Left everything to Clare to do with as she saw fit. Only Clare never did see fit. He sucked on his cigarette again.

Julie didn't say anything, so Brian said,

Then a while after that I lost my job. So Christine went round to Clare's – not to ask for her share, anything like that, you understand – just a loan, a few hundred to tide us over. You know what your Aunty Clare said?

Julie's stomach felt bad. She knew with a sick certainty what was coming.

She said she didn't have any money to spare just then, it was all tied up in the house, and Brian laughed shortly. She was just buying that nice little bungalow she took you off to. That was why she took you on, you know, and why she turned up here after all these years – guilt. Pure and simple. He raised his eyebrows in exaggerated surprise. But don't say she didn't tell you.

Julie's head ached. She didn't want to be sidetracked like this.

Have you kept anything? she said.

Kept anything? O, aye – I've kept the lot, and he waited for her to ask to go upstairs.

There's not much, he said when she didn't ask. Not a lot to show for a lifetime. So I reckoned that what there was were mine – I kept you both all those years.

Julie couldn't believe what she was hearing.

My mother worked, she said.

She kept you, she added silently. Brian's face hardly changed at all.

O aye, she did, he said. She knew she had to do something to make up for the fact that she didn't have owt of her own.

Julie didn't want to hear any of this. Brian was filling her head like bad smoke.

I'm surprised you haven't called round before this, he said. I'm surprised your Aunty Clare hasn't sent you round before now for the pickings. Didn't she want a little something to remember her only sister by? After all, she got everything else.

Julie closed her eyes.

I'm not with Aunty Clare, she said.

Are you not? Now there's a surprise. She didn't throw you out when you fell pregnant, did she? Ne'er darken my doors and all that. She always was one for the high moral ground was Clare. Eh, he said, and stopped as if a new thought had struck him. Is that why you're here? Don't tell me you need a roof over your head –

No, Julie said. She didn't say, *I wouldn't be paid good money to live with you*. Everything she had tried to forget had come back in a powerful rush and she wished it was Brian dead instead of her mother, she wished she had never come.

I just wanted something of hers to keep, she said. Then the way he looked at her with the old contempt made her say, She was my mother.

I'm very glad you remembered that, Brian said. And you can remember this an'all. This is my house. Not yours, not your mother's and certainly not Clare's. It's my house and legally everything in it's mine. Now then.

He leant back.

Julie hated herself for going red. He had always been able to make her do that, all he had to do was look at her with that old dislike and she would burn and crumble before him. She wasn't going to do that now. She stood up.

I'd better be going, she said faintly, and she turned to leave the room.

But when she got to the door Brian said,

You can go up if you like.

With one hand on the door Julie stopped.

It doesn't matter, she said.

No, go on. You might as well. It's all up there. I haven't touched it. Yet.

Julie wanted to leave. She hated the thought of being

upstairs when Brian was down, like the old days when she stayed in her room if her mother and Brian were shouting at one another, or if Brian was in the house and her mother was out. She could remember the fear if he came upstairs, and the knowledge that she couldn't leave the house without having to get past him. But she had come this far.

All right, she said.

Slowly she made her way up the stairs.

Was it the stairs or the smoky smell that made it hard to breathe? Something in the air was stifling Julie and she had to stop. Her head was full of voices saying all the things she hadn't said.

You never kept her, she kept you.

She worked herself into the ground for you.

You killed her.

These were the things she would never say. She had never been able to tell the truth there, even when it was her home. They had told her lies all the time, and now there was just Brian, with the lies he told himself. For all she knew it was a lie about Aunty Clare, otherwise why hadn't he told her before? It was like Eric said about memory, it wasn't the truth. Over the years in that house any number of lies had festered, any number of things that hadn't been said. It made her feel ill. That was what home was, Julie suddenly thought, a place of lies, where you couldn't tell the truth, or even if you did, if you followed people round screaming it, as Julie sometimes did in her dreams, they didn't or couldn't listen.

That was what she had had to live with.

After a moment Julie made herself press on up the stairs, through the bad air that was partly old unwashed things and partly Brian's bitterness. He always had been a hard bitter man, as if life had never done him a good turn. That was the atmosphere Julie had grown up in, although grown was probably the wrong word, not even a plant could have grown in this. She had shrivelled in it, it had shrivelled her, as long as she lived here she never could have grown.

Breathing hard, Julie went into the room her mother had shared with Brian. Apart from the mess everything looked the same. But Julie could hardly think any more why she was there for the jumble of voices in her head. She sat down heavily on the bed.

He had never liked her, she could see that now. He had never wanted her there. And the way he had been with her had somehow caused the jumble of voices in her head, so that everything she said or did was always wrong. But why had he taken on a woman with a daughter when he couldn't like the child? And why had Julie's mother stayed with him when he wasn't even providing for her? She had always had to earn the money. And why had Julie had to live with it all until it had climbed into her head and nearly driven her daft?

Why, Mam? Why, Mam? said the thoughts in her head, Julie almost thought she had said them aloud. She opened her eyes. In front of her was the wardrobe, the plain old fake teak wardrobe which held her mother's clothes. She didn't want them, she didn't want anything. She hated herself for having thought, when she was desperate at Uncle Si's, that she might come back, just for a little while. Because however bad it was at Uncle Si's she didn't feel shrivelled by it the way she did here.

Julie opened the wardrobe. She was going to make herself get on with it now, not for Julie or her mother but for the baby. She didn't want a keepsake, she wanted something she could sell.

There wasn't much worth saving. Most of the clothes were only fit to be thrown, or for Age Concern. But there was one good thick jacket in a heavy, knobbly material, astrakhan her mother had called it. Julie picked it out and folded it on the bed. She thought of the new dress agency near the precinct and rummaged through again until she found her mother's best skirt. Then she stuffed them both into the carrier bag she'd found in the bottom of the wardrobe and turned to the drawers.

Julie went through the drawers thoroughly, almost violently, looking for things to sell. She knew now that she had been betrayed, made to live with a man who had never liked her, whom she was frightened of, frightened that when they were alone he would do something to her, the terrible, obscene thing, it wasn't stupid to think that, because where there was no love anything was possible at all. She pulled her mother's things out of the drawers and crammed them back in. There was nothing in most of them but underwear. Then, in the last drawer she found her mother's jewellery box and remembered the brooch, a small cameo, her mother had said it had been Julie's grandmother's, a wedding gift. She opened the box and there it was, a lovely thing. Julie held it against her jumper.

The rest of the jewellery wasn't worth much, but there were two big mock pearl earrings, that Julie thought might be the kind of thing they would like at the dress agency.

That was it, there wasn't any more, apart from the photos Julie didn't want to look at and a phial half full of perfume. Julie remembered what Brian had said, about it not being much to show for a lifetime, but she was beyond feeling soft. She found a small cardboard box for the earrings and put the brooch into her purse. Then she picked up her bags. There was a feeling behind her eyes as though she might cry, but the tears didn't come. And when she went downstairs to Brian, who was still sitting where she had left him, his head bent forward, she felt very cold and hard.

I've just taken a jacket and a skirt, she said, and a pair of earrings. She didn't mention the brooch.

They kept things from me, she thought.

Brian didn't look up.

Take what you want, he said, flicking more ash onto the carpet. Take the lot.

Julie's voice was like chips of ice.

I don't want anything else, she said, and she turned and left without saying goodbye.

The woman at the dress agency, Dominique's, was very thin. She had close-cropped platinum-blonde hair, long lilac nails and a tight-fitting purple dress. For all that, she looked like a man, Julie thought. She took the skirt and jacket out, then the earrings, and the woman said, Hmm . . . hmm, without really looking at them at all. Then she said that astrakhan wasn't selling, and the skirt obviously wasn't the best jersey wool, and the earrings were neither here nor there. Julie would be lucky to get ten pounds for the lot.

Fifteen, said Julie, and the woman pursed her lips and said she could try for twelve.

Then, not without a pang of pain, Julie took the brooch out of her purse. She wasn't sure that the dress agency was the right place for it, but the woman seemed a lot more interested now. She looked at it in the light from the window and said it was a nice piece, she might be able to get Julie twenty pounds for it.

Then she wrote out a receipt and asked for Julie's phone number, so Julie had to say she didn't have one, but she could call in. And she took the receipt and went out, it was all over, over and done with, she had done it. And she felt unutterably tired now, and weak and depressed. Because nothing had changed, she hadn't found the answer to her many problems. She had only managed to sell some of her mother's things, probably for a lot less than they were worth. But she needed money for the baby, that was what she had to think about now. She had already opened a building society account and had a little less than twenty pounds in it from money she had put aside from the shopping every week. And she would carry on putting money in it when she could, she didn't care now she knew Mick had been spending money on drugs, but as she walked and stopped and walked and stopped along the road that led to Uncle Si's yard she knew it wasn't enough, it would never be enough. Her baby needed a home, somewhere to grow up in, not like Julie had grown up, trying so hard all the time to be liked, waiting and waiting for any sign of affection. And she still hadn't got anywhere else to live.

As Julie pulled herself up the stairs she felt the bitterness of defeat, because all the time she had wanted, more than anything, to protect her baby from the hard, loveless world, and now she knew she couldn't. She had done everything she could and it wasn't enough. She went into her room, sank down onto her mattress, rolled over and lay on her side.

Some time later she woke up to a knocking on the door and Uncle Si's voice.

Julie?
– What.
Are you well?
Yes – thank you.
Can I come in?

Julie didn't say anything to that and Uncle Si came in. He sat down at the far end of the mattress. Julie sat up.

Is it the little one? he said.

Is what the little one, said Julie.

I – we – thought you might not be well, because of, you know, the little one.

Julie shook her head and Uncle Si said, O, and looked down. There was a long silence, then he said,

You know – if you wanted to put your name down – for the council – I'd come with you.

Julie looked at his grey, unshaven face.

Do you want me to go? she said.

No, said Uncle Si. That was all he said. He didn't say the place had been much nicer with Julie there, or that he'd miss her. Julie thought about the waiting list for houses, seven years long, and the flats where they put people they couldn't house anywhere else. Maybe she'd end up near Jean, she thought. Then she sighed and turned her head away, and tears began rolling down her cheeks. It was a funny kind of crying, her breathing hardly changed, but more and more tears rolled down. Uncle Si patted her hand once, then rubbed it, then looked away. He stayed with her though, and when she finished crying he looked at her again and said,

Will you come down now? and Julie nodded and blew her nose.

Downstairs the telly was on. Mick was talking and there was a panful of stew on the table. Darren looked up at her quickly then away.

Hiya, Mick said. Have some stew.

What is it? Julie said, sitting down.

It's very good stew, said Mick. I made it, and he went off to get her a bowl.

You're eating late, Julie said to fill the silence when he left.

We got in late, said Darren, apparently to a dumpling in his bowl. Julie didn't ask where they'd been. Mick doled out some stew. It was brownish, with pale greasy specks. Julie knew they didn't always wash the bowls, but she also knew she was very hungry. She didn't look at it while she was eating, she kept her eyes on the telly.

A man was saying that the number of murders committed by the homeless was going up all the time. He asked another man what the government might do about it.

Mick jabbed his spoon towards the telly.

Now why do you think, he said, that God would allow such bad things to happen?

Julie couldn't see Darren's face but she thought he was smiling.

I mean, wouldn't you think, Mick went on, what with God being all-powerful and that, he might think to himself, Now here's a bad situation, I could do something about that. Or the war in Eastern Europe maybe – I could definitely do something about one or the other – or even both. Yeah, why not? After all, it's not Sunday.

God gave us free will, said Julie in spite of herself.

What for? said Mick. I mean it's not the most useful

thing to have, is it, eh? Maybe he thought, I'll bugger this lot up, I'll give them free will – what do you think, Uncle Si? But Uncle Si said he had no opinion about God whatever.

And I'll bet he feels the same way about you, said Mick. And me if it comes to that. Now –

I don't think God's like that, said Darren, and they all looked at him in surprise.

Like what? said Mick.

All-powerful, Darren said without looking up. I don't think God has power.

Well, who has then? said Mick. Mr Blobby?

That's just what we're told to think about God, Darren said, like he's a big person in the sky who could do something about all the mess if he wanted to. I don't think it's like that.

This was almost the longest speech Darren had ever made. Everyone waited for him to say more but he didn't.

Well, go on then, said Mick. Tell us about your friend God.

Darren sighed and broke up a dumpling with his spoon.

It's just that once like, he said, once when I was on the streets and it was raining, pissing it down, and I had about twelve p someone had given me –

The good old days, said Mick.

– And I couldn't find anywhere to kip, and I think I had flu.

Mick laughed.

– Anyway, Darren said, I must have fallen over. I don't remember much except lying there, then rolling over and looking at the sky. There weren't any stars, just clouds and street lamps, but I kept on staring at the sky and I felt – empty.

Is that it? Mick said after a bit.

Darren went back to the stew.

It was the best feeling I ever had, he said with his mouth full. And I remember thinking, this is what God is.

Yeah, right, said Mick. A strung-out junkie with flu.

I wasn't stoned, Darren said. I just thought, this is it, you know. Like all the time we're full of something, thoughts or feelings or just shit, and then, just for once I wasn't full of anything and I felt great. And Darren actually looked up and round at them all, Julie could see his eyes were brown, she'd never seen his eyes before.

Mick said,

So we're all worshipping this big blank space in the sky. Dear Blank Space who art in heaven, Hollowed be thy name, and he laughed but no one else did.

Uncle Si said,

I thought I saw an angel once, and he told them that when he was a little boy, playing on some waste ground where a church used to be, he'd felt a rush of light.

You mean you saw it, Mick said.

No, I felt it, said Uncle Si, and he looked at Julie. Not like the pictures in books, not like anything, but I knew that was what it was. And it's funny, he said, because all the time I went to chapel I never saw one there.

Mick laughed.

That doesn't surprise me, he said. The last place any self-respecting angel'd be is in church. He picked up his plate and Darren's. I must say, he said, I didn't know I was living with the three wise men, sorry, one woman. Or is it the three wise monkeys?

It's all right you laughing, said Uncle Si. It'll happen to you one day.

That it won't, said Mick and he carried the plates through.

Julie stood at the bottom of The Rise in the rain, hoping that Sylvia had remembered what she'd said about picking her up, because she didn't feel well enough to get up the hill. She'd brought Sylvia's book back, *Astro-Geography*. It had caused a great row with Mick.

Can't you tell when someone's trying to make a few

quid? he'd said, turning the book over in his hands. This'll be sponsored by Thomson's Travel. See chapter six for why everyone should move to Torremolinos. Jesus, he said. Twelve ninety-five for this crap.

I didn't buy it, Julie said.

I should hope not, said Mick. We're not so overloaded with money we can start throwing it away.

Julie wasn't going to take that from Mick.

It's better than spending it on drugs, she said.

Mick hardly blinked. He tapped on the book with his hand.

This is a drug, he said, and all those meetings you go to. A bunch of rich wankers looking for easy answers. They're walking around in a bloody daze if anyone is. They wouldn't know a real problem if they fell over it.

How do you know? Julie said. You don't know anything about them, and she told him about Jean's cancer and Sylvia's son and Margery's daughter. Mick waited for her to finish.

They deserve it, he said.

What? said Julie.

They deserve it – a bit of real shit in their lives.

Julie stared at him. For the first time she saw how sick he was. He was sick and stupid from hating.

I mean it, Mick said, following her as she started to walk away. What do they know about sleeping rough when it's pissing it down, or going hungry for days? What do they know about having a habit you can't kick, and even if you do kick it you're never free? What do they know about having your hand cut off because you can't pay your dealer?

He was shouting after her up the stairs. Julie turned and faced him.

You never had your hand cut off, she said.

For a second she thought Mick would explode, come running up the stairs after her and beat her round the head, but he just lifted both arms and dropped them again.

Cracked, he said. Just fucking cracked. What are you looking for, Julie? he shouted after her as she locked the bathroom door. God and all his angels? Well, just keep on looking, I hope you find him, because he sure as hell isn't looking for you. It's not that he couldn't find you if he wanted to, he shouted. He just forgot to look.

Julie dampened a cloth and wiped her face. Mick went on shouting for a bit, then stopped. She had never seen before how sick he was, now she could see it clearly. It was a terrible thing to see, but at the same time it cleared her mind. There was no point talking to him any more, explaining the way she felt about anything. It was a waste of time.

But Mick hadn't finished, and when she went downstairs again to pick the book up he started again, more calmly.

I've heard you do a lot better in life if you live in Hampstead, he said. Or even at the top of The Rise.

Julie ignored him.

In fact, all you really have to do to get on, he said, is to become an enemy of the working class.

That was a phrase he used all the time, Julie was sick of it.

There are a lot of enemies around, aren't there, Mick? she said. What are you going to do with them all, come the revolution?

What do you mean? he said.

Well, how are you going to get rid of them all? said Julie. String them up? You'll need an awful lot of rope.

Mick stared at her.

Well, maybe we'll join hands and dance round them all in a circle, he said, and left the room.

That was the one conversation they'd had together since talking about God. Mick and Darren were busy all the time making new units for the kitchen and fixing some of the old ones. Julie still didn't know where they were getting the materials from, and at the back of her mind there was still the fear that Mick or his friends would raid one of her friends' houses. She had never heard before of kitchen units being taken in a break-in, still the thought chilled her when it came.

You do better in life if you live up The Rise, he had said.

It was a wet cold night. Julie pulled the edges of her coat together. She could only fasten the top two buttons now, and she had to wear pumps because her shoes were too tight. Her feet were getting very wet, her head ached and she knew she was starting a cold. She had missed three of her weekly visits to the hospital, and she was too afraid to go back now. But sometimes she felt very ill.

Sorry I'm late, Sylvia said, opening the car door for Julie. Last-minute phone call.

This woman is always on the phone, Jean said, and Julie passed her the book for Sylvia.

O thanks, Sylvia said. It's interesting, isn't it? And I've brought an article I thought you might like to read as well, from *Psychic News*, about how the angle of your bed in the bedroom can affect your health.

Julie couldn't help sighing. There did seem to be a lot of things to think about all the time. Jean said as much.

Good heavens, Sylvia, she said, you don't mean to say that that's what I've been doing wrong all these years?

They were nearing Eric's house now. Julie could see Esther's car pulling up, and Esther and Josepha getting out. She looked round at the houses, lawns with no fences, windows with lots of tiny white frames. She didn't like them, she realised.

Then, when they caught up to the others at the door, Pierre opened it and Julie felt her heart slip.

Hello, Pierre, Jean said, and she reached up to kiss his cheek. He kissed everyone then, Esther and Josepha and Sylvia. Julie looked, but he didn't kiss Josepha any more than anyone else, and when it was her turn she touched her lips lightly against his cheek, then hurried inside.

Surprise for you tonight, Eric said as they went into the lounge.

Everyone was conscious of the difference, having Pierre.

So Pierre, Sylvia said, what part of France do you come from?

Pierre said he came from Aix-en-Provence.

O it's beautiful there, Sylvia said.

It is, said Pierre, and when he described his village to them Julie felt it was the place she most wanted to live in the world.

So what made you come here? Jean said, and everyone laughed.

O well, I wanted to travel, Pierre said, see the world.

See the world and then come here, Jean said, and everyone laughed again.

All the conversation centred on Pierre and he seemed quite happy with that. Eric didn't seem to mind either. He sat back smoking a strange-looking pipe, his feet up on a little stool. Even Esther got quite talkative, telling Pierre that she had been to Aix-en-Provence many times and stayed in a village near Pierre's, it was surprising that they'd never met.

If we had, I'm sure I would have remembered, Pierre said, and Esther blushed.

They were all flirting with him, Julie thought, it was just happening naturally. It was because he was French, Sylvia said later. Only Julie and Eric were quiet. Julie looked round for the others who weren't there, Gerry and Annie of course, but Suzi hadn't come either, she'd only been to one meeting. There were just the five of them left, Julie thought. All women.

When they did the meditation Pierre's voice was very easy to listen to, easier than Eric's or even Medbh's. It was like a meditation in itself, just listening. He didn't do the visualisations like Eric, but he did use images.

Let your neck and spine flow into each other, he said.

Imagine a column of light passing through them. Let your forehead become broad.

Julie was almost asleep before they started the breathing practice.

Then afterwards everyone felt much better. They came out of the meditation into the blurred feeling that followed and smiled at one another and the room felt very warm. Pierre went into the kitchen to help Muriel with the drinks, people yawned and stretched and smiled at one another all over again.

I've been meaning to ask you, Sylvia said to Julie, when is the baby due?

Everyone looked at Julie.

Well, Julie said, I've been given different dates.

Everyone groaned.

They gave me four different dates for Stanley, Josepha said, and in the end he wasn't born on any of them.

When do *you* think you're due? Jean said, and Julie said in about five weeks.

The light at the end of the tunnel, Sylvia said, but Julie didn't know if she felt that way or not.

I keep thinking how nice it is that we have an unborn child with us at these meetings, said Jean, and Josepha said,

I wish I'd known about them when I was having Stanley.

Yes, it's the perfect environment, Sylvia said.

Pierre and Muriel came back with the herbal teas and coffee.

We were just saying, said Jean, how nice it is to have an unborn baby here at the meetings.

Pierre looked at Julie and Julie went very red.

Yes, it is the best possible atmosphere for the new spirit, he said.

That's just what we were saying, said Sylvia.

But I keep thinking, said Jean, that it would be nice to direct some of the energy from the meditation towards the baby, you know, when we send it out for healing. Or even do an entire meditation just for Julie.

O yes, said Sylvia, and Esther smiled at Julie, who was very embarrassed.

After all, Jean said, babies come into this world with precious little to help them, and Julie felt a real pang.

It would be like a blessing, Josepha said, and Sylvia said it would be the spring equinox soon, that would be the perfect time.

Where I come from, Pierre said, there is a ceremony to celebrate the life of the unborn child.

Everyone wanted to know what it was.

Pierre told them they would have to find an open space, on a hillside, near an ancient monument if possible, and bring a gift for the pregnant woman to celebrate her fertility. Then they would dance round her in a circle and finally place their hands upon her stomach and ask the spirits of earth and water to bless her fruitfulness and the actual delivery, and the spirits of air and fire to bless the spirit of the baby and aid it to fulfil its destiny.

O yes, said Jean, and Sylvia said,

How marvellous.

Julie said nothing. She felt nervous and yet she wanted them to do it, she felt as though the baby needed all the blessing it could get.

Esther said,

There's a stone circle near my house, overlooking Shiny Clough Moor, and suddenly everyone was talking at once. They all agreed they must do it, they loved the idea of an open-air ritual, and at the spring equinox, too. Sylvia was very enthusiastic.

This is what it's all about, she said. I've said so before. We don't celebrate nature enough in these groups.

She had said it before, about meeting in the open, on the hills, or by rivers, or going on long walks to celebrate the seasons. That was what she thought about when she thought about nature. But when Julie thought about it she remembered going to stay on her grandmother's farm on Pike Moor around the time that her mother and father split up, and feeding the hens, and how they fought. And how one day the pigeons that gathered in the yard had all climbed on top of one pigeon and pecked it to death, the way it sat there patiently, how long it seemed to take.

What about you gentlemen? Jean said to Eric and Pierre.

Well, I don't know about you, Eric said to Pierre, but I think this is one for the ladies myself.

O yes, it is definitely a feminine ritual, said Pierre.

Well, then, said Jean. Shall we fix a date? And they all got their diaries out. Julie sat in the middle of everyone, feeling nervous and shown up and pleased all at once. Pierre smiled at her.

It is a wonderful way to welcome the new baby, he said, and Julie went red all over again.

The equinox fell midweek so there was some trouble fixing a date between Esther's shiatsu and Jean's yoga and Sylvia's meeting with the Friends of the Rainbow Trust, but eventually they fixed on the early evening of the twenty-third.

Then, if the weather's bad, Esther said, you can all come back for cocoa and cake instead, and everyone agreed that would be a good alternative.

Is that date all right for you? Sylvia said to Julie.

Julie wasn't booked up.

Well, then that's settled, said Sylvia. I'll give you and Jean a lift and we'll all meet up at the stone circle, and she beamed around the room.

So can we get back to the meeting then? Eric said, and he told them he was going to do the final meditation with a candle. Everyone sat back on their chairs, but this time Josepha sat next to Julie, Julie could smell her perfume and she remembered it from Esther's aromatherapy oils. All through the meditation Julie could only think about the ritual and what it might do for her and what she might have to do. Then at the end Josepha turned to her and smiled.

Julie smiled back.

You'll have to come up to my place some time, Josepha said, and she told Julie where she lived. Maybe you could come up before the ritual and have some tea, and we could go up to the stone circle together, if you're free.

Julie was always free.

She could hardly believe, as she left the meeting, that all this was happening to her. It was like a sign, that while things were bad at Uncle Si's, she still had the group. If she turned to Mind-Power more and more things would open up for her and show her what to do. She wondered what Josepha's house was like. It would be beautiful, she thought, and she felt a bit worried about the pain she would feel when she saw it, but she couldn't let that stop her going. She wanted to be friends with Josepha, and Sylvia, Jean and Esther. It was very important to her now that she had friends.

Julie had finally remembered Annie's pram. She had woken up in the early morning needing to wee – she always needed to wee in the night now, four or five times, and couldn't get back to sleep. So eventually she'd got up and started to wash. Then she'd remembered her dream.

She'd dreamt that the post had come and in it there was a cheque from Brian. He'd written,

This was in your mother's box, I thought it would come in useful for the baby. And the cheque was for four hundred pounds. And in the dream the whole world had seemed to open up for Julie, she remembered saying to the baby,

Look, we're all right now, we can buy a nice little house in the country.

The snowy light in the bathroom was just like ash. So much for dreams, Julie thought. Very bloody funny. Brian didn't even know where she lived. She damped her hair and fluffed up her lost perm. Four hundred pounds wasn't that much anyway, she told herself. Not when she still had everything to buy. And then she'd remembered Annie's pram.

She'd gone out early to catch Annie in, and had helped her to comfort one twin who was crying all the time and the other who kept being sick. Now she was pushing the pram home, very carefully, because it was piled high with all the things Annie had given her.

Behind Julie a car tooted loudly and several things fell off the pram at once.

O I'm sorry, Sylvia said, pulling up. I thought for a minute you must have had the baby. I wasn't thinking straight, was I? she said, unbuckling the seat belt and getting out. She helped Julie to pick up the things, a sterilising unit and several bottles, a bottle warmer and a knitted shawl.

They're from Annie, Julie said, and they had a short conversation about Annie and the twins, and how hard it must be. Then neither of them had anything else to say, but Sylvia went on smiling at Julie in her vague way until Julie felt that she wanted to go.

I was just on my way to Jean's, Sylvia said, would you like to come?

Julie looked at the pram.

Would it go in the back? Sylvia said, and together they tugged at the pram and it's rigging until the top bit came off, then Julie struggled to fold up the rest.

Annie's just shown me how to do this, she said.

Let me see, said Sylvia, and together they tugged and pushed and unscrewed things until Julie was sorry they'd started, then it suddenly collapsed. Julie was a bit worried that they'd broken it but Sylvia loaded it into the back so cheerfully she didn't like to say anything.

I must say I was always glad I didn't have twins, she said pulling out. Five single children were quite enough work. I hope Jean's in, she said, narrowly missing a parked car.

Jean was in, but it took her a long time to answer the door, they heard her footsteps dragging over the carpet. Then when she opened the door Julie was shocked by her face, which was all yellow and puckered. She was still in her nightie and a blue robe.

Good Lord, Jean, Sylvia said. Have we called at a bad time?

Jean didn't answer, but fell against the frame of the door.

Sylvia moved quickly, half carrying and half dragging Jean back into the lounge. She called to Julie to get a glass of water.

Julie ran into the kitchen and stood still, unable to see what to do. There was a mess of pots in the sink, then she saw a mug amongst them and hastily rinsed it, filled it with water and carried it back.

Jean was on the futon, holding onto Sylvia's arm and moaning.

Shall I call the doctor? Sylvia said. Jean, shall I call the doctor?

Jean shook her head. She clutched Sylvia's arm and moaned and gasped.

Bottle, she said, nodding towards the small table. Julie grabbed the bottle and between them they shook some medicine into the glass of water. Jean swallowed it quickly, her hands shaking so much that the glass knocked against her teeth. Then after a few moments she leant back on the futon and closed her eyes. A dribble of medicine ran down her chin.

Sylvia said, Well, Jean, then she didn't seem to know what to say. Julie sat down on the chair. She could see Jean relaxing, unclenching like a fist. Sylvia held onto her hand and stroked it.

Are you feeling any better? she said.

Jean opened her eyes.

I'll never be better, she said, and closed them again.

O now that's nonsense, Sylvia said. You're bound to get better, you're doing all the right things: the diet, the yoga, the meditation –

Uncle Tom Cobbley and all, said Jean, and Julie laughed

though she didn't mean to. Jean opened her eyes again. I haven't offered you a drink, she said.

O sod that, Sylvia said, and Julie was surprised to hear her swear, but Jean said,

Julie, be a love and put the kettle on, and, glad to be given something to do, Julie hurried into the kitchen.

It took a while to sort out where the tea bags and teapot and sugar were, but eventually she got it together and carried it all through on a tray.

Sylvia was sitting back on the futon now and Jean was leaning her head against her shoulder. They looked odd but right together somehow, like an old married couple, but Sylvia got up to help Julie with the tray.

Now this is service for you, she said, pulling up a small table. You're a spoilt woman, Jean.

Jean wasn't listening. She twisted round on the futon so that she could see out of the big window.

I stood on the balcony last night, she said, and the stars were so big and close, you know, there was one really big one, and I stood watching it and thinking, I'm made out of the same stuff you are, and when I die, some of the particles that are me might return to the stars, for other people on balconies to watch.

O well, there you are, Sylvia said. No wonder you're ill this morning. Out on the balcony in the freezing cold.

I've thought that about stars before, said Jean, ignoring her. But it only seemed real last night, that when we die we do eventually get to heaven, because we're made out of the same stuff as the stars.

What's brought all this on? said Sylvia, and Jean was quiet for a while, then she said,

I've been told I'm going to die.

Sylvia snorted.

Again? she said. Who told you this time?

Jean was very quiet and Julie really wanted her to speak. Finally she said,

Aaron Li.

Aaron Li was her Qi Gong teacher.

You what? Sylvia said, then she stopped as if she had lost all her words at once. When Jean didn't say anything either she said,

I thought he was supposed to be helping you to get better.

He is, Jean said, then she covered her face with her hands. Julie felt her own face burning, she hated to see people cry, but Sylvia took Jean in her arms and rocked her.

What did he say exactly? she said, and Jean sobbed,

It's not his fault, he thought I was ready to take it.

Bit by bit they got the whole story.

Two days ago she had gone to her Qi Gong practice. She went every fortnight for an hour, then afterwards they always sat together and drank ginseng tea. It was one of her favourite things, to see Aaron Li and sit with him after the practice and talk. He was a very gentle man with big soft eyes. He had looked at Jean steadily and had said, Jean, I have something to tell you. And Jean had felt really good and glowing after the practice, but he'd said,

I have to tell you this because you are paying me a lot of money, and because I know you can take it, and Jean had looked at him and felt all the energy draining from her, she'd known he was going to tell her the worst thing she had ever heard.

He had taken her hand.

Jean, he'd said, I have to tell you that I can't help you to get better, or even to prolong your life. I can only help you to die.

When Jean told them this she let go of a long shaky breath.

So then we talked, she said. I was very sensible and matter of fact. We talked wills and insurance and about how I'd like to die. And I felt all right talking, she said. But then we stopped and I had to go home, and I didn't feel all right any more. She looked at them with a shaky smile. I've been in bed ever since.

O Jean, Sylvia mourned. You should have called me.

Jean shook her head. I didn't even want to think about it, she said. Let alone talk.

Sylvia looked helplessly at Jean. She didn't tell her not to listen to Aaron Li, who was he anyway, so Julie leant forwards and said,

But you don't know he's right. How can he know something like that?

Jean had covered her eyes with the heels of her palms. She uncovered them and rubbed at them with the tips of her fingers, then she said,

But you see, when he told me, I knew it was true.

She looked at Sylvia and Sylvia looked away.

They told me two years ago at the hospital that I had about six months to live, but I didn't believe them, did I?

Sylvia shook her head.

I thought, I'll show you, I remember thinking that. But when Aaron Li told me, I just knew he was right. He thought I was ready, you see, she said, and her face began to pucker again. But I'm not ready. And I don't want to die, and she leant against Sylvia and sobbed.

All Sylvia could say was, O, Jean, Jean, but Julie was outraged.

He had no right saying that, she said. Why don't you tell her not to believe him?

Julie, Julie, ssh, Sylvia said, and she took Julie's hand. Julie nearly withdrew it she was so angry, then she saw that Sylvia was crying. Then Sylvia buried her face in Jean's hair and kissed her. Julie sat where she was, with Sylvia still holding her hand. She couldn't think of a thing to say. All the meditation, she was thinking. All the yoga.

Look at us, Jean said, sitting up and blowing her nose. The three stooges.

Sylvia blew her nose too.

That was a bit before your time, she said to Julie.

Let's have another drink, said Jean. I'll get it, she said as

Julie started to get up. I'm not dead yet, but they went into the kitchen with her anyway and Jean sang,

Together, we belong together, and Sylvia laughed and Julie laughed a bit.

Then, when they sat down with their tea, Jean talked about what she'd like to have done with her ashes.

I want them scattered over Shiny Clough Moor, she said, above the reservoir.

You don't want much, Sylvia said. Can't we just flush them down the loo? They'll get to the reservoir eventually, and Jean elbowed her and they giggled like girls, then Jean said,

I was thinking of having a party before I go.

O yes, Sylvia said. Like Socrates.

It'll have to be after Julie's ritual, Jean said. I was thinking of April Fool's Day, and Jean and Sylvia laughed again, and Julie laughed, though she couldn't help thinking it was very strange.

We could all bring presents, Sylvia said, and Jean said she couldn't see why, but Sylvia said it would be like the Egyptians. Then she said they couldn't possibly have it in Jean's flat, it was too small, it would have to be at her place, and they would have to get a move on if they wanted it on April Fool's day. Then they began to talk about food. Julie didn't join in.

It doesn't work, she kept thinking. *None of it works*. She couldn't join in a conversation about party food. But anyway Jean soon began to look yellow and tired again. She took some more of her medication and said she'd like to sleep now.

O, of course, Sylvia said, looking round for her things.

Julie didn't want to leave Jean all alone, but Sylvia said,

All right, sweetheart, you get some rest, I'll call you later, and she held Jean for a moment. Julie didn't go in for all the kissing and hugging they did at the meetings, she just couldn't do it, but when she looked at Jean, Jean hugged her.

Don't look so sad, she said. You take care of yourself. You've got a little life to bring into the world.

Poor, poor love, Sylvia said in the lift. She's worked so hard.

Julie didn't say anything because the lift doors opened and a big man with a Rottweiler got in. They all stood together in a compressed way, not looking at one another, with Julie's stomach practically touching the man's and the Rottweiler stench in their noses until Julie didn't know if she wanted to laugh or be sick.

And the worst of it is, Sylvia said as they got in the car, once someone's told you you're dying, and you take it in, you inevitably do go downhill, I've seen it before.

He shouldn't have said it, Julie said, pulling the seat belt around her with difficulty.

Sylvia's eyes were red and weepy.

There's a time for everything, she said. We don't know that it wasn't the right time. Then she started the car and the radio came on.

– the death of a little boy found near a golf course can almost certainly be linked to a paedophile ring . . .

Julie felt a sickening movement in her stomach and Sylvia said, Good Lord. She fiddled with the dial.

Let's have some music, shall we? she said, and a high, pure, chanting voice came on.

Ah, Scarlatti, Sylvia said, pulling out.

Julie felt the pain of the little boy like a rush of heat, all tangled up with Jean's pain. She closed her eyes and shook her head as if trying to clear it, then suddenly she burst out,

How can it happen?

How can what happen? Sylvia said, swerving the car a little in surprise.

That, Julie said. She couldn't bring herself to say it. How could anyone die a worse death than that?

Then she was crying, she leant forwards against the seat belt and sobbed.

Sylvia managed to find a parking space. She passed Julie

some tissues from the glove compartment and put an arm round her, but Julie only cried harder, at all the inexplicable suffering of the world.

Sylvia didn't seem to know what to say. Finally she said, I don't know why these things happen, then stopped. She waited a minute, then started to laugh quietly, Julie looked at her in surprise.

I was remembering something Medbh said, she said, at the time of the Ethiopian famine. People were very worked up about it, you know; in fact we'd talked about nothing else all evening, and I think Medbh was getting a bit cross, you know the way she does. And suddenly she said, Well, for all you know, these famine victims could have been Nazis in their past lives.

Julie felt a stab of outrage.

That doesn't matter, she said, but Sylvia was still laughing.

It caused an absolute furore at the meeting, I can tell you, she said. Sometimes I think Medbh stirs things up deliberately, but she got more than she bargained for that night. People left the meeting, and others said if that was all Mind-Power was, a short-cut to an easy conscience, they wanted nothing to do with it. Even Medbh was a bit thrown by it all I think, and she tried to retract what she'd said – well, not retract it exactly, but you know, she said the whole thing about how you can't really know what another person is going through or why they're going through it, and you can't really help them, except in minor ways. All you can do is –

– Look after your own garden, Julie said, but that just seems selfish.

Yes, I know, Sylvia said. I suppose Medbh would say that people who help others are just being selfish in a different way. But what I remember thinking that night was that neither Medbh nor anyone else has any real answers. She started the car again.

Julie struggled to say what she meant.

But –, she said, – all the work you do – those photographs –

O yes, Sylvia said. I've done it for years. And I used to get terribly cross with Medbh for saying that charity workers poke their noses in and add to the problem. But I had to admit, even then, there was something in it, relieving one's own guilt, not really doing any long-term good, and worst of all, ignoring what's right under our noses in favour of more exotic forms of calamity. I can certainly see that here in the West we suffer different kinds of pain and we don't seem able to do anything about it. Maybe we can't see it clearly enough. Or maybe it is easier, helping other people, I don't know. At any rate, I've gone on doing it. I seem to need it somehow, it's opened my world out tremendously. I don't kid myself that I'm any use in real terms, but then it's not something you can measure, is it? she said, turning her large eyes on Julie. How much use one's been? And then I tell myself, maybe the kind of work I do *is* my garden, and she smiled and pulled up at the lights.

If I park just up there, she said, I can help you with the pram, and when Julie didn't say anything she patted her knee.

I can see why all this is bothering you, she said. Here you are, about to bring a child into the world, and you keep hearing about all this pain and gloom. But in the end your baby will have to make his or her own way. Life is a mysterious thing, and she shook her head and pulled up the hill.

Julie leant back in her seat. She was so tired suddenly she couldn't think of any more questions to ask, she just wanted to go to sleep. And if Jean with her diet and meditation and Qi Gong hadn't got anywhere, then she didn't think that she, Julie, ever would. Sylvia was right, she thought, getting out of the car. It was no use looking for answers because there weren't any. So she would stop looking, she thought as Sylvia opened the boot and hauled the pram out. She would just stop looking.

Josepha looked very sad.

But maybe it is a kind of healing in a way, she said.

They were sitting at a little table beneath the window of Josepha's front room, looking out as great curtains of rain swept the valley.

Julie didn't think much of what Josepha said. You could do anything to anyone, she thought, and call it healing. But Josepha was so serious she didn't like to contradict. She lowered her eyes and concentrated on the soup, which was made from vegetables Josepha had grown herself and frozen. It was very nice, though Julie might have added salt herself, but Josepha had only put pepper on the table.

Stanley sat at the table with them, eating very seriously and breathing hard. He played with his spoon in the soup, then lifted it to his mouth and sometimes turned it over before it got there so that the soup ran all down his chin and bib. But he was very good and quiet, and Josepha didn't interfere at all with the way he ate. Josepha was quiet as well, so Julie hardly knew what to say, but after a while she found she didn't mind. She broke up her bread as Josepha was doing, spread the pieces with cashew nut butter, and something called olive and herb tapenade, and dunked it into the soup. And all the time she was eating she took in the details of Josepha's house and the view outside.

Josepha's cottage was very small, but it stood on its own overlooking the pike on the opposite hill, which was near where Julie's grandmother used to live and where, Josepha told her, they were doing the ritual later on, if the rain cleared. Josepha hoped it would clear, but Julie wasn't sure. She felt less and less happy about the ritual and really hoped they could just go to Esther's instead. Esther's house was at the end of the road that wound up the hill and disappeared, Josepha said.

It's a fantastic place, she told Julie. Esther's husband's an architect.

Julie tried not to feel depressed by this. In fact she thought that Josepha's house was the nicest she had seen so far, though it was also the smallest. There were just two tiny rooms downstairs and two up, with one of them cut nearly in half where the bathroom had been put in. You didn't feel compressed though, because of the views. In front of the house and to one side there was a garden where Josepha had grown the vegetables for the soup, though as it was still only March you couldn't see much. But she was getting hens from Esther and one day she thought she might be almost self-sufficient.

Would you like some olives and tomatoes, Josepha said, and Julie said she would. She was still hungry, even though the heartburn meant that she ate less these days. She burped quietly when Josepha went out of the room and Stanley regarded her silently for a moment.

Instead of curtains Josepha had hung beaded strings of different lengths in the window, each ending in a wooden star or sun or moon, and on the table there was a bowl of floating candles. Julie admired this and the vases with large paper flowers very much. The walls of the little cottage were painted apple green or a pale, sunshiny yellow. There was a real fire with a tiled fireplace and a rag rug. The settee and the table with its two chairs were the only furniture, but the room seemed full. There was a shelf with books on vegan cooking and yoga, the settee was draped with a big flowery shawl, and Indian flute music was playing on a CD player. It was very soothing.

Josepha returned with a plateful of sliced tomatoes and a small dish of olives.

I used to really miss meat and cheese, she said, but now I hardly notice. But I thought keeping my own hens so that I know they're free range would be okay, and eggs would be good for Stanley. Julie agreed, her mouth full. I've got some herb tea brewing, Josepha said, slicing more bread.

Of all the houses she had seen so far, this was the one Julie could most imagine herself living in. If she closed her eyes she could see the home that she had inside her as a cross between this one and the houses near the park. But it was no use thinking like that. She opened her eyes.

I like the music, she said, and Josepha got up again to bring her some CDs to look at.

Stanley looked round as his mother disappeared, then he looked at Julie and reached for the pepper.

Car, he said, holding the mill up.

No, Julie said, pepper.

Car, said Stanley.

Pepper, said Julie.

Car, Stanley said. Julie gave up.

Josepha came back with the CDs, *Sublime Soul Music*, *Seventh Chakra*, *Music for the New Age*.

This music will gently cleanse your aura and tune your psyche to the divine, the booklet in the first box said.

I started playing them when I was pregnant, Josepha said. It's important to create the right vibrations, and she told Julie how she'd massaged her stomach every night with aromatherapy oils whilst listening to the music.

You can borrow them if you like, she said, and Julie told her she didn't have a CD player.

O, well, you can get the tapes, said Josepha, and Julie didn't like to say she didn't have a cassette player either.

You have to be careful which oils you use, Josepha said, but she still massaged Stanley every night with a mixture of lavender and rose to keep him balanced and calm.

Stanley certainly seemed balanced and calm, especially when Julie thought about the twins, or Sadie. She couldn't think about Sadie without pangs of guilt, and the image of that terrible fall. She hadn't forgiven Alison, but she felt she should have found out about Sadie. Maybe she would phone the hospital, she thought.

She couldn't feel troubled for long in this calm, quiet

house. When the music ended the only sounds were soft slurping noises and occasional gasps from Stanley as he finished his soup. When he had finished Josepha told him he could get down and he did. He was the best-behaved baby Julie had ever seen and she said so. Josepha smiled. She clearly felt it was all down to diet, music and aromatherapy.

Meat makes people aggressive, she said.

She didn't pick Stanley up or hold him and Julie didn't feel she could either. He was like his mother, beautiful, serious and remote. Julie realised that though she had been in Josepha's house two hours now she still didn't feel that she knew her any better.

Isn't it hard bringing a baby up vegan? she said, and Josepha went into a long explanation of how it had to be done. Julie watched her and thought about how she could have been a model or an actress, but she didn't seem to think about herself that way at all. She never wore make-up and never mentioned men. Julie wanted to know about Stanley's father, but she didn't like to ask. She felt that Josepha would only want to talk about the spiritual things she believed in, but she did wonder all the same. She wondered if he had left Josepha when she was pregnant, but it was hard to imagine anyone leaving Josepha.

Stanley, who had wandered into the kitchen, came wandering back in with a welly.

Out, he said.

Josepha went with him to look for the other welly.

Does he go out in the rain? Julie said, surprised.

Of course, said Josepha. Rain never hurt anyone, and she let Stanley out of the front door, then started to clear the pots.

Julie thought Josepha's ideas were very strange, but they seemed to work. She watched Stanley toddling down the garden path and for a moment was watching herself and her own little boy, they would do the garden together, and listen to spiritual music. But she couldn't help wondering what Josepha did for money.

Don't you find it hard, bringing up a baby on your own? she said, carrying the remaining pots into the kitchen.

O no, Josepha said, as if surprised by the question. They watched Stanley from the kitchen window as he sat on his heels and poked at the plants with a stick. Josepha brought out a cake.

I don't let Stanley have sugar, she said, and she explained to Julie how she'd made the cake without eggs or milk.

Julie couldn't keep her eyes off Stanley.

He seems so good, she said, wiping a dish. Doesn't he ever give you a hard time, you know, throw tantrums or keep you awake at nights?

Josepha shook her head thoughtfully and the little stars in her earrings tinkled and shone in the thick folds of her hair.

I never knew much about babies before I had Stanley, she said. I'd never even held one. But I was twenty-eight and I felt it was the right time.

Josepha must be thirty, Julie thought in surprise.

Did you have a job? she said.

O well, at first, Josepha said, I worked in an organic wholefood collective called Green Earth, and I went back after Stanley was born, but they weren't all supportive. Some of them were, but one of them said I shouldn't be breast-feeding when there were customers to serve, and someone else said they didn't think Stanley should be there at all. It wasn't on really. I'd told them all about my decision to have a baby and they'd promised support, but when the time came they couldn't handle it. Not everyone – I'm still in touch with one or two of them. Rose comes here a lot and she always brings stuff – soya milk and organic fruit, though I don't ask her to. But in the end I let the others buy me out. So I had some money from that, and then of course this place is my father's, you know.

Julie began to see.

Buddha was a prince, Mick's voice said. He could afford to sit on his arse all day and smile.

Where's Stanley's father? Julie said, and Josepha paused before replying.

He's a free spirit, she said. He had his own path to follow – I knew that at the time, and she put the plate she was wiping lightly back onto a shelf.

Julie wondered if he paid any money, the place didn't run itself, but she couldn't bring herself to ask. She was beginning to see though how it was that Josepha could seem so remote, and absorbed in her world, untouched by the troubles of Julie's own.

Don't you ever get a break? she said artfully, to find out more, and Josepha said her parents were very good. They only lived half a mile away and they had Stanley every weekend, from Friday night till Sunday after church. He went with them to church. And if Josepha had anything midweek, meditation or yoga, they had him then too. They would be taking him tonight, for the ritual, Josepha and Julie would take him there together on the way.

He's their only grandson you see, she said.

Julie did see. She saw that she would never be like Josepha. She caught sight of herself in the small, enamelled mirror above the sink, perm grown out to a greasy flatness ending in frizz, folds of fat around her chin, and felt a powerful ache for the person she would never be. She thought about Mick. Lately she'd thought a lot about confronting him, just saying right out,

I think Darren should go.

Any way she imagined it, the response wasn't good. She didn't know really why she wanted to say it at all, except that nothing ever got said. Even the pram, up and working now, by Julie's bed, hadn't made him say anything. She had almost given up on Mick.

Josepha moved the kitchen curtain to one side.

The rain's clearing, she said with a smile.

If possible, Julie's heart sank even further.

Julie stood with the others on the wind-blasted hill, wishing she'd stayed in.

Sylvia was very happy.

When you're up on the hills, she said, you know you're living in a spacious world.

And a cold one, Jean said. She looked much better than when Julie had last seen her, but her teeth were chattering with cold. She was wearing corduroy trousers as usual, a thick anorak and walking boots. Julie only had her cagoule and pumps, with her blue top and flowery leggings stretched tightly over her stomach. She was freezing.

Sylvia, dressed in a long sheepskin jacket which had attracted a shocked look from Josepha, had left the car near the turn-off to the standing stones. Julie and Josepha were waiting for them and, as they trekked up the ragged footpath, the wind blasted them from all sides.

All of the others were carrying packages. Julie knew they were presents for her. She felt funny about receiving them, and very conscious that she hadn't brought a bag.

By the time they got to the circle the wind was so bad that Julie was amazed the stones were still standing. She stood with the others, huddled inside the ring, and Esther shouted something no one could hear. Then she turned, pulling Jean along with her, so that the rest of them followed.

They went down a winding path. Julie was cross now, because she didn't know where they were going, and tired. Sylvia held her hand to stop her skidding in the mud or on loose stones, but Esther was entirely sure-footed. It seemed to take a long time, and Julie was considering sitting down where she was and refusing to move, when Esther stopped.

They were in a hollow in the hillside with thick bushes, overhanging rocks and, some way below, a stream. Esther still had to shout.

We can't possibly do anything up there, she said. There's too much wind.

Julie didn't care. She sat down thankfully on a stone out of the wind, but she could tell Sylvia was disappointed.

There's water here, Esther said to Sylvia, almost pleading, and flowering branches.

Yes, we've got all the elements, Sylvia, said Jean. What are you waiting for, a burning bush?

Well –, said Sylvia, but Jean cut in.

I'm too cold to stand here arguing. Let's get the thing started.

Then they all, except Julie, had a bit of an argument about which part of the ritual came first, until Jean said quite sharply that they should probably do the circle dance first before they froze to the spot, and everyone joined hands.

It wasn't a big circle. They kept bumping into one another and slipping on the rough ground.

This is awful, Jean said. Whose idea was it?

Yours, I think, said Sylvia.

Julie stood in the middle, trying not to look at anyone. First Jean bumped into her then Josepha, and everyone apologised. Jean said,

You'd better join in Julie, this is ridiculous.

So Julie joined hands with Jean and Esther, and immediately the circle moved more easily, though no one knew the steps, then Sylvia said,

You know, this might work better if we sing something.

Ring-a-ring-a-roses, said Jean.

How about the 'Song of the North Berwick Witches'? Sylvia said. Jean snorted and said she was trying to get them arrested, but Sylvia began in her deep voice,

Cummer go ye before, cummer go ye . . .

It was easy to pick up, though Julie had never heard it before. It was a kind of chant, and as they circled round singing their voices got louder and louder and Julie definitely felt better. She began to feel the same glow she had felt when Medbh did the circle dance, and even Jean's mood seemed to improve. When they stopped, breathless and laughing, Sylvia said,

Now for the presents.

Josepha went first. She had baked one of the vegan cakes Julie had eaten at tea, but on the top in thin icing she'd piped Happy Birth Day.

Thank you, Julie said.

Then Sylvia gave her a wooden box full of some kind of herb.

Raspberry leaf tea, she said. It'll help with the contractions.

Esther gave Julie a beautiful square of crocheted lace for the baby. She had made it herself years ago, she said, and Julie remembered what Josepha had said, that Esther couldn't have babies of her own, she had had to adopt, and she hardly knew what to say.

Then Jean came up.

I might not get to see the baby, she said, though I hope I do, and she patted Julie's stomach. I've brought you this, she said. You said you liked it, and from a carrier bag she took the little tree from her miniature garden.

O thank you, Julie said. She didn't know what else to say.

It needs a sunny position, Jean said. And don't water it too much.

Julie stood, looking down at the presents. She hoped she wouldn't cry. Jean hugged her and so did Sylvia, then after a moment, Esther and Josepha.

We mustn't forget the blessing, Sylvia said. We must all put our hands on Julie's tummy to bless the baby.

Everyone put a hand on Julie's hard, bumpy stomach.

Julie didn't feel so self-conscious now. Everyone was smiling and she looked round at all their faces.

Our mother earth, Sylvia said, bless this labour and this child, that the birth may be painless and swift and the child beautiful and strong. Bless him with air, water, fire and earth.

Suppose it's a girl, Josepha said, and Jean said,

It's a boy, you can tell from the way she's carrying, and at that moment the baby kicked out at all the hands and everyone laughed.

O he's a strong one, Sylvia said, and Josepha said,

Have you chosen a name yet?

Julie hadn't. It seemed daft to say it but all this time she had been waiting for Mick. Now it struck her how daft that was.

Esther said,

I've got a book on the numerology of names at home. I vote we all go back now for some cocoa and cake, and I'll get it for you if you like. That is, if we're finished.

You mean, unless we want to strip ourselves naked and run round the hills in a Bacchic frenzy, said Jean. No, I think I'll settle for cocoa and cake, and since they were all getting cold again everyone agreed. All the presents fitted into Jean's carrier, and as they set off back along the path Sylvia said,

You know, it's a full moon tonight, I checked on the calendar.

O I've got a wonderful window for watching the moonrise, if it's not too cloudy, said Esther.

Just don't start howling, Sylvia, said Jean. Her mood seemed to have improved no end, but as they reached the crest of the hill Julie saw her pause and gaze over the valley. Though there was no light in the sky, just a mass of blue cloud, the hill opposite was lit up by a weird, very cold light. Julie waited and Jean said,

They are fantastic, aren't they? and Julie knew she was thinking she wouldn't see them many more times. She took Jean's arm and together they tried to catch up to the others. Although it was less than half a mile to Esther's, they both had to be helped over the last bit, Josepha holding onto Jean and Esther and Sylvia pulling Julie along.

Esther's house was the most impressive Julie had ever seen. There was an entrance hall with a domed ceiling, and an enormous room with brick walls and pillars down the centre, and set in every other pillar there was a glass panel with flames leaping behind. The whole of the back wall was one great arched window looking out over the moor. There were three cream-coloured sofas in the room and a polished mosaic floor.

I can't believe you ever let your children in here, Jean said.

O I do, Esther said, looking quite hurt. She pulled up two sofas so that everyone could see, then hurried up the spiral staircase in the centre of the room.

You're supposed to be in bed, she said, and Julie just caught sight of two heads with shiny black hair disappearing back up the staircase.

They're from Brazil you know, Sylvia said in hushed tones, and they actually are brother and sister. Esther and Greg made a special journey out for them, it cost them a fortune I believe.

Now the two children were called Naomi and Luke and they were seven and five.

They're such a happy family now, Sylvia said, and Julie couldn't see how anyone could be unhappy in that house.

Esther's husband helped her make the cocoa and brought the cake in. He was dark and quiet like Esther. Esther passed Julie the book on numerology and said she could borrow it if she liked, then they all sat round the window.

It's too cloudy, Josepha said, but Sylvia said, No, I think it's clearing over there.

Shreds of moon appeared and disappeared. Julie had never watched a moonrise before, she hadn't known it happened so fast, but each time they saw the moon it was in a different place. There it is, Josepha said, and Esther said, There.

In the centre of the sky a big space appeared, clouds rolled back like stage curtains. No one spoke or moved and the moon rolled straight into it, white and glowing.

Everyone breathed out at once.

Julie was so happy it had happened, the ceremony and the moonrise. She really did feel different, as though it would make a difference to her life. She was there in the beautiful room with all her friends, drinking cocoa and eating cake, and when she looked round at them she really felt that the blessing had worked, she really had been blessed.

Julie didn't go out much any more. Days passed slowly in her room, punctuated by trains. By some agreement that was never fully sorted out, other people began to do the shopping and cooking; there was always food in, of a sort, but Julie knew the laundry wasn't being done, and if she didn't clean the toilet nobody would, so she went on doing it most days, with the brush she'd bought, until one day she couldn't be bothered any more.

Downstairs Mick and Darren were busy with the kitchen when they were in, but they were going out a lot again. Uncle Si hadn't been in for some days. Julie didn't speak to Mick or Darren, she didn't know what to say. Sometimes they called up to ask her if she wanted a cup of tea, then sometimes they forgot to bring it up. Julie always waited until the house was quiet before going down to make some food. She stayed in her room and ate the cake Josepha had made and read the book Esther had given her and went through all the things in the pram. The baby would have to sleep in the top bit of the pram, since there wasn't a cot. She would leave the bottom bit downstairs and carry the top down when she needed to go out. But there were still many more things to buy, and she also had to buy something for Jean's party, which had been moved now to the seventeenth of April, Jean's birthday. Julie didn't know whether she would be able to go by then or not. She felt a peculiar depression, a listlessness about everything, as if somehow she really had expected everything to change. She looked down at the things

Aunty Clare had bought her, the coat, and the cardigan she'd made. Everything seemed sour now, since seeing Brian, she didn't think she would ever get back in touch. Once she decided she would go out to look for a present and for baby things, and she tugged her pumps on with some difficulty over her swollen feet, then pushed them off again. She couldn't be bothered. She moved with difficulty between her mattress and the toilet, rolling onto all fours first, then pulling herself up by the windowsill. She held her stomach and wondered if she would still be pregnant by Jean's birthday, it was hard to imagine not being pregnant any more. But all she had to do was to go to the hospital and they would look at her swollen fingers and feet and induce her, Julie knew. But they would ask her about the four visits she'd missed, so she was afraid to go. She was afraid to count the movements of her baby, she was afraid to choose a name. She read the book of names page by page, Hepsibah, Chrysippis, but since in her mind the child had no face it was hard to give it a name. She wondered what had made her mother pick a dull name like Julie, it wasn't in the family. Sometimes she held the book and stared out of the window and wondered how Jean was, or what Josepha or Annie was doing. When she listened to the noises of her room she was surprised by how many there were, it was never entirely quiet. Joints creaked, trains rumbled past, sometimes she heard laughter below.

Mick and Darren never seemed to sleep at night, they sat up smoking and talking, and sometimes, when Uncle Si wasn't there, started work at three in the morning. Julie slept on and off throughout the day and night, in between visits to the toilet. Once, waking from a deep, muggy sleep, she saw Mick standing by the window, his hair a shaggy darkness against the whirling snow, but when she woke up again he was gone. Then another time she saw him standing by the window again, looking at the night sky and the railway tracks stretching far into the night. Julie raised herself slowly on one elbow but she didn't say anything.

He didn't move, but behind the stillness Julie could sense the restlessness in him. He would be off if he could, through the window, along those tracks to the hills, or maybe hitching a ride into another town. And it came to her then, as she watched how little Mick liked being in a house at all, how much he missed being homeless. That was why he filled the house with homeless people and why the work on the house was never done. And seeing this, Julie felt she had known it all the time.

Mick sighed and muttered something under his breath, then he turned away from the window. Julie lay down quickly and closed her eyes, but she followed all his movements in her mind. He walked over to his mattress and lay down, sighed and shifted and rolled over. Then after a moment he rolled back and lay still.

Julie knew he wasn't asleep. She wondered if he knew she was awake. She wished he would say something, at the same time part of her was afraid. She lay listening to him sigh and cough, then after several moments he sat up. There was another pause and he lit a cigarette, then went back to the window. Then, as if remembering that the smoke might waken Julie, he left the room.

Eventually Julie went back to sleep.

She woke up again, or thought she woke, and Mick was there, not by the window this time but at the foot of her mattress, staring at her. As she stared back she realised as she had never realised before, how hard it was for him having Julie there, and the baby, how easy it would be to get rid of her, who would ask any questions? But even as she thought this she had already fallen back into sleep, she tried but she couldn't open her eyes. She moaned and shifted and tried to talk to Mick. But when she managed to open them again he wasn't there.

This time she needed the toilet. She tried to walk but felt peculiar and pulled herself along. Despite her fears there was no sound from anyone in the house. When she got back she lay awake for some time. A train passed, there was the reflection of light and branches. Julie watched the moving shadows in a dazed way and eventually fell back into a deep, awful sleep.

When she woke up she felt sick. Not the ordinary sickness of pregnancy but a deeper kind, as if all the organs of her body were sick at once. She crawled to the toilet and crouched, retching, partly from the smell, then she crawled back without throwing up at all.

Every time she slept it was harder to wake up. One time she was sweating heavily, as if she was losing all the water in her body. That time when she slept she dreamt she was on the scales at the clinic and Sylvia, Jean and Josepha were next to be weighed. They all told her how much weight she'd lost. Julie felt very happy, but then she realised they thought she'd had the baby, they were sending her home, and she knew it was still inside.

I haven't had it yet, she told them, but they told her she must have, she must have left it at home.

Go home and have a good look, they said.

Julie woke up, still sweating so heavily she could hardly see, but the effort of waking was too much and sleep pulled her back. When she woke up again the window was a pale blur in the deeper blur of the room. I'm going blind, she thought, and a small part of her felt afraid, but not enough to keep her awake.

The next time she stayed awake quite a long time, staring hopelessly at things she couldn't see. It seemed to her as though she knew this helplessness, as though all her life she had been travelling towards it. She remembered her mother's face in hospital, and closed her eyes.

The next time she woke up, Mick was leaning over her. She knew it was Mick, though she couldn't see his face.

Jesus, Julie, he said.

Water, Julie said, and immediately Mick went away. He was away so long Julie lapsed back into sleep, and then she thought she must have dreamt him being there, but finally he came back. He held the glass to her lips and the water bubbled round her mouth and ran down her chin and chest.

What is it? Mick said, and Julie gulped loudly.

I'm sick, Mick, she said, and giggled at the way it sounded.

I'll get a doctor.

Julie could hardly believe Mick was saying that, he hated doctors.

No, she said.

You don't look good, said Mick. I'll call someone out.

Julie shook her head. She didn't want to be induced, she didn't want the baby yet.

I'll be all right, she said, lying back and gazing at the ceiling she couldn't see.

Do you want anything? Mick said. Julie shook her head. It was funny, she thought. All this time all she had to do to get Mick to notice her was to get sick, like Darren, but now he was there, taking notice, she didn't care.

The next moment she was awake with him shaking her.

Julie, Julie, he said, for Christ's sake.

Julie felt bad everywhere. She leant over and vomited hugely, all over Mick's feet.

Christ's sake, Mick said, stepping back, then he ran for a cloth. I'm getting the doctor, he said, coming back.

No, said Julie. She grasped his hand. They'll induce the baby. She couldn't say why it was so important for them not to induce the baby, she could only hold Mick's hand and stare at him.

I have to do something, Mick said. He was really scared, Julie could smell his fear. She struggled to sit up but failed.

After tonight, she managed to say. You can call the doctor tomorrow.

Then she closed her eyes and fell into a deep sleep, with dreams that were full of light and space, and somewhere in the background her mother's voice was humming, twinkle, twinkle, little star.

When she woke up, Mick and Darren were both there,

and she could see them, though there was still some blurring.

What time is it? she said.

What day is it, you mean, said Mick. You were asleep all yesterday and most of today. Talking to yourself and singing. I was going to call the doctor, but I waited.

Thanks, Julie said. She felt very weak, but the deep sickness had gone. She wondered if the baby was all right.

Darren was holding the book of names.

Yggdrasil, he said. Someone must actually have called their kid that.

I always thought Mucus was a nice name for a boy, Mick said.

I used to know a girl called Incandescent Freedom, Darren said. But she changed her name to Ann.

Mick laughed.

That guy Archie, he said, always said his name was short for Archetypal Energy.

They went on, talking to each other about people they had known with daft names. They didn't talk to Julie, but she knew they were doing it for her. She didn't feel strong enough to join in. She lay back and listened to their voices, to the sound of the radio downstairs and to the faint rushing noises in her ears.

One day Julie went downstairs. Darren was there on his own, reading the *Socialist Worker*. He jumped up when Julie came in.

Are you all right, he said.

Yes, thanks, said Julie, and she told him she had to go out.

I'll come with you if you like, Darren said, and Julie was surprised and pleased. They were all getting on so much better now. She told him he didn't have to, she wasn't going far, but Darren insisted. He was going out anyway, he said, to the unit. Then he poured out a cup of tea for her. He told her Mick had gone out for some plywood. They didn't say much after that. Julie sipped her tea and Darren looked away from her, down at the table.

It's not long now, till the baby, is it? he said, and Julie was surprised again. She hadn't even been sure that he'd noticed she was pregnant. She told him it was due at the end of the month, and they lapsed back into silence. Julie had never spent any time alone in a room with Darren before. She stared down at her tea and wondered what Mick had said to him about the baby.

Before she had drunk half the cup the heartburn started, so she got up and said she'd have to be going and Darren got up too. Julie couldn't think what she'd say to Darren all the way into town but he didn't seem worried and as they went out into the cluttered yard he even offered her his arm to help her past. They walked down the road looking almost like a couple, Julie thought.

Then Darren started talking to her. He said he didn't think they were too far off being ready for the baby, a bit of plumbing and heating work, some carpets maybe.

Julie could hardly believe he was talking like this, as though they would all live together and everything would be all right. He still stared at the ground when he was talking, not at Julie, and mumbled a bit, but it was plain he meant what he said. Suddenly Julie felt the pressure of wanting to say the right thing back to him, to be friends. She had never walked out like this with Mick, she thought. And Darren was considerate. He kept stopping so that she could catch her breath. She joked, It's like being disabled, this, and Darren smiled, he didn't seem impatient at all. They were silent again and Julie racked her brains for something to say. There were so many things she wanted to say, she didn't know where to start. Finally she said,

How are you going on, at the unit?

Darren didn't seem surprised. He said,

All right, I suppose.

They've not stopped the methadone then.

O no. One of the doctors said they would be stopping it but he's gone now. They'll run out some time, I suppose, but not yet.

What happens when they run out?

Darren shrugged.

Well, don't they want you to come off it in the end? Julie said, but Darren shook his head.

That hardly ever happens, he said. It happens sometimes. That's supposed to be the idea of methadone, that you come off it eventually and you're normal again like, but no one ever does. Some people reckon methadone's more addictive than smack. You're hooked for life once you start. Like me, for instance. I wouldn't be talking to you now if I hadn't had some. It's what makes me seem normal, if you like. People who come off it just hit smack again.

Doesn't it bother you, Julie said, being hooked for life?

Darren shrugged again.

That's just the way it is, he said, and he stopped, not looking at Julie.

I have to go this way now, he said.

See you later, said Julie, and he smiled. Then she realised he was waiting for her to go first, he didn't want her watching him. Bye then, she said, and walked away.

Julie walked slowly towards Dominique's, thinking about Darren all the way. Maybe they could all live together, she thought. Darren was a nice person really, and she didn't have anywhere else. So long as she accepted him and Mick there didn't have to be a problem.

Dominique wasn't in. The girl said they'd only managed to sell the brooch so far, she could have the money for that if she liked, eighteen pounds. Julie took it and didn't say that it was less than she'd thought. She was still thinking about Darren, and about them all living together, and being friends. People needed one another, she thought, then she thought about him only being able to talk because he'd taken the methadone, and about him being hooked for life.

Her back and lower belly ached as she waddled across the road to the building society. There was so much to buy she would have to draw out the bit she'd saved. The tops of her legs rubbed together and her heart banged. The bloating hadn't stopped, though she hardly ate anything any more, she was like a great bloated monster. And suddenly she was so sick of being pregnant she almost lay down in the middle of the road. She would go to the hospital, she thought, and get herself induced.

In the end it was the thought of the nightie she hadn't got yet that made Julie carry on from the building society to the market, where Annie had said there was a stall full of cheap baby things. She couldn't wear the old purple dress in hospital. And she still had to get something for Jean.

Julie didn't know what to get for Jean. At the baby stall she bought baby oil and baby bath and sterilising tablets in case she couldn't breast-feed, and nipple cream in case she could, and nappies and some extra vests and a nightie that buttoned down the front. She couldn't afford baby milk that week, so she wandered over to a stall that sold cheap perfume instead, and sprayed on one tester, then another. Then she saw Alison.

Julie considered walking away, but Alison had seen her.

Hello, Julie, she said. She looks terrible, Julie thought, then, *She's on her own.*

Julie was afraid to ask, but she said,

Where's Sadie?

Alison didn't say anything, she looked away. Her face looked as though she'd been crying. Julie felt sick, she didn't know what to say, then Alison said,

She's in hospital. They're keeping her in.

Relief washed through Julie. She said,

What's wrong with her?

Alison looked as though she was going to speak, then she stopped. She looked at Julie without saying anything and Julie could see she was going to cry. She stepped forwards and took Alison's arm.

Come on, she said, leading her away from the stall towards McDonald's, reckoning her money up all the way.

I'll buy you a drink, she said eventually. She could run to a cup of tea, she told herself. Though she hadn't forgiven Alison. She sat her down near the window and went to the counter to order tea for one and some hot water for herself.

We don't do hot water, said the girl behind the counter.

What do you put in the tea then? said Julie.

The girl stared at her.

It's not listed, she said.

Julie took tea for one. When she got back to the table Alison hadn't changed position at all. She was staring out of the window into nothing. But when Julie started to sit down she said,

Aren't you having one?

Heartburn, said Julie, and Alison said, O. She took the little plastic stirrer and bent it backwards and forwards, then she said,

Everything's wrong with her. She's got injuries.

Julie steadied the tea.

Alison didn't look up. She let out a long trembling breath.

They said she had injuries down below.

Then she was crying, very quietly, her face screwed up and the tears ran down, but Julie couldn't hear a thing.

Julie felt her own baby kicking. She held her stomach and whispered,

What happened?

But Alison couldn't speak for crying. Eventually she said,

Alan did it. He didn't even deny it, then she let her head fall forwards into her hands and her hair fell forwards too, Julie couldn't see her face.

A hundred things ran through Julie's mind but all she could say was, O, God. It was like an attack. She waited until the feeling of panic died down, then she said, Her own father.

Alison stopped crying. Her breathing quietened, but she didn't take her face from her hands. She said,

Sadie isn't Alan's.

Now Julie really didn't understand. At the same time she felt she had known it all along. She stared at Alison helplessly. Alison looked up, but not at Julie. She said, as if she had rehearsed saying it,

Alan liked me to go with other men, it turned him on. She stopped, then in the face of Julie's blank silence, said,

We hardly ever slept together, he just wanted to watch. She lowered her face again.

Terrible thoughts went through Julie's mind, words she never used. She sat back in her chair and said,

Whose is she? in quite a hard way.

O Jesus, I don't know, Alison said. Then she looked up and laughed a bit.

Look at you, she said. You don't understand. How could you?

Julie didn't understand. She had never even imagined anything like this. It was so far outside her own experience she felt almost as though she was watching the whole thing on telly. She tried to think, would she do anything for Mick, anything at all? She used to think so but not any more.

Alison was talking again.

The first time we went together, she said in a tired kind of way, I thought it was my fault that we couldn't get it on. I tried hard enough. Then one night we went to the pub and this bloke we met there came back with us and we opened some cans and smoked a bit, and Alan started saying, Alison's kisses are ambrosia, and all that stuff, you ought to try her, and we ended up kissing. I think I was doing it to nark Alan, to see if he'd get jealous. Of course, it didn't work. This bloke got more and more keen and I kept looking at Alan and waiting for him to stop it, but he didn't. He didn't want to, I could see it in his face. And after, when it was over, he was really kind and loving to me, saying how beautiful I was, and if he couldn't enjoy me himself it was the closest thing. He felt privileged, he said, and Alison looked up quickly to catch the expression on Julie's face, then looked down again when she did.

Anyway, she said after a pause. It wasn't just Alan. I liked doing it. I liked it and felt bad at the same time. I felt like I was betraying Alan. Crazy isn't it, she said with half a laugh. I felt bad and afterwards I couldn't do enough to please him. And he couldn't do enough to please me.

Alison looked away again.

That's the way it was anyhow, she said, and she sat back.

Julie stared down at the table. Then suddenly she was struck with a terrible thought. She didn't know how to say it, but she had to ask.

Is that why Mick was there? she managed to say.

Alison laughed.

O shit. No.

Julie didn't know whether or not to believe her. Alison said,

If you ask me, Mick's too much into Darren.

She didn't say it unkindly but Julie felt bad. She was surprised to find it still hurt her, but it did. She steered the conversation away.

What about Sadie? she said.

Sadie got sick, said Alison. They let her out of hospital after she banged her head – she was only in for observation. But a week after that she was ill again. She cried all night after I'd been out and when I looked at her I thought there was something funny with her arm. And Alan wouldn't let me call the doctor. He went screaming mad – I've never seen him like that before. He said if I called the doctor he'd tell everyone what a filthy whore I was, he'd burn it into my face with his fag. I was scared shitless. He must have been doing temazzis or something – he was off his head. And Sadie screamed all night, I nearly killed her myself.

But in the morning he crashed out. I took Sadie and ran all the way to the hospital. They x-rayed her arm and said it was broken – not an ordinary break but like someone had been twisting it. And then they told me about the other stuff. A ruptured cervix. Alison's face twisted with pain. Before I knew where I was, she said, I was in this room with a social worker. She asked me if I'd ever done drugs. And I was so dropped on I told her everything. She said Sadie was probably dependent on them through me, that was why she kept crying. And they couldn't let her go home with me, I couldn't even see her. And they asked me if I wanted to press charges and when I'd finished crying I said I did. I hate him. I want them to put him away.

Julie could see from her face that she meant it. It was the same look Mick had had, she was sick from hating.

I thought of killing myself, Alison said. It sounds daft, but I did. I just couldn't think what to do. I couldn't go back to the flat. I told them where he was and that, and the police went round and pressed charges. And I went back to my mum's. They took me back. My dad and Steve wanted to kill Alan. They said they'd get my things but I went back with them, I made them wait at the bottom and I went in on my own. And Alan was there – he'd got himself bail, the bastard – I never knew he had that much cash. He was lying on the bed with his eyes wide open – I thought he'd OD'd. Then he looked at me. And I started shaking – I don't know if I was angry or scared. He just looked at me and said, Traitor. That was all he said. Then he got up and went into the kitchen, and he starts brewing up as if nothing had happened. I followed him in and he said, Tea? Just like that. And I just said, Why, eh, why? and he wouldn't say anything, but I kept on at him, I started screaming and shouting, everything the hospital had said, all the proof. And he just stood and looked at me, like he was just waiting for me to stop. And when I did, you know what he said?

Julie shook her head. She couldn't imagine what he could say.

He said, *It's a sick society that denies the sexuality of infants*. I could have killed him then, there was a knife right there on the side. But I suddenly felt dead calm, and all I did was look at him. And he turned away. And I got my things and left. Steve and my dad went round later for my other things, the cot and stuff, and Alan wasn't in. So I'm living at home now, Alison said. And I want Sadie back. I never thought I would, but I do. And there's a chance, if I stay away from Alan and off drugs, and prove I can support myself and her. And I can, she said. I want to get a job. I've heard they're taking part-timers on at Woolworths, I was just on my way. She blew her nose and wiped her eyes.

Julie didn't speak, she couldn't. She could only think about Sadie and about everything Sadie had been through in the four short months of her life.

After a pause Alison said, So there we are, with a bit of a smile, but Julie still didn't say anything.

You know the worst thing? Alison said after a bit. Julie didn't want to know about anything worse, but Alison went on, You know what I thought when they told me about Sadie? I thought, He couldn't make it with me but he could with her, and her face twisted up again and she looked away.

Julie thought about how happy Alison had been when she first met Alan, and her eyes filled up. Alison looked at her.

What's up with you? she said.

Julie could hardly speak, but she took hold of Alison's hand.

Everything went wrong for you, she managed to say. Everything went wrong.

Alison didn't take her hand away from Julie's. They sat together at the window table in McDonald's, looking away from everyone else and holding hands, and crying.

Mick's very worried you know, Julie said to Darren. They sat facing one another at the kitchen table, eating the soup Julie had made. Mick was out.

Darren looked surprised.

What about? he said.

Looking at Darren it was hard to say. But she had to say it. She had thought about nothing else since seeing Alison, she couldn't get what Alison had said out of her mind. She looked away.

He's worried about you, she said. And the baby.

What do you mean, Darren said.

With the drugs and that, said Julie.

There was a long silence, then Darren said,

He never said anything to me.

No, he wouldn't, Julie said. He asked me not to either. But he is worried. He thinks – he thinks it'd be better for all of us if you got a place of your own. She looked at him without blinking.

Darren's face was very pale in the pale snowy light from the window, but he smiled.

Mick wouldn't say that, he said.

He says it all the time, said Julie. He just doesn't know how to say it to you. He cares about you, Darren, we both do, she said. He just thinks – we've got to do the best for the baby, and she leant forwards earnestly. She believed what she was saying. They did care for Darren, but they did have to do their best for the baby.

Darren stopped smiling. He pushed his chair back a bit.

He never said anything, he repeated.

Julie's face was compassionate.

No, she said. I know.

Darren looked at her. He looked as though he was going to say something, then he looked away. Then suddenly he stood up, knocking his chair over, and went out.

Julie stood up to stir the soup.

I've done it now, she thought.

She had done what she had meant to do and she didn't

feel any better. But she hadn't been able to stop herself thinking about Alan, and Sadie. It was because of drugs, she thought. She couldn't think of any other explanation. Now she looked out of the window, at the wet snow splashing into the yard. It was April, and still snowing, and both Mick and Uncle Si were out.

Work doesn't stop for snow, Mick had said.

So there was no one in but Julie, and all Julie could do was wait, and she waited all day with a peculiar, weighted-down feeling.

Where's Darren? said Mick.

Julie didn't look around.

I don't know, she said. He was in earlier.

He might have gone to the drughouse, Mick said, and he went upstairs.

Julie stirred the soup. She was turning it into curry by adding a lot of curry powder and boiling up some rice. Darren hadn't been in for over six hours. She wanted to tell Mick but didn't know how.

Uncle Si came in.

By, it's cold, he said.

I'll make you a cup of tea, Julie said. The kettle had already boiled for Mick. She got the tea and sugar from the new units. Uncle Si took his mug into his room.

Julie served the curry, in a small bowl for herself, and larger amounts on plates for Mick and Uncle Si. Then she knocked on Uncle Si's door and carried the plates through.

Mick, she called up the stairs. Tea's ready.

Mick clumped down the stairs.

They sat near the fire in Uncle Si's room as the snowy rain dripped from the eaves outside. It didn't come in any more. Mick and Darren had seen to that.

Mick talked about the bad day he'd had, trying to sell the *Socialist Worker*. He'd only sold two, then when he was packing up someone had come along and Mick had thought he was going to make one more sale, but the bloke just wanted to slag him off. Why should people like you get free handouts? he'd said. He'd worked all his life and been in the army. Mick couldn't believe people were still coming out with the same old shit, but he'd been too tired to argue. Change the record, Dad, he'd said, and he'd packed up his papers and left.

Uncle Si said that he'd thought the army was a nice place, and Mick nearly choked, explaining why you couldn't say that about the army.

Well, I had a nice time, Uncle Si said when he'd finished. They gave me all my meals. And there wasn't any fighting.

Mick started patiently to explain again, and Julie carried the dishes back into the kitchen. She washed up, thinking all the time about Darren. When she went back Mick had finished explaining and Julie sat down again. There was a long pause, then Mick said,

I wonder where Darren's got to.

Julie couldn't stand it any longer.

He's been out a long time, she said. I didn't think he looked too good when he went.

Mick looked at her.

What do you mean? he said.

You know, Julie said quickly, not quite himself.

Mick stared.

Why didn't you tell me? he said.

Well, he didn't say anything, said Julie. He just walked past me and went out. She felt sick in the pit of her stomach.

Mick stood up.

What time did he go out? he said.

Julie couldn't look at him.

About twelve, she said. Or half past.

Mick looked as if he couldn't believe what he was hearing.

Half twelve? He said. Half past fucking twelve? Jesus, he said. He looked as if he was going to say something else, then he left the room, Julie heard the bang of the back door as he left.

Uncle Si looked at Julie.

Will there be trouble? he said.

No, said Julie.

Late in the night Julie heard voices and a crashing noise downstairs. She struggled up, trying to see in the dark. There was Mick's voice and the crashing noise again. Julie wouldn't be caught like this, in the dark. She rolled onto her knees and got to her feet, clutching her coat as if she might have to run outside. Then she crept onto the landing.

At the same time the light went on. Julie stared straight down into Mick's face, yellow in the light from the bulb. He stared back at her, then shoved something, and a great pile of rubble collapsed over the stairs. A thick smoke of dust went up, and by the time it cleared Mick had gone, there were more smashing noises from the kitchen.

Julie was afraid to go downstairs, afraid not to. She didn't know where Uncle Si was. There was another great crash and she gripped the stair rail hard. There was the sound of glass shattering. Julie clung to the stair rail and lowered herself carefully past the rubble.

Mick held a hammer in both hands. He raised it shoulder high and swung it at the double-glazed window he had put in last week. More of the glass shattered.

Mick, Julie cried.

Mick didn't even pause. He swung at the frame this time with a great grunt. All round the kitchen there were piles of glass and rubble and shattered units, Mick was smashing up all the work he'd done.

Julie knew she should get out and save her own skin. Instead she took a great lungful of air and screamed at him,

Mick! Stop it!

Mick looked at her with livid eyes, then strode over to

where she was, raising the hammer, but instead of swinging it right at her he pushed past her, hard. Julie overbalanced on the rubble and the baby lurched inside. She struggled up again and followed Mick into Uncle Si's room.

Mick was overturning the furniture, laying into it in a systematic way with his hammer. Julie closed her eyes.

Mick, she said weakly. This isn't your room.

Mick ignored her.

Mick, she said. Where's Uncle Si?

Then,

Where's Darren?

Mick stopped mid-swing.

Don't you talk about Darren, he said. Don't you *ever* talk about Darren.

He smashed the hammer into the telly.

Julie's baby lurched again, inside her head she could hear him crying.

Then Mick pushed past her again, going upstairs, to where the baby things were, and the pram.

No, Mick, Julie said. Her voice came out too weakly. She clambered after him, slipping on the rubble, scraping her hands. When she got to the bedroom Mick had tipped the pram over and all the baby things were on the floor. Julie's voice came shrilly,

Leave that bloody pram alone!

Leave that bloody pram alone, Mick said. Bloody this, bloody that. Why can't you say fucking, Julie? I can say it, why can't you? Fuck the pram, and he hit the base of it with the hammer, a glancing blow that didn't go through.

Come on say it, he said. Fuck the fucking pram.

Julie hadn't meant to start crying but now she was.

Leave it alone, she said, and she went all the way round Mick to the pram and tried to pick it up.

It's mine, she said.

Mick kicked it out of her hands.

Fucking say it, he said.

Julie bent down over the pram. She didn't think she could save it, or herself, or get away, she only knew she wasn't leaving the pram. Then Mick grabbed the hair on the back of her head. He wrenched her upwards and into the wall.

Say *fuck* the *fucking* baby in the *fucking* pram, he said, banging her face into the wall each time he swore. Julie could feel the blood running down and hear a kind of moaning noise in her ears. Then abruptly he let her go, and she sank down onto the mattress, then slid from the mattress to the floor. She reached forwards blindly and somehow found the handle of the pram.

When she could see through the blood and dirt of her face she saw Mick standing in the middle of the room with his back to Julie, the hammer hanging loosely at his side. Julie wiped her face on her sleeve, then wiped it again.

Neither of them spoke.

Then Mick walked away from her to the far wall. He pressed his forehead briefly to it, then straightened.

Shit, he said.

All the tension sagged out of him, Julie had known all the time it was her he needed to hit. She went on dabbing at her face with her sleeve, though she knew she was ruining the coat.

Mick shook his head. Then he walked away from her towards the door, but Julie couldn't just let him leave. She said,

What happened to Darren?

Mick stopped. He still wouldn't look at her. He took a breath.

Darren's all right – he'll be all right. He'll live.

Then he sat down on his mattress.

He had found Darren in the park, stoned out of his head, not moving. It was dark, he couldn't see him clearly. He thought Darren was soaked with the wet snow, then when he got closer he saw that Darren's trousers were covered in blood.

Mick lost it. He ran to the gates of the park screaming for an ambulance, then, when someone heard him, he legged it back to Darren. From somewhere the memory came that you had to lean on a wound to stop it bleeding, and he tugged at Darren's trousers. They weren't fastened, and he saw where the needle was stuck in the groin. He pulled it out and leant with all his weight. He said, Come on, Darren, come on, over and over again for a long time, it was all he could think of to say. Then the ambulance came. They made a tourniquet and rushed Darren and Mick to hospital. They told Mick he'd probably saved Darren's life.

Mick was silent again, gazing at the wall.

Julie said,

Why was he injecting himself there? and Mick said it was the femeral vein, his other veins were knackered. There was another silence, and Mick stared at the floor, then Julie said,

I told Darren you wanted him to leave.

Mick nodded slowly.

I thought that might be it, he said.

I didn't mean to –, she said and stopped, then started again. I didn't mean it to happen. I didn't mean any of it to happen, she repeated, and there was an edge of bitterness in her voice.

No, right, Mick said, resigned now.

I didn't, Julie said. You think I planned it all, the baby and everything, but I didn't. I didn't plan on having a baby any more than you did.

She'd wanted to tell him that for a long time. Mick said,

You could have done something about it – once you knew.

Julie sighed. She'd known that was coming. She remembered when she'd first known she was pregnant, standing at the front door of Uncle Si's just because she was tired of looking out at the back. All along the path in front of the house rose bay-willow herb was growing, four feet high and a pinkish-purple colour. Behind this there was the track, then the disused sheds and garages, and behind everything were the hills, coloured a different purple with the heather. She'd stood at the front door looking at it all and known she was keeping the baby, though she didn't know how, or why. She couldn't explain this to Mick. She thought of one way of explaining it, then another, then she said, No, I couldn't, in a tired kind of way.

Mick didn't say anything. Julie said,

I can't have an abortion now. The baby's here now. We've got to accept it – and do our best.

She'd said everything finally, everything she'd been meaning to say for months. Over on his mattress Mick shifted himself and lay back, staring at the ceiling.

There's this guy, he said. They call him Soft Matt, you know, like the emulsion. He's been homeless years, most of his life. He started selling for *The Big Issue*, and they helped him to get a flat and a job on one of the newspaper stands. So that was him set up. Except that he kept not turning up for the job, and wandering off early, and one day when money was missing they turned up at his flat. But it turned out he never used the flat. He kept the key, paid some of the rent, but every night he slept out, behind the railings in Victoria Park, where he always used to sleep. So in the end he lost the job, and the flat and he's back on the streets.

Mick paused and Julie waited.

He couldn't hack it, you see, he said.

Julie said nothing and moments ticked over. It was so quiet that they could hear one another breathing, then Julie said,

I just think we've got to do our best.

Yeah, right, said Mick.

What have you done to your face? one person then another asked Julie, and she was just about to give the same explanation again, about falling down the stairs, when at the other side of the room Jean clapped her hands.

Everyone turned to look.

I want to thank you all, she said, for your lovely presents. Today, as you know, is my fifty-fourth birthday. But that's not the only reason for this party. I'm also celebrating the end of my life.

Julie looked round at the faces of people there. Some of them she already knew. Certainly everyone from the meditation group knew, and Aaron Li, of course. He stood beside Jean at the head of the oak table, looking shifty, Julie thought. But there was the yoga group, and the two women from the health shop, standing in an electrified silence, as if they half expected Jean to spontaneously combust there and then, or at least slash her wrists. Jean looked nervous now she'd made the announcement. She looked from one face to another but didn't say anything, Julie thought she must be losing her nerve. And the party was having a hard enough time getting going as it was, this wasn't likely to help.

I've been told I don't have long to live, Jean said, and Julie saw her gripping Aaron Li's hand. A murmur ran through the yoga group.

I'm sorry, Jean said. She seemed overcome with confusion. In the silence that followed, Julie stared at the pale sunlight gleaming on the oak panels, then jumped violently when someone rang the front doorbell.

I'll get it, Sylvia said, and hurried out.

Moments later there were shouts up the hall and Annie entered, dragging a twin in either hand.

They're a nightmare on the bus, she was saying. It's easier staying in – then she stopped because of the silence in the room.

Am I interrupting something? she said.

Somehow the silence relaxed.

No, no, Jean said, going over to one of the twins and kneeling down. Come and get some food. She took Jamie's hand.

People started talking again and moving round. Annie

tugged coats, hats and wellies off the twins. Julie was very glad to see her. She moved herself over slowly.

Hi, Annie said. What happened to your face? and Julie began her story about the stairs, but Thomas disappeared and Annie gave up trying to listen. Julie went to get a drink for her instead.

The twins were walking now. They pulled themselves round the furniture and held onto the knees of anyone who was sitting down, then they found Stanley and all three babies crawled round after one another. It gave everyone something to talk about apart from death, and Annie was able to sit down for a minute with Julie and Josepha.

Not long now, she said, to Julie. Just another few decades.

Feels like it, Julie said, and they were off, talking about how long nine months could seem. Then Jamie fell over a chair leg and a glass toppled from the table. Both Jean and Annie ran to pick the glass up.

I shouldn't have brought them, Annie said. They're causing havoc – I knew they would.

Not at all, said Jean. I'm glad you brought them, they've broken the ice. Look how everyone's talking.

Julie looked round and it was true. People all over the room were talking to each other, picking the babies up and putting them down again. There was an energy in the room Julie hadn't noticed before, as if the announcement of Jean's death had made everyone feel more alive. The party was really taking off. Someone was dancing with Stanley, someone else was crawling round the floor after the twins. There was a bump and a roar as one of the twins bumped his head, and Annie ran to pick him up.

You know sometimes I think I'll get my own back on these two when they grow up, she said coming back. I think I'll go round to their houses at four in the morning and scream in their ears and run round their front rooms throwing coffee everywhere.

How old are they? said Josepha.

Thirteen months twelve days, Annie said.

Time to think about having some more, said Julie smiling.

Ho fucking ho, said Annie, and went off to get the other twin down from the shelves.

The trouble with being a parent, Jean said to Julie and Josepha, is that if you ever do get revenge you don't actually feel good about it, and she got up as the doorbell rang.

It was Medbh, looking very exotic in what she said was the Icelandic national dress. She'd been over there on a tour with the Mind-Power programme to defeat depression, and a party of women had presented it to her as a gift. She kissed Jean, Eric and Pierre, then disappeared in a group of people.

Can't be long now, Sylvia said, sitting down next to Julie. You know, she said to Annie and Josepha, I always think of this baby as being partly ours. When are you due?

Julie said she thought she was due some time in the next fortnight.

You'll have to take better care of yourself then, Jean said, coming back into the conversation and touching Julie's bruised cheek. Julie smiled at her. She wanted to ask her something but felt a bit shy. She'd thought of calling the baby after Jean if it was a girl, only she didn't like the name much. So she'd been wondering if Jean had a middle name.

Jean filled everyone's glass, including her own, Julie had never seen her drinking before. Then Annie went over to see Medbh, who had picked up a twin in each arm and was rocking them as she talked. Josepha rocked Stanley who had climbed onto her knee and seemed to be falling asleep, and Sylvia was called away to be introduced to someone.

Jean, Julie said, do you have a middle name?

Jean is my middle name, Jean said. My first name was so God-awful I never used it. I was christened Elsie Jean Makepeace. Isn't that wonderful?

Julie couldn't see anything nice in that name at all.

Why, said Jean, then, You weren't thinking –, and she squeezed Julie's arm. What a lovely idea, but don't you dare. I wouldn't wish my name on a member of Parliament. Besides, we're all convinced it'll be a boy.

Josepha said,

You could call him John.

Yes, John's a nice name, Jean said, and I read somewhere that it's going out of use, which would be a pity.

John Fegan, Julie thought, turning the name over in her mind. She still felt she should have a girl's name ready in case, but she didn't like her mother's name either. Or Clare.

Jean filled her own glass again.

This baby's very important to me, you know, she said, and she leant her head against Julie's shoulder and Julie didn't mind at all. All babies are, more so now than ever. I never used to like them really, until they got older. But this one's special, I can tell. And he'll need the very best care.

Julie thought about Uncle Si, and about Darren, who'd be out of hospital soon. But while she was at the party, though she was only sipping water, she could almost feel that she didn't care.

Do you know what all this has taught me? Jean said, sitting up.

No, what, said Julie, and Josepha leant forwards a bit, anxious not to miss out on the mysterious wisdom of the dying.

It's taught me to stop trying to avoid suffering, Jean said. We're all so busy running away from suffering and asking questions that really boil down to *why* do we suffer, that we don't notice that we're carrying the suffering with us all the time. I mean, cancer is just an obvious form of what the whole world is suffering, all the time.

Josepha looked disappointed by this, as if she thought Jean might be drunk, but Julie thought she would try to remember it.

The important thing, said Jean, is to remember the dead.

More and more I feel it's very important to remember the dead, not just because I'll soon be one of them, but because I think, if you remember them, it stops you asking questions. So that's my whole philosophy in a nutshell, she said laughing. Stop asking questions and remember the dead. And she drained her glass and went off to talk to Medbh, who was talking to Sylvia.

Julie admired Stanley who was fast asleep, his breathing hoarse against his mother's embroidered shirt.

Am I interrupting you ladies? Pierre said. He stood behind Josepha, looking very handsome in a silk shirt and waistcoat. They both said no, of course not, and he sat down. He asked them what they thought of the party, and if they knew all the people there. But it seemed to Julie that he was mainly talking to Josepha, and after a while she excused herself and went over to the food. Then, when she was sure they weren't looking, she sat on her own in a corner.

The party went on and the food was disappearing fast. Julie hardly ate any, mindful of heartburn. She sat on her own for quite a long time watching different groups of people come together and disperse. She didn't mind being alone. The heavy, dreamlike feeling of late pregnancy deepened. She thought about her mother and Aunty Clare, and about remembering the dead. Everything that had happened seemed a long time ago. Even her stay with Aunty Clare seemed a lifetime away. It was before the baby's lifetime, she thought. And she thought again about giving the baby a family name, though she didn't like Christine or Clare. But she did like John. And Christian, she thought, though she knew what Mick would think about the name Christian. John Christian, she thought, then Christian John, and Christian John Fegan, and while she was thinking this the doorbell rang again and Jean went to answer it and when she came back Julie thought she had never seen her look so happy. She was with a pale, awkward-looking young man with mousy hair.

This is my son, Michael, she said to everyone, and Michael looked very embarrassed. Julie thought how ordinary he looked. She'd expected him to look a bit wild, or unconventional at least, but he looked like Jean, only without her spark. He slid into a chair at the back of the room and Sylvia went over to rescue him and take him food.

Two people left, kissing and hugging Jean, and were shown to the door by Sylvia. Medbh started talking to Michael, who seemed to cheer up a good deal. Julie couldn't see Annie or the twins, but Pierre was still with Josepha and Stanley was still asleep on Josepha's knee. Julie was struck by how good they looked together. Sylvia came back and started showing Michael her photographs, just as she'd shown Julie all those months ago. Julie sat back and almost dozed, then was brought back by the sound of Medbh's voice.

This woman, Medbh said, holding up Jean's hand, is preparing to leave her life in style. It's a lesson we could all learn, and she paused until people started clapping, and then held up her own hand.

Think what a difference it makes to your afterlife if you don't start off frightened and unwilling, she said. When you go you want to go with banners flying. I'll bet they're looking over from the other side right now and saying, She's all right, this one, she's a fighter, we need more of her sort on our team.

There was laughter, and more clapping.

So I'd like to propose a toast, Medbh said. To Jean. We've all loved you in this life, our love will be with you as you pass into the next and for a long time afterwards. We won't forget you easily, love, and we wish you the very best for your next life. To Jean, she said, and everyone stood up and raised their glasses and said, To Jean. Then someone started singing, Should auld acquaintance be forgot, then everyone was singing it, and Jean stood in the middle, smiling and close to tears.

When everyone had finished singing they clapped again, then Jean said,

Thank you. Thank you all so much. I want to thank Sylvia especially because when I had my doubts about the party and wanted to back out she wouldn't let me – laughter – and she was right. It was a good idea. I wanted to be surrounded at least once by all the people I feel close to, who have shared my journey in some way, and here you all are. I want to thank all of you for being such good company, and to give my especial thanks to my doctor, Dr Bill Radcliffe, who couldn't make it, and to my faithful nurse Sheila, who could and did.

Everyone clapped Sheila, then Jean said,

And now I'm going to retire, but the party must go on. I want everyone to eat, drink and be merry in my absence.

Three cheers for Jean, someone said, and everyone cheered, then Sylvia led Jean away, stopping several times while people hugged and kissed her. Julie didn't go up. She felt as though she'd already said goodbye. At the door Michael took his mother's arm and they went out together, Jean leaning on him quite heavily and Sheila following. Julie watched them go. It might be the last time she ever saw Jean, she thought, and she felt very lonely.

Annie sat down next to her.

Am I missing something? she said. I thought it was her birthday.

It is, said Julie, and tried to explain.

O God, said Annie. O, God. She listened as well as she could for Jamie, who kept pulling at her face and slapping it and shrieking in her ears.

Jesus, stop it, will you? she bellowed suddenly, and people nearby stared in alarm. Annie was embarrassed.

I can't think, she said. It's like having dustbin lids clanging about in your head, and she left Julie and took Jamie back into the garden.

Julie looked over at the presents. She had been pleased with her present in the end, though it had cost more than she'd wanted to pay. It was a small stained-glass panel from Krishna, with a picture of the moon and a lotus flower on it. Wherever you are, it said, there the light shall be also. Other people had brought tapestries and herbs and crystals.

So is Jean really dying, Annie said, coming back.

Julie picked Thomas up.

Looks like it, she said. That's what he says anyway, and they both looked with disfavour at Aaron Li, who was talking to Medbh. Then Annie started to ask Julie about Alison, but Julie didn't want to go into all that, and she was saved by Thomas, who suddenly lunged out of Julie's arms towards the table and grabbed at a plate of quiche, which fell all over the floor.

Shit, Annie breathed, and Julie hurried slowly over to Sylvia for a cloth.

Sylvia and Julie scraped the quiche up while Annie grabbed the twins and their coats and boots. Across the room she signalled to Julie that she was leaving and she left, pulling the twins behind her and apologising to everyone, before Julie could get to her. She had meant to see if she could get a lift back with Annie and Chris, who was picking Annie up, it was Sunday and she wasn't sure which buses were running. She didn't want to trouble Sylvia again. After a bit she sat back in her chair and fell into a kind of inertia. Something would sort itself out. She didn't really want to stay, but she didn't want to go either, she felt the old reluctance to go home. She thought of Jean going home with Michael and Sheila, and how most nights they wouldn't be there, she would be on her own with her thoughts of death. Home is where the pain is, Julie thought. It was where you were on your own with your pain.

Eventually, pressed by the need to wee, she got up and climbed slowly up the stairs. When she came out of the toilet Pierre was there.

I did not mean to startle you, he said, and his face was very serious.

O no, said Julie.

You are going? he said.

I'd better be getting back, said Julie.

How are you getting back? said Pierre, and Julie had to tell him she didn't know.

You must let me drive you, said Pierre.

O no, Julie said. I don't want you to leave the party because of me.

No, he said. I came to look for my jacket.

It was settled then, and Julie went to get her coat and to say goodbye to Sylvia. Pierre excused himself and went over to speak to Josepha, who looked briefly at Julie in what Julie thought was a surprised kind of way, then they were leaving together, and Julie didn't know what to say at all.

I always drive the long way round, Pierre said, because of the view.

Julie looked at the view. The sun was a red disc in a misty sky, some of the hills glowed with it, others were grey and dull.

It is beautiful, Pierre said, and Julie agreed with him. Then he stretched out a hand and patted her stomach.

And this too is beautiful, he said.

Julie wasn't alarmed, but it felt strange. She said, I don't feel very beautiful.

All pregnant women are beautiful, Pierre said smiling. His eyes were on the road. Julie thought briefly of men who only fancied pregnant women, but then he said,

And you are also very tired. I think you have been tired a long time.

No one else had said that to Julie, but now Pierre had said it she knew it was true. She leant back and looked at Pierre with eyes that were huge and dark with tiredness.

I can't stop worrying, she said.

You worry about the birth, said Pierre.

No, said Julie, though she did sometimes. I worry about – afterwards.

I see, said Pierre. He said nothing more and Julie closed her eyes. She could just go to sleep, she thought.

Afterwards, Pierre said, will take care of itself. Just as your baby will take care of himself. All parents are fooled into thinking it is they who take care of the baby, but really it is always the baby who arranges his own parenting.

Even if it's bad, said Julie.

Of course, said Pierre, and Julie sighed. It sounded like the kind of thing people were always saying at Mind-Power.

But you will not be bad, he said.

No, but –, said Julie and stopped.

But, said Pierre.

It's more the situation, Julie said. She didn't want to say any more.

Whatever situation you are in, you will do your best.

Julie sighed again. She could only see the hopeless gap between what Pierre knew about her situation and what she knew. She thought about Darren.

Sometimes you think you're doing the right thing, she said, but it all turns out wrong.

For sure, Pierre said. That is often so.

Julie couldn't make this fit with her idea of karma, that whatever you gave out, good or bad, came back.

Then how do you ever know if you're doing the right thing? she said. For karma.

Karma is not about right or wrong, Pierre said. That is Christian. Karma is only about change, and the consequences of change.

Julie tried, but she couldn't make all the bits fit together.

Stop asking questions, Jean said, and remember the dead.

We're here now, she said quickly, as they came to the lights. She didn't want Pierre seeing the yard. He pulled up at once.

I may not see you before the baby is born, he said, but I hope you will bring him to a meeting afterwards.

O yes, said Julie. She had stopped reminding people that she might be having a girl. Thank you very much. She shifted herself out of the car with difficulty.

And remember, Pierre said, no matter what your situation, it is about to change. There will be a new factor and who knows how that will affect everything else. Everything may change.

Yes, Julie said. Thank you.

Now the days and nights were hardly different from one another. Julie slept a lot in the daytime and was awake a lot at night, going backwards and forwards to the toilet. She didn't go out any more, she was too tired. When Mick had explained to Uncle Si what had happened he had cried, and Uncle Si had held onto him awkwardly, then he had started slowly to patch things up, sometimes when Julie lay awake at night she could hear him. He was sleeping in Darren's room while Darren was away. Julie didn't mind too much, it meant they didn't disturb one another. Besides, she wanted to be on her own.

Then one afternoon she heard voices below, Mick's voice and someone answering, and she knew Darren was back.

She had to go down.

Darren was sitting on Uncle Si's settee, looking very pale. As Julie went in, he looked at Mick as if for support. Uncle Si looked down. Julie walked right across the room towards Darren, she could hear her own heavy steps. When she was only a couple of feet away she said,

Darren – I'm sorry. I shouldn't have said what I did. I thought I was doing the right thing for the baby – but I was wrong.

There was a drawn-out silence. Darren took his eyes off Mick and turned them to the floor in his usual way.

It's all right, he said.

No one else said anything, and after a moment Julie turned and walked out of the room, her heavy tread sounding thud, thud, thud across the floorboards. She went back to her room and stayed there again, leaving only to go to the toilet once or twice an hour. She washed her great, swollen body carefully. No matter how softly she cleaned her teeth her gums still bled.

Then, in the early hours, Julie sat staring into the dark. She had been dreaming about her mother. She got herself to the toilet and sat on it, staring at the tiles, and remembering what Jean had said. It came to her that she had never been to her mother's grave.

She had never been. In the early dark the enormity of this struck her. Nothing would be right if she didn't go, and she went back to the bedroom and walked over to the window, and back to her mattress and sat down.

She wished she hadn't sold the brooch.

The darkness pressed around her as though she was still dreaming. She had tried to forget her own mother. She knew something bad would happen because of it, and she tried to lie down, then got up again. She couldn't sleep.

Finally she tugged on her pumps and made her way downstairs. It seemed to take her a long time to get there, like one of those dreams where you can never get where you're going. And when she got to the kitchen she kept bumping into things and she picked up a cup and dropped it with her great swollen fingers.

Uncle Si came in.

What is it? he said. Is it the young one?

Julie, flushed and unsettled, looked at him.

No, she said.

Uncle Si stepped carefully over bricks and planks of wood. He was wearing his usual shirt and trousers, which were very crumpled because he'd been sleeping in them. Julie was wearing her purple dress.

I have to go out, she said.

Mick had cleared all the smashed glass and patched over

the window with a board so she couldn't see outside, but she could hear it was raining. Uncle Si picked up the kettle.

Will you have a cup of tea? he said.

Julie sat down. Uncle Si had never made her a cup of tea before. She watched him as he found the tea and milk and sugar, then he sat down facing her.

This isn't a good place for you, he said, and Julie thought, *He's going to ask me to go*, and she knew that while she had resisted going until now, if Uncle Si asked her she would have to leave.

When you first came, he said, I thought you were Mick's girlfriend –, he trailed off and coughed a bit. But now you're here, and the little one – I want you to know that no harm'll come – if I can help it – no harm, and he stared at her earnestly as if trying to convince her of his protective powers.

Julie blushed and swallowed. She saw that he meant what he said, though he might not remember it later, and she felt great pangs of guilt and gratitude.

Thank you, she whispered. Then she felt oddly quiet. Uncle Si sat back.

Where is it you have to go? he said.

O nowhere, said Julie, then, I want to go to the cemetery, to see my mother's grave. She died, you know, she said, smiling foolishly, but Uncle Si only nodded.

My mother died too, he said.

Julie thought of saying, when was that, or how old was she, but she didn't really want to talk. So she stood up instead and poured the tea out of habit, stirring plenty of sugar into Uncle Si's cup.

You'll not go out then, he said unexpectedly as she passed him the mug, and Julie shook her head.

I'll wait till morning, she said.

Later she lay on her mattress, sure she could feel an ache. Not yet, she implored the night, and she promised she would stay awake and go to the cemetery first thing, without knowing who she was talking to.

Later still she struggled awake, and the first thing she saw was the little orange tree Jean gave her. It didn't look too healthy. Julie knew suddenly that she should take it. It wouldn't last long in the cemetery, but she felt better about it dying there than in her room. She felt better having something to take.

The air was clear and the sunlight sharp as a lemon as Julie made her way, stopping and starting along the road to the bus stop. The sharp air hurt her throat, she hadn't been out for so long, but she was glad she had come out, it made her feel alive. She pressed on doggedly along the road. On the bus she sat on the front seat clutching her little tree and watching brilliant splashes of sunlight suddenly fade, then flare out again. It had been the worst April in years, but now the weather was changing. Julie was glad she was having her baby in spring.

When she got off the bus she had to walk up a long incline to the entrance of the cemetery. There were railings all along and Julie held onto these trying to breathe. Please, God; please, God, she said. She couldn't give up now. On the other side of the railings pushing through were all the new pale leaves with water trembling in them from the recent rain.

By the time Julie got to the gates she felt bad. And she still had to find the grave. She was mad, she told herself, it was a mad idea. Then she made herself read the inscriptions.

In memory of Albert, loving husband of Edith, one said. 1914–1959. *Safely gathered in.* Then there was the grave of a family who had lost four sons called Walter, 1907, 1908, 1909 and 1911. *In thee we trust*, it said.

Julie remembered from the funeral that there was a bench near her mother's grave with a view of the valley below between two tall chimneys. She went slowly along the paths sitting on each bench she came to. Donated by

George Hirst, said the brass plaque on one bench and, In loving memory of Margaret Wetherby, on another. Julie sat among all the memorials to the dead and was just beginning to think she would have to go all the way to the office on the other side when she realised she was staring at two factory chimneys. And nearby there was a laburnum tree budding, it had been in bloom at the funeral. Even so, she went up and down the nearby graves twice before she saw the little square of marble with, Christine May Morris, Beloved Wife and Mother, written on the plague. It looked lost among the bigger stone slabs with crosses and angels, but in front of it there were newly dead flowers in a small iron holder. Brian, Julie thought, and she knelt to put the orange tree next to them. He would see it the next time he came, she thought. She stayed kneeling a while, looking at the little slab. Her mother's middle name was May, she'd forgotten that. She had died in the month of May and it was nearly May now that Julie's baby was ready to be born. Perhaps May was the name she should pass on if she had a girl, Julie thought, then felt a quiet chill at the thought that her baby might be born on the day her mother died. She touched the plaque with one finger and wanted to feel something else, but didn't. She got up stiffly and thought of Brian. *Not much to show for a lifetime*, he'd said, and she stopped looking at the plaque and sat on the bench instead.

She looked over the valley. It was an ordinary view, full of factory roofs and terraced streets and shops, where people lived and worked now as they had done for the past two hundred years, all those small lives, all that relentless work. A cold breeze blew and the little drops of rain collecting into bigger drops along the branches of the laburnum tree shivered and dripped. Suddenly Julie said,

I need to be brave, Mam,

I need to be brave, and it came out in a whimper.

She closed her eyes and when she opened them still all she could see was the valley framed by the two chimneys.

There was smoke in one of the great chimneys, the other factory had long since closed down. There was noise from the builders' yard and from the yellow crane clearing wreckage along the banks of the canal. Julie could see people on the streets shopping, making deliveries, taking children to school. Someone was driving a load of bricks over to another crane, new houses were being built on Mill Brew, there were roadworks on Trevor Street; work went on and on, the ordinariness of life went on. New people were moving in all the time into new houses, or into houses built and lived in by people who would now be dead. Most of the town had been shaped and built and carved by people who were now dead, you couldn't walk along a street without seeing their work, except that most of the time you didn't see it at all. But in streets and shops, houses and gardens and canals, churches and railways, the work of the dead remained, in the odd shape of a hearthstone or a cupboard that wouldn't close they left their mark. Julie had thought that it was the ordinary, humdrum affairs of life that wiped you out, taking up your energy and time, never leaving you alone until there was no time or energy for anything else. But it was the routine work that lasted, she could see it now. All the world around her had been left by people who cut stone and washed clothes and swept pavements, so that more work could go on. And if you wanted to change the world like Mick you had this to change, not just the world you could see, but all the unending labours of the dead. Everything the dead left behind changed the living world in unseen ways. And if you wanted to change the world like Julie you had this to understand, not just karma, or what was left from your own past lives, but what the dead had left, and the presence of the dead in what was left, on the streets, or in photos like Uncle Si's, or in newborn babies. Julie sat on the bench beside her mother's grave marvelling that she had never seen any of this before. It was like looking at one of those pictures where the shaded areas made one shape and the white areas another, and just sometimes you could see both pictures together, the image of the world made by the unending labours of the living and the dead.

Julie stood in the middle of the kitchen.

Mick, she said.

Mick wasn't there.

Water poured uncontrollably down Julie's legs, just like the books said it would, but she couldn't remember what to do.

Her bag, she thought, she had to get her bag, and she made her way out of the kitchen and up the stairs, water dribbling all the way.

At the top of the stairs she felt her first pain, low down, she had to bend over with it, then slowly she straightened. This was the moment she had imagined many times, only Mick was always there, taking her to hospital, holding her hand, telling her to push. Now she didn't know what would happen.

Julie went through all the things she'd bought and stored over the weeks, the nightie, breast pads, a towel. She didn't have a dressing gown but she rolled up the cardigan Aunty Clare had made and then went through the baby things, the nappies and vests and socks, all the things Annie had passed on and the ones Julie had bought herself. That was it only it didn't seem to be enough. She hadn't managed to get baby milk in the end, she was counting on being able to feed the baby herself, her mind went blank at the cost if she couldn't. When she finished packing she couldn't close the case, she had to take everything out and start again. And when she finally got it closed, stuffed and bulging, it still didn't seem enough. All these weeks she had been waiting to feel ready, and now it was happening she still didn't, she still felt as though she was waiting.

Maybe it wasn't happening, she thought. There were no more pains, labour did start and then stop, she knew, it had happened to Julie's mother. I was three weeks in hospital waiting for you, she used to say, very regularly, to Julie. That was horrible, and for a moment Julie wished she'd been induced after all, except for this peculiar feeling of not being ready. She held her bag and gazed out of the window. Then the second pain came, worse than the first, Julie gripped her stomach and gasped. She had forgotten how to breathe. When the pain went she knew what she had been waiting for, why the thought of being induced was so terrible. All this time she had been waiting to want her baby, and now it was coming whether she wanted it to or not.

She wanted Mick.

For the last few weeks she hadn't known what she would do when the time came, now she did. She was going to wait for Mick, she had to see him at least before she went, even if he wouldn't come with her, and she picked up her bag and coat and went to wait in Uncle Si's room for as long as it took, even though it was only eleven o'clock now and he was never usually in before tea.

When Mick came, Julie was doubled up and sweating.

Jesus, Mick said.

Julie was so glad to see him she almost cried.

Get an ambulance, she said, and Mick left the room without a word.

That was twenty past five. When he didn't come back immediately it struck Julie that he might not be coming back, and she felt a pang of terror. But the nearest phone box was right down the street and there might be a queue, Mick would come back. For once he had come in without Darren and Uncle Si was nowhere around, it was just Julie and Mick and Julie took this as a good sign. He would be back as soon as he could, she should try to practice her breathing. Then the pain came again and she clung to the settee.

Bastard, Mick, bastard, she screamed in her head. Why was he waiting in a queue? It was an emergency, he should batter the door down and shout.

At five to six Mick came back, out of breath. The nearest phone was broken, he said. He'd had to run all the way to the next one. The ambulance was on its way.

Thank God, said Julie. The relief was so intense she forgot to shout. Mick sat down.

How long has this been going on? he said, and when Julie told him he shook his head. When the next pain came she gripped his hand and hung over it and he didn't pull away.

Come with me, Mick, she gasped, and Mick didn't say anything. When she looked up, Darren and Uncle Si were both there, staring at them.

The baby's coming, Mick told them, and Julie moaned, Why doesn't the bloody ambulance come?

It's here now, Mick said, and through the window Julie could see a flashing light.

Then everything seemed to happen at once. Everyone helped her into the ambulance, but Julie clung onto Mick. On the ambulance steps Mick hung back.

Are you coming in, son? the ambulance man said, and Mick started to say something, then Uncle Si stepped forwards and took Mick's arm.

Go with her, he said. His face glowed with a weird light from the lamp. Someone has to go, he said.

Mick looked as if he didn't know what to say, but he couldn't refuse Uncle Si. Slowly he climbed into the van.

Julie didn't look at him or touch him on the way, she held onto the steel rail and then the ambulance man as she was getting out. They went into the hospital the same way Julie used to go when she visited her mother, then down a different corridor to a desk, and a nurse asked Julie's name.

Julie Fegan, she said, not looking at Mick. It was the name she'd used all along for the records. She thought Mick would say something but he didn't. As they were shown down more corridors to a room she caught sight of the expression on his face, white and tense.

Then different sets of people came in to ask the same questions: was it her first baby, what was the expected date of delivery, had the waters broken, when did the contractions start?

Jesus, Mick burst out, don't you people ever communicate?

Then Julie had to get changed, and the nurse examined her and it felt funny Mick being there, she still wouldn't look at him and he didn't look at her, but when the pain came she forgot to be embarrassed.

So it's coming on the expected day, the nurse said. That doesn't often happen.

It's late, Julie thought, but she didn't say anything. It wasn't the date of her mother's death, that was good enough for her. She was examined twice, but no one asked her why she hadn't been for check-ups. And for some reason, all the pain seemed to have stopped.

Six centimetres, the nurse said. And no further contractions. We'd better set up a drip.

Minutes later, with the drip and the foetal heart monitor stuck in her, the pains started again. Julie bellowed aloud and was offered pethidine or an epidural.

Both, she said.

We don't do both, said the nurse. Pethidine's quickest.

After the injection everything became blurred. People came and went, prodding her stomach, washing their hands. The pain was still there but it was blurred as well. At one point Julie became aware that she was hanging onto someone's hand, she hoped it was Mick's. She rolled over towards him and cried, We haven't got a name yet, then saw Mick's face, white and angry at the back of the room.

Finally she woke on a rising wave of pain and only Mick was there.

You've been out of it over an hour, he said.

Julie had never imagined such pain.

Another nurse came in and examined her and said she was fully dilated, she should be feeling the urge to push.

Pushing made it worse. Julie rolled from one position to another, in spite of the drip.

You're disturbing the foetal heart monitor, said the nurse.

Fuck off, cow, Julie thought.

O God, O God, O God, she moaned, then unexpectedly Mick gripped her hand.

You don't have to be polite in here, for Christ's sake, he said.

Try to push from the abdomen, said the nurse.

Julie knew she was going to be sick, or die. With the next spasm all her body seemed to go into a long cramp.

Push, said the midwife and nurse.

I am pushing, Julie screamed at them.

Push again now, they said.

O Jesus, Joseph, Mary, Julie sobbed. Then the pain gripped her and she screamed,

Jesus fucking Christ.

I can feel the head, cried the midwife. Keep pushing now, keep pushing.

Come on, Julie, Mick said, push.

That's it, that's it, said the midwife.

Keep going, love, keep it going.

Push.